HYPNOSIS

A RETURN TO THE PAST

Maria Inês Rebelo

To my grandfather, Francisco Rebelo,
who turned his shoemaking
into a real art

Look at the nature that surrounds us and see each being -
a plant, a stone or an animal -
as something like a particle of an alphabet,
considering then a word built from this alphabet:
you will find Man.

Paracelsus
Physician, alchemist, physicist and astrologist
(1493 – 1541)

CONTENTS

ACKNOWLEDGEMENTS

A journey usually has an itinerary, and a book usually has a soul.

You cannot write a book without life experience and the people who accompany you on that route.

Therefore, I would like to especially thank Alexandra Figueiredo for her constant suggestions and motivation.

Thank you to Lino Galveias whose persistent and dedicated work over the course of many months enabled the translation of the book, *Hypnosis: A Return to the Past.*

I want to thank Carlos for his constant support. He has always patiently waited for a daily page to eventually turn into a book.

To my parents and my sister, who are a part of this life-long journey; I hope this book will return us to the past.

These are voyages into the past, but also the future, which is around the corner.

This version of the book is now available to every reader thanks to the intense proofreading efforts that were carried out in two phases throughout 2018 and 2019.

Phase one was completed by the I AM Self-Publishing editing team. I would like to extend a sincere thank you to proofreaders Lisa Woodford and Tim Russell. for their dedicated, detailed and thorough work, which required great patience translating the Portuguese version to English.

Thank you also to Leila and Ali Dewji for their willingness to accept my project and continue supporting it, even after its initial publication in September 2017. Last but not least, I must to express all of my gratitude to Rachel Lawston for the beautiful cover she created.

The second phase was carried out by Amanda Adams with Pen and Ink Provisions. I would like to convey my deep appreciation for her efficiency and thoroughness. The changes she made, including adjusting from British to American spelling and style, created a more fluid and optimized text.

HYPNOSIS

I have no doubts that this latest version of the book will be easier to read and more appealing, which is what I wish for all of my readers.

Lisbon, November 2019

Focus here and now...

The story you are about to read tells the life story of Anne Pauline Roux, not only in the past, but also in the present and the future.

Anne Pauline has a destiny. One that only reveals itself when she makes the crucial decision to begin hypnosis sessions with famous hypnotist, Marcus Belling. Her intention is to confront her fears and anxieties, knowing that only through hypnosis and past life therapy, will she understand her inexplicable feeling of not belonging anywhere and her inability to establish her own identity. The experiences of her past lives appear to have contributed to the person she is today, while giving her the coordinates to find her future.

Throughout a nine-month therapy period with Marcus Belling, Anne Pauline will discover that she contains a mighty force within herself, which reveals its power only while she is under hypnotic trance. The realization that Belling is the person responsible for her crippling anxiety leads her into an alliance with his opponent, Josef Salvaterra. The partnership gives her the opportunity to use her power to put an end to Belling and his practice. However, this decision will weigh heavily on her conscience, propelling her on a quest to forgive her own past and build a future full of happiness.

The search for truth will require Anne Pauline to accept the consequences of her search, which sometimes may be inevitable and unpredictable. Anne will understand it much later. Until then, her indecisions and dilemmas will be part of this journey and will demand that she make brave decisions to achieve the biggest goal of her life; her freedom. Specifically, liberation from her past.

I ask you now to take a deep breath, choose a comfortable seat and relax... Feel the whole of your body preparing for this journey that lies before you... and then turn the page whenever you feel ready.

CHAPTER 1

THE MEDICAL HYPNOSIS CLINIC ON SUN AVENUE

1

At the exact stroke of noon, Anne Pauline Roux rang the bell on Marcus Belling's medical clinic at 27 Sun Avenue. It was mid-July and very warm already. A fresh breeze was blowing, and the city was bustling with activity, as waves of tourists invaded for the summer season.

When Anne Pauline rang the bell, she didn't know who she was looking for, though Marcus Belling was a renowned hypnotist. Years before, he began appearing on national television to talk about hypnosis. The most famous of his public presentations was Therapy of Past Lives and Regression, which had become legendary. It wouldn't be an exaggeration to say the entire country stopped to listen when Belling spoke.

Anne was afraid of the unknown, so before she made her appointment, she bought a book on the subject to help reduce the dread she felt when she thought about being hypnotized. Its title, *The Mysteries of Hypnosis*, created a certain feeling of suspense for her, but she had been enchanted by the words she read. It was as though she had been given a peek into a world which she knew nothing about. She tried not to think any more about it as she steeled herself to ring the bell.

Since Belling started his work, people had developed new ideas and perspectives about hypnosis as a therapeutic method and alternative to traditional medicine. Hypnosis had been seen as a kind of occult practice, so its practitioners and followers had been shunned by the conventional system of medicine. Some have argued with conviction that Marcus Belling is responsible for the change in perception.

Belling was not the only one in the public eye. Another hypnotist, Josef Salvaterra, had also been the focus of national attention, although he wasn't as charismatic or beloved by the media. Salvaterra, like Belling, attracted huge crowds through his work with hypnosis. Theirs was a symbiotic relationship. Disputes between the two constantly fed newspapers and various magazines, especially the ones who exploited the duality of their personalities. Marcus Belling and Josef Salvaterra were quite different from one another, and so were the patients who came to their respective clinics. Belling typically attracted men and women who were fascinated by his charisma and wanted him to use his particular hypnotic techniques to improve their lives. These patients varied according to their social status, political views, and religious convictions. Many families came specifically for the techniques he used on children to solve typical childhood anxieties and fears. Marcus Belling took great pleasure in treating young patients, perhaps because his career in hypnotism had begun in the pediatric units of hospitals where he had championed the use of hypnosis to facilitate the diagnosis of certain diseases.

Belling began his career in the field of clinical hypnosis 15 years earlier, when the subject was barely spoken of, let alone welcomed in hospitals. He took part in an experiment with other hypnotists from the National Council for Hypnosis. For this trial, hypnosis was tested on children with epilepsy. Marcus Belling would induce the children into a hypnotic trance to create an altered state of consciousness. Later, an analysis of the changes in cerebral wave patterns was made, and the patients' brains were then screened by an imagology device. Results led hypnotists to conclude that some of these children's symptoms corresponded with typical symptoms of other diseases, so these children didn't, in fact, suffer from epilepsy. For the first time, evidence suggested that hypnosis could be a fundamental means of clinical diagnosis, as well as a crucial tool for the application of the most effective treatment. As with all specialists, Belling knew that an error in diagnosis would extend suffering for patients.

Marcus Belling's experience with hypnosis had been decisive in the shaping of his convictions. By looking at current perspectives in the field, he quickly understood that young hypnotists didn't show much interest in the subject; probably because they were in close contact with human suffering, both of the body and of the soul. Belling's opinion, though, was that all acquired knowledge in this field was vital to training good hypnotists in the future. He resisted accepting the commercial attitude that permeated the profession; he supported the idea that a broader approach to clinical hypnosis would release some of the pressure there was on hypnotists to make quick, constant profits from their sessions.

Over time, it would be the merging of these professional experiences that would make Belling known for having developed household therapies to help whole families to overcome internal conflicts. He had become a hypnotist and therapist who had a good balance of abilities.

Josef Salvaterra had a more antiquated style, old-fashioned was a term many people used to describe his techniques. He often saw the more conservative, middle-aged men and women who were either unsure about, or downright against, Marcus Belling's methods. Salvaterra knew that some of his clients came to him precisely because they didn't like Belling's excessive media attention, preferring a different kind of hypnotist. Marcus Belling's charisma had become uncomfortable for them. Each of the hypnotists' groups of patients (Salvaterra called them clients) belonged to distinct social classes, and this might have had led to conflict. This had, however, become normal for both Belling and Salvaterra, who had been practicing hypnosis for more than two decades.

Over the years, the public had also shown an interest in the political affiliations and ideologies of the two hypnotists. They believed both would be good politicians, even though they had no political experience. In fact, emotions ran high at their public appearances – some defending Belling, some Salvaterra. In the eyes of many, Belling would make a good minister of Social Welfare, while Salvaterra had been offered, by popular vote, the post of Minister of Labor. The mass media, as usual, always tried to simplify their differences. To put it briefly, Belling leaned to the political right, and Salvaterra had more left-wing ideals. The public and the press, normally classified their ideologies in this way so that they could more easily comprehend their personal and political differences. Marcus Belling tried to ignore these descriptions of himself, but Josef Salvaterra cared much more about how people described him politically. Despite their differences, the two hypnotists refused to participate in the political struggle because they believed that this would simply not be beneficial to their careers. However, Salvaterra had more ambitions in this field than Belling. In fact, he had only stayed away from politics in order to avoid disagreeing with Belling's position. In this sense, it could be said that Josef Salvaterra was nervous about treading a path that was too different from that of his competitor.

This example clearly shows that Marcus Belling and Josef Salvaterra limited their own areas of influence. Both hypnotists would unknowingly take similar stands before the public and the mass media, even if they had very different personalities. They therefore tried not to diverge on crucial issues, including their personal, political and ideological convictions. This might have been limiting for both of them, but they unconsciously decided not to emphasize their remarkable personal and professional differences. There seemed to be some sort of league of gentlemen that would use actions and not words. For that reason, each of them set up a kind of espionage network that studied the other's movements and tried to limit their influence on a national scale. Then, out of the blue, Anne Pauline appeared and totally undermined their working methods. She also unintentionally changed the personal and professional dynamics of the two men, which had been built over the course of more than twenty years.

It also became important for the public to know about the past of Marcus Belling and Josef Salvaterra.

Marcus Belling was born into a middle-class family. He was the son of a country doctor who knew nothing about hypnosis before his son started practicing it. Marcus's father, Elias Belling, was one of the few doctors at the time who preferred to practice medicine outside the major cities to help people who lived a long way away from the healthcare available in towns, and didn't have the necessary financial means to pay a doctor from outside their village. Country doctors were also called nomadic doctors and only a few existed 60 years ago. Years later, Belling's father was recognized by the National Medical Commission as one of the best doctors in the country. He was anguished, however, by Marcus Belling's decision to start practicing hypnosis and took all the polemics about his son personally. At the beginning of his career, Marcus Belling's struggle to become a national reference point in hypnosis seemed to conflict with his family history, which was tied to traditional medicine. Conventional healthcare was seen by most as the only kind of therapy to cure any kind of disease. Then, as the media began to focus on Marcus, the clinical professionals opposed the theories that were spread about the therapeutic effects of hypnosis. Many attempted to discredit the work of the now famous hypnotist, and Belling's father was advised to stay well out of the controversy. He decided to withdraw from traditional medicine earlier than was usually expected, despite a successful career that was recognized at a national level. This inevitably meant his career eventually exerted a dominant influence on the son's life. Marcus, who was still a little afraid of relying solely on hypnotism, completed a course in medicine.

Josef Salvaterra's past was very different than Belling's. He was an orphan, a subject he avoided as if it were the worst of taboos, and therefore rarely addressed it in interviews. He had been brought up by an uncle, his father's brother, who paid for the studies that permitted Josef to follow a stable professional career. Contrary to Belling, Salvaterra had never had any contact with medicine, not even during his training in hypnosis, though it was considered by many to be a major foundation in hypnosis. Some people saw this as an obstacle for him in his attempt to surpass Marcus Belling as a practitioner.

We now know about the backgrounds of both Belling and Salvaterra, but still have little information about Anne Pauline. The first time the young girl met Marcus Belling was on this hot summer's day when she rang the doorbell of his medical clinic on Sun Avenue. Until then, she had only known him from television programs, and the two had never met each other. At least that was what they thought, but the truth was that they just hadn't met each other in *this* life. It is, therefore, essential to talk more about the mysterious Anne Pauline Roux, the 25-year-old woman, with large, vividly green eyes and long black hair. She had an oval-shaped face and sometimes wore glasses, which, gave her character greater depth and mystery. She also had quite a past, just like the two hypnotists.

"Each one of us has a past. Our past lives are important. They enable us to define our very identities," her father once told her.

"And if I don't know what my past was? What will happen to me?" asked a curious, 10-year-old Anne Pauline.

"In that case, you won't know who you are," answered her father.

"That seems frightening," she said meekly.

This conversation with her father remained a strong memory for Anne Pauline. The young girl promised herself that she would discover her past. She was so afraid of not knowing who she was, the search became an obsession.

Anne Pauline's life was connected to the sea and she always returned to it when she couldn't see a clear way forward because of her inner anguish. There were good reasons for this; her father had been a fisherman all his life, and her mother worked tirelessly as a fishnet binder, a job that was rarely done by women and was at risk of disappearing. The truth was that she was an excellent fishnet binder, and many people in the fishing community referred to her as the best in the country. She would arrange and tie the nets so well that her husband said that it was thanks to her that he caught so many fish. It was also often noted that Anne Pauline's father was an excellent angler. Something, maybe intuition, would tell him where to throw the nets, making him catch more fish than his competitors. He rarely made mistakes. When he decided to throw the nets into some given spot of the sea, he would usually get a larger amount of all kinds of fish, which would mean a better profit at the end of the month.

The family owned a fishing boat (as did all of the families in the community) called *Argo*. This had belonged to Anne's grandparents, who also had been in the fishing trade. After being kept on land for many years, it had begun to deteriorate. After thoroughly repairing the boat, Anne Pauline's father had decided to name it *Argo*. This was a very divisive issue among the locals as they said the name was a reference to an illegitimate son born to a girl who had joined the community quite suddenly, and then disappeared without a trace a few months later. The pair had been seen together but no one could confirm the facts. In any event, *Argo* was returned to the sea in its full splendor. The beautiful boat was painted in all the colors of the rainbow. On one side there was a painted fish and the word *ichthus*, and on the other side – for the more curious minds – was a serpent holding its own tail and the word *ouroboros*. No one knew exactly what this meant. Anne's father was considered to be an intelligent and knowledgeable man. Although he had no formal education, some in the community were afraid of addressing him as he had a paternal quality that everyone respected and was rarely questioned. It was for this reason that no one confronted him about the question of his illegitimate son, or the meaning of the strange words he used to decorate his boat, not even his daughter.

As a child, Anne Pauline had many opportunities to travel with her father aboard the *Argo* as it sailed across the horizon. At the end of the day, some shoals would surface from the water, as if in a last effort to see the sunset, as if they were in awe of the beauty of the world. Then, far away on the horizon, the majestic and beautiful seagulls would appear. They were attracted by the fish who turned the sea into their own balcony where they could watch the sun go down. During these trips, Anne Pauline wondered if she really had a brother, or if it was just a rumor that had been made up by the locals to satisfy their own hunger for scandalous news. However, she was afraid of facing her father with this story.

This was a tiny piece of Anne Pauline's past. The sea gave the green-eyed girl a precious gift, which was now something that she felt only rarely; her inner peace and mindfulness. Something haunted her. Something immense, which she could barely understand. Anne did remember dreaming as a child of strange images that caused her anguish and which she couldn't explain. Often, there were moments of anxiety and sadness, which she struggled to explain because, despite the poverty, she had enjoyed a happy childhood; certainly, in terms of her memories of her travels with her father in the family boat. The truth was, however, that *something* would not leave her alone.

Nobody knew that she had one life by day, and another one at night. She never mentioned this to her parents, who would have had difficulty understanding it, given that their greatest concern was to feed the family physically. When the main concern was daily survival, everything else seemed to pale into insignificance. Nothing was more important than surviving to work the next day. Perhaps that is why Anne Pauline's parents didn't know what was happening with their daughter's past, a past that insisted on showing itself to her whenever it could. Very often, at night, she could clearly hear a man's voice asking her incessantly;

"What is your true name?"
"Do you know your past well?"
"Are you honest?"
"Do you desire good for others?"
"Do you have values?"

"If one day, you find a secret place, will you be able to keep it secret?"

"Can you keep secrets?"

The voice of the man came from a world she didn't know. The questions were always the same and she gradually began to doubt her own identity. In the back of her mind, she could see the face of someone shaking his head; no, she wasn't being honest, that was what he was trying to say. How could she convince him otherwise? How could know her so well that he was able to make her doubt herself? And might she have other names? Why should she have other names? The questions began to invade her mind and they never left her. Even to this day, she didn't know who she was, in spite of the promise that she had made to her father.

On the day that Anne Pauline could no longer fulfil her promise to her father, to never forget her past or where she came from, she found that neither the boat trips nor the sea brought her the happiness and tranquility she needed. The *Argo* remained moored more frequently, and even the seagulls began to feel the lack of the young, who now only observed the horizon on the beach, wondering who was the man that spoke to her at night, asking her so many questions. Often, in the distance, the tides left a strip of land that rose out of the water and formed a small island where all the birds in the vicinity looked for the appetizer of the day. It was an isolated island made of sand, where the sounds of nature reigned. Anne Pauline called this place the Island of the Birds.

As Anne Pauline grew up, this feeling got bigger and bigger, until it became so intolerable it reached a point where she really needed to find help. Having been skeptical about the therapeutic benefits of hypnosis for many years, Anne Pauline finally made the decision to ask for help from the famous and charismatic Marcus Belling. She didn't question the statistics, and she couldn't resist Belling's charm and natural attractiveness, although she mainly saw him because he was a good hypnotist. She didn't for a moment consider Josef Salvaterra when she decided to use hypnosis as a treatment to her inexplicable anguish. However, Anne Pauline didn't choose hypnosis because she wanted to meet some past love or find out if she had been an important historical figure. Something inside Anne told her that her sadness, which was irrational, was related to a variety of past lives that kept sending her subliminal messages (even if only through her dreams). Anne's past had this brutal way of communicating with her, as if it wanted her to constantly return to a specific location to live those events once again, but from a different perspective. However, the past was now asking her to look at the world around her in an altogether different way.

But how could the past communicate with Anne Pauline? And how could she be sure that an unknown past was now trying to get to her? The dreams of past lives invaded her nights, year after year. Try as she might, she couldn't prevent the familiar voice in her mind of a man putting a set of questions that didn't seem random;

"Who are you?"

"Do you know the true history of the *Argo* and your father?"

"Do you have your own convictions, or have you lost your values?"

"Are you able to travel to the past? Do you want to discover what exists there?"

"Are you a respectful person?"

"Could you believe in something that you can't see?"

The same man appeared in the shadow of her dreams and shook his head. No, she wasn't a respectful person. She was now certain that it was necessary to travel back to the past, but how could she do that? And what was there in the past that she might discover? Every time, it became clearer that she should go back to her past, but she didn't know if it was possible to believe in something that she couldn't see. Had she lost her values; did she know who she was? Seeing her so thoughtful, her father had said to her once, "Nowadays, people are finding it increasingly difficult to believe in something they can't see. I liked that you were different. It's important to believe in your intuition and your convictions. None of this can be seen, but it can be felt," he concluded.

The man who appeared every night of her life made her doubt herself. Strangely, when he asked about her past, he questioned her honor and dignity. The young Anne Pauline could not understand the negativity of this man, who never showed his face. Who could he be?

2

One day, he posed a unique question, "Imagine that you had the ability to return to your past. You wouldn't look at the events the same way, for you would have a different view."

Anne Pauline faced the challenge and thought about the question. It would be physically impossible to return to the past, what has gone has gone. Human beings have no control over time. There was one alternative, however; past lives therapy. When Anne Pauline searched for a specialist in past lives therapy, she became aware of the two decades long rivalry between Marcus Belling and Josef Salvaterra. She couldn't care less, all she wanted was a helping hand.

It was generally accepted that Marcus Belling's charisma affected everyone. He was a statuesque, 45-year-old man with a head full of dark hair and deep brown eyes that flashed when he spoke on hypnosis, either on television or in conferences organized by the National Council for Hypnosis. His presence at such events meant that his celebrity spread far and wide. Women were especially thrilled to see him, and he attracted media attention with his natural charm, not to mention his internationally recognized competence in hypnosis and regression. Belling's specialization was focused on two specific areas; clinical hypnosis and hypnotherapy. He had studied past lives therapy in the United States, where he had acquired most of his knowledge of the subject. Despite the merit of his work, consensus on the subject was a distant goal.

At the start of his career, Marcus Belling was more salesman than hypnotist; he did as well as any professional in making a sale. He was criticized for that on several occasions. It was his opinion that traditional medicine was no cure-all, and that one had to take the entire nature of man into account, as only a holistic approach could provide people with what they need. Many, though, considered him to be a charlatan. Hence, it was difficult to legitimize his name as a professional in the field, which made his early years rough ones. Superstition and prejudice plagued Marcus Belling's career, but he was lucky to have his wife, Patricia Murio, a family physiotherapist, who was a precious support for him.

For all these reasons, the first decade in Belling's career was very tough and not even his easy, empathetic way with people helped him to adapt to the modern times. He wanted to deliver the message that hypnosis could be applied in diverse traumatic, physiological or emotional contexts. Within a few years though, people started to see Belling as a serious contender, noting that his research was both exhaustive and rigorous. His responsibility in the daily practice of his profession was unquestionable, and so the idea of him being a charlatan or a salesman slowly faded away. As misconceptions about hypnosis were gradually corrected, a slow, yet sustainable rise in Belling's national recognition was noticed. Years later, he would be the most famous hypnotist in the country.

It was easy to tell waiting patients from bystanders on Sun Avenue; the wide-eyed ones glowed with an anticipation Belling saw in most of his clientele. He also recognized a different group among the crowd. A different tell for different intentions; an envy-green-tinted aura surrounded those who wanted access only to sell their story to the tabloids for cash. They would be filtered from those who suffered genuinely; it was these people who were Belling's priority.

Just like his father, Elias Belling, Marcus Belling wanted to help people in his profession, and he saw it as his mission to use hypnosis as an instrument to do that. Apart from those who were merely curious, people suffered from sleeping difficulties, anxiety, being over or underweight, chronic pain (both emotional and physical) or were generally restless souls. In the last of these cases, regression helped them to understand what was going on in the inner layers of their consciousness. This consequently nullified the trauma from their past and, helped them to live a fulfilled life. This was the case with Anne Pauline.

Many regression patients, Anne Pauline included, were not completely sold on the therapeutic effects of hypnosis. For that reason, they almost always went to a psychologist first to look for answers. It was only when their symptoms didn't change after years that they sought out a hypnotist. Past lives therapy was, in reality, the only solution for the most complicated of cases.

Marcus Belling was not a one man show, however. This was part of his recipe for success. To prevent fraudsters from ruining his career, he worked only with a small, faithful team. They filtered his cases in order of priority and evaluated the real intentions of those who asked for help.

Belling would not have become so successful without the help of Sofia Estelar. Tall, with jovial eyes, she was his secretary from the beginning of his career and had developed a motherly relationship with him. Mrs. Estelar had witnessed the decline of Elias Belling's career, as she watched his son mature and grow competent in his profession. They worked together in that clinic for twenty years and naturally became emotionally dependent on one another. The two families were very close, spending personal time together at the home of one or the other.

Inside Belling's clinic was an old, enlarged photograph, taken on the day the clinic opened for the first time at that location. Since then, Sofia and Marcus had changed, both physically and emotionally, but they both knew that people could have no such influence on time.

One of Sofia's defining personality traits was her natural predilection to distrust. It had always been in her and had helped her greatly in the early days, when Marcus was beginning to present hypnosis as a legitimate therapeutic treatment for the soul. From their very first meeting, Sofia drew Belling's attention, as he admired her strong personality. He could see that she was someone who would not give up easily. Her contagious smile, which he saw often, provided confirmation that she was firmly dedicated to what she believed in. So, Belling knew that she was the right person to be his secretary right away, that she would focus all her attention on detecting and filtering out the truly suffering from those seeking a brief moment in the spotlight.

It was no easy task to manage the professional agenda of Marcus Belling. There was never enough time for all the appointments requested, so prioritizing was essential. Belling chose well when he gave Sofia that sensitive role. The two worked together to bring hypnosis to all who needed, seeing this as a public mission.

Sofia had, therefore, stayed with Belling throughout his first harsh decade of work, when he had to make a name in the country as a reputed hypnotist. His career had, of course, taken off since then. She had always been a major source of support, and his success was inevitably connected to his personal secretary's efforts to protect him from harm and the danger that could be thrown at him. We could also say that her natural suspicion had always been a decisive aspect in his career. The two trusted one another implicitly. On Sofia's part, she had taken an oath many years ago to protect the illustrious hypnotist from various external hazards. All of this happened because, more than anyone else, she knew the immense amount of work that lay behind the management of both his image and career. She successfully worked according to that oath until the day Anne Pauline came into their lives. In this case, not even Sofia's suspicion and acute intuition could prevent the coming damage.

Sofia had been, and always would be, faithful to Marcus Belling. At night, at the foot of her bed, she repeated the words of that oath to strengthen herself mentally for the challenges she might face in protecting Marcus. She wasn't just his secretary, but also his confidant and friend. So, when Belling's professional life was threatened, he took comfort from her, as she gave her sincere affection freely. Sometimes, though, their complicity resembled a different kind of relationship that not even his wife, Patricia Murio, could quite understand. Over the years, the relationship became increasingly complicated to the point some might think the two were lovers, when in fact, they were only ever friends. There were no words to describe the harmony that existed between the two. Anne Pauline's entrance into their lives would, however, force them to discover that they, too, had been connected in the past.

In the beginning, it was only he and Sofia working in his clinic on Sun Avenue, but with time, she realized that the hypnotist needed more help, someone to improve his image. Belling was quite naïve and trusting in terms of his relationship with others and sometimes put him in harm's way due to his fame. His relationship with Josef Salvaterra, for instance, had been bitter even in the early days, which created dreadful scandals that often took years to assuage. Over the last two decades, their personalities inevitably changed, keeping pace with Belling's blossoming career. Unsurprisingly, they are very different people than those in the picture taken the day the clinic opened.

Sofia encouraged Marcus to be more suspicious and to consider his career, but his personality could hardly have changed simply on the recommendation of others. She constantly reminded him to be more aware of the people around him and his actions and reactions in public. Her words had no effect, however, and his conflict with Salvaterra grew in intensity over the years. With the situation out of her control, Sofia turned to Maria de Burgos, an intelligent and discerning 38-year-old woman who had already worked with other professionals managing their public image. Belling wisely agreed with his longtime coworker and extended an offer. There was a chemistry between the two women, so Maria quickly accepted the position. and they easily began working together to build a team of staff loyal to Marcus Belling.

Maria de Burgos soon started to manage all issues related to the Belling's image, not only in the media but also in the minds of the general public. She advised him about posture, eye contact, and how to be confident without the air of arrogance. His relationship with Josef Salvaterra was also changing due to more control, and there were no more major scandals.

As the years passed though, Maria de Burgos came to accept that she could not fully impose her professional opinions on Marcus, as he wanted to retain a certain degree of his personal approach to his public. This sometimes risked his career to such an extent that Sofia and Maria feared the collapse of the entire organization. And that is precisely what happened when Anne Pauline came into his life. Despite the mystery swirling around everything about her, Belling decided to continue hypnosis sessions with the young woman. For him, practicing his profession meant accepting risk, even unforeseen risk.

One thing was for sure, after the first decade, Marcus Belling was more confident in his professional skills, and the support of Sofia Estelar and Maria de Burgos had completely changed the public perception of his Sun Avenue clinic. The team would not be complete, however, without someone to be manage the clinic's complicated finances, and this was done by Ruben Mortsel. The young bookkeeper had been working with Marcus Belling only a short time yet had quickly mastered handling the significant amount of revenue that Belling's practice generated.

Torquay and Mortsel worked there together for a year, constantly informing and advising Belling on the monthly financial health of the clinic. Those reports mattered little to Belling, who trusted in the professional honesty of both accountants. He knew a lot of money was pouring in, but for a long time, he chose to remain ignorant of his net worth. Josef Salvaterra, on the contrary, knew every figure in his books.

This much trusted staff had sworn to defend Belling and fight for the spirit of his mission, which was to use hypnosis to help people find their path to mindfulness and inner peace. Despite his pleasant nature, Belling expected humility from his staff and an atmosphere of composure and confidentiality in his clinic.Any question about the practice of hypnosis was expertly answered by him or one of his colleagues in order to neutralize any misconceptions. A sort of mantra used in his professional life enabled him to form a connection with all of these people who had signed a work loyalty contract with him. Although degrees of loyalty would naturally vary, that core value was the foundation on which the clinic and Belling's work rested firmly.

Everyone expected great things from Marcus from his early beginnings His years studying in the United States were a time of accelerated learning. In the university's medical facility, he used his developing hypnosis skills to relieve student anxiety related to academics and social angst. Though his specialty was clinical hypnosis, it was there that Belling had his first experience with the therapeutic method of past lives regression. His initial reaction to past lives therapy was apprehensive, as it was relatively unknown back home. Ultimately his focus was diverted from hospital work toward research into hypnotherapy and regression therapy. This new focus would go on to give him soaring success among the public.

He returned home with a degree focused on Regression Therapy and soon married Patricia Murio, a charming and talented physiotherapist. Patricia had her own medical clinic a good distance from her new husband's. They made their home just outside the city, where they raised two children and lived a comfortable, happy life.

Marcus Belling was grateful for all the ways he was blessed that he'd never dared to expect. However, his relationship with Josef Salvaterra, though more tranquil than it had been before, was still troublesome and Belling felt the situation marred the otherwise perfect life he'd made for himself. Maria de Burgos had the daily task of keeping a safe distance between the two men; a feat which sometimes proved more difficult than one might expect. Josef Salvaterra was obsessed with the younger and less experienced hypnotist's career successes; mostly because despite those perceived shortcomings, Belling had somehow overshadowed Salvaterra. In addition to their polar opposite personalities, they had also had quite different working methods, which seemed to be the crux of the conflict between them. Many of Belling's patients felt that he had a preferable bed-side manner to his method, while Salvaterra adhered to a more rigid form of therapy, demanding patients enter the trance he led them to rather than gently coaxing them into it.

Though their methods differed, both men knew it was the confidence that they established within their patients that promoted the true healing of the soul. The effectiveness of their treatments was similar to the placebo effect. The purpose was not to create illusions, but to help people in the process of building an internal conviction that, through the techniques employed, could actually work in the soul and heal the wounds created by each patients' worst traumas. Gaining the trust of the patients was a fundamental element of successful treatment. These tactics worked, but skeptics had difficulty accepting this idea. The National Council of Hypnotists and its members all believed in and practiced this to the desired effect on the regular.

Belling and his team had long been familiar with Salvaterra's hypnosis strategy but were surprised at the contempt and arrogance it brought out in the specialist.

It was thought that the pasts of the two men might explain why their methods differed so widely.

Joseph Salvaterra had endured a difficult childhood, tempered only mildly by the financial support he received from a rich uncle to attend school. Six years older than Belling, he had a shock of dark brown hair and his dark eyes only intensified the broodiness of his overall facade.

Salvaterra had been the first hypnotist on the public stage when he offered hypnosis as a whole treatment plan rather than something to aid other treatments. If truth be told, people only knew that hypnosis was an alternative therapy to conventional medicine. 20 years ago, hypnosis had been *complementary to* and not *an alternative* to existing methods, regarding the treatment of harmful life habits and the diagnosis of diseases. The difference in the terminology used increased the credibility of hypnosis.

It was the altruistic uncle who initiated the push for his nephew to become a hypnotist, thinking it could be a ticket to success, if he was courageous enough to explore it. The first form of hypnosis was only just beginning to bloom, so there was an opportunity for the young man to become a pioneer in the field. To urge him in the right direction, his uncle presented him to Marbella Gorey, who was daring, ambitious and greedy. Josef fell in love with her deeply. Making use of her cunning character and her own charm, she helped to convince Josef Salvaterra to become a hypnotist, and obviously, she benefited from his success. His uncle and Marbella were happy, and so was Josef, who found this practice to be the best way to forget his difficult upbringing. Everything was going well until Marcus Belling rose to fame. By this time, Salvaterra's profile as a hypnotist was already set and his arrogance prevented him from continuing to research and change with any developments. While Salvaterra's authoritarian tone was the norm at the time, Belling was using a more coddling approach that would become very popular with patients.

Marabella and his uncle never imagined that someone like Marcus Belling, who had an innate talent for hypnosis, would emerge as a popular national figure in the field. Marbella was as unhappy about Belling's media attention as her husband was and although she would never say it, Belling's popularity made her feel like her marriage to Salvaterra was a failed project. But she had fallen in love with Josef and didn't want to split with him, at least not for the first 10 years of their marriage. Her restless spirit would not let her be and she was uncomfortable with the situation. It was Marbella who stirred up the rivalry between the two hypnotists, as the need to improve her wealth and social status dominated her life. She was particularly venomous, feeding his hatred while sparking envy and greed. No one could stand Marbella Gorey. Her body grew increasingly frail with the passing years, as if her unachievable desire for vengeance was eating her away inside.

But Joseph Salvaterra didn't fear his wife. He knew her character very well and could impose his authority on her. He loved her deeply, and because he knew her so well, he did not easily accept her suggestions when Marbella tried to control or manipulate him and lead his work in another direction. Once she had suggested that he worked with collaborators, but they were no more than spies that aimed to control Marcus Belling and his team. She kept telling him, "You have to make sure that you have profits at the end of the month."

But Marbella would not actually really insist on this as she was afraid to lose her golden goose. By then, their marriage was merely one of convenience.

Unlike Marcus Belling, Josef Salvaterra didn't have a loyal team defending and promoting his work. He quickly got rid of the people chosen by his wife to improve and control the logistical part of his profession. Like Marbella, Salvaterra needed to dominate that business as hypnosis was effectively only a business and his patients were clients, and not his patients. There was no spirit of public mission to move them, and the receipts that were produced by the hypnosis sessions were the main reason that kept the clinic open. This was located at the opposite end of the city to that of Belling, far away from Sun Avenue.

At the time, Marbella had a secret desire, which she had never revealed to her husband. There was an exclusive club in town, which was known as the Factory Club. It was known to be highly exclusive and only the richest women in the nation were members. It was a great honor to become part of this club, and there were rumors that these women controlled a large number of cultural and educational institutions, which only gave them more power. Being a highly selective club, it would not allow just any woman in, only those who had the highest income levels. Josef knew of his wife's desire to be part of the Factory Club and disapproved. He wanted her close to him. Although he sometimes felt suffocated by her constant presence, he was lost when she got caught up in her other interests. He feared that if she joined the club, she would have less time for him and find him less interesting.

Jasmine was Marabella's friend and she was the only person capable of controlling Marbella; to the point of manipulating her for her own purposes. Jasmine was an unusual person; she was an oracle, a visionary and a fortune teller with extra-sensory perception, which is why people turned to her when they were in need. By the time Anne Pauline reached Marcus Belling's clinic, Jasmine's own life was changing, her present as well as her past.

Marabella frequently told Jasmine that her husband was destroying her dreams, and about that time is when the desire for revenge began to develop within her. By then, Marbella and Josef Salvaterra enjoyed a marriage of convenience, though the hypnotist still loved his wife. Both, of course, hated Marcus Belling and were committed to destroy his career.

To make things worse, Marbella excelled at making her husband feel envious of Belling. Josef loved his wife, but sometimes couldn't understand her motives. He was getting older and his disputes with Marcus Belling just made him tired now. He started locking himself in his clinic when his wife wanted him to be there. When Anne Pauline started her appointments with Belling, the couple could barely agree on anything, and each focused on different goals in their lives.

Life and personal experiences of the two hypnotists shaped their respective methods of practicing hypnosis. Inevitably, they established diverse levels of trust with their patients as well. One was considered to be more lenient, the other more authoritarian. This was but one of the issues that intensified their struggle for the limelight.

When Anne Pauline rang Belling's clinic doorbell that day, she didn't know any of their life stories. She had her own story, which was sometimes divided between present and past. She had no idea of the loyal and dedicated team that worked with Belling, nor of the elaborate operative system that made the Sun Avenue clinic run so well. The personal and professional feud that her hypnotist had been locked in with Salvaterra and his wife for decades was also unknown to her. Anne Pauline couldn't have known what her arrival would put into motion.

Marcus Belling's clinic was located in an old building, one that closely resembled many others that had been built during the 18th century on the city's main avenue. Stretching over a mile were cafés and restaurants with crowded outside terraces, as well as ornate fountains that were true architectural masterpieces. Not far from number 27 was an early twentieth-century statue of a phoenix that seemed to rise from the floor, preparing to take flight. To the side were its ashes, which signified rebirth. Anne Pauline had been looking for her own identity for a long time, and desperately needed to know what had really happened in her past. The man who had been appearing every night in her dreams for so many years had almost demanded that she return to her past. He had also destroyed her inner confidence, making her doubt who she really was. She needed to rise up again, just like that phoenix.

On her way to Belling's clinic, Anne Pauline stopped in front of the statue to admire its architecture. The paint that covered the bird had faded with time, but the statue remained intact because of the strength of the stone, which was a metaphor for it was always being necessary to hope for a better future. The young woman took a deep breath and felt some hope for herself, just as she did when she was looking at the Island of the Birds from her beach.

Wide and splendid, Sun Avenue was the city's main road. Belling and Sofia often spent time in the cafés and restaurants there. Women who recognized him took the opportunity to ask for an autograph or take a photograph, which bothered his personal assistant. Their close relationship led her to feel jealous, like a secret admirer who couldn't reveal her true feelings but resented those who approached him. Though he worked with her every single day, Belling remained ignorant of this turmoil in his colleague.

That attraction was why Sofia was cold and unrelenting with the women who came for hypnosis treatments with Belling. She harbored a nasty, manipulative streak and would insist that many procedures were mandatory, forcing them to jump through hoops before they could begin hypnosis treatment. Sofia's ability to sort out the priority cases, though, allowed Marcus Belling to remain ignorant of the shady antics of a woman he depended on both personally and professionally.

Anne Pauline rang the bell of 27 Sun Avenue, and after a moment's silence, rang a second time. The sun and the heat seemed to have slowed the pace of people walking on the street, as if they could sense what was coming. The red and gold colors on the statue of the phoenix seemed brighter, as if the bird wanted to fly again. The electrical mechanism inside the statute triggered the movement of plates twice a day so that where the ashes had been, clear, fresh water would flow, making the statue into a water fountain. While she waited for the door to open, something of major importance to her life was happening in another part of the city.

Georgine Gunderson was 5 feet 3-inch-tall librarian with dark green eyes and an oval-shaped face. That day she had been called by the council library's archives director and informed of her temporary transfer to the old national library building. which had been empty for more than seven years. The nineteenth-century building had been home to the library for many years, but now only processed special orders and stored books that couldn't be housed in any other council facilities due to lack of space. Gunderson would be the only person working there,

Georgine couldn't understand why she had been given this lonely task, which seemed inappropriate, given her professional experience. She worried that it had something to do with what she'd been hiding. Yes, she had secrets, but she also wondered if her research on Sun Avenue, though outside working hours, had irked her bosses and this was a way to refocus her attentions. Georgine would never know the true reason – that she was now the only officially city council-appointed employee who could inventory the books at the library. Her boss promised her, "It's temporary. We do need someone who can organize the existing materials in that building, but today, we have an important order. We need you to help sort out the books that have just arrived. You'll stay there for nine months and then take over the full-time librarian position at the new library."

She could do nothing about it, so Georgine reluctantly went to the old library that morning. A small truck full of boxes of books was waiting for her there and she helped unload them into the building. All the boxes were put on top of an old table that was covered in dust. Something about the place scared Georgine, she didn't like being the only person working in a place that was now closed to the public.

She carefully opened all the boxes that had just arrived and found that all had been numbered by the city council. She didn't know the origin of the books and never learned any more information about them. Finally, and after two hours of work, the last box was opened; it was marked **BO18**. Gunderson slowly and carefully started to stack the books on the shelves. Our librarian didn't know it, but she'd been tapped to hide a secret. She would have to keep it for the next nine months, the duration indicated by her boss. In the meantime, a lot of work was expected from her.

These nine months would be significant to both Anne Pauline and Georgine. Meanwhile, Anne Pauline would have the chance to understand the trauma of her past and finally discover her true identity. It was beyond their imagination that their destinies would actually intertwine. Georgine wasn't used to hiding things, but she would keep a major secret one about Anne Pauline. Georgine closed box BO18 and returned home with an unnerving feeling.

CHAPTER 2

THE MYSTERY OF ANNE PAULINE

1

The door was now open, and Anne Pauline was finally allowed to meet Marcus Belling.

Being asked to enter the consultation clinic meant that the patient had already gone through a rigorous selection process by Sofia Estelar. The assistant had kept exactly the same ritual for many years. When patients started with Belling, Sofia waited at the main door to greet them personally, and to prove that she really could choose the right people. Sofia took a fierce pride in the process.

When the secretary saw Anne Pauline, she realized that Anne was much more beautiful than the photograph on her chart. This consisted of compiled data from a single form that all patients who applied for sessions with Belling filled out. People who came to Sun Avenue could, therefore, range from dazzling to monstrous and there were times when she had to hide her reaction. There were few women who looked as good on their arrival as they did in their photograph so, Sofia learned not to trust the picture attached to the file. As for Anne Pauline, Sofia Estelar felt a strange shiver as the green-eyed patient got closer. At that moment, she realized that she had chosen the wrong person for sessions with Belling, and that her selection methods, which were a combination of intuition, cunning, intelligence and insight, hadn't worked well in this case. She was suddenly fearful at the thought and wondered if she'd lost her gift for selection.

Her intuition was telling her that Anne Pauline Roux was different than what she had expected when she had read her letter, but there was nothing more she could do. Anne Pauline sensed the discomfort she had caused Sofia, but greeted her kindly, nevertheless. The secretary took Anne down the corridor to a door, behind which the hypnotist awaited her. It was beyond Anne Pauline's imagination that she would change the lives of everyone who worked at Sun Avenue. Anne was a mystery and Sofia regretted ever opening the door to her.

When Anne Pauline entered the treatment room, she found that Belling was much more charming than she had imagined. *He looked taller on television,* she thought. Marcus welcomed her with both an enchanting smile and warm affection. Sofia rolled her eyes, then closed the door behind her and left the two alone for the session.

When Marcus Belling saw Anne Pauline, he felt something strange. A momentary sense of affection rapidly turned into mistrust. It was rare that this happened to him, because he usually easily established a rapport with his patients. He had been warned by Maria de Burgos to protect himself a little more, but he never followed the advice. Belling understood the look Sofia had shot him before closing the door. Anne Pauline didn't notice, but the message was clear between the two; I made a mistake. Belling thought to himself, *this is not a trustworthy person, I should be careful with this one.*

Marcus put his hand out silently to Anne Pauline in a friendly fashion, still not understanding why she made him uneasy. "Sit down, please. Welcome to the Medical Clinic of Hypnosis on Sun Avenue. Today, your way of discovering your past begins," he said, and smiled.

The patient remained silent, as if she were memorizing the short speech. His voice was familiar to her, but she had difficulty working out where that sensation was coming from. She sat on the sofa and Marcus Belling started by introducing himself. He was trying to direct the patients' attention away from their personal drama and onto their sessions, preparing them to build a trusting relationship as he did so. Belling often told the people who sought him out that trust is a fundamental pillar of their relationship. As a hypnotist, he always tried to delve deep into the soul of each person and get to know them, more than anyone else had tried before. For these reasons, and despite the opposition of Sofia Estelar and Maria de Burgos, he refused to be less authentic than he actually was or appeared to be. There were times he felt like his team just didn't understand him. Sofia had once courageously told him, "Marcus, sometimes you ask the impossible from people. No one is as authentic as you would like people to be."

Deep in his heart, Marcus Belling knew she was right.

Being that Belling's goal was to delve so deep, it was important to build a relationship of confidence with his patients. The same was not true of Josef Salvaterra, however, who only looked for the right moment to induce a hypnotic state. He preferred not to know more than he absolutely had to. He didn't deal well with moodiness and fled from demonstrations of emotion. In contrast, Belling wanted to know all their fears, sorrows, temptations, inner thoughts, and darkest secrets. In many cases, his patients resorted to hypnosis to forgive themselves for one thing or another. This was something Marcus Belling knew quite well, as he was an exceptionally good observer and extremely perspicacious. Because of this, people sometimes contacted him to share their shame with someone who wouldn't judge them. As he knew well, human nature is difficult to understand.

Marcus Belling tried to make Anne Pauline comfortable so that she could tell him why she was there to see him. That was the first thing he asked her. The answer came as follows, "For all of my life, I have felt that I have a past I don't understand at all. I have memories of a life that doesn't feel as though it was really mine."

"Are you trying to tell me that you can sense things from your past lives?" asked Belling.

"Yes, that is what I am saying," she answered.

"It might seem strange to you, but did you know that many dreams are linked to episodes of past lives? Most people never realize it. When the past life is full of unexplained events and memories, dreams can help you relate," Belling replied.

Anne Pauline was intrigued and surprised by what he had just told her. This meant that a portion of what she had dreamt of over the course of her entire life was connected to her past lives. However, she had had many dreams during her life, and it was making it difficult to specify which of them were connected to her unknown past. Belling caught on to her enthusiasm for the subject and continued the session.

"That happens to many people. Most of us know that some of those dreams are related to past lives. If you are able to remember those images, it's because they cause some level of discomfort to you. The Anne Pauline of today feels discomfort because you've lived such intense experiences, and they were stored in your subconscious. That's a simplified way to explain Regression Therapy. Perhaps there is something in your past that is still waiting to be clarified in your future?" said Belling.

Anne Pauline thought about the question for some time, but she was no expert. She didn't know the reasons behind her restlessness. Perhaps there were past lives, with traumatic moments or situations that demanded she go back to the past. She wanted to live in peace. Belling understood that she might not be able to answer his question. He didn't have an answer. The illustrious hypnotist tried to calm her and, in an attempt to gain her confidence, formulated a new question,

"Have you always felt like this?" he asked.

"Yes, I have always felt continuous anxiety and agitation. I hope to discover my past through hypnosis," said Anne Pauline as she lowered her eyes.

"And that is why you came here. You decided to start past life regression to find the peace of mind you've been looking for," added Belling.

"Yes, it is precisely that," answered the young lady, her eyes still lowered.

"I would like you to give me some examples of what you tell me. I see that there's a past, or several pasts, trying to reach you, by using your subconscious. This form of liberation is achieved so that you tell me, through dreams. Could you tell me about the experiences you had?" asked Marcus Belling.

"One night, I dreamed I was in a place with three doors. I decided to open one of these doors, one with Unknown Destination written on it, and I was pulled through. I felt an overwhelming sense of peace and tranquility that I first felt when I was sailing on the *Argo* with my father. When I woke up, my bed was filled with needles, herbs and leaves, as if I had been in that place before. It seemed to so familiar. It was an extensive golden plain," said Anne Pauline, visibly moved.

"What is the *Argo*?" asked Marcus Belling.

Marcus Belling didn't know what the *Argo* was, but he could deduce that it was a boat. He knew little of the history of his new patient, but since she remained silent, he concluded that *Argo* was much more than a boat. Finally, she spoke, "The *Argo* is the fishing boat of my family."

Whoever started an appointment with Belling knew that they were accepting a loyal relationship with him. Trust was crucial in this rapport and Belling tried to reinforce the idea with Anne Pauline. It was essential there was an open and clear connection between the two of them. Marcus Belling guessed everything that Anne Pauline wanted to say. As she spoke more about herself and her unknown world, Belling was feeling a restlessness inside her. Once more, the desperate look on the Sofia's face came to his mind. But the conversation with Anne Pauline had been very natural up to that moment. She was a young woman of 25 years who needed his help to understand if the past was indeed trying to somehow send her a message through her mind.

Anne Pauline still didn't know his professional history, but he had been dedicated to Regression Therapy for only the last 12 years of his career. He was an expert in clinical hypnosis, but gradually developed an interest in past life regression over the years. Belling then became aware that it was equally possible to treat serious physical or psychological symptoms (such as depression and other disorders) through regression. Some of his fellow hypnotists continued to doubt this therapy's success, however, which had raised a commotion within the National Council for Hypnosis.

Belling didn't devote much of his time to clinical hypnosis anymore, as he was slowly moving away from his investigations in the field, and yet he was still in touch with the children in the hospitals. The hypnotist used hypnosis to help them overcome their trauma and anxieties. Belling turned his thoughts to the clinic so that he could explain the purposes, the conditions, and the therapeutic methods used in his sessions of hypnosis, "For your information, and before anything else, hypnosis is a mental state that is usually induced through what is known as hypnotic induction, of which you must have heard before. A hypnotic state corresponds to the so-called alpha waves that are connected to tranquility and receptivity. That is why people feel a lot calmer while they're in a trance. And that is what we'll be doing in our sessions, dear Anne Pauline. I will induce you into a hypnotic trance, but you'll always be under control."

Anne listened to everything that Belling had to tell her. Her hypnotist went on, "In past life regression itself, and with the use of hypnosis, you'll return to a past or different pasts that are beyond the limits of your current life. This will then take us to what we call extra-cerebral memory. As we reach this deposit of memory, it will be possible to reach the core of your trauma, and your unconscious will release the psychic substance named catharsis. We will then be able to understand the trauma that got locked in your past and, afterwards, we'll free those memories. From this moment, you'll then feel a significant relief of your symptoms," Belling concluded.

"And everything that I tell you here, what happens to that information?" asked Anne Pauline.

"In my sessions of hypnosis, I maintain the confidentiality of everything that is discussed with my patients. In this sense, my colleagues and the other hypnotists work within the framework of law, which in this case is the Code of Ethics of the National Council of Hypnosis," replied Belling.

Anne Pauline listened and understood everything that he told her. She had never really believed in the therapeutic effect of hypnosis, however. But, as the years went by, and traditional medicine couldn't help with her anxiety, Anne started to think about hypnosis as an alternative to her cure. Having heard Belling speak about regression on that day, she immediately understood that this was the right option to choose. Marcus Belling was the only one who could help her. But Anne couldn't help feeling scared at the thought of being hypnotized. There were many questions inside her head. How would it feel to be hypnotized? Would she go into another dimension? Could a hypnotic trance be called a near-death experience? What if Belling died during one of her sessions; would she be able to wake up from her trance? On the one hand, and like many other people, she was afraid that secrets from her past would be revealed. Everything would be clear if no filters were added. On the other hand, she didn't want anyone to know her personal history and she had to repeat the mantra to herself many times; I will trust, I will trust. Anne Pauline would trust this time. Marcus Belling then told her, "I would just like to reiterate that it's quite important to a hypnotist to know what happens to their patients during the hypnotic trance. This state is induced through the power of suggestion. At this stage, only the patients can say what they see, feel and hear. I ask you then to trust me."

It all seemed so simple, but Belling's request would make Anne Pauline face a dilemma, as she would understand some months later. This time, though, she had nothing to fear. Belling followed his professional ethics and was obliged to secrecy regarding the content of the appointments. The first of many appointments in those nine months happened. What both Anne Pauline and Marcus Belling would discover was well beyond their imagination, and none of the two was prepared for the revelations that would arise in the upcoming months.

Trust between the patient and hypnotist has always been fundamental to the success of this therapy. The lack of this factor would make it impossible for the patient to overcome any anguish that is caused by his or her past lives. However, there was an understandable fear on the part of some patients about reporting everything that was happening during the hypnotic trance to their hypnotists, as some of their memories were very deep and intense. In addition, there were some reported cases where professional ethics had been violated. In these situations, the National Council of Hypnosis applied the appropriate fines and disciplinary proceedings against those who had broken their professional ethics. One of these cases involved Josef Salvaterra.

The Salvaterra Case, as it became known, seemed like a work of fiction. A few years previously, a retired banker had come to see Salvaterra in his medical clinic, wanting to understand the feeling of guilt that had inexplicably persecuted him for the whole of his life, and to learn from the master. These feelings were mysterious, as he had always lived a respectable life with both his family and friends; plus, he had nothing to be ashamed of. However, something told him that his life wasn't immaculate, and so he looked for the reasons behind that strange intuition.

As the banker started his regression to a past life, he learned that he had been an outlaw who had constantly run away from justice and survived as well as he could. One day, though, he found the directions to some treasure that had belonged to a man who had died and left behind unimaginable wealth. Part of this fortune had been buried at a hidden location, together with his other belongings. The banker found the treasure but was then murdered by others who wanted to get their hands on it too. Salvaterra then asked the retired banker for the coordinates of the treasure while he was under a hypnotic state and used the information to search for it himself. Josef Salvaterra was sure that he was going to find a fortune. The treasure did actually exist, but it had been dug up years ago, and was now part of a private collection on display at the city museum. The banker was informed of Josef Salvaterra's action and reported the facts to the National Council for Hypnosis. The hypnotist was then suspended for three months, to the despair of Marbella Grey, who thought their end was near and they would both fall into misery.

This didn't happen, but the hypnotist never tried such an action ever again. The professional code had been broken, and Marcus Belling and his team very soon knew about the whole story. Belling was obviously not at all surprised about the facts he had heard. Salvaterra's episode was an exception amongst hypnotists, though, and not repeated. Trust was necessary for past life regression therapy to be successful.

While he was hearing a little of the personal history of Anne Pauline, Belling was also looking at outlines of the so-called Salvaterra Case. Then, at the very moment, his patient finished speaking. It was incredible, but an hour had already passed since the young woman had reached the medical clinic and the session was now over. At this, Marcus said, "Speak with Sofia to make a new hypnosis session appointment. And remember what we spoke of today. A new case is always a beginning for me too, in the field of hypnosis."

Belling could never have imagined that this sentence contained the whole truth about both Anne Pauline and himself. His patient now was staring at him, not understanding where the words were coming from. That tone of voice was familiar, and only now was she sure of that. It became clearer and clearer than she had heard that voice before in some way and, after thinking a little, she finally realized it was the voice of the man in her dreams, who had questioned her dignity and her honor, while asking for her to return to the past. With this assurance, Anne Pauline knew that this man was, very probably, Marcus Belling.

Anne Pauline said goodbye and thanked him for his explanations of hypnosis and past life regression. Something much more intense was now entering her soul. On the one hand, she was anxious to initiate this new journey into hypnosis, but on the other, she wasn't keen to carry on with it with the man in her dreams. Anne Pauline was in a dilemma, but even so, she knew that she would return the next day.

2

When Belling closed the door to his clinic, Sofia was at reception doing some paperwork, or so she pretended. She saw Anne out of the corner of her eye as she walked away from the clinic, without even greeting the patient. Sofia regretted admitting Anne Pauline, and all she thought about now was, *how could I have fooled myself in this way?* As she heard the door closing, she knew that she needed to warn Marcus Belling of the strange feeling that haunted her concerning this particular patient. Sofia didn't usually make such mistakes. When someone applied for sessions with Belling, she could rapidly evaluate the person really well and then decide on whether to grant them consultations or not. Belling counted on his assistant's intuition and intelligence as it stopped him from having problems in his work. There were obvious risks to fear. Many intruders tried to abuse his privacy by photographing him with hidden cameras or would even blackmail him. Sofia knew that once the patients had started therapy, they would have regular contact with the hypnotist and get to know him very well over the months; including his routines, way of life, work methods, and some of his life. It was essential to know which cases could reach him, and that made Sofia's work so important.

It's a fact that she knew Marcus Belling quite well. This knowledge came not only from the years in which she had worked with him, but also because she had herself been hypnotized by Belling. In a way, she had been a sceptic about the effects of hypnosis until that moment, although she had never confessed this. She knew that such a confession would grieve Marcus Belling. Her experience of hypnosis had occurred several years ago, when he had asked her personally.

He had been practicing past life regression for the past 10 years and felt the need to test it on someone he really trusted. The goal was to check if the beliefs or myths could influence memories that his patients had from their past. That was indeed a challenge, as the National Council for Hypnosis rejected regression as a way to cure certain symptoms and disturbances. Salvaterra and Belling were different from their fellow hypnotists as they both practiced hypnosis with a focus on regression, but some of their colleagues refuted the therapeutic effects of such a practice. These same hypnotists backed the idea that the memories of past lives were just memory failures in memory, with the human being using his firsthand experiences and beliefs to recreate images of a past that had never happened.

Neither Mark Belling nor Josef Salvaterra had ever the opportunity to refute these theories. On the one hand, they ignored the arguments, but on the other, when they had to defend their work before the public, they tried to confirm through real cases that regression therapy worked effectively in their patients. Therefore, there was a certain amount of discrediting going on by some hypnotists and, for that reason, Belling decided to perform a test with Sofia. The goal of the first session was to try to induce a set of beliefs and myths while Sofia was in hypnotic trance. In the second session, regression therapy was used, and he asked her to remember her past lives. He did this by resorting to the extra memory-brain. Marcus Belling would be given the opportunity to test the effectiveness of this therapy, although he had no intention of disseminating the results of his experiment. Despite being fully convinced that this therapy worked, and it wasn't a system failure of memory, he needed this last confirmation. When Sofia sat on the clinic's cozy green sofa to be hypnotized, something extraordinary happened; without ever losing touch with the outside, she quickly went into hypnotic trance. She hadn't expected to be hypnotized by Belling so easily. However, through the techniques and extensive experience of Marcus Belling, Sofia quickly slipped into a deep trance without realizing it. Despite their long working relationship, she had never thought seriously about what made him such a competent hypnotist. She knew of his dedication but had never witnessed his innate talent. From that day on, Sofia understood why people sought him out so desperately. The test was a success as the beliefs that Belling had introduced in the first session of hypnosis didn't influence his secretary regarding her real memories of her previous lives. She was able to remember a relationship she had once had with a man who seemed to be connected to typography and the name Christopher Beck appeared in her mind. After reading a few pages about a specific period of time, Belling realized that she had regressed to a time where he could remove concrete memories. Listening to her words, he realized that all she had reported was absolutely true. Sofia was not influenced, or contaminated, by the ideas that Belling had placed in her mind during the previous session of hypnosis.

This experience with Sofia strengthened Belling's will to continue to practice the regression therapy without letting his work be questioned by some members of his professional class. The test only served to reinforce his convictions. It was his intention once more to disseminate the results of these tests, having just reviewed what had happened with his wife, Patricia Murio.

Patricia Murio had been surprised at the courage her husband had shown in carrying out this experiment. She knew him quite well but would never have supposed that he would resort to Sofia to prove his theories.

She was marked by this experience of hypnosis, which not only confirmed Marcus Belling's competence, but also the therapeutic effects and success of regression. The truth is that she felt an enormous tranquility soon after this session. She felt a profound sense of relief when the sessions ended. As was reported by the other patients, it seemed that the memories were released from a spiritual force that overloaded their souls and it now flowed outside their subconscious. Sofia was actually a very rational woman and would, had it not been for Belling, kept her skepticism about hypnosis and past life regression to herself. She had never told him, but when she saw Anne Pauline closing the clinic door, she immediately remembered all the events from her past.

After the green-eyed woman left Belling's clinic, Sofia ran to talk to the hypnotist. She looked impatient. Belling didn't let her lead the conversation, but instead he did so himself,

"Sofia, I had a strange feeling with this person. Based on the look you gave me at the door, can I deduce that you felt the same?" he asked.

"The first time I saw her, I felt something really strange," she answered. "I can't stop thinking that I might have made an error with this particular patient, which doesn't usually happen. I deeply regret opening the door to her."

"Don't worry. I didn't ask the question to blame it on you," Belling said, to keep her calm.

Both Marcus Belling and Sofia Estelar were sure of one thing. They had the same strange feeling when they saw Anne Pauline for the first time, even if they didn't totally understand it. This woman's large, bright green eyes hid a past that either would not come out very easily or was too complex and traumatic. The question now was should Belling continue to do therapy with this person? Both thought about this question, but it was Sofia finally broke the silence, "Do you think she should come back again?"

Sofia's question demanded a quick answer, but she knew it would put him in an awkward position that was even unfair. But her feeling of responsibility for the situation he was in made her ask the question. Belling followed strict professional ethics, and never refused to continue sessions with a patient who needed him. Denying help to someone in need was against his principles, so he made his decision. He would take it to the end. He had never refused to help a patient in his career, and despite the chilling feeling he had experienced, he accepted the risks of his decision. Sofia understood his dilemma and accepted it, despite the fact that she disagreed with it. She was his personal assistant and there had been only complete trust between the two of them for many years, but Marcus Belling always made the final decision.

Two major events had marked this hot July day; the arrival of Anne Pauline and with her, the final test of Belling's personal convictions. Sofia knew this for sure. Belling was willing to continue with Anne Pauline's therapy, free her from her trauma, and with the help of hypnosis, free her to enjoy the happiness she had never experienced before. As always, he took his work as a public mission, without exception; however, as his team knew from past experience, there would be consequences to his action. Nothing, however, could prepare them for what was to happen in the following months.

As events rolled on, 27 Sun Avenue swarmed with movement and life. Anne Pauline left the clinic, walking down an avenue packed with restaurants, cafés and Victorian-style terraces at either side. There were many fountains, which delighted the children during the summer. Belling's clinic was in a building located at exactly halfway down the central boulevard. It was a magnificent eighteenth-century building of white lines, painted ceilings and walls shaped into baroque figures. On that day, just after Anne Pauline walked down the avenue, Marcus Belling and Sofia Estelar came out to have lunch at one of the restaurants in Sun Avenue.

At his clinic, Belling kept a library whose shelves were full of a wide range of books on hypnosis, which Anne Pauline had noticed. But his interests were wider than just that subject, as he was a man of many skills, and curious about many areas of knowledge. For a number of years, he had been interested in the connection between medicine and astrology, the therapeutic and medical properties of plants, the healing powers of faith, alchemy, and experimental science. Belling considered that knowledge of minerals and plants could, in practice, provide a therapeutic effect that should not be ignored. He accepted natural and homoeopathic medicine as a form of therapy, that was no less valid than hypnosis itself. Considering that the two served the same purposes, Belling started to try out both simultaneously for the benefit of his patients. Having started in clinical hypnosis, he decided to use his expertise from that period to take past lives regression into a whole new level of wisdom and skill. His library was, therefore, full of books on alchemy, regression, and the healing power of body and mind, medicine, astrology, and botany for the occult. All these books were a source of inspiration in his daily work, which Sofia didn't always understand.

But Marcus Belling was also passionate about the world of literature, and not only technical works. He was very keen on books in general, as long as they could make him a better hypnotist. Belling had even spent some periods in the city library, where he got to speak to Georgine Gunderson. A few days afterwards, the librarian was selected to work at the former city library. Belling would use some ideas from fictional or technical literature to help him in the most complicated cases. The theoretical study of scientific studies wasn't enough to solve certain traumas of the past. Traveling around the world and having different experiences, even if it was through books at times, was also a big requirement. Aldous Huxley's *Brave New World* was a splendid example of that. Belling used it to develop his critical mindset, which he considered to be fundamental throughout his career. He would sometimes use reading to question the pattern techniques that were used in hypnosis, and then suggest innovative approaches. His passion for this book, which started in his youth, sparked an interest in him regarding the construction of a pattern of society that was ruled by progress, without any notions of the past or concepts of morality and the family – a society divided into castes in which members were ruled by the same genetic and psychological principles, and also permanent controlled by the same social rules. As Belling grew and his interest in hypnosis developed, his mind naturally took him to this book. As he never forgot a good book and used the writer's ideas to understand his role in the world, the hypnotist got to understand that his work was a valuable way for people to look at themselves without the rules of social convention. Hypnosis meant freedom. The notion of liberty, as well as trust, was then developed by Marcus Belling throughout his practice as a fundamental pillar of his moral duty.

Belling saw hypnosis as an empowering tool that could be used to see beyond the soul itself, including within its own limits, the illusion of progress and established social rules. The hypnotist would start to transmit this powerful idea of his own power to his patients, which could cause him serious problems in his career; an idea that people are responsible for their own destiny and had the capacity to change their own lifelines, even if it was with the help of a hypnotist. Belling was a pioneer in recognizing that people might misuse this tool of power and change that was totally within their reach. The hypnotist only helped them to discover it. That was all there was to it. All these people reached out to Belling to help them to achieve felicity, and Anne Pauline was no exception.

Despite his success, the National Council for Hypnosis didn't fully approve of Marcus Belling's message and his position about his role. Some fellow members who had taken higher roles within the Council had warned him that he was giving false expectations to people, making them think that a hypnotist was dispensable during their treatment. The Council saw this attitude as underestimating the crucial role of its professionals and asked him to refrain from making this speech. He was warned that people will start self-hypnosis at home and then practitioners won't be needed. But, despite his respect for the Council's recommendation, he continued with his own work methods.

The approach used by Marcus Belling didn't just bother the National Council for Hypnosis, but also Josef Salvaterra. On a radio broadcast several years previously, Salvaterra had inflicted considerable damage to Belling by declaring that his colleague fooled people with his prophetic ideas. Josef defended the idea that the role of a hypnotist was irreplaceable, because sometimes, people need someone to guide them. He spoke this last sentence on a radio program about hypnosis and caused a torrent of calls from people who insisted on speaking to Salvaterra. "They must be mad *fans* of Belling's," said a witty Salvaterra to the program's producer.

Noted for having views that were a marked distance away from Belling's position, Salvaterra had a different status within the Council. Marcus Belling gradually developed his own work methods that were both more distant and innovative from those recommended by the Council, which created great enthusiasm in his patients.

Salvaterra and Belling started to move further away from each other, even within the Council. Unlike Belling, Josef Salvaterra didn't just want to become the most respected hypnotist in the country, his ambitions exceeded this. He aimed for more of a *status quo* within the National Council for Hypnosis, as it could give him advantage inside the professional guild. And for that same reason, he presented his candidacy for the Presidency of the General Assembly. He wanted to manage the destiny of the organization and, therefore, remove Bellin from his path. The only way to do this was to take over the management of the organization, which would mean controlling the whole Council. But he won only a small number of votes in the elections, which just infuriated him more. The events following the vote were disturbing. Josef Salvaterra cursed all of his colleagues, calling them ignorant, and promised to lodge a protest before the International Council for Hypnosis, claiming the election was a fraud. A few days later, to everyone's shock, his wife Marbella entered the Council's headquarters during a meeting of the General Assembly and tried to poke her nose into their internal affairs; specifically, the revenue obtained from the yearly fees paid to the Council by its associates.

Everyone knew how greedy Marbella was and all the hypnotists realized that she had been ejected from the premises of the Council, much to her anger. Marbella Gorey was, therefore, known as the mole who sniffed out money, wherever it was and at long range, looking in each and every single corner to see where she could get it, and by any means possible. She could use any resources if money was involved, and only one thing really bothered her – that her husband didn't earn much of a fortune. Marbella and Salvaterra had quite a good, but far from luxurious lifestyle and, therefore, she even used unethical means to reach her goals. She would do anything to harm Belling and push him out of the limelight and had tried to do more than once. A quick response by Maria de Burgos did, however, efficiently blocking the publishing of misleading material about Belling. But for some years, Marbella had the helping hand of a partner called Alfonso Rúbio, who was her cousin's son and frequently implicated in small-scale criminality. Despite being only 23 years old, his criminal report was full of different acts of robbery and was sometimes called a lost cause. He had occasionally agreed to help Marbella, for a fair price, to spread information which she found important to move the media's attention away from Belling, or to some other illicit activities. Alfonso charged little, which was great for Marbella, who found him the ideal person to achieve some of her plans. Nevertheless, this complicity no longer existed on the day that Anne Pauline rang the bell of Marcus Belling's hypnosis clinic, as Alfonso had disappeared some time ago.

Marcus Belling seemed immune to all of this, perhaps because of his loyal team, who had set up a complex system that allowed him to focus totally on his work as a hypnotist. He was told one day at an international conference, "Belling, you believe in hypnosis. It's as if an unbeatable faith worked inside you. I also had those illusions once. Don't think that you can know all about a world into which you can only enter through our minds," said a colleague.

"I believe in my job," Belling answered.

Not all hypnotists were convinced that their therapy was accurate enough for the public domain, even if they made their living from it. It was a contradiction to them, but some professionals did not believe in the efficiency of their work. But Marcus Belling couldn't conform to their views and always tried to keep true to himself. But it hadn't been an easy road, and he also doubted himself, his work and his mission at times over the years. At certain points, he needed seclusion to believe in those convictions again. Neither Marcus Belling nor his career would exist if it wasn't for his convictions. He also knew of the many limiting beliefs around hypnosis, which were made up by people or the media, and it wasn't easy to deconstruct those ideas. He had no idea that Anne Pauline would leave a mark on his life. Before she came into his clinic on Sun Avenue, Belling remembered one of the most striking cases in his career, one that helped him to believe in his work again.

One day, a woman called Carla reported sleeping issues to Belling. With the passing years and without any cure in sight, her disturbed sleep led her to somnambulism. This worried her son, as he heard her walking around their home at night. She was a single mother and had been since the birth of her son, and she rarely had stable work. This left her in a permanent state of anxiety and stopped her sleeping, sometimes for several days in a row. Carla, therefore, thought of hypnosis and, obviously, of Marcus Belling. She knew it was hard to get an appointment with him because of the long waiting list that everyone knew about. But Carla tried her luck, and Sofia considered her a high priority case. Due to her financial situation, the price she paid for her sessions was halved, allowing her to continue the therapy. Marcus Belling had a special price for such situations and offered lower rates. Although Belling was pragmatic, he was also sensitive to people who were in a less favorable economic situation and had set up the logistics to give them quick aid and therefore answer the most sensitive cases.

Carla confessed to Marcus Belling that she was afraid of using hypnosis to cure her somnambulism and wondered if she would sleepwalk during her trance? He calmed her down, saying it was just a myth and there was no reason to fear something happening while she was under hypnosis, as she was in a controlled atmosphere. As time went by, Carla felt much more at ease with Belling and started to feel increasingly comfortable about starting and allowed herself to go deeper into her trance, guided by Belling's smooth and hypnotic words. Belling would always tell her, "Carla, imagine that you are in a very comfortable position, now take a deep breath… feel your body at rest… close your eyes… and now imagine that you are Robinson Crusoe on a desert island…

the sea is at your feet and the waves bring you the sea air… take a deep breath and feel your eyes closing very slowly…"

Once more, Marcus Belling was using literature to help his patients overcome their inner problems by adapting quotes or characters from books. In this way, the power of suggestion could work. The writings of Daniel Defoe helped him to use a powerful metaphor on Carla. By suggesting to her that she felt like Robinson Crusoe during her trance, roaming alone on this desert island, where she had to rebuild her life using just the few resources available, he was restoring her self-confidence that had been shaken during her life.

Crusoe did save her life. Belling sometimes thought that this fictional hero, who saved himself from death and privation, had a glorious destiny of saving others who fell into the same situation. What better destiny could this character have, Belling thought to himself. For month after month, Carla saw herself on a desert island and, amongst the silence, gradually recovered from her anxiety. This powerful metaphor helped Carla to recover from her sleep disturbances and gain a quality of life that she had never experienced before.

In her last session, Belling told her, "I hope you find your happiness and fulfilment from this moment on. Our soul only understands itself when we start to look inside of ourselves."

This meant, therefore, that Carla had just awakened. She was waking up to life, which resulted in the sleepwalking problem eventually disappearing. Her sleep was now relaxing and revitalizing. This was one of Belling's most successful cases. In time, she even became close friends with the secretary. Marcus Belling also followed a certain pattern. He would invite some of the most remarkable people in his career for regular visits. This helped to keep their friendship with Belling and his working team fresh, at least for those who got to know the team better.

The day Carla left Belling's clinic and walked down Sun Avenue after curing her symptoms, she immediately looked for a second-hand bookshop, where she bought an old copy of

Daniel Defoe's book. Carla read it thoroughly and took major teachings from it, which would help her keep her wellbeing in the coming years. Next to this shop, which had sold old books for over 15 years, an antique shop, whose owner was called Argus Dubois, could be found. When Carla passed by this shop, she dreamt of owning a *gueridon*, a small, round table with a marble top. She would leave *Robinson Crusoe* on her table at the end of that day. The following day would be one more discovery to be made, one more journey to take.

It was not just Carla who learned something with Belling. Her case taught him the true power of imagination and of suggestion. He had already used it in other cases, though not with so much success. The so-called anchor-images were used with some patients to give them a bigger sense of comfort and safety during their trance. Belling then learned that these images were connected to the power of symbols. Here was an important field connected to hypnosis that had never been researched before and which now, with Carla's example, should not be ignored anymore. The knowledge Belling gained through Carla's case superseded everything known by the National Council of Hypnosis. Symbology was now an active research area in this field of work.

Studying symbols was now a fundamental tool that Marcus Belling used to better understand each case that his patients presented at his clinic and, therefore, to become a better hypnotist. As he studied, Belling became aware that the study of the origin, interpretation and art behind the creation of these symbols was more relevant than he and other hypnotists had considered, as symbols and their representation helped human beings to have the world in their hands. He saw that all myths, facts and beliefs were represented through symbols, and these showed reality. How could this reality have been ignored for all these years, he wondered?

Symbology didn't seem related to hypnosis and his interest wasn't connected to his work. There was no reason to assume that someone like Belling, who had studied clinical hypnosis, would choose to interpret his work in a more spiritual and less rational way. Though he now considered himself to be more open-minded, Belling's mindset had been logical and analytical when he had started to study medicine and neurology. He learned that humans were a set of nervous connections and specific organizations made up by a brain, spinal cord and nerves. The body is controlled by a complex system of movements and sensations. Of all human organs, the most important is the brain. In fact, despite representing only two percent of a person's body mass, it receives a quarter of the blood that is pumped from the heart. This blood, a fluid that flows through the circulatory system, takes the necessary nutrients to the cells and all the organs. As a good hypnotist, Belling felt the need to know about the brain's functioning and, most of all, the frontal lobe or the prefrontal cortex, which is responsible for the management of executive commands. This part of the brain is essential for attention, thought and task resolution, as a predictor of future behaviors and to gain consciousness of our decisions. Belling found that it was essential for every hypnotist to be knowledgeable of the overall functioning of the human body.

One could say there is a paradox when trying to describe hypnosis. It isn't only an art, but also, somehow, a science. An art, because not all hypnotists have fully mastered the technique, and because not everybody can be hypnotized. The hypnotic trance also differs in each individual and so it can be deeper or lighter, to the point where a patient might not be relaxed enough to go into a trance. It is, however, taken as a science too, and Belling thought that any skilled professional needed to know the human physiology, the nervous system, and the functioning of the brain. This was how Marcus Belling viewed his work.

As for the power of symbols, Belling believed that symbology was fundamental for a better understanding of the potential of hypnosis. He was incredibly grateful to have had a patient such as Carla, who had shown him another world beyond this one he knew as a hypnotist. It was really possible for hypnotists to become wiser as a result of caring about their patients. This was an extremely fulfilling experience for both parties. Belling also knew that symbology and language were interconnected as well, with each depending on the other. Belling warned his other fellow hypnotists of the importance of their speech on the patient and all the training they required to improve their language skills for hypnosis.

Belling's practical experience showed the importance of persuasive language, which, when it was brought into hypnosis, helped conversational hypnosis. The use of two remarkable words during the trance seemed to make a notable difference to the patient. These exact words were WHY and REALLY. Marcus Belling would introduce these words early in the sessions and immediately noticed that the trance would become deeper as a result.

He normally told his patients, "I would like you to sit comfortably, close your eyes and try to relax because it's very important that you listen relaxed and with no hurry."

By using the power of language, through words such as because and very during special moments of speech, Belling could hypnotize those patients who had managed to resist the treatment of other professionals. Some of these patients, though they didn't say so, were demotivated after having attempted sessions with Josef Salvaterra. It was for this same reason that, little by little, these personal reports made the media turn their spotlight on Marcus Belling. His innovative approach to hypnosis was, therefore, decisive. Belling used all of this knowledge to develop a captivating language that worked with patients and brought him fame and fortune. This was much more than Josef Salvaterra could earn in the end, which only made Marbella more envious.

The appearance of Carla changed Marcus Belling's perspective on hypnosis and his career, but the greater change would come with Anne Pauline. In both cases, the patients would undermine their conviction. This would give him dilemmas and doubts, which showed a different world in terms of how the human mind works. However, this was the beauty of his profession.

There is no doubt that Marcus Belling and Josef Salvaterra were two quite different people and hypnotists.

Their routines were different too. Salvaterra had tastes and habits that could be considered traditional. He liked to collect antiques and tried not to share public space with his rival. Like Marcus Belling and Anne Pauline, Josef had a library at his disposal. This was located in his home, which was not the case with Belling. Salvaterra had for the past few years brought many works on hypnosis, past life regression, magic, mysticism and spirituality. Marbella also brought his attention to other subjects beyond those issues, such as the occult, necromancy, tarotology and futurology. He had recently acquired books on metal transmutation that showed a more visible interest in chrysopoeia, the art of transforming metals into gold. Josef Salvaterra couldn't understand why Marbella was interested in this issue and would occasionally set up a domestic laboratory to try to distil gold from lead.

Marcus Belling, on the other hand, had more modern habits, and the great difficulties he faced in his career were the natural consequence of his exposure to the public. Once, during an interview for public television, a daring journalist asked Belling if he used hypnosis on his wife at home. This question sparked laughter amongst the audience. This moment left a mark on that year's television scene, but Belling's answer didn't feed the controversy any further, "Hypnosis is based on the premise that no one, with no exception, is free from being hypnotized. You can't oblige a person to do what he doesn't want to do. This means that hypnosis means liberty, as you are freeing another being to transform his thoughts and attitudes and allow him to live a meaningful and joyful life."

Unsurprisingly, scores of women called the clinic on Sun Avenue the next day to make an appointment with the handsome hypnotist, much to his secretary's dismay. The jealousy his secretary showed caused Marcus Belling to decide, from then on, to only give televised interviews in exceptional circumstances. Marcus Belling had taken the opportunity to have some fun with the situation, but it was down to Maria de Burgos to manage the consequences of his public actions. The same thing happened to both Sofia

Estelar and Patricia Murio; especially the latter, as she was his wife. From that day on, the tabloid press exploited the issue endlessly, speculating on a possible extra-marital relationship between the show's host and Belling himself. Some satirical magazines showed the black-haired reporter being hypnotized by Marcus Belling as he suggested the couple's therapy. Maria de Burgos had a full week's work ahead of her afterwards and repeatedly wondered why he hadn't said things differently. He could've done so, but then again, he would not have been the Marcus Belling that everyone knew.

Patricia Murio did know how to prudently manage these situations. She obviously didn't feel comfortable that the press was suggesting extra-marital affairs between her husband and some journalists, but there was no truth in the suggestion. Unlike other women, Patricia hadn't only fallen for Belling's charisma. Her stripped-off soul had caught Belling's attention and it became the main reason he had fallen in love with her. Patricia Murio helped him to look for the essence and leave the superfluous behind, among all the chaos that was brought on by his mediatized life.

On the day that Anne Pauline came into Marcus Belling's life, he felt the need to come home earlier than usual. For many years, his wife and Sofia had maintained an alliance, with the secretary controlling any woman who could potentially get closer to him. This alliance had been successful in detecting the danger signs of him getting close to females and then rapidly and effectively getting these women out of the way. Thanks to this system, all the movements of her husband and of those around him were controlled. It was with surprise and even some shock that she got that call from her husband, telling her that he would arrive home much earlier, as Marcus Belling was a restless worker. Both talent and constant work were essential in a career that was filled with professional success; even those who despised him couldn't accuse him of laziness. There was a reason for his early return home on that day, though, and Patricia Murio knew it. She didn't know what to think for a while, and even thought of calling Sofia to ask if something bad had happened at her husband's clinic. But she refrained from doing so as she didn't want to sound frail to his personal assistant.

When Marcus Belling finally got home, Patricia Murio hugged her husband and was surprised to see him crying. He then remained silent, without speaking a single word. He faced deep and inexplicable feelings that seemed to be transmitted from his patients to him while they were back in their past lives. These traumas from the past seemed to have an impact on Belling's spirit and to hover in his clinic, sometimes for days until they either disappeared or entered his body and soul. It seemed like a bizarre, surreal situation at first, and made Marcus Belling ask his fellow hypnotists if they had the same feelings while doing past life regression. Many of them were afraid to confess that it had happened to them as well and, for some reason, kept this from the National Council for Hypnosis.

Performing past life therapy was highly misunderstood in terms of the occurrence of certain phenomena. Not only did feelings seem to transfer from the patient to the hypnotist, but also the professional really felt the pain of the person lying on the couch. There was no comfort in this situation. Belling convinced himself that some emotional transfer took place, and that he and his fellow hypnotists were not immune to their patients' past lives. He had never spoken to Patricia Murio about this, but she also felt everything. He didn't need to tell her, because she knew that her husband experienced such a phenomenon.

The two quickly climbed the stairs and fell passionately onto the bed. The sheets slowly muddled around their entangled wet bodies in a confusion of gestures, while murmured words and loving sentences were whispered. After one last breath, the two held hands, stretched their bodies and vanished into their own fiery passion. Patricia then noticed that Belling had continued crying, not convulsively but innocently, in a more controlled fashion, as if he needed to throw off the intense feeling that had taken hold of him. He was now sure that the strange feeling he had experienced upon seeing Anne Pauline for the first time was much more than mere intuition.

CHAPTER 3

THE FIRST SESSION – FRANCE, 1785

1

The big day arrived. Anne Pauline would finally start her sessions with Marcus Belling, and it was beyond her wildest dreams that these appointments would change both her life and that of Belling… forever.

The sun was shining brightly on that day. The woman was anxious for the return to her past through regression, as it could open the door and enable her to understand her anxieties. But for the moment, it was no more than mere speculation. Anne wasn't sure if she had lived any past lives, despite her intuition telling her that she had so. She didn't know if her anxiety was related to any traumas from the past, but her intuition said yes to this as well. Anne was also not sure if Marcus Belling was the right person to help her, especially after having discovered that he was the mysterious and obscure man of her dreams. Once more, however, her instinct was right; the hypnotist would be able to find her lost memories, those mementoes that made her feel lost, guilty, anxious and incapable of defining her own identity. She belonged to those different times, especially when she dreamed. This was truly a different dimension of life that wasn't always so accessible to others.

Anne Pauline wondered how she could be healed by someone who had created so much harm. The man in her dreams had asked a set of questions every night that made her doubt if she even deserved to know her past. Was she worthy enough? Her true self was considered to be so, but she didn't know if it was necessary to look for the help of the famous Marcus Belling at this stage in her life. For many years, she lived with this dilemma, up until she finally built up the courage to ring the bell of 27 Sun Avenue.

Anne Pauline Roux had a strange mixture of feelings. She lived for many years with her parents in the village where she learned to listen to the sounds of the world, and where she admired the horizon at the end of the day; it was only that sight which brought her peace of mind. But during the night, everything changed. Her dreams were trying to grab her once more, and she didn't know if she should open the door to the unknown. At times, she felt a lack of freedom, as if someone had imprisoned Anne at a certain point, and there was no space left for critical thought to develop within her. This was the worst possible thing one could do to her. It seemed that her mind and capability of thought were chained, even if it was hard to define this feeling. She was also daunted by some kind of treason, though Anne could not really define this feeling, which seemed lost somewhere in the remote past. The combination of all these circumstances created a mixture of sensations within her that was not easy to define and made Anne Pauline's soul enormously unstable. After several years, this discomfort made her look for help and try past life regression with Marcus Belling. On this day, just as Anne was heading downtown, Marcus got ready to leave home. He kissed Patricia tenderly and made his way to the hypnosis clinic.

Marcus Belling had decided to see his friend Thaddeus Borba before starting his sessions. The man was over 70 years old and Sun Avenue's shoemaker. He was a tireless worker who kept doing his work with the same dedication as he did more than 40 years ago, and so shared many affinities with Belling. They had a friendly relationship, something the old man didn't have with all his clients. On his way to the clinic, he tried to sniff of a summer morning. He was a regular client at the shoemaker's workshop and normally trusted him to repair his shoes. Belling really liked to help those who worked on Sun Avenue by using their services, such as buying a book, an old chest of drawers or, as on this occasion, simply having his shoes polished. This purpose led to the creation of the Sun Avenue Free Club, an open organization that was formed years ago and brought together all those who worked, lived or simply loved and admired the famous avenue. It was far from being a closed, elitist group, as all of its members openly promoted their membership, as well as the culture and arts that had developed in that central artery, and its history. Marcus Belling obviously belonged to the Club but wasn't its most regular attending member due to a lack of time.

Georgine Gunderson had also decided to join but did so to develop her research into the history of the Avenue. Legend had it that large amounts of gold existed under this street, which had become the heart of the city. It was a myth such as this which was behind the construction of the statue to the phoenix, a tribute to the forgotten history of Sun Avenue. It could be that it was a forgotten history by convenience, Georgine thought, for if the legend was true, there could really be tons of gold to extract. But she would never know if this was true and there was no other alternative than to continue her search through local history, with a special focus on Sun Avenue. Georgine finished her lonesome work at the library before she closed up the building.

As usual, Belling used some of his spare time to visit Thaddeus. The shoemaker was a special person, who was different from all the others. Just like many other clients, Marcus Belling considered him to be one of the best shoemakers in the entire country, as he could make each client a special person. Everyone admired him, though some found it sad that he would not teach his precious knowledge to anyone who could then keep it alive. Belling hadn't forgotten Thaddeus on this particular day, but he didn't bring any shoes to repair this time. He just wanted to greet him and see that remarkable smile Thaddeus showed to every single client.

"Good morning, Thaddeus, how do you do?"

HYPNOSIS

"Good morning, Mr. Belling. You're quite early today. What can I do for you? Don't tell me it's because of those shoes I fixed last time Didn't it work?" the shoemaker asked.

"Don't worry, Thaddeus, I really appreciate what you did. Today, I'm not bringing you shoes, I just wanted to see how you're doing," a smiling Belling answered.

Thaddeus wasn't only recognized as the shoemaker of Sun Avenue but also as one of the last of his generation. He never married nor had any children, and therefore, no descendants would inherit his workmanship. To make it worse, he was the only shoemaker who played the lute. As he sang verses on the truth about people's lives (or so they said), they gave him the nickname of Troubadour of Truth. For others, he was not a troubadour but rather, an oracle, as each of the verses contained a vision of what the person's future would be like. The words of the trova, held a hidden prognosis about future times, which often materialized, and to everyone's knowledge, an apparent lay hid the prospect of future events, which could very possibly become true. Thaddeus Borba brought these up to entertain his clients while they waited for their shoes to be fixed, instead of asking them to take a walk while he serviced their shoes. This innovative method made him even more famous and brought him more clients. Playing the lute and singing those verses were quite a common occurrence for him, and that's exactly what he did when he saw Marcus Belling on this day. Thaddeus had known the man for many years and could tell when he needed advice to guide him in the future. His words came out to the sound of the music:

> *It is better to know at times*
> *Then just to wait and see*
> *The one who will arise*
> *Will forever change your mind.*

Marcus Belling was astonished, for he didn't expect to be the object of a lay of truth on that day. It was actually quite rare for a verse to be dedicated to him, and Marcus knew well what it could mean. He needed to be aware of his future and silently listened to this poem that summed his situation up:

It is better to know at times
than just to wait and see

But what did the shoemaker mean with those words? Just like the others who knew Thaddeus Borba, he thought that this man who shoemaker was a true oracle. Everyone knew that each lay corresponded to a piece of truth, which meant that memorizing and keeping it was important, though it was hard to understand its content. Marcus Belling was unable to hide his doubts when he asked his friend, "Why do you tell me this, Thaddeus? Who is it that will change my judgement? You speak in codes and I can't understand what you tell me. What do you know about my future?"

"Your whole future lies in these verses. Don't forget them!" the shoemaker briefly answered.

Thaddeus Borba did know quite a bit about the future of Marcus Belling, although he couldn't tell him. True oracles are only allowed to warn about upcoming events or provide clues about a way forward, but nothing more, as this would interfere with the freedom of each person. It was essential not to reveal everything to a person. This made Belling very uneasy and uncomfortable, as he didn't know how he should deal with the situation in his life after he had listened to this lay of truth. Once more, Marcus stared into the shoemaker's eyes, which seemed very sincere to him. The sun was at its peak, and the hubbub on Sun Avenue was growing, as more families came out for a coffee. As Belling saw the shoemaker put his lute away, he knew it was time to get back to his clinic. He gently waved goodbye to Thaddeus but knew that he had to keep those enigmatic verses that were in his mind, to himself.

He arrived at 27 Sun Avenue and greeted Sofia with an apprehensive smile. He could still hear Thaddeus singing his lay of truth in his head. His personal secretary could tell his state of mind just by looking at him, but thought it was related to Anne Pauline. The two knew that she would come for her first day of hypnosis later. The first appointment of the previous day had only served to clear some of her doubts about hypnosis and regression, and Belling had to assure her of its safety by focusing on the importance of trust between the hypnotist and the patient. Anne would obviously need to be looked at very carefully, but that wasn't what made Belling uneasy when he entered his clinic that day.

Marcus Belling had planned well to ensure his day flowed easily, for it was hard to imagine a situation, such as the one that Thaddeus Borba had announced would get out of hand. The shoemaker had now told him of a person, who would appear and change his future. At least, that was, if the hypnotist had understood him well. It would not be easy to break the verse's code.

The famous therapist felt the need to vent his emotions to Sofia. She had noticed Belling's worried look since he arrived. Belling told her of his meeting with the Troubadour of Truth, and then repeated the coded verses that the shoemaker had relayed to him earlier. Sofia had heard of the myths surrounding the lays sung by the shoemaker, but she didn't believe in the occult, nor did she believe that Thaddeus was a true oracle. Sofia refused to believe that any circumstance could affect the safety net that had been built around Belling and was maintained by the secretary herself.

She couldn't conceive of the occult entering their clinic, though she easily understood that some people could link such ideas to hypnosis or regression, including those verses by Sun Avenue's shoemaker. Sofia put it straight to Belling, as she wanted to stop this bothersome conversation. "Forget what Thaddeus told you! Don't let yourself be influenced by the verses he sang. Even if they're called the lays of truth, they're not scientific, as you may well know."

"Sofia, a lot of people have reported that some of the events he sings about in those verses go on to become reality," said the hypnotist.

"First Anne Pauline, now this! You really need to forget these verses. Concentrate on your own work and put this behind you," Sofia pleaded.

Marcus Belling looked into her eyes and decided to follow her advice. It seemed impossible to imagine that the shoemaker could know exactly what would happen soon. The hypnotist saw Sofia's point, though he had questions about many situations that had occurred in his work involving past life regression. In particular, the strange feeling that occurred when certain patients began to report their experiences of past lives, as it allowed him to question the extent to which the souls had traveled in time. He had, however, developed a spiritualist perspective after leaving clinical hypnosis, and had discovered at some point that the human mind had broad potential. Nothing, though, could have prepared him for what would happen with Anne Pauline.

After sharing his thoughts with Sofia, Belling opened the door to his clinic. It wasn't big, but each work area was well defined. On the right, there stood a set of shelves that his personal books, on the left sat his Victorian-style desk, and on the wall next to it hung the picture of him with Sofia on the day he had opened the clinic's doors for the first time.

In the middle of the room was the cozy green sofa that Sofia procured 10 years ago. Belling knew that the couch was the most scrutinized piece of furniture at any hypnosis clinic, and he insisted they find one that his patients would feel comfortable on. Traveling into the subconscious meant patients needed to feel at peace and secure on the couch, something that most people who came there struggled to find anywhere else.

In another corner stood Belling's private library, a tool he utilized often throughout his career. In addition to books on medicine, alchemy and astrology, he owned a broad collection of works on hypnosis, regression and the neurosciences. In a section dedicated to Regression, Belling kept one of the most acclaimed books on the subject, *Regression: A New Understanding* by Thomas Hommas.

Hommas became a pioneer when he wrote about regression at a time when so little was known about this issue. The first theories about the survival of the soul relative to the body were developed from 1857, and formal recognition of past life regression only occurred in 1967. The book by Hommas, edited in 1950, was a true encyclopedia, as it deciphered the language that related to regression and past lives. Hommas had graduated in Humanities and Psychology, before becoming keen on hypnosis and studied the field in depth. He explored the procedure of regression therapy to treat emotional instability and even psychological derangement. Hommas tried to develop a non-conventional treatment that was close to past life regression. He believed that he could expose the potential of the human mind to remember the events of a previous life.

This led Hommas to take an interest in neurology, though many of his books focused on regression when applied during a hypnotic trance. Years later, after further research, he would publish another book called *Psychology and Mind: Therapy in Hypnosis, Its Concept and Approach.* This was a first attempt to gather people's experiences and was available in Belling's library. It was told by people who had sworn to have memories from previous lives. These testimonies had been recorded for examination of results of the therapies applied by Hommas at his own consultations. It was the first time that a hypnotist openly approached the subject by exposing real situations.

Throughout his career in hypnosis, Belling had learned much from this work and had even helped in cases such as Carla's. In the book written by Hommas, he found reflections and conclusions that caught his eye, such as those ideas about the so-called regression guardians, the animal or plant-like figures that accompanied people from life to life, without changing much in form. These guardians kept the secrets of people's past lives, the passing of souls through times and their own timelessness. In effect, a vague memory of the guardian would remain, as it was unique to each person. It could be a bird, a land animal, a mammal or a plant. From these theories, other authors developed new ones by relating them to astrology. Some even wrote that the birth of a person under a given sign would determine one's regression guardian. As examples of these guardians, one could find the eagle, the lamb, the crab, the giraffe, the pigeon, the chameleon, the lion, or, quite possibly, the phoenix. Anne Pauline didn't know her guardian, but unlike most people, she was sure she had two instead of one, having two birth signs and all. It could only mean that she would have to accomplish a mission that started in her first consultation with Marcus Belling.

The book by Hommas shared some more thoughts, with the most interesting conclusions being related to real testimonies that had been shared by Belling's patients. At the time it was written, people stated that they could see themselves in different time periods while they were in a trance, and frequently in different social classes. Social status seemed an aspect that varied greatly when people were reincarnated. Other patients remembered dying in childhood in their past lives; such cases were particularly sensitive, as people had extremely intense remembrances of premature death that were only freed by hypnosis. This trauma of dying in infancy could pass through different lives, as it was hard to find the root of the problem and tranquilize the troubled soul. Hommas reported dozens of such cases. His final conclusion was that present-life traumas are directly related to negative experiences that have occurred during past lives. The individual would face extreme anxiety and pressure because of the psychological barriers that were passed on to their future incarnations.

Hommas dedicated his life exclusively to developing his research on hypnosis. He had become an expert to Marcus Belling, who took this book from his clinic that day to read at home. You never know when I will need to consult it again, he thought to himself.

Anne Pauline was born under two astrological signs, which did little to calm her sensitivities. She hadn't told Belling about her dreams in her first consultation, keeping it a secret because it was difficult to talk about. It has all started when she quit living by the sea to move into the city. The sea had always calmed her inner troubles, which continued to haunt her when she decided to move away from her family's fishing village. Anne had many dreams, but the intense ones related to a particular aroma that she could never identify. She only had a vague memory of a fresh scent that was similar to cinnamon, cloves and jasmine. It was like a fresh breeze of inner peace that she couldn't find anywhere else. This smell was associated with her past.

Because of these dreams, she started an obsessive and unstoppable search for this aroma in every perfume shop she visited. Sometimes, however, she felt quite discouraged. Anne knew that it would be hard to identify the scent of her dreams, which would mean she could be forever lost in emotional turbulence. Over time, Anne Pauline became very keen on perfume chemistry and traditional self-production methods, which she used to try and recreate that fresh aroma from her dreams repeatedly. Despite her many failed attempts, she learned the various processes of traditional perfume production. Soon there was only one other person in town who could compete with her; Jasmine.

Six compounds and endless combinations stood between her and that scent. Anne Pauline tried to recreate many fragrances by combining these ingredients, but she still couldn't achieve the special aroma. She knew that aromas were related to our remembrances and so were connected to the past. After some reflection, Anne decided that hypnosis and past life regression were the correct choices if she really wanted to know the true reason for her restless soul, as she knew the answers to her interrogations did reside in her past. Anne consulted many books in this field, as she tried the new perfume components. From *Secret Perfumes and Fragrances*, Anne Pauline acquired enough knowledge to produce a handcrafted perfume. Attempts would always fail, however, as the last component was missing; the essence that Anne didn't know about. The mysterious woman only knew that this essence had to exist in its pure form in nature, and that it should be possible to distil it. By doing this she would be able to recognize the aroma that had existed in her memory for so many years. This was one of the secrets she kept from Marcus Belling.

Over a year had passed since she had started trying to reproduce the remembered fragrance, when Anne Pauline arrived to the Sun Avenue clinic for her first hypnosis consultation. She rang the bell once more after arriving. After hearing the familiar ding, Sofia allowed the green-eyed girl to come to the third floor, despite distrusting Anne's intentions. Marcus prepared to welcome her to the clinic after meeting with Thaddeus Borba. The hypnotist didn't correlate the verses the shoemaker had shared with this mysterious patient's arrival:

The one who will arise
will forever change your mind.

After entering the front door, the new patient climbed the stairs to be greeted by a grim-faced Sofia Estelar. Anne ignored the underlying hostility and followed her to Belling's office, where the door was already open for her.

"Welcome, Anne Pauline. Please sit down," said Belling.

"This is my first session of hypnosis," the patient said, reassuring herself.

"Yes, I know. Don't be worried. You're not going to lose your freedom and won't do anything that you don't want to. As I said before, the most important thing is that there is confidence between us. There are always the usual fears in a first session of hypnosis," Belling answered.

After this brief conversation, Anne Pauline sat down on the green couch and prepared to be hypnotized. She had lost her freedom before she was even hypnotized, and once again she confessed her fear of being eternally lost in a trance, never returning to the present. Belling tried to calm her down for there were no reasons to fear any traumatic event; the situation was under control and she was free to ask him to end it at any time.

As Belling already explained to Anne Pauline, the Therapy of Past Lives would allow them to discover the traumas and anxieties that hadn't been resolved in her past lives. The release of these memories would significantly contribute to an improvement in her health and well-being. However, before starting the session, her reminded Anne Pauline that during the period of the trance, she would have to be honest with him; as it was the only way he could guide her the properly. Both thought hypnosis sessions could obtain positive results over time, but this was only possible if there were trust between them. The young woman seemed to have understood what she had just heard. As she moved through her different past lives, it was important that she described her experiences to the hypnotist, who would not have access to these extra memories. The collaboration between hypnotist and the mesmerized patient became crucial. Anne Pauline nodded her head in subtle assent. She understood perfectly that it was important to establish a relationship of trust with Belling and, without realizing it, she was influenced by the hypnotist's words, "Now, you'll be listening to my voice and start to feel very relaxed. As you hear my voice, you'll feel increasingly comfortable, and your eyes will slowly feel much heavier. I would now ask you to concentrate, as we are starting our trip back in time.

2

This was the first session for Anne Pauline, and with these words, she and Marcus Belling headed on a trip back to the past without a destination in mind. It always started like this. The patients never noticed that they were being induced into a trance during the sessions, as it always seemed like they were engaging in an informal chat with a friend. This was most probably an innate talent that Belling had mastered. It was also the reason quite a few people had told Sofia that they didn't notice the exact moment when they fell into a trance. Of one thing they were sure; the phenomenon was most probably linked to language and its persuasive power. The truth was that Belling had been, for all these years, taking his patients back to remote periods of time and making them live through their traumatic experiences again, as well as help them to understand the events. 27 Sun Avenue had somehow become a pilgrimage site for all those who were curious about hypnosis and regression techniques, but also as a sanctuary to souls of the past for refuge, tranquility and comprehension. As she fell into a trance, Anne Pauline stopped feeling those spiritual wounds. The hypnotist told her to imagine a tunnel with a window at its very end. Making use of his hypnotic words, Belling gently instructed her, "I would now like you to walk along this tunnel, open the window that you'll find at the end, and then describe to me what you see."

Anne Pauline followed his words exactly and, feeling a combination of both courage and fear, opened that enormous window that lay ahead of her. An intense light immediately flashed before her eyes, which dazed Anne Pauline and made her believe that she had gone blind. After opening her eyes, Anne noticed she had entered a laboratory in an old building, which seemed like a university. The girl had unconsciously traveled back to the 18th century. The year was 1785. It didn't take much time before she heard steps and suddenly, to her surprise, a man and a woman walked into the room without noticing her. Though she was in trance, Anne Pauline could clearly see and hear the couple. To Anne's surprise, the woman was her, but she was living in another time! Anne Pauline was astonished as she saw herself accompanied by a man she didn't know, although he seemed close to her. They should be husband and wife, she thought. He suddenly ordered the woman to pass him the test tubes and the filtering towers.

"Pass me those flasks, Aurélie," he said.

By using regression to travel back in time, Anne Pauline had discovered that she had been Aurélie Caen, an illustrious scientist from the 18th century, who was married to Gabriel Caen. The couple had been working for many years to search the chemical elements of minerals and of some plants, with the goal of finding a natural cure for some of the typical diseases of their time. At that moment, Anne Pauline found it exceedingly difficult to believe that the Therapy of Past Lives would have its effects; however, the presence of these two people was proof that it was possible to observe a past life by using hypnosis. Anne Pauline couldn't believe that the past life regression was really working, but she was living proof that hypnosis could be used to observe a previous life. There was no doubt that this woman in the laboratory was her... but living at a different time. Consequently, Anne Pauline tried to focus on that moment, as traveling back in time didn't happen every day.

The Caens had been working on clandestine experiments for some years at the university's laboratory; the academy where they both taught chemistry. Their goal was to prove the theories developed by Paracelsus about the transmutation of metals into gold. Paracelsus had lived in the 16th century, but his ideas on natural medicine, alchemy, transmutation and the power of minerals were still updated two centuries later. Both Aurélie and Gabriel had been interested in the studies of this alchemist and doctor for a long time, even if they didn't know what their destiny would be after they finally proved their theories about the natural world in the laboratory.

The university's internal rules and its Dean forbade professors from carrying out alchemy experiments. The couple ignoring the prohibition, having been long consumed by avarice and ambition. So, the plans remained private in order to put some of the theories of the alchemists of Antiquity and the Renaissance into practice, with the purpose of discovering how to transmute metals. Given the secretive nature of their project, Aurélie and Gabriel didn't have many chances to work in the laboratory (where they kept all their materials). This meant Anne Pauline arrived on a special day, as this was a major date when the two would conclude the research that had taken two years. It was now time to put these studies into practice and find out if the transmutation of metal into gold could effectively work.

At Gabriel's request, Aurélie passed him the test tubes and the filtering towers, as more lead melted into a flask, which would later be alloyed with other metals. The Caens hoped to transform this metallic alloy into silver and then into gold. This would be potable gold, also called *argentaurum*. Anne had been hidden behind a table next to the wall all this time, even though she knew the scientists could not actually see or recognize her.

Both Aurélie and Gabriel were focused on the experiment they were conducting and hadn't really noticed the girl who had just arrived from the future. Anne Pauline was frankly astonished. She had never supposed she would see herself in the middle of the 18th century. Now she had the opportunity to observe the work of specialists in chemistry anxiously try to discover the process of transformation of base metals into gold. The mysterious girl was also aware that she was witnessing an act that was forbidden by the rules of this university. The couple were so avid about the experiment it was worth the risk, however. For the last few years, Aurélie Caen had felt frustrated about the laboratory experiments that sought to discover a cure to diseases by combining natural elements; herbs, plants or minerals. In effect, there were so few successful results that the director of the university had declared four years previously that the institution's laboratories would be closed. Their costs hadn't been met by the very few discoveries that had been made in natural pharmacology. Aurélie and Gabriel had, however, decided to present a pioneering project to their director, informing him that there was a stream of water nearby that contained rare and unique minerals that could cure several illnesses. From the manipulated data given to him, the director was convinced of the importance of such a project, but with one remark; they would need to present him with solid evidence of the therapeutic properties of the water at the end of the research and convincing results. However, as Aurélie and Gabriel already knew, this would never happen because the stream had, in reality, no therapeutic or healing effects. Even so, they had convinced the director of their theory and the deadline he had set was running out. In fact, the day that Anne Pauline entered the laboratory in a trance was the last day they had to test the transmutation of lead into gold. Fortunately, Anne Pauline had arrived to witness the conclusion of this process. That was why she was hiding behind a desk and leaning into the wall, while still noticing her physical resemblance to Aurélie, who was actually her... but living in a different period. The hidden girl suddenly noticed a calendar that showed the date; May 5, 1785. Hypnosis had made her travel more than two-hundred years back in time, though she had doubted that she could really observe one of her previous lives in such detail using this process. In the meantime, Anne Pauline still heard the voice of Marcus Belling and reported back to him, explaining each aspect in detail. She was respecting the trust that she had promised to him.

This was a secret project she was watching. Aurélie and Gabriel were trying to discover the exact formula for gold and would fool the dean by leaving the city with the results they had obtained. But first, the couple needed to prove if their theories followed the ideas of renowned alchemists, including Paracelsus. Time was running out and the Caens were under pressure from the clock. They would have to present fake and forged conclusions the next day about the healing properties of the minerals contained in the stream near the city. Apart from that, the report would need to be well prepared to avoid any distrust.

Despite the secrecy of their project, Aurélie and Gabriel told Rosalie, who had worked as their assistant at the lab for many years, what they were doing right from the beginning. She had been called by the Caens to quickly come to their laboratory, and Anne Pauline saw a blonde woman with deep brown eyes arrive. Belling's voice now sounded crystal clear, as if to tell her this was the moment to watch closely what would happen during this experience. The lead had now been alloyed and crushed with other metals, such as zinc, mercury, copper and nickel, which would form a liquid solution after cooling down, but this didn't correspond to the expected result. The alloy had been tested many times by Aurélie, who, despite Gabriel's opposition, had insisted that all the elements should have been previously heated and then distilled. This procedure caused an argument between the two, as Gabriel had in mind a different theory regarding the metallic league.

"We have already tested your theory, Gabriel, and we saw that it didn't work," Aurélie told him.

Gabriel had to accept that his wife was right, they would try a new technique, but this time, they would follow her instructions. The time set by their director was running out and Mr. Caen had to swallow his pride. This meant that they had to reach the right formula for gold that day, leaving them with no margin for errors. So, Rosalie helped Aurélie to add water from the nearby mineral-rich stream, after which she combined all the elements, followed by powder alabaster. She then added the mixture to the minerals that had been crushed and absorbed by the water. Gabriel promptly helped Aurélie and Rosalie to heat up a small laboratory stove for the experiment, letting the mixture boil until it reached the right temperature, as described in some of the formulas from Antiquity. At that moment, the strange smell of melted material was now all over the room and Anne Pauline decided to go under the table, as Rosalie opened some window to let the fresh air come in. As she passed by the table that Anne was hiding under, something made the assistant stop for a moment; it was as if she had sensed someone else in the room. She searched for the mysterious person with her perceptive eyes, and a few minutes were enough to find a vulture under an old table that was in this laboratory because there was a lack of space in the university's other rooms. Anne Pauline and Rosalie faced each other, and their eyes met, the latter had to bite her lip to remain silent and not reveal her shock to the two scientists about the intruder in the room that day.

"Please don't tell anyone," Anne Pauline whispered, as she started to cry.

She had never imagined that someone in a past life would recognize her while she was under a hypnotic trance.

She didn't know how to react, but the green-eyed girl from the future was sincere as she begged the Caens' assistant to keep quiet; no one could know that she was there. Rosalie was moved by the despair of this mysterious hiding woman and decided not to denounce her to the scientists. Shortly afterwards, she was called by Aurélie to help finish the experiment that was being concluded on that day. The three kept stirring the mixture that had been placed on the heat by the Caens. It was now time to drop it into a flask. This would be left at a cooler temperature, after which the distillation would occur. The combination was then cooled down by using ice and water, and the team would then wait outside for the temperature to fall.

When the eyes of Rosalie met those of Anne Pauline on May 5, 1785, something extraordinary happened; this stare activated a power that was beyond the imagination of either of the two women or Marcus Belling. This simple action was enough to spark changes in the psychiatric structure of Anne Pauline, which enabled her to regress to her past lives in a unique way. This was an unheard-of situation. Though it was the first time she had experienced hypnosis, Anne Pauline knew that it was impossible to be seen or recognized during hypnosis. She hadn't heard of it happening in the articles that she had read in recent years on past life regression, plus, nothing that Belling had told her could predict such events. Anne immediately knew that she had experienced something unique and pondered if there was enough trust between her and the hypnotist to report the events that had just happened.

Anne needed to think quickly, but Belling kept asking her what had really happened when Rosalie came close to her, and she ended up hiding the truth from her hypnotist.

"Anne Pauline, what are you seeing now? Communicate with me," he said.

She told him it was nothing special and that the Caens' assistant had just opened the window for the smell to be vented out of the laboratory. Anne Pauline had decided to hide her power from Marcus Belling; the capacity for interaction with people from her past lives. As a result, the promise of trust with the hypnotist had just been breached. The patient had just kept a major secret, one which not even the experienced therapist could decode. Anne, however, kept focused on this past life. Within a few minutes, Aurélie, Gabriel and Rosalie returned to the laboratory and took the cold mixture. In under 15 minutes, a golden liquid began to drop into the flask from the thick, grey sludge they'd started with. This seemed like gold to them, but more tests were still required. Gabriel Caen took the flask to analyze the substance that lay in his hands and found there was no doubt that the combination of the metals with rare mineral-filled water had produced gold. Transmutation had really worked!

Aurélie, Gabriel and Rosalie were absolutely stunned by the results of their experiment and couldn't contain their joy, as they had put four years of arduous work into this project. However, they knew that there was no time to lose. Gabriel Caen kept this sample of gold with him, while Aurélie and Rosalie picked out every material that had been used over the last few years to transmute metals, which had now been successfully achieved. The group ended up faking the results to be presented to the director regarding the healing power of the stream water, which they had been preparing for months if the transmutation really did work. Finally, after concluding their experiments, the three ended up locking the laboratory.

These events in this room should have been kept secret, but Anne Pauline now knew the whole truth. The next day, Aurélie and Gabriel Caen left the university for good and traveled all over the country with their formula for potable gold, without ever returning.

After the laboratory was locked, Anne Pauline came out from under the table and felt disoriented. The young girl now knew that she had been Aurélie Caen in the 18th century and that she had just committed a fraud. What she didn't know was that Rosalie was a past life of Patricia Murio, the wife of Marcus Belling. It was impossible for her to recognize Patricia, though, as they had never seen each other, but this event left an open door to what would happen in future appointments.

It was true, Anne Pauline had committed a fraud in this past life. With the help of the husband, she had duped the university's director to develop the formula for the transmutation of metal into gold. She now knew now that this project had been delayed for four years, and that the water of the brook had no curative properties. Quickly, she remembered the man of her dreams who continually asked her; was she a respectful woman? Apparently, no. Now she understood those words.

As she wandered into the laboratory and tried to understand what had just happened in this regression, Marcus Belling called her to come out of her hypnotic trance. She would have loved to stay longer, after being one of the first people to witness the process of metal transmutation. There was nothing she could do, however, as the words of het hypnotist brought Anne back to the couch.

When Anne Pauline finally opened her eyes, Marcus Belling was curious as he watched her, while also trying to find out how her first-time experience of hypnosis had been. He obviously couldn't keep the inevitable question for much longer, "How did you feel during your trance?"

"I felt comfortable and safe," Anne Pauline answered quickly and sincerely.

"Now, that is how I expect you to feel during our next sessions. There is no reason for you to fear hypnosis. It's a very safe practice and you'll never be lost during your trance, as you'll always hear my voice," Belling assured her.

"I did hear you the whole time," Anne answered.

"We'll speak about what you experienced today in your next session. We'll slowly release those extra-sensorial memories to solve the trauma from your past. I once more underline the fact that our collaboration is fundamental," said the hypnotist.

"Yes, I understand that," Anne Pauline told him.

Anne knew perfectly well that her collaboration with him and trust had now been breached. She then lowered her eyes, feeling ashamed about lying to her hypnotist. The young girl felt that he had both read and understood her vague answers and nervous moves, but that hadn't really happened. Anne got up from the green couch, and as she tried to give him confident answers, a shocking thing happened. On top of Belling's Victorian-style table was an old photograph of Patricia Murio, which Anne immediately recognized as Rosalie, the young assistant who had helped Aurélie and Gabriel Caen to produce the potable gold in the 18th century. For a moment, Anne felt despair after realizing that Belling's wife had taken a role in one of her past lives and lowered her stare once again. Fortunately, the voice of Sofia Estelar resounded from outside, telling Marcus that the next patient had been waiting for over 20 minutes. Realizing that he had taken too much time with Anne Pauline, he waved her a quick yet friendly goodbye. They would soon meet for another session in this same clinic.

After her appointment, Anne Pauline decided to consult a few books at the city library, where Georgine Gunderson was working at that time. If she had been a famous scientist and chemist, more information should be written about her past character, Anne Pauline thought, which would help her to decode more about her life in the 18th century.

Upon entering the library, Anne Pauline went directly to the reading room, where she thoroughly consulted every register that had Aurélie and Caen on it at that time. One book in particular caught her attention, and Anne immediately asked if she could consult it. It was named *The Life and Work of Aurélie and Gabriel Caen: The Chemists of Illuminism*, and as she read it, Anne Pauline understood that the couple's fraud at the university had devastating consequences for them.

A few months after the experiment had taken place, the Caens left the country with the formula and their sample of gold, and the dean ordered that the laboratory where their experiments had taken place should be closed. Rosalie ended up confessing their project and that they had faked the evidence of the stream's healing properties. A major scandal, though, would arise only a year later. Gabriel Caen was now known all over Europe for discovering transmutation of metal into gold after giving the formula to a few celebrated chemists. Aurélie Caen was totally ignored from the annals of history and the rupture between the couple became unbearable after such treason. After finishing the experiment, Gabriel became responsible for keeping the sample of gold, which he did. However, a year later, he claimed it was an exclusive personal discovery. Their history was well documented in this book, which included testimonies from that period, and in other works Anne consulted at the public library.

Anne Pauline quickly understood that Gabriel Caen's betrayal might be one of the personal traumas she had from the past, which could explain her permanent lack of trust in anyone else. This lack of trust brought her incomprehensible anguish.

Anne Pauline realized that she had betrayed and was betrayed. On the one hand, she had tricked the university where she was working to develop a prohibited project and, on the other, she had watched Gabriel appropriate that discovery for himself. she was increasingly convinced that Marcus Belling, her hypnotist, was the enigmatic man of her dreams.

As she continued her exhaustive study about the life and works of Aurélie, Anne knew that she had learned more of her past than she could ever have imagined. Night had fallen and it was nearly closing time, but as Anne turned the last pages of this book, she discovered that according to its author, that the university where the experiment had taken place had been transformed into the city's well-known Museum of Gold, due to the chemistry work done by the Caens. Effectively, the museum had been inaugurated several years ago. The history of Sun Avenue had now begun to interest people, like Georgine Gunderson. As Anne Pauline would discover later, gold drives people and makes them excessively ambitions, and this greed was being kept secret by Marcus Belling's medical clinic.

Before returning the book to the library's internal catalogue, there was one last page she was curious to see. In the left-hand corner, something was written that surprised her; *To Anne Pauline CNPP.14.1.* The mysterious message was targeting this young woman, as if someone had known that she would read and study this book while she looked for her own identity in the past. Anne Pauline wrote the code on a piece of paper. Though she didn't know what she would do with it, she felt that it would be necessary someday. She hadn't much time to think, but she believed that something was in the way of her destiny.

When Anne Pauline left the library long after it went dark knowing that her first appointment with Marcus Belling had already changed her life forever. The former city library where Georgine Gunderson now worked stood two blocks away and the Museum of Gold only a few meters away, which she now felt was part of her own personal life.

It had been several weeks since Georgine Gunderson had been relocated to the archive of the former library, and boxes full of books arrived each day for her to put away on the still dusty shelves. Since the library had closed, its doors hadn't been opened again until the day that Georgine arrived. The shelves were covered with a thick layer of dust and the cabinets had a strange but unique aroma. The whole building smelt of abandonment, but the librarian still had important work to do. She needed to organize all the books in order of their theme, title and author, and give this sterile, empty space a new face. The city council had helped her by turning the central heating system and power supply on again, which made the old library less of an abandoned place.

As the weeks went by, the solitude she had felt in the first few days became less overwhelming, as her work required more concentration and care. She was the only worker from the old library, and the management of the whole bibliographic collection and the full archive had been entrusted to her, because of her two decades working as a librarian and archivist. She was used to the loneliness, but the smell of a library that had been closed for more than seven years affected her. Gunderson had a particular relationship with scents. Having been an archivist and librarian all her life, she had found that the effect of strong aromas was the hardest part of her work, whether that be the smell of printing ink, dust floating in the rooms, wood from the cabinets, or books, both new and old. As anyone would understand, this was extremely hard to cope with, and yet Georgine Gunderson had to deal with these smells every single day, as she executed these tasks. So Georgine thought of visiting someone who was known for producing handcrafted perfume, whose intense fragrances would last much longer.

However, they were in town only twice a year, using the rest of their time on major trips around the world. After her move to the former library, Georgine noticed that her sensitivity to odors had gotten worse. The lack of a good cleaning service and the abandoned aspect of the building impregnated each book and piece of furniture with a smell, torturing her more as the days went on. Her desperation grew as she worked at the old library. So Georgine decide to visit this special person in September to buy more of that essence. The librarian's situation was now unbearable, and she didn't know if she could hold on for two more months with such a smell surrounding her. This time she would have to but more if she wanted to save her job. Aversion to odors was increasingly like a disease, which she hid from her boss and the city council, so no one could tell that she was suffering from such problems.

Over the years, it had seemed a contradiction that a librarian should struggle with the smells of a library. Georgine Gunderson was afraid that she could lose her job for not adapting to her workplace. So, she kept her issues secret, hiding her aversion to smells from everyone.

This happened until now, even as Anne Pauline came to the library to research Aurélie Caen. It wasn't hard to find out that the Museum of Gold had been a place of major importance in her past, which helped Anne discover more of her own identity.

When Georgine Gunderson decided to visit the person from whom she bought artisanal perfume, she couldn't have imagined that this simple action would change the course of her entire life.

Now that you've met Anne Pauline and Marcus Belling, I invite you to keep following our history, and to feel your whole body as it slowly relaxes...

*I now ask you to grab a piece of paper and a pen to write down the codes **BO8** and **CNPP.14.1** that will help Anne Pauline to find her identity. It isn't always easy to know who we really are. Sometimes, the truth hides behind encrypted codes, as well as secret messages. For that reason, you should register those other codes that were hidden in the book to arrive at the same destiny as Anne Pauline does.*

The task isn't as complicated as it seems. Once more, calm down, move your legs and your arms a little bit, and, if you like, stand up to feel lighter. Do you feel more tranquil now? Relax.

Now, close your eyes and imagine Marcus Belling's clinic on Sun Avenue. On your left side, by the Victorian-style desk where the old pot was found, you will see a door. Please open it. Now you will see a chair. Take a seat, leaving the door open. Now you can watch as Anne Pauline is hypnotized by Marcus Belling throughout her therapy.

As you can imagine, this is a rare occasion. You are about to become the first reader who will enter the lives of the characters in a book. Leave the door half open. Nobody can see you, not even Anne Pauline, not even the famous hypnotist, Marcus Belling. The two are much too attentive to the session of hypnosis to consider the hypothesis of someone sitting down in this chair, where you are sitting down now, watching them. How do you feel? Remain relaxed.

Calm down... Feel your body as it is slowly rocked by our tale and, with tranquility, you can turn the page.

CHAPTER 4

THE FORGOTTEN ISLAND – THE DRUIDS TIME

1

On another day, Anne Pauline heard of a mysterious island where no humans lived. A phoenix also lived within that singular community, a unique bird that is reborn from the ashes at the end of each day. This bird kept a precious secret. History showed that the phoenix had to escape from mankind. Coveted for its magical powers, the bird was hunted by humans for thousands of years, and could only find peace among the seagulls, where it still lived. No one knew the exact location of the island, however, as its latitude or longitude never matched human prediction. Some written sources even stated that one could only find this island through hypnosis.

Anne Pauline could not remember how she had learnt about the existence of this Forgotten Island. It had been through her dreams, though it was necessary to resort to hypnosis to know about this piece of land, which was so far away from the world of men. She heard it repeated many times; the Forgotten Island is a piece of land that man had forgotten. Once the last man forgot, the island left the water of the oceans and became incorporated in another dimension, taking refuge from the battles and conflicts that develop between people.

Anne Pauline had never been to the Forgotten Island but had seen it in several dreams. She had many different dreams throughout her life, not only about her past lives, but also about places that she had never been to. The blurry visions she had were imperceptible, which only seemed to reinforce this subtle demonstration. This was a mysterious way to communicate, and it was what happened when Anne dreamt of a luxurious, green island with golden beaches and thousands of seagulls flying over its peaks. It had a rugged coast, surrounded by the ocean, and there was no man to be seen. These seagulls knew something about humans, which they had tried to reveal for ages, but with no success. For this reason, the place was known as the Forgotten Island.

Though hypnosis was the only way to access it, there were few practitioners who were aware of this non-terrestrial world, including Marcus Belling. But Anne Pauline had knowledge of it and knew that she could only understand the meaning of her dream by traveling back to her previous lives through hypnosis. Something inside Anne Pauline told her that the unveiling of her past was the way to make her inner discovery, which would lead to her felicity. This got Anne ready to find the mysterious island as soon as she went into a trance, though she didn't know when it would happen.

Deep in his heart, Marcus Belling was now certain that Anne Pauline would leave a mark on his career, though he didn't know that she could interact and communicate with people from her past. Although he couldn't imagine that the Forgotten Island was involved with hypnosis, Josef Salvaterra did know that a non-earthly and less mundane world existed, one could only enter it through an altered state of consciousness, with hypnosis being one of the ways. However, this other world was merely inhabited by plants and animals, as there was no sign of humans on it. Another dimension had been built to protect it so that it couldn't be destroyed or contaminated by the human spirit. One of these human-free locations was the Forgotten Island, which was kept away from human malice and cupidity. Salvaterra knew of its existence and that not everyone had access to it, even under hypnosis.

Conscious that Anne would leave a mark on his career, Belling was aware that she could make him question his own beliefs, and he was not ready to meet such a patient. There is always someone who reacts to hypnotic trance in a different manner than anyone else, and he knew that this had happened to all his colleagues. The National Council for Hypnosis pursued an investigation in all of these cases and collected the testimonies from hypnotists in manuscripts, which sometimes took decades to be studied and analyzed. There was never a short-term answer. There were no certainties in this field. It seemed like the time had come for Marcus Belling, as Anne Pauline seemed to be one of a kind. From the day of her arrival, Marcus had felt some strange, familiar and inexplicable connection with his patient, which made him feel uneasy and disturbed, without ever understanding why. Belling felt that he wasn't ready to accept Anne Pauline as a different case and tried to keep his worries at a distance, while also trying to hide his intuition and predictions from Sofia, who also seemed disturbed by the presence of this mysterious young woman.

A week had passed since Anne Pauline had discovered that she had been Aurélie Caen, the chemist betrayed by Gabriel and Rosalie. After this first session, she decided to visit the Museum of Gold, which was only a few meters from the former city library where Georgine Gunderson was working. Anne entered a building that had been adapted to its new functions, but she recognized the old university laboratories, which were now a wing used for the exhibition of works by Paracelsus and the other alchemists. This area demonstrated the theories about metal transmutation, as well as the formula used by Gabriel Caen to achieve the production of gold. Aurélie Caen developed further studies on transmutation after their shared experiments but would never see this museum being built in the town. The recently discovered past events were how Anne Pauline knew this place so well. After leaving the Museum of Gold, she walked to Sun Avenue for another session with Belling.

Her fear of hypnosis had vanished her mind during her first appointment with the acclaimed hypnotist. Anne Pauline was now fully aware that her fear of this therapy was unfounded. There was no transcendent phenomenon hiding behind this technique, as the hypnotized patient didn't lose control of their spirit and soul. The individual's consciousness remained intact, and so they could understand everything that happened. The look on Rosalie's face was still fresh in her memory. The assistant had recognized her. Anne had somehow become visible to someone in her previous life, which showed that she had a power that she could still not understand Anne Pauline did know some of the myths surrounding hypnosis, and just like many others, had her own preconceptions. She had, however, overcome the hardest obstacle, which was to fully believe the hypnotist in order to give him access to extra-sensorial memories from her past. Trust truly was the most complicated aspect of this and made it a major challenge. Anne Pauline arrived at 27 Sun Avenue, went up the three flights of stairs, and entered Marcus Belling's clinic in the company of Sofia Estelar. After sitting on the green couch, Anne let herself be guided by his words, "Now, feel your eyes as they slowly close… you're starting to feel very tired…"

Before she knew it, Anne Pauline fell into a deep, hypnotic trance. Her consciousness was open but dormant. Each time she entered this state, it felt like her mind had accessed a whole new world in which the transmitted signals were different from the ones she usually knew. Everything sounded different, even the voice of the hypnotist. What at first seemed like normal talk quickly became a deep trance, thanks to Belling's innate talent and his thorough study of this sort of language, which gave him a special talent for words. One could say that words were everything in this kind of work, but many years of practice were also necessary to refine the technique, and it could only be perfected by daily practice over the decades.

Like his patients, Belling never knew the destiny of these trips into the conscious and the past. Just like Patricia Murio, he knew he was influenced by these interactions and the souls that he encountered through his patients as he applied the past life regression therapy. In Anne Pauline's case, Belling was very curious to know where this session would take them both this time. In their first session, he found out she had been a famous chemist called Aurélie Caen but didn't know half of the power that had been used, nor its influence on the rest of his life. Today, however, everything was going according to the plan.

Marcus Belling had put Anne Pauline into a trance and then asked her to follow the narrow tunnel that she could see. At the end of it, there was a door. Anne Pauline followed her way to the sound of his voice. This time, however, the door referred to by the hypnotist didn't exist. Instead, Anne Pauline said there were three parallel paths, as well as other ways that in this tunnel to establish contact with other worlds. Marcus Normally, his patients didn't have such a creative capacity to deconstruct his therapy, but this time everything was different. Anne Pauline subliminally suggested the way to get to her past was different to the one that he suggested. Marcus Belling decided to let her wander freely, as freedom was at the heart of his *modus operandi*. Freedom was everything in hypnosis. Whereas Josef Salvaterra would not appreciate Anne Pauline's creative ways, Belling allowed himself to learn from his patient, though he was quite fearful of what might happen. For past life regression to work, he would need to respect the patient's will to operate the process. Belling asked Anne to follow her instinct and choose any of these parallel paths, and so she did.

"In this case, you should follow your feeling," said the hypnotist.

Her choice was not random. One of these passages caught Anne's attention as she could smell the ocean at the entrance. As she had always lived by the sea, this was an easy choice. Marcus Belling decided not to interfere. She clearly where she intended to go and had the tools to show her therapist a whole new world. Marcus Belling, however, would have a tremendous difficulty understanding how this related to Anne Pauline's past.

The green-eyed girl wasn't walking but flying. She flew between the sky and the Earth and could see everything from the golden plains to the blue ocean. This was only possible because Anne was sitting on the back of a giant seagull that graciously took her on a trip to distant lands. The seagull had large, light-brown eyes and a yellow beak that stood out from his whole physiognomy. Of every single animal in the world, the seagull is the freest of them all. Anne now knew that the seagull could read her thoughts and understand her fear, which could only mean that this was a magical animal. She let herself be taken over by the trip's tranquility and delivered her spirit to the seagull. The two were now one.

When she awoke from this journey, Anne Pauline saw herself on a deserted beach and the seagull watched her tired face lying on the sand from afar. She couldn't hear Belling's voice when she entered this path and suddenly felt like she was betraying her therapist, not only by choosing a different path in the tunnel, but also because she had entered a dimension that didn't seem related to any her past events. What was she doing on this island, after all? Once more, the seagull seemed to read Anne Pauline's thoughts and extended its wing to guide her. The young woman didn't recognize this place but knew that she had come to a remote island, and the surf of the waves was still at her feet as she tried to stand up. This was a location that one could only arrive at by air. Anne decided to follow the seagull, going deep into the forest that covered the whole island. The two now traveled side by side along the island, moving away from the beaches, which extended for miles and miles. There was no geographical indication of where they were, and it seemed to Anne Pauline that the seagull would remain silent. This was a secret place. After a few miles, the seagull took Anne Pauline on its wing and pushed her forward through the dense vegetation, behind which a vast, bright glade was hiding. They had now arrived at their destination. Anne Pauline opened her eyes in astonishment. There were hundreds of giant seagulls in front of her that form a community on this island. The vegetation was different, as it was less dense but greener and fresher, and she could hear the small stream that passed along the glade. Anne Pauline was now sure that this was indeed a sacred location. One of the seagulls, a notoriously adventurous and daring member of the group, came to her and said, "Welcome to the Forgotten Island."

The bird extended both her wings as she spoke, as if to tell the other seagulls to trust their new visitor.

Anne was in shock over the seagulls' ability to speak, their capability to read her mind, and their larger size compared to seagulls from her world. Not forgetting, of course, how she had arrived there through hypnosis.

Anne had heard of this island and how it was lost from the human world, which was why it wasn't registered on any map or geography known to humans. The island was sacred and a true secret. It had been forgotten by the terrestrial world and become a mysterious corner that was only inhabited by giant seagulls. She realized that this was the island she had dreamt of all her life, had never doubted but didn't have much time to think about it. Anne tried to memorize everything she could, as she knew that it was a rare and unique occasion. She was suddenly surrounded by the seagulls. In a coordinated way, they formed a long, wide corridor that connected the end of the clearing to a wooden house that stood a few feet from the ground. An awkward silence now filled the area. The door of the house then opened, and two seagulls came out of it. Anne immediately recognized one of them as the bird who had brought her to the Forgotten Island during her hypnotic sleep. The other, however, was much bigger and looked much older than the rest. It had some prominent role in their community.

The two seagulls quickly came closer to Anne Pauline and took a long look at her. The eldest one, covered in darker feathers, protected her with its wing. As Anne looked deep into its ocean-colored eyes, the young woman saw her entire childhood, including the trips with her father on their family's fishing boat under the bright blue sky. Anne Pauline realized that this wise seagull knew about both her destiny and her past, and that it was responsible for bringing her to the Forgotten Island. Given this, Queen Seagull then told her, "This is the Forgotten Island. I know that you dreamt of our land many times over, as it holds a key function in the human world, even if they usually ignore this. We fly around the world to spread wisdom, and when someone falls into a hypnotic trance, we bring this person to our island. This is the only way for them to meet us. Not all people under hypnosis are chosen to visit the Forgotten Island, however."

"So why was I chosen to find out about the island?" Anne Pauline asked immediately

"Because we want you to help us spread wisdom throughout the world," answered Queen Seagull.

"Just that?" a curious Anne Pauline asked.

"This is already a major task. It's a complicated mission, and for that reason, we have flown around the world for ages. Humans, however, always repeat their mistakes. We try to teach man to live wisely. Wisdom implies forgiveness. In your case, you possess a unique power and a past that you'll have to understand so that you help us with this mission. That is why the Forgotten Island always came up in your dreams," said the Seagull.

This revelation left Anne Pauline speechless. The Forgotten Island was only accessible through hypnosis and the seagulls spread wisdom around the world. She recognized that this was a grueling task. It was quite probable that the seagulls had had this role for many centuries. Only that could explain why she'd had dreams of this island for so many years.

"We have been doing this for two millennia. For 2,000 years, we have tried to get man to turn his attention towards wisdom, generosity, friendship and other values that seem to be lost in the human world. We need someone who has learnt from their past to help us with our mission," said Queen Seagull.

"In that case, I don't think I am the right person," said Anne Pauline, still not understanding how she had been taken to the Forgotten Island.

"It's clear that you're the right person. The past doesn't tell you what you can be today, if it's your will to go on this way. It is so with all men," answered the seagull.

The truth was that the dark-feathered Queen Seagull had managed to read our young woman's thoughts. Anne Pauline then understood that she had always dreamt of the Forgotten Island because it was intrinsically related to her past. The seagulls knew of her anguish, her inner unrest, and that Anne had started doing hypnosis under the guidance of Marcus Belling. That was why they had brought her to the island during her second appointment; they wanted to let her know that the island of her dreams did exist, and that the seagulls knew her secret. Anne Pauline once more felt a sense of tranquility, as she always did after dreaming of this magical location. But Anne couldn't leave them without knowing about the history of the island, so she had to remain in a trance for longer.

Beyond the fact that the island was only accessible by hypnosis, it was written that the one in a trance could only return there one more time. The place was so well kept that the seagulls could not allow its existence to be revealed to anyone else. The birds decided to tell the history of this place to Anne Pauline, something rarely offered to visitors. She now had an important mission to undertake and the seagulls wanted to relieve some of the distress that had been caused by her dreams. They summoned a general assembly and unanimously decided that Anne Pauline had the right to know more about the Forgotten Island.

Anne Pauline wasn't aware of what had happened around the island, as it was the task of the seagulls to keep the island's existence mysterious. The Queen Seagull took Anne Pauline into the wooden cabin and asked her to sit down by a small bonfire at its center.

"Please sit here now. I will have to tell you the history of this island so that you understand your mission," said the seagull.

The seagulls that formed this community followed the *Book of Rules*, which was a collection of the most important rules that governed their community. It was kept in Queen Seagull's wooden cabin and could only be consulted by her. When she died, the wisest seagull would take her place.

Rule #18 in the bool set out one of the most fundamental rules of the community; the history of the Forgotten Island can only be transmitted in one of three ways, that each made sure that its history was well kept. Queen Seagull explained that the history of the Forgotten Island could only be explained through dreams, hypnosis or being induced into an unconscious state by smelling hypnotic fragrances that worked as a sedative. Anne had already seen the island through her dreams, and, at that moment, she was under hypnosis, so the alternative was to fall into a deeper dimension, far from that of the seagulls. This was another dimension that showed the past of the island. So, to tell Anne Pauline the truth about their world of luxuriously green hills and golden beaches, Queen Seagull applied the scents by using a plant that was only native to this location.

Before preparing the recipe for this fragrance, she took one of the dark feathers from her opulent body by using her beak. This was a sacred element, the Feather of Mercy, which wasn't given to everyone who was allowed onto the island. The wise seagull explained this to Anne and decided to proceed differently with this young woman, as she would certainly change the perspectives and the lives of others. This made it essential that Anne forgave her past. The leader of the seagulls gave the mysterious young woman the feather, which would protect and guide her, and turned it into a sacred object.

"It is required that, someday, the feather will come back to its origins. But only when your mission is accomplished," said the wise seagull.

It was now time to use the herbal fragrance to recreate that hypnotic scent so that the history of the Forgotten Island, or Island of Wisdom, as the seagulls knew it, could finally be told. Anne Pauline now knew that this place had two names, the first one being the most common. Queen Seagull then opened *Book of Rules* and turned to rule #19, where the recipe for the hypnotic scent was written. Anne Pauline was rapidly taken to another state of consciousness, one even deeper than the one she had been induced into by Belling.

The other seagulls outside the log cabin soon understood what was happening and silence fell on the community, for this was a unique moment.

The history of the Forgotten Island, also known as the Island of Wisdom to the seagulls, unfolded before Anne Pauline, from the moment she heard the Queen's voice rather than Belling's. There were no sea routes to the island or any known maps of it. But it hadn't always been like that. Many centuries ago, a lonesome man who was navigating the oceans without a route, arrived at the island in his wooden canoe. This was unprecedented, for no such thing had ever happened to the truly astonished seagulls, who had been living there a long time. The first seagulls on the island had been expelled from the world of humans, for they didn't want anyone else to have moral rule over their actions, and so decided to ban these wise animals from their lives. As they had gotten rid of the wise seagulls, humans were lost forever, despite thinking they had achieved a greater freedom. Despite this, the seagulls decided to continue their mission of spreading knowledge around the world and kept following the tragic developments down there, every single day. Living on their island meant they were protected from human malice and incomprehension, so they decided to keep access to it from outside limited, and only through the process of hypnosis. For over a century, the community grew. No rules had been written, the log cabin hadn't been built, the recipe for the fragrance hadn't been created, and there was no leader of the seagulls. But the community was strong and firm in continuing its mission to teach men what the most relevant things in life were.

When this solitary man with no name arrived on the Forgotten Island, everything changed. The seagulls knew that this island belonged to another non-Earthly world that couldn't be accessed by using latitude or longitude, as it was on Earth. The island was located in a world different to that of humanity, and only seagulls could connect the two worlds of different dimensions by flying low between them. But as this solitary, exhausted and naked man arrived on the island, he began to yell, "I know the truth! I know this island, for I saw it in my dreams! I have learned and forgiven!" after which he fell on the sand and rapidly lost his senses. The seagulls knew that humans were resentful and vindictive, and that some of them couldn't forgive their past after they got to truly know it. However, this wasn't the case with this man, as the community could prove after hearing the story from him moments later, as they all sat in the clearing of the forest.

The lonesome man who had come ashore on the Forgotten Island earlier in the day was the first and only man who had managed to arrive there without being hypnotized. He had lost his family at sea in a previous life, for which he spent a troublesome life with dreams of a terrible sinking. He had forgiven that past life, however. But as the seagulls knew so well, although he said he forgave, a human would often not say it sincerely. Resentment and pain over traumatic or dramatic moments can always remain in one's memory. But the seagulls rapidly recognized the honesty in this man. This led them to draft *Book of Rules*, in which the first page promptly established the only two possible paths to the Island of Wisdom; under hypnosis and after fully forgiving the past. Fully forgiving the past was the hardest path to the island, but possible, as the lonesome man had shown them. The nameless man got a new name from the community; Felix. He stayed and lived with the seagulls until his passing, and as his ashes were scattered into the sea, he transformed into a beautiful orange and red-colored bird that reflected the colors of the sunset. At the end of the day, Felix returned to ashes, before turning into a bird the following day. Within a few years, he had become known as Phoenix. Queen Seagull took this moment to give Anne Pauline a feather of the phoenix while she was under the effect of the fragrance. She kept it with the seagull feather inside the pocket of her jacket. These were two sacred feathers that she needed to keep with her along the path to the discovery of her identity. Anne Pauline was obliged to resist avarice and greed, and to protect the feathers until the end of her journey.

In the meantime, Queen Seagull kept telling Anne the story of the island. After Felix passed away, *Book of Rules* was written by the Scrivener Seagulls, inaugurating the School of Wisdom, where younger seagulls were now taught how to transcribe wisdom into text. The *Book of Rules* grew as an orienting guide for the community. In addition to the Scrivener Seagulls, there were the Messenger Seagulls, which would transport people under hypnosis to the Island of Wisdom. Not all those who were hypnotized around the world were allowed onto the island, though; only those who the seagulls thought were apt to help them spread wisdom to every human. Then there were the Listener Seagulls. They were much quieter, but which could listen to every sound that was made in the world, allowing them to warn the others if the community was in danger. Among these, the Sentinel Seagulls arose. They adopted a more militaristic posture and were trained to defend the island. The community was organized by distinct functions and tasks. Everyone helped to maintain and preserve the existence of the Forgotten Island. Throughout the centuries, the Scrivener Seagulls would add new facts and wisdom to the *Book of Rules*. As the community grew, it required a leader, and a Queen Seagull was chosen, being the wisest amongst them and a bird that showed better group leadership. This event only occurred a hundred years after the lonesome man arrived on the island. He was now restricted to a specific area of the island, where he was a bird during the day and became ashes during the night.

After all this time, Queen Seagull decided to inaugurate one new era in their mission of spreading wisdom to the humans. Once in every 50 years a new person, under hypnosis, would receive the feather of mercy, and take it to the world of humans to find a way for their knowledge as well as their felicity. Those who received the feather of mercy would not only forgive their past, but also show the others the way to a more fulfilling life. The chosen one would require an inner potential to change the others' pasts. This was why, on that day, Queen Seagull gave one of her feathers to Anne Pauline.

This was how the seagulls found to believe in their own convictions. At times, the effort they took to transmit knowledge to humans didn't seem to show the desired results. They rapidly understood that they had to ally themselves with man in order to make their actions come true. The seagulls would need to unanimously agree that the chosen person deserved their trust to use their capacity to set a new path to the past event, by pardoning the past to find a better future. To achieve their mission, humans were required to show the seagulls a sign to receive their trust.

Anne Pauline listened carefully to the history of the Forgotten Island. The fragrances exhaled inside the log cabin still produced their effect, while the history of the island was told to her by Queen Seagull. Her voice whispered among the silent scents. It had been determined in the *Book of Rules* that the history of the Island of Wisdom couldn't be verbalized. There was no oral tradition among the community, so the truth about the world and the humans was transmitted through stares, scents, premonitions and dreams. That was how their system worked. Anne Pauline was still in an even deeper consciousness. After first being put under hypnosis by Belling, Anne sensorial perception had become deeper. She could feel the aromatic power as if it could speak to her. The truth was that the scents were communicating with Anne Pauline and once more, they showed a connection to her past. Queen Seagull then put out the fire, extinguishing the hypnotic trance. Anne opened her eyes, still incredulous that it was possible to communicate through silence. Her hand now held the Queen's feather. All that had happened and everything she heard was true. The feather of mercy did really exist, and the lonesome man was part of the history of this island. Now it was time for her to leave.

Queen Seagull showed the young woman the door and they both left the hut, towards the enthusiastic community of seagulls that had waited for 50 years for this moment. Queen Seagull's wing landed on the shoulder of the patient of Marcus Belling, and said to her, "Only Anne Pauline will be able to know with security the person you are. The whole of mankind is complex in its nature, and it can take decades to know this depth. If you receive glances of suspicion while entering that medical clinic in Sun Avenue, promise to yourself that you'll be true to your own history."

In that instant, the other seagulls rapidly surrounded the young woman. A Scrivener Seagull came close and asked her to read an important writing in *Book of Rules*. Anne Pauline audibly read, "The Forgotten Island is a secret that should be kept. After traveling to this island and taking the feather of mercy with me, I promise I won't speak of its existence to anyone."

The seagulls opened the way for the Messenger Seagull, who waited for Anne at the other end of the glade to take her back to Marcus Belling's couch. Anne Pauline walked the improvised corridor and sat on the large back of the seagull. Queen Seagull had gone back into her log cabin. The seagull rapidly flapped its wings and took off. Once more, Anne had a birds-eye view of the golden plains and the blue ocean. She was very tired, and her eyes became heavier and heavier.

A few minutes had passed before Anne Pauline recognized Marcus Belling's voice. Sounding distorted, it told her, "You'll now slowly awake and your eyes will gradually open. Your body still feels like it's flying."

2

Anne Pauline returned to Belling's clinic to the sound of these words, still startled about what had happened to her and not knowing what to tell her therapist about the experience that she had just had. Anne clearly remembered that she had just promised the seagulls not to speak about the Forgotten Island's existence, the feather of mercy, the log cabin, or the hypnotic scent to any other human. So, what would she report to her therapist, to whom she had sworn honesty during the sessions? Anne had promised him that she would tell him everything that happened during her trance. The young woman felt catharsis but knew that it was difficult dilemma to solve. Once more, Anne's green eyes were directed at Belling's Victorian-style desk. Something that was related to her past hid in it, but whatever it was, she didn't know. Anne rapidly took her eyes away from it, as she understood that Belling wasn't fond of her excessive attention towards his furniture.

When Anne Pauline awoke from her hypnotic trance, she realized that she was crying. Belling was sat in front of her, still perplexed by her silence during the entire session, as she hadn't answered a word to his questions about her experience. Belling waited for her to fully awake from her trance so that he could face her, as it was such an unheard-of situation in his career. Never in his whole career had anyone ever kept silent for the whole trance, as if one had gone into a non-earthly world, but there was always some physical movement that showed him that his patient had traveled back in time. Belling didn't pretend to be tough on Anne Pauline, but the lack of collaboration of the person on the couch was the worst thing that could've happened to the hypnotist. Honesty was an important value for Belling, so when a patient didn't trust him enough to share their experiences during regression, this meant more to the hypnotist than a mere lack of confidence; sincerity was at risk. The hypnotist waited for Anne to recover from her catharsis and asked her, as soon as she was ready, to tell him why she had kept silent for all that time. She understood the embarrassing situation but knew that she couldn't speak about the existence of the Forgotten Island. As her hand searched the pocket in her jacket, she knew that Queen Seagull's feather was there and felt relieved. Anne had to keep her secret, but she was required to give an explanation of what had just happened in the session.

"I didn't go back to a past life this time. I also didn't see Aurélie Caen. I flew on the back of a seagull, though, and couldn't hear its voice. The wind blocked all the sounds in my direction," said Anne Pauline.

"You flew on the back of a seagull?" Belling asked with curiosity.

"Yes, I believe that it wanted to show me other lives from my past, but we flew around for two hours and I couldn't hear anything else," said Anne Pauline, while covering up all facts about the island.

"I am rather surprised. That wasn't what I expected with past life regression," said Marcus Belling

"I understand," answered Anne.

"In my opinion, this seagull is connected to your past, even if it isn't connected to the past of Aurélie Caen. Did you ever dream of seagulls?" asked Belling.

The experienced hypnotist was muddled. He couldn't understand how the session could have led to such a situation. How could Anne Pauline's past be related to a seagull, after all? Marcus Belling couldn't connect the dots. He needed her to tell him what had actually happened during the two hours that she spent on the back of the seagull that showed her the world. Anne Pauline decided to keep her explanation short, as she still didn't know what to report. It was essential that he couldn't tell she was keeping secrets despite swearing honesty to him. Anne then spoke of flying in the company of a seagull that knew her past lives, but without referring to the Forgotten Island or, as she preferred calling it, the Island of Wisdom. Marcus Belling listened carefully to what Anne said told her that he now realized this regression had gone differently somehow. This time, her past had used wings to come to Anne Pauline.

Belling wasn't satisfied by her version of the facts. For the first time in his life, he was feeling that he still hadn't established a relationship of confidence with this patient. However, he was resilient. Many sessions of hypnosis were to come, and he was sure the young woman would come to trust his words, and so trust the treatment.

After the session, Anne waved goodbye to Marcus Belling, aware of having breached the agreement they had sealed on her first day. As she came down the three flights of stairs, the green-eyed youngster was reminded of the seagull feather that she had put in her jacket pocket. It seemed unbelievable, but the feather had crossed time and accompanied her through the hypnotic process. Anne Pauline knew that she had been given this feather to accomplish a mission, but still didn't know how to carry this out. This question, as well as the fresh breeze, followed Anne on her way back home.

In the meantime, Marcus Belling was alone in his clinic. He looked again at his Victorian-style desk. Something in this piece of the furniture had caught his patient's eye and the hypnotist didn't like to think that something had slipped through his fingers. He kept thinking of what he might find in the drawers.

It didn't take much more time for him to finally get his hand on an old magazine that stood out from the wooden drawer. Marcus took it out for a better look. It was a first edition from 1930, he read on the upper right corner of the cover. It was a specialty issue on nature, animals and marine life. Belling would need to consult Sun Avenue's second-hand seller, but he was sure he was holding a rare magazine. He could tell by its worn-out aspect, as if its pages had been turned over many times. He was right. This first edition had been issued in 1930 and there had only been two editions, so it had become extremely valuable. A lack of readers and a lack of public curiosity about such a specific issue, which only concerned a small elite group, had brought about the end of this magazine only a few months after its first issue. This publication, published on November 3, 1930, had an article on the most recent discovery of a rare species of plant in some remote part of the planet. Back in the day, only two or three scientists minded about such a discovery. They were living in the aftermath of World War I, and both the political and economic instability of the time was felt all over Europe and would soon lead to World War II. This background was clearly not suitable for the development of further interest in this subject and the article went unnoticed.

What Marcus Belling did not know was that the article announced the existence of a plant that only grew on the Forgotten Island. This was the one place that was beyond his knowledge, but which Anne Pauline had gotten acquainted with during her second session of hypnosis. At the time of the article, the Forgotten Island could still be found in the Pacific Ocean. A few years later the island would belong only to the world of hypnosis and vanish off the maps and memory of men. Now nobody knew of the Island of Wisdom's whereabouts, as it had never been lived on by men, only by seagulls. These birds were able, through flight, to lift the island off the ocean and transport it to a world away from men. From that moment on, the Forgotten Island was hardly accessible through hypnosis. Indeed, a few days later, the second-hand book dealer on Sun Avenue would confirm to the hypnotist that this unique magazine had only been printed twice, which made this object a rarity. Marcus Belling was slowly becoming aware that Anne Pauline was indeed a distinctive patient.

After this session, Anne Pauline would return in about two weeks for a third hypnosis session, without ever suspecting what Belling had found in a drawer of his desk. She had been facing a dilemma for these past two weeks and had felt embarrassed about the situation that had occurred. The Forgotten Island, however, needed to remain a secret.

As she got to the consulting clinic, Anne Pauline was taken to Marcus Belling's consulting room by Sofia, who still disapproved of her presence. The secretary couldn't do anything about this, though, as Belling insisted on finishing his patient's treatment, and he had never anyone of his services who needed to clear their minds about their past. After the usual greetings, Anne Pauline sat back on the dark green couch and, before being guided into trance, heard the following words by the hypnotist, "I do hope that, this time, we can go back to one of your past lives so that we'll start to release those extra-sensorial memories. I also ask you to weigh the meaning of everything that you've seen and experienced in your second session. I guess the seagull is a symbol of freedom for you," said the therapist.

Anne Pauline looked deep into his eyes, and he looked as if he had guessed that there was something so deeply rooted in her soul it would not come out easily. Precisely so. Anne wanted to be free, as she had never wanted before. She didn't understand who or what circumstances she so desperately needed to be free. Suddenly, the green-eyed girl snapped to attention, as Marcus Belling was speaking about the therapeutic effect of past life regression, "That is why hypnotists also refer to this therapy as retro-cognotherapy, which consists of doing active hypnosis that lets us get to the extra-cerebral memory. This therapy allows us to release your traumas by pushing this psychic material out. I must confess that I didn't immediately understand how the flight of that seagull could be related to your past, although I admit that there could be some connection, or else you would not have had this experience."

To Anne's surprise, Marcus Belling had used those last few words to give all his trust back to her. One could say that her dilemma was now partially solved, which made the young patient feel more relieved. The relationship with Belling remained unchanged but, the island would remain a well-kept secret, as the seagull community had requested. These thoughts were followed by a fresh breeze from the open window in the clinic. Marcus Belling felt it too. It smelled of the sea, the beach, and of wet earth. It was a very intense aroma that was quickly gone. Anne Pauline and Belling looked at each other as they tried to decipher the meaning of this event. They could find no words to explain it, or it was simply not a subject to be spoken of. Marcus Belling took his eyes off his patient. It was time to start the therapy.

As the third session of hypnosis began, Anne Pauline felt herself being rocked by the sound of Belling's words. Her consciousness quickly entered a deep trance and the hypnotist asked her to come down the stairs of the tunnel. At the bottom of the stairs, Anne Pauline found a wooden door that was locked. Marcus Belling asked her to search in a pocket of her jacket for an old key, which would open this same door. Anne was suddenly frightened for she remembered that she had kept the feather in this same pocket. The young patient was careful enough, though, to successfully take out the key from deep inside the pocket. Carefully minding her gestures, Anne inserted the key in the lock and opened the door. A ray of light flashed temporarily in her eyes. A voice that seemed familiar kept telling her, "Come this way, don't be afraid."

When Anne Pauline opened her eyes, she realized that she was in a circular room with a woman in the center who resembled her very much. Her name was Guinerve and she was dancing. Her eyes were green, and her hair was black, just like Anne's, and it was actually her in another of those past lives. Guinerve did a sensual dance but her situation seemed to make her unhappy and anguished. Someone occasionally called her the Gaul, and another voice called for dubra, which in the Celtic language means water. Finally, she would be known like Guinerve Dubra was, revealing another part of her own personal story, which combined battles, victories and defeats in the conflicts between the Gauls and the powerful Roman Empire.

Guinerve had lived in southern Gaul during the second century A.D. This was a territory where great cultural and economic development was taking place, adding to the particular richness of its soil and trade. At that time, Gaul was inhabited by a Celtic population, organized by a tribal system, although it was dependent on the richness created in Massalia, the site of present-day Marseille. What Anne didn't know was that Salvaterra's wife, Marbella, was born in this city, which connected their past lives by a very subtle coincidence. Guinerve Dubra, however, had a dramatic past. Romans confiscated Gaulish territory, sometimes using the natives for slave work, and looted indiscriminately. But they always implemented a local Roman administrative system in these same regions. Such events happened in the village where Guinerve lived with her family. This woman was taken as a wife by a Roman military commandant (mostly because of her beauty) after she was taken from her community.

Guinerve Dubra ended up in a village only a few miles from her hometown. She had become the lover of a Roman leader and was obliged to regularly dance to a packed crowd that was anxious to watch her sensual moves. When Anne

Pauline returned to this ancient life of hers, Guinerve was dressed in a dazzling green dress and covered in gold-made jewelry. Once more, a connection between her past and gold existed, as Gaul was a territory where vast amounts of gold could be found, mainly in the riverbed sand and other fluvial sediments. The local druidic religious centers also accumulated large sums of gold in the form of nuggets or crafted materials, which the Romans also laid their hands on. Anne Pauline remembered this wing of the Museum of Gold, where she could see some of the objects from the second century. She now remembered the Museum, where she discovered for the first time that she had been Aurélie Caen. Once more, her past was trying to return to that place close to Marcus Belling's medical clinic. Once again, a familiar voice was asking her to come closer and then her arm was brutally pulled as Anne Pauline got dragged into another room. She couldn't figure out the face of the sacerdotal and authoritarian vulture who spoke due to the shade that covered his face. He turned to her and said, "I knew you would come back."

"Are you able to see me? But… I am under hypnosis; this isn't possible! I can't speak to people from my past," replied an incredulous Anne Pauline.

"You can indeed do it. You're able to do it for you have this immense power," answered the person, who was really a druid.

After Rosalie stared at her in the laboratory, Anne Pauline did know that she had some different power while under hypnosis. What Anne didn't know, however, was that she could use speech during this state of mind, or that someone from her past lives could recognize her. She still couldn't see the face of this priestly figure but was soon aware that it was a respected religious member of this community. Once more, Marcus Belling's voice resonated, asking her to describe whatever she saw, but just like in the Forgotten Island, Anne Pauline didn't know if she could tell him the truth. Once again, she felt this dilemma, not knowing if she could respect the alliance and honesty pact that she had signed. The druid used that moment to continue telling the truth about her past, "All that I am telling you has already been part of your dreams, throughout your life. You did live here as Guinerve Dubra, daughter of Gaul farmers and the sister of Sianna, who was killed by the Roman legions. I know that these dreams keep bothering you."

"Was my name Guinerve?" asked Anne Pauline.

"Yes. I saw you many times in my dreams and knew that you would return here. You must have listened to a voice that asked you to come here, though you didn't know where that voice would lead you. It was all prepared over the centuries. When you were Guinerve, I made you drink this herbal potion so that you would not forget your past. I did it to make you return again someday."

"How was it that possible that you were so certain of my return?" asked Anne.

"Simply because I see the past," answered the Druid.

Anne Pauline still couldn't believe that she could interact with people from her previous lives. But the truth was that she couldn't be hypnotized by any person, so this unique power could work out during her trance. The druid had promised the Druidess, who also lived in the community, that he would not reveal the whole potential of her gift to the young, green-eyed woman.

He was not alone. An older and wiser woman, dedicated to the preparation of healing herbs for many decades, had begged him to not reveal everything to this woman, who had now returned to this distant world through hypnosis. The Druidess was named Antha and she remained hidden as the Druid spoke to Anne Pauline, while carefully listening to the whole dialogue. She could see both the past and the future, and knew that another dimension of the world existed, one in which the human body is influenced by the state of soul. The soul itself is influenced by nature, which, in turn, is influenced by the occult power of its four primary elements; water, earth, fire and air.

In this moment, Anne Pauline was reminded once again of Marcus Belling, for she hadn't heard his voice since falling into a deep trance, as she was immersed in a world that she didn't know so well. Without her therapist to help her, Anne was now by herself. It was still impossible to see the druid's face, but Anne understood that he hadn't yet completed whatever he had to tell her.

"I know that you flew to the Forgotten Island in your last session. I need you to give me that feather from Queen Seagull," he ordered.

"How is it possible that you know about the feather?" asked Anne.

"I have never been to the Forgotten Island, but I know of its existence. Most of all, I know that there is this sacred feather that gives enormous power to whoever possesses it. These are powers you won't know how to deal with," replied the druid

"I won't give you the feather. I received it to keep it safe," answered the young woman, while firmly holding the feather that she still kept in her jacket pocket.

"I can't waste all this work I did for centuries only for you to decide it by yourself. All that I did; the voices in your dreams, the self-suggestion I induced that made you look for a hypnotist who made you return to the past... it was all from my own initiative. I wanted you to come back with that feather," the now angry druid explained.

"I can imagine that this feather will make you a druid with immense power," Anne answered back, defying the priestly figure.

"You should know that I exert enormous power through dreams. I am capable of coming to you by other means to make sure that you'll never find the tranquility that you so look for if you don't give me that feather," answered the menacing druid.

Anne Pauline was now getting frightened. The druid had managed to call her to the past through her dreams and made her relive those traumatic experiences of that remote life. Anne knew that if she didn't give the feather to the druid, as he was asked, his voice would continue to resonate in her head during the night, and doubts and restlessness would continue to torment her. Despite all that, she could not allow this priest from olden times to be granted access to such enormous power that could change the course of events in her future life and the lives of others. With this feather in his hands, the druid could force his authority onto that entire Roman community. He also desired vengeance. Most of the druids who lived in ancient Gaul had disappeared after the Roman invasions, although a pact that benefitted both sides had allowed him to survive. However, the druid wanted total freedom and required this feather to control all the others around him. Anne Pauline decided not to give him the feather, despite risking hearing his voice resonate in her dreams. In any event, Anne was under a hypnotic trance and Marcus Belling could always use his words to help her leave that state at any moment.

Anne Pauline tried to call for her hypnotist, but soon realized that the druid was blocking her communication with her therapist. The priestly figure did know how to manipulate every circumstance around him. At that moment, the druid held the pot he always carried with him and raised it high above his head. Then, as the smoke from the herbs spread around the room, he started whispering mysterious and indecipherable words. He had fallen into a trance and was rising to another dimension, trying to reconnect to Anne Pauline's present, to make it impossible for her to wake up from her trance and free herself from this menace. Young Anne Pauline now feared for her life for the first time ever. She didn't know how to contact her hypnotist to warn him of dangers if this trance continued. Anne could not hold back the tears that slowly came down her face as the druid kept whispering such incomprehensible words that she couldn't identify the language he was using for this rite.

Suddenly, the chaos in her mind gave way and she saw a window for her escape. By means of a quick and sudden gesture, Anne raised her arms and jumped, pulling the pot to the ground, where it broke into a thousand pieces. This made the druid come rapidly out of his trance and the voice of Marcus Belling could now be heard throughout the whole room. The power of his voice had never been this audible until now. Anne Pauline slowly became aware that the druid was increasingly disoriented in consequence, as Belling's words were now heard all around that room.

The famous therapist's hypnotizing language took the druid into the deepest hypnotic trance, and Anne Pauline started to get control over her own body and mind back. Before fully regaining control over herself and finally leaving this ancient life, the green-eyed girl decided to look at the druid's face from another angle. Anne turned his head up by the chin and toward a lit corner of the room. Suddenly, perplexed by that sight, she let his head suddenly drop. The druid in her past was none other than… Marcus Belling, her own hypnotist!

The truth had been revealed. The druid was Belling. Anne Pauline could never have imagined that, while searching for her own truth by using hypnosis to discover her past, she would ever face such a situation. The young woman was no longer in control of the process though. When she opened her eyes, still in shock, Anne found she was sat down on the green couch in that Sun Avenue consulting room at with Belling himself at her side.

CHAPTER 5

THE SECRET ALLIANCE – THE ROMAN PERIOD

1

When Anne Pauline left the consulting clinic after her session, Marcus Belling felt helpless. After what she had discovered, the young woman didn't know how she could continue the hypnosis sessions with the prominent hypnotist. On the other hand, when she woke up from her hypnotic trance, he seemed increasingly suspicious that something was going on in her subconscious, but he did not perceive the great power that the young woman possessed when she was hypnotized. Marcus Belling found it increasingly difficult to apply the treatment, but always asked Anne Pauline to relax so that she could interpret the contents of those extra-sensory memories. Her past life mixed seagulls, scientific discoveries and the life experiences of Celtic and Roman communities, and was somehow linked to gold, though he still didn't totally understand this connection. As a result, it was time to ask what happened in the past life therapy.

"I ask you to close your eyes, Anne Pauline. We will now try to interpret all those memories. Do these experiences make you somehow feel guilty of anything?" asked Belling.

"Yes, somehow, I think so," replied the young woman.

"I think your life as Aurélie Caen and her ambition to produce gold is what gives you that sentiment. However, you should understand that we all have different facets, but at present, we have the choice of being the person we want to be," said Belling with conviction.

"The other day, I went to visit the Museum of Gold," confessed the young woman.

"Oh yes?" This answer surprised Belling. "And how did you feel in this place?"

"After seeing all that gold, something inside me made me want to take it and that's why I left there quickly," answered Anne Pauline.

"I understand that," Marcus Belling replied consulting room at. "So, let's relax and think more slowly of all these experiences."

When the treatment was finished, Belling asked his patient to relax once more. At one point, she opened her eyes and again and looked around hypnotist's medical clinic. As on previous occasions, her eyes were fixed on his old Victorian desk, as if she was avidly looking for something. But he knew what to do now. When the young woman closed the door behind her, the hypnotist sat up from his couch, unlocked the first drawer and opened it, after which he careful searched it with his hand. As he expected, there was something more than a rare magazine from 1930 inside the drawer. The second-hand dealer on Sun Avenue had confirmed that Belling had a relic on his hands; more specifically, an old, short-lived specialty magazine, with a high market value.

As he put his hand deeper into the drawer, Belling noticed another object and took it out for a closer look. It was an antique pot with a red beveled edge. It was of apparent religious usage and gave off a scent like a strange mixture of herbs. These may have been heated at an elevated temperature, with the smoke used for many different purposes. Marcus Belling had obviously never seen such pot before in his life. It was becoming clear that Anne Pauline was a unique patient. As usual, the hypnotist was driven by a tireless curiosity that now made him eager to know more about the history of this object. He hoped it could tell him more about the mysterious history of Anne Pauline. Or at least of the past she refused to speak about. Only one person could help clear up his doubts, and his name was Argus Dubois, the famed second-hand dealer whose shop was on Sun Avenue. He was the only one who could reveal more to the hypnotist about the real history of this artefact and, consequently, the hidden truth about his patient.

After finishing another session of hypnosis, Marcus Belling informed Sofia that he would not be returning to the m office that day.

"Today, I have a meeting at the National Council of Hypnosis," he said.

"Should I clear the afternoon sessions?" asked Sofia.

"Yes Sofia, please. This unexpected commitment has come up, so I won't return this afternoon," he replied.

Effectively, Marcus Belling didn't know what was going on with Anne Pauline when she was induced into a hypnotic trance. However, he had still not had the opportunity to address his suspicions and insecurities about her with another hypnotist colleague. In some ways, Belling was a loner in his profession, as he didn't comply with most of the policies that were adopted by the National Council of Hypnosis. On the other hand, he considered the new generation of hypnotists to be little prepared for the challenges of that profession and criticized the mercantilist spirit of some of his colleagues. Still, like Josef Salvaterra, he was the one who gripped the public with his words and ideas on hypnosis. The truth was he hadn't ever known in his professional life a person like Anne Pauline Roux.

Belling closed the door of 27 of Sun Avenue and walked towards the premises of the National Council of Hypnosis. In a few minutes, he passed the workshop of Thaddeus Borba's, who was very focused on the shoes of his customers, the store of Argus Dubois, and the old bookstore, which had assessed the market value of the rare 1930 magazine that had appeared so mysteriously in the drawer of his desk. They were all were part of a small world that centered on that specific location in the city, and they all had their own stories to tell. Later that day, Georgine Gunderson would order books at the bookstore there, without knowing how her fate would cross paths with the patient of the famous Marcus Belling.

HYPNOSIS

There many hypnotists at the door of the National Council of Hypnosis at that moment. However, to the great surprise of Marcus Belling, Josef Salvaterra was not present. The topic of discussion that day was related to the Code of Ethics that applied to all professionals in the field. This debate must be of little interest to Salvaterra, Marcus Belling thought immediately, and wondered how the meeting would be that day. However, before he could formulate any more thoughts, the hypnotists were called by the President of the Council to start the meeting as soon as possible.

This was a historic day for the Council. After long years of debate, there would be substantial changes to the Code of Ethics in order to adapt to modern times. In recent years, questions had arisen about the use of hypnosis in innovative areas, such as the field of medicine. There was a new current of thought within the Council which argued that the application of past life therapy should be limited to only two or three hypnotists, since these hypnotists believed that accessing memories from past lives could constitute a violation of the privacy of patients, even if they gave their permission. Therefore, Marcus Belling knew well that he would have to present all the arguments that he had formulated during a professional life of twenty-five years if he was to counter the ideas of these hypnotists. This would not be an easy task.

Anne Pauline made her way home, certain that she didn't have total command of her own power. Although she had noticed that she could interact with other people in her previous lives, nothing could prepare her for the shocking discovery that the druid was, in fact, Marcus Belling, her own hypnotist.

Both shared a common past. He had betrayed her before, using his expertise and the functioning of her dreams to come after Anne throughout her subsequent lives, obliging her to return to the past through hypnosis. Marcus Belling had done all that to hold the sacred feather from the Forgotten Island. But what mighty power could this feather contain? The seagulls had only given her an orientation guide to her life, but it hadn't been clear what the true influence was of any person who, like her, did understand the circumstances around it. He had made her doubt if it was the traumas and insecurities, she faced in her past that had made her submit to past life regression. "Could this be possible?" Anne Pauline asked. At the base of this chaos was something that she kept in her pocket; an object that could make the druid an extremely powerful man, one that had traveled between the past and the future. The feather could not, by any means, fall into the wrong hands.

Anne Pauline knew that she had made a promise to the seagulls from the Forgotten Island, assuring them that Marcus Belling would know nothing about the island; though he was in a different dimension. They knew the truth. It isn't recommended to doubt the word of a seagull, she thought. Due to their common past, Anne was now aware that she could never report her trip to the Island of Wisdom, nor reveal that her own hypnotist had created the circumstances in a past life that had led to the trauma that made her recently look for help. Anne Pauline once more faced a dilemma, which she had regularly encountered since she started therapy with Marcus Belling. She was now at a crossroads, as she didn't know whether to pursue her sessions. Vengeance was brewing inside the young woman and was taking control of her, making it pointless to continue therapy with the famed hypnotist. Anne Pauline walked quickly down Sun Avenue without knowing how to deal with the revelation that she had stumbled upon.

As she walked, the young woman didn't notice a man watching her. Her mind was caught up in so many thoughts that she didn't realize that this man in restaurants and cafés along Sun Avenue, almost every day, watching her. He was a middle-aged man of medium height, who wore a long, brown jacket and sunglasses. Every single day, he spent hours watching the windows of number 27. His name was Rolland Ulm. He'd been a detective and private eye for many years, closely watching every action that Belling had taken since he had set up his clinic on the city's main boulevard. Rolland had been hired by Josef Salvaterra and Marbella to transmit every piece of information to them about Belling's life.

Both Belling and his staff knew that they were being spied on for many years but had no means of stopping it, as Rolland was always very discreet. He was also sneaky and not always on duty. He had other clients besides Salvaterra, some of whom were even more influential than him, but Belling's pace of life had always interested him. Ulm kept a special focus on Sofia, towards whom he felt something more than simple interest. He had always admired her figure, unable to take his eyes off her well-shaped legs. However, Rolland had never mixed business with pleasure. Her presence had become uncomfortable for him as the years passed by; as Maria de Burgos used to say, it was like a thorn in his side.

Through the precious information supplied by his spy, Josef Salvaterra became aware of Anne Pauline. During the recent National Council for Hypnosis meetings, he had noticed that Belling seemed disturbed and caught up in increasingly distant thoughts. Josef's suspicions grew from the moment that Rolland confirmed to him that young Anne Pauline had caused an upheaval in Belling's clinic. Some indications existed, all too exhaustive to be detailed, that something abnormal was happening to him. Salvaterra decided to do some research of his own. He demanded that his spy should focus his search on Sun Avenue and ordered him to watch closer than ever before and to forget his desire for Sofia. The spy quickly understood that Anne Pauline was one of a kind. Whenever she came for hypnosis, Belling closed the door of his office with an unusual look in his eyes and stared at the sky for quite some time.

One day, he saw the hypnotist walk into the antique shop owned by Argus Dubois, which was quite rare. He left some minutes later with a puzzled look on his face, as if he had just unlocked a hidden secret. His whole body had changed, like something bothered him. On another occasion, Ulm heard a conversation between Marcus Belling and Thaddeus Borba, during which the shoemaker revealed facts about someone from the future. Rolland Ulm felt that he had entered an unknown world. Something had happened in the consulting room since Anne Pauline arrived and, as she finished another of her appointments, the spy waited for an opportunity to move into action. He waved discreetly with his hand to someone else across the road. This other person was Salvaterra, who had decided to discover more about the mysterious young girl who had seemed to bring so much distress to the most celebrated hypnotist in the whole nation.

With this new challenge on his hands, Josef Salvaterra discovered a new purpose in life. His career had been stagnant for over a decade, as the spotlight had turned to Marcus Belling. As a result, some of Josef's clients had switched to other hypnotists, who now searched for advanced techniques abroad. Such events had given Salvaterra the urge to take back his place in the world of hypnosis, and Anne Pauline's case was a unique chance to build an alliance that would make him a success again. This being a personal issue, Josef was cautious and decided not to tell his plans to Marbella. At the subtle sign from his spy, the rival hypnotist sat up from his chair and decided to follow Anne Pauline. He took his time to admire her long, black hair, which was being blown by the soft summer breeze. A particular floral scent now spread across the city and a flock of seagulls could be seen flying across the horizon.

However, Rolland Ulm was back and sitting at a coffee shop with a terrace on Sun Avenue. In the distance, he saw Sofia and looked at the time; she was leaving early. Rolland was powerless to contain his desire so; he rose from the chair and followed her home.

As Anne Pauline walked down Sun Avenue, Josef Salvaterra needed to hurry to keep up with her. He was much older than her and his age meant he couldn't walk as fast as he did in the past. When the young woman reached the end of the boulevard she turned into a narrow street and hid in the shadow of the buildings. Her hypnotist's rival still followed her, though. Anne Pauline lived in the outskirts but was still within the city limits, having walked for about half an hour. In the meantime, the spy had been ordered to watch Belling's clinic, as it was essential to keep an eye out when Anne Pauline had an appointment. However, that's not what happened that day. Rolland Ulm had fallen in love with Sofia Estelar and decided not to follow the orders of Josef and Marbella.

Anne finally got home. She lived in the mansard of a modest building that had been recently refurbished. From her little balcony, she could see the city lights, the moon and the universe. For a brief moment, Anne Pauline felt like she owned the city and her own world. She lived alone but was always illuminated by the stars, but this was different from sharing these moments with a man. As Anne would later know, this man lived in her past and not in the present.

As Anne Pauline opened the door to her building, Josef Salvaterra stood right behind her, forming a strange shadow that scared her. For one moment, Anne thought that the druid had come from the past to take the sacred feather of the Forgotten Island from her. The young woman quickly turned back and was ready to use her self-defense skills to fight the druid, but her arm was held by Salvaterra, whose face was instantly recognizable to her. Anne Pauline was startled. As many people in the country knew, Marcus Belling and Josef Salvaterra were the two leading hypnotists with the most recent media coverage. Josef took the moment to introduce himself to her, although he guessed that she already knew him, and invited her to accompany him to the nearest café for a talk. There was no time to lose, for he needed to act quickly. The smiles on both of their faces showed that a common empathy had been established. There was an exchange of intense and familiar looks, as if they had met a long time ago. Anne Pauline had no doubts that she could trust this man and accepted his invitation.

To tell the truth, it was also Anne's rage towards Marcus Belling that pushed her to accept so easily, though they had never met each other before. The two sat down and Anne gave him a long look. He was a few years older than Belling, with big, dark eyes. He was dressed in an old-fashioned style, but still had some charm that didn't show at first, unlike his rival.

Anne's long, black hair and deep green eyes caught Josef's interest, who wasn't expecting her to have the magnetic personality she showed him. He lowered his stare and tried to focus on the reasons that made him come after her, while using the precious information that Ulm had given him.

"I think you'll know me," said Salvaterra without humility. "Usually, when people refer to Marcus Belling, they also mention my name," he said finally.

"Yes, I recognized you," said Anne Pauline.

"Josef Salvaterra, hypnotist."

An hour had passed, and they were still at the table. Josef Salvaterra wanted to know more about the sessions that Anne Pauline was taking with Marcus Belling. He decided to take a risk and put the question to her, though they had only met for a brief time.

"Tell me. I'm very curious about your sessions with your hypnotist," he said. Anne Pauline was silent. The young woman didn't understand the purpose of such a question, but truth be told, she increasingly felt each step she had taken since visiting the clinic for the first time had been carefully studied by him. She already suspected that someone was watching all of her moves and Belling's for at least a month. With fear growing inside her, she questioned herself as to whether Salvaterra knew what had happened to her after falling into the hypnotic trance. Anne looked back at Salvaterra. His eyes shone as her black hair danced in the summer breeze. Looking at his reactions, he didn't seem to know her inner power. He just seemed delighted to be in the presence of this young woman. Anne then suddenly took courage to question him, "Have you been spying on me?"

"I can't answer that question," said Salvaterra, who felt ashamed about being taken by surprise. "I propose, however, an alliance, a true collaboration between the two of us," he answered.

Anne Pauline felt these words had answered her question as to whether this man had spied on her since she first entered Belling's consulting room. However, she didn't really expect the proposal of this alliance with Josef

Salvaterra, but the look on his face told her that he was to be taken seriously. It seemed, nonetheless, that he didn't know her secret, which was related to the power that she only showed when she was under the hypnotic trance. But after what she had gone on in her therapy, this proposal did look very tempting. Knowing what really happened during her trance would have been impossible. Anne Pauline had just discovered, earlier on that day, that Belling had been a part of her past and had contributed to some of the traumas that still tormented her. In addition, he was the druid who intended to take the valuable commodity that was now in her hands; the feather of the Island of Wisdom. She had also found out that the men of her dreams, who had asked her questions overnight for many years, during which she questioned the righteousness of her personality, was also Marcus Belling. It would be impossible to confuse that hypnotic voice and his calmness with the voice of another man. Despite the hatred she now felt against her therapist, Anne still needed to know more about the proposal that Josef Salvaterra was presenting her with.

The two now sat comfortably together in their chairs. Far away from the café, a group of seagulls blocked the sunlight, and for a moment, it felt like summer had turned into autumn. Salvaterra knew he owed his rival's patient an explanation if he wanted her to accept his proposal of an alliance that would benefit both of them. Salvaterra took courage and prepared to clarify Anne Pauline's doubts about the results of his studies on hypnosis.

For over two decades, Josef had carried out thorough research into the process of hypnotic trance, despite the recommendations given by the National Council for Hypnosis, which forbade any independent studies by any researcher. Salvaterra knew that he had breached the rules and that what he was going to tell was an absolute secret. These conclusions, though, were what allowed him to have a different perspective on hypnosis compared to studies by his colleagues.

As he took a deep breath to explain all that he had learned during his life and career, Josef Salvaterra sensed an enormous power that emanated from her. He didn't know that this green-eyed, black-haired girl had the ability to interact with people from her past lives, but after looking deep into her eyes, Josef could sense this enormous gift. He was now sure. Her power was strong enough to dominate Marcus Belling. This made it worth it to know her better and explain his accumulated knowledge to, which was kept permanently deep in his memory, but was now ready to wander around the free world. Anne Pauline was silent for a few moments and took a deep breath. She immediately understood that Salvaterra was preparing to say something of major importance, something that he would not share with common people. The hypnotist made himself comfortable in his chair, but retained that stern, rigid pose that anyone would use to tell such a secret.

For over twenty years, after he had followed hundreds of people return to their past lives through past life regression, Salvaterra had developed a set of four theories, which explained how this cosmic connection between people worked out. Some would call it empathy while others prefer to call it synchrony.

"Did you know that hypnosis can help us to discover what connects every one of us?" he asked her, while not actually expecting an answer. Anne Pauline was getting more interested in the conversation for she felt his words could help her to find her core identity, and the truth about herself. She made more effort to pay attention to the forthcoming ideas, while Salvaterra tried to adopt a better position in his chair before starting to present his ideas. He stretched his legs and took a gulp of air, and then knew that the moment for his revelations had arrived.

Over the years, Salvaterra had developed a theory that related to occupations, which somehow explained, in an indirect way, the different synchronies that people establish between each other. For that reason, he named it the Theory of Vocations. As he observed and analyzed his patients in a hypnotic trance returning to their pasts, the hypnotist concluded that their talents and callings (which would someday be used for some designated function) originated from the sequence of experiences they had accumulated from different lives. The example could apply not only to artists, but also to any other professional. Anne Pauline was suddenly confused, and so Salvaterra tried to clear her doubts. According to his studies, careers developed during people's lives as they learned from their personal experiences, and those experiences would create the conditions to let a special talent develop. It is, in other words, an innate talent for something. So, a calling is no more than the accumulation of experiences and habits that accumulate throughout one's reincarnations. As we observe the different previous lives, we can see a specific vocation form itself. For the same reason, Josef Salvaterra had called this the Theory of Vocations, which was the one out of the four theories that most fascinated him. This could be related to Josef finding a way to reach his rival, Marcus Belling. At that moment, Anne Pauline understood it all. Salvaterra concluded that Belling's calling for hypnosis might have been learned and mastered through the different experiences of his previous lives. Anne was now silent, keeping Belling's past as a druid secret from her correspondent. In the meantime, she kept listening carefully to his ideas.

"If you wanted me to define what a vocation is, what would you say?" challenged the hypnotist.

"I'd say vocation is a talent, a calling to undertake a career," said Anne Pauline, feeling that she was being tested by her teacher.

"But how do you, Anne Pauline, define innate competence? Where does this competence come from? As you can see, the questions don't end," replied Salvaterra. Then he finished, "The theme is more complex than you can imagine."

Once again, Josef took a deep breath. Other than Marbella, his wife, no one had ever heard his vocational theory, which only showed the trust he had in Anne Pauline.

This was already a good principle for an alliance, as trust became fundamental for this relationship. Now more relaxed, Josef kept explaining his thoughts. He then told her that, after verifying that a match between his theory and experiences with his patients, he had acquired enough motivation to develop new theories on hypnosis and Theory of Past Lives. Although he knew that he was violating the Ethics Code of the National Council for Hypnosis, he decided to keep his private research.

As the years went by, Josef managed to progressively learn from his patients and further developed his Theory of Vocations. It became increasingly evident to him that people who excelled in their professional areas faced notable and defining experiences in their past lives, which stimulated certain intellectual and psychic faculties. These faculties, along with the following incarnations, grouped into specific sets that formed the so-called innate talent. Salvaterra then applied hypnosis to discover these talents as he helped his patients to bring their inner callings into the light. Through this research, Salvaterra managed to help many of his patients find their correct professional paths and contributed to restoring their confidence and trust in themselves. However, he cared little about these issues as he was interested in something else. When a patient discovered their calling in the sessions, the hypnotist would charge a further commission for their professional activities. As they stood out more in their professional lives and earned more money, Salvaterra would receive an advantageous percentage of these profits.

Marbella had told him a few times, "Very soon, this clinic will not be for hypnosis, but rather for professional orientation."

She was frustrated with her husband's professional choices, although he earned a lot of money with his unethical scheme. Truth be told, almost nothing about the work fascinated her anymore. When they got married hypnosis was a truly under-explored field of knowledge with only a handful of practitioners, but once Belling entered the scene, everything started to change.

After the vocational theory was discovered, years would pass before Josef Salvaterra developed a new theory about time regression. Once more, this went totally beyond the conventions established by the National Council for Hypnosis.

After years of research, the Theory of Bonds was complete. Once more, Anne Pauline felt confused. Those theories that Salvaterra explained seemed unlikely, but she kept silent and listened to whatever more he had to tell her. For a moment, the hypnotist was enchanted by this young woman's long and shiny, black hair, but then returned to his thoughts once more. According to Josef Salvaterra, the Theory of Bonds could be summed up by a simple idea; that connections between people are sometimes immutable and strong feelings like love are able to endure life after life. This was a daring idea, mainly because the theory tried to explain complex interconnections that exist in life, such as love and friendship, one's natural empathy or displeasure, and rage or hate. It could also explain simple aspects, such as why some faces look more familiar to us than others, though we have never seen that person before in our lives. Salvaterra knew that he had entered an unknown world, which involved the existence of invincible ties between people who end up in a "web", which then connects an entire community of different lives. Publishing these innovative ideas could even have put his career at risk.

Josef Salvaterra had dared to explain how the feelings between people worked out, which made it impossible for him to openly speak about them with his colleagues or the Council for Hypnosis. The Theory of Vocations and the Theory of Bonds were, so far, a secret that only he and Marbella possessed, though she didn't understand its full meaning.

Josef Salvaterra felt true emotion while explaining his new ideas to Anne Pauline. He could finally present his new theories, which were the result of decades of research, to another person without fear of being judged. The fresh breeze that was blowing at that time brought a new sense of freedom to the hypnotist that he had never felt before. It was a great sensation, he thought to himself. He then smiled and got ready to explain his last theory to Anne Pauline.

As he continued to defend his ideas on regression, Salvaterra referred to a third theory, which he named the Theory of Casualty. The young, dark-haired woman was much more interested in this new perspective on hypnosis, he had created. The Theory of Casualty demonstrated that a link to the past did exist, generating a set of consequences that would influence the circumstances of the future. For that reason, Salvaterra pointed out that a change of past events would inevitably trigger modifications in the following lives. On the other hand, a positive action always caused a negative action, which also left the possibility for the opposite to happen, allowing one to find a balance in the past. For this reason, the Theory of Casualty could also be named the Theory of the Opposites, but Salvaterra only rarely designated it as such. The three theories he had presented could all apply to every person who submitted to past life regression and they all tried to explain some of the enigmas of human existence, which the hypnotist knew was an extremely daring task. Belling's rival also felt proud to share those ideas (to which he had dedicated so much time of his time) to someone other than Marbella, who knew them well enough, though she didn't fully understand them. He showed a subtle smile, as if he was hiding something. Josef had shared much more with Anne Pauline across that coffee table than he had ever done to any other person. Once again, his eyes observed her long, black hair and her slightly open lips. He wished to kiss her so much.

Josef Salvaterra's eyes were shining brightly. He felt free next to Anne. Up to that moment, she had listened carefully to each word he had told her. The hypnotist was now silent. Sitting back in his chair, he asked her, "What do you think of what I just told you?"

"These theories are very interesting," answered Anne.

"They're much more than interesting, dear Anne. My professional experience proves everything that I hereby defend. As for past life regression, any therapist should take these theories of vocations, bonds and casualty into account," said Joseph.

"I believe so," agreed Anne.

Anne Pauline once more remembered those bizarre experiences she had gone through in her appointments with Marcus Belling. Everything she had gone through made her easily accept these theories and the conviction he showed meant she didn't doubt his honesty. However, it also became clear that sharing his secret didn't come free of charge. Marcus Belling's rival wanted something from her. Up to that moment, the conversation had been amicable, sincere, and their rapport was good, without any mention of Belling. But Anne's hypnotist was the thing they had in common, and the reason Salvaterra had spied on the young woman with shiny, black hair. Anne Pauline felt that listening to his theories was the beginning of a kind of ritual of introduction before he revealed ed his real aim. The three theories did make sense to her. After what she had gone through during her trance, Anne knew well that hypnosis" potential was powerful and that, contrary to what most people and hypnotists believed, the connection to the past could sometimes be overwhelming. Anne once more looked into the eyes of Salvaterra and tried to read his soul.

"Anne, if you consider that we know only a tiny fraction of how the human mind works, you'll also agree that we still have a small knowledge of hypnosis. Contrary to what many of my colleagues think, I do believe there are experiences and consequences that are unknown to whoever is hypnotized," Salvaterra continued.

Anne Pauline felt shivers down her spine as she heard those words. Was it possible that he knew what she had experienced in her sessions? It seemed improbable. Either way, it was clear that he found she was a unique patient. She had reacted to a hypnotic trance in a way that left a strong mark on Marcus Belling's state of mind. Now she was comfortable communicating to Salvaterra and felt he understood her, she decided that lying about whatever had occurred, or hiding details of it, wasn't the best choice. They both felt free next to each other. She now had all the conditions she required to listen to the demands of Marcus Belling's rival.

Josef Salvaterra realized that this was the right moment to get the information he wanted on what had happened during her sessions with Marcus Belling. Words flew out of the young woman's mouth as she had no intention of hiding any of the facts. As she spoke, Salvaterra was increasingly surprised and happy with what he heard. Here was this young woman, a patient of Belling, who could interact with people from her past and even change some events from her previous lives. Anne Pauline was fully sincere with him but, even then, didn't speak a word about the Forgotten Island, for she considered the promise to the seagulls to be sacred. When the young woman finished reporting what she had experienced during her hypnotic process, Salvaterra took the chance to inform her that he had formulated a fourth theory, but he had never found a patient to try it on. This was his only theory that had never been put into practice, but his luck could now be changing. Anne Pauline was surprised about the existence of this fourth theory. After sipping some water, she looked fascinated at everything that was going on around this table. She was now ready for one more revelation.

"The fourth theory is the Theory of Nonsense," after which Josef Salvaterra laughed his head off.

Anne Pauline realized that Josef Salvaterra was vastly different from Marcus Belling. Both were equally intelligent, but Salvaterra was more open-minded about understanding certain phenomena that are beyond the capacity of the logical man. This made it easier for her to explain what she was living through at that time. Anne now understood that Josef Salvaterra didn't live on the income he earned from his hypnosis session, but through unethical schemes, in which he charged his former patients a commission for their "Vocation".

Salvaterra now laughed aloud; he couldn't control the impulse. When he had conceived his last theory some years ago, Josef could never have imagined that he would find someone like Anne Pauline. But there she was, across the coffee table, not knowing what was going on with him. He looked more deeply at the special young woman, and after a long breath, was ready to continue his explanation, "Anne Pauline, you're the first person who can prove that my theory is correct. This is unseen, I should confess. For this reason, I now feel that I should change its name to Theory of Change," said Salvaterra.

Josef continued arguing about how this theory explained why some people could interact with others from their previous incarnations when doing their past life regression, and even change events. This idea made total sense to Anne Pauline. She could prove that this theory corresponded to her own experience on that green couch under Belling's orientation. Salvaterra kept informing her that if the hypnotist was aware of the situation, he should induce some suggestion to the patient during the trance to undo the actions committed in the past. He added that another suggestion should be induced so that the patient would gain an aversion to hypnosis. In this way, the patient would lose the power to intervene in the past. Anne was in awe of his discoveries, mainly because he could elaborate a theory about hypnosis, though none of the patients could confirm its content. She was there, however, to tell him that everything he had theorized was true.

Salvaterra knew that he had mentioned all the circumstances that had brought distress to Anne Pauline for quite some time. This beautiful woman with green eyes and dark hair had the ability to change the course of her past lives while doing past life regression. She was the first person he knew who was capable of such an achievement. Up to then, this idea was no more than a simple theory that he had formed after reading a few confidential documents someone had forgotten at the headquarters of the National Council for Hypnosis. He remembered that night very well, even after eight years. He was still beginning his career in the field and starting to deal with the Council's matters. Salvaterra took on different roles within its governing bodies, the organization of conferences being one of them. These tasks meant he had to work late hours in its clinics to arrange details for each event. One night, by accident, he found a document inside the drawer of a desk that hadn't been used for several years, which had belonged to a retired hypnotist. Salvaterra kept few memories fresh in his mind, but he did remember this tall man, over 65 years old, with a grey beard. He had an immense reputation among his colleagues, having written works on the Theory of Past Lives. Those documents were kept inside a folder classified as confidential. Salvaterra couldn't control his curiosity, so he opened the folder to see what the results were of recent medical examinations. On the last page, the names of several people were written down, and above this was a brief handwritten note that read;

This shows, in this specific case, that therapy contributed to an increase of the neurological capability. Brain data shows some instability. Among the symptoms, patients reported the ability to speak to people from their past.

After reading this, Josef put the folder back in the former hypnotist's desk and immediately left the building, not able to control the fear that engulfed him. The simple idea of interactivity with the past through hypnosis seemed like nonsense to him.

Some months after this experience, Salvaterra used this discovery to improve the design of his Theory of Nonsense, which he hadn't allied to his other three theories... until Anne Pauline appeared. He could now confirm that those tests 10 years ago had uncovered an inconvenient truth for many hypnotists. The document was locked in this old desk, either on purpose or by mistake. It was impossible to know for sure, but he now realized that his other colleagues and the Council still didn't know the full potential of the hypnotic trance.

Anne Pauline was really surprised with what she had just heard, mainly because it was so directly connected to her life. Despite listening carefully to every word, she still couldn't understand what he wanted from her. The day was ending, and the summer temperature had now cooled. Salvaterra once more admired her green eyes and suddenly felt an attraction towards her. He didn't expect this. He wanted to kiss her. Anne Pauline heard his words carefully, stoutly, and without complaint. Salvaterra was somehow enchanted by her. The two had shown an inexplicable chemistry. It was time, however, for Josef to explain the reasons why he followed the young woman home, what he wanted from her, and why Rolland Ulm had spied on her all that time. After this conversation, the two now felt a common bond of trust and freedom. I want you to tell me everything that happens after each session and to keep this meeting hidden from him, as well as the partnership that we might establish. If my theory is correct, it will clear away any doubts about how he became such a good hypnotist. "Do you have any idea how important it is for us to know this?" asked Belling.

"You'll probably want me to intervene in the past to change it, will you?" asked Anne. "Your real intention would be to test the validity of your four theories."

"I can see that you've fully understood it," answered the hypnotist.

Josef took the unique chance to explain to Anne how the Theory of Vocations could be adjusted to Belling, whose talent had been refined over the course of his different past lives. It had now become essential to know when and in what life he had started to develop his innate talent. Salvaterra was fascinated by the idea that Anne and Belling had shared a common past. Something told him that this had happened many times over the centuries. Only that could explain the reaction by Marcus and Sofia when they first saw Anne Pauline. As Anne Pauline had described beforehand, "I feel like they're uncomfortable when they see me."

He then told her how his Theory of Bonds explained that the connections between people continue all along their future incarnations, and it would not surprise him if Belling had been part of Anne Pauline's other lives. The hypnotist explained to her that, after finding out the origin of Belling's calling, he wanted her to change those facts. These were his real intentions and the reason Rolland Ulm had spied on her for some time. The implications of this intervention were still not visible, though. Anne Pauline tried to find a more suitable position, took some more water, and asked him, "What if Belling discovers my intentions while I am in a trance?"

"Relax, he won't discover it. He didn't read those documents I saw at the Council's headquarters, nor will he have the slightest idea that some persons like you can control the hypnotic processes. Keep hiding most of the events from him that you see while you're in trance and do not tell him anything except for what is necessary," he replied.

"Why should I want to sign a pact with you?" she asked assertively, her eyes now wide open.

"If Marcus Belling was a part of your past, and has contributed to your anxieties, then this alliance you're signing with me is your ticket to freedom," said the rival hypnotist.

"Freedom," Anne whispered, as she let the magic word flow until it faded away…

After discovering that Marcus Belling had taken part in her life and had an influence on her incomprehensible traumas, Anne Pauline didn't hesitate to agree to this alliance with Salvaterra. She also knew, however, that this would oblige her to turn back on the consulting clinic on Sun Avenue. Such an obligation made Anne feel extremely anxious as she had previously decided not to go back. There was no other option, though. There was an explanation as to how Marcus Belling had built such a reputed career as a hypnotist. According to Salvaterra, his rival's firsthand experiences in the past had led to the expertise he had developed. Anne had the power to intervene in her past, interact with other people, and even change the circumstances that made Belling such a powerful hypnotist. Deep in her heart, Anne knew that the journey ahead would be dangerous but, it was also new and thrilling for her.

HYPNOSIS

This was what Josef Salvaterra had planned as he started to follow Anne around the city and ask her to go for a coffee. After her last appointment, the young woman wanted to accept anything that he proposed to her. From Anne's perspective, Salvaterra had come into her life to relieve her from a secret too heavy to carry. Now Anne didn't feel as alone as before.

Anne and Josef finally stood up and shook hands. Their pact required a close relationship and permanent communication between them. The two would meet after each of Anne's sessions for a full report, as planned. The young black-haired woman and her new ally exchanged a deep stare as they waved goodbye. Josef Salvaterra looked at Anne for the last time that day, with her hair dancing in the sea breeze and those lips he so craved. Anne Pauline began to run, scared of a secret that couldn't be revealed.

Salvaterra walked down the street and came back home, always thinking about Anne Pauline and what he had just heard. Although he showed tranquility next to her, his heart was really pounding with anxiety as he thought of those revelations. He knew that this situation went against all the written knowledge of the human mind that had been written until that moment. Such facts could even jeopardize the work of the National Council for Hypnosis. Not only would the Council's studies and research work need to be reviewed, but also all the knowledge there was of the effects of hypnosis. To tell the truth, most of the hypnotists across the country were not open to accepting the assertion that someone like Anne Pauline could control her own hypnotic process by using her ability to communicate with certain people from her past lives. Salvaterra's position was assured, however, as he decided not to present the case to the Council and his colleagues, letting him use the Anne Pauline's power as freely as he wanted, without being questioned for it.

However, this young woman's personal history could be even more complex than it seemed at first glance. Salvaterra suspected that each member of the group that worked with Marcus Belling had a connection, even if it was tenuous, to the previous lives of Anne Pauline. Destiny let her take sessions with Belling and showed her that he had helped in the search for her identity. But who was Anne Pauline Roux? From Josef Salvaterra's perspective, this young woman was an inconvenient truth. Her ability to intervene in the hypnotic process should, therefore, be kept from the public. For this reason, the hypnotist should only be a supervisor during Anne's trips into her subconscious.

At last, Salvaterra had a competitive advantage over Marcus Belling. Now that he knew Anne Pauline, he was granted access to her power of intervention over the past. This allowed Belling's rival to put his vocational theory into practice and explore its myriad of potentialities and facets. It was Josef's ultimate attempt to confirm his theories. He was sure that Belling had improved his skills as a hypnotist along the course of his successive incarnations.

2

After a few days, Anne Pauline returned to Belling's clinic, but now with a new mission. It was not easy to return to the room where she had discovered more of her own history, and this made Anne struggle with inner doubts. The mysterious girl now knew that her task, other than discovering more about herself, was to transmit all the information to Salvaterra so that the two could take away those twenty years of accumulated power from Belling. Salvaterra's words, ticket to freedom, were ringing in her head in his deep and hollow voice, pushing her to respect and follow their agreement.

Now it was all making sense. After walking up Sun Avenue, Anne Pauline finally rang the bell, climbed the three flights of stairs, and greeted Sofia Estelar without showing any signs of the anxiety that she felt. It didn't take much time for Anne to be called into the clinic, where an unsuspecting Marcus Belling asked her to sit down on the green couch.

"Are you ready for a new session?" he asked. Another appointment was about to start.

However, the day before, Rolland Ulm had followed Sofia. For a while, she hadn't detected his presence. However, using her wit, she had turned back and seen a man retreating quickly to the corner of a house; clearly, he was following her. In this way, she met him. The spy never thought he would meet Marcus's secretary face to face but realized he had been discovered. In reality, he had always intended to be discovered. The wedding ring on her hand left him in no doubt that she was a married woman and she returned that afternoon to her family. However, she fascinated him for many years, and that day, he was no longer able to contain his desire. He raised his face and looked into her eyes with an interrogative depth. He then heard her authoritative voice, "What do you want from me?"

"Good afternoon, I don't believe we've met."

"I think we have met, you're Salvaterra's spy!" exclaimed Sofia Estelar.

"I don't belong to anyone," Rolland Ulm grumbled. "I answer to my soul and my feelings."

At this, the spy grabbed Sofia tightly by the waist and kissed her passionately. As he said, he didn't belong to Josef Salvaterra or Marbella Gorey, only to that feeling. Knowing that this woman couldn't be his, he ran down the street, with eyes full of tears.

When Anne Pauline entered the clinic next day for another session, she easily fell back into a deep trance. Her mind once more traveled in time, leading her back to the old Gaul village where her reincarnation was born, just after the invasion by a Roman legion. Anne was once more reminded of her conversation with Salvaterra just a few days before, as they sealed their pact. Josef's Theory of Vocations predicted that Marcus Belling had developed his talent as a hypnotist all through his past lives. She immediately thought of the wisdom he had built up as a druid, when he was seen as an authority by the entire community and had gathered much more knowledge than the average person.

This brought him a major advantage. Such a function gave him enough preparation and expertise about both humans and the world to help him as a hypnotist in the future. He would also have increased his natural authority from his time as a druid, working for the Romans to guarantee his own survival and using that capacity to guarantee the respect of others. In both situations, everyone saw him as a wise man. Druid or not, many listened to what Marcus Belling had to say about past lives. Anne Pauline was now gathering all the characteristics of both of his incarnations to find if there were any coincidences between the druid and the hypnotist. The theory, as proposed by Salvaterra, did show there was evidence that it might be correct.

The druid had set an efficient plan to make Anne Pauline return to the past to make her give him the sacred feather of the Forgotten Island, which would give him immense power over the world and humans. He could only achieve this in secret through the occult and, obviously, hypnosis. He had Antha, the druidess, by his side, and they could both see the future of Anne Pauline and Marcus Belling. They immediately understood that the fates of these two people of the future would be tied together, sharing a common past. They would require a connection between the two lives if they were to obtain the secret of the Forgotten Island.

The druid and Antha belonged to different social classes within the Gallic priesthood hierarchy. Whereas the druid was an oracle who predicted the future, the druidess was a member of the Vaccaei, who took charge of sacrifices and dogma interpretation. The two had their own influence in areas, which when brought together, created an immense power. Both have acted together to change Anne Pauline's past and future by reshuffling her identity so that she couldn't guess that she had such power. A magic potion was produced to tie the lives of Belling and of the young woman together. It all seemed so simple, yet it would have a tremendous impact on their lives. The druid and druidess knew the mysteries of nature well and decided to combine this unseen combination of different herbs, which were known for an array of therapeutic effects. Those plants were not prejudicial to humans. Instead of curing illnesses, this new mixture changed the human spirits. Their goal was to confuse both the soul and the spirit of Guinerve so that the future reincarnations of the young Gaul woman couldn't find their past. This would lead her to seek hypnosis at some time in her future. It was a daring act that had never been tried by the druids, who were eager to keep the sacred feather, even if they had to wait many centuries for it. Once the potion was ready, they convinced Guinerve Dubra the Gaul to drink it, which she did one night, without knowing that she was changing the course of her current and future lives.

This was the past that Anne Pauline saw as soon as she entered the hypnotic state. She couldn't contain her feelings. The druid had poisoned her spirit, turning it against her, in order to stop Anne from discovering her own identity. Marcus Belling was to blame for all this. As Guinerve drank the potion, her soul became increasingly anxious, desperate about not understanding her corporal stimulus and the reasons for her constant distress. The druid had always been a mysterious figure and enigmatic presence, and as she regressed under Belling's guidance, Anne noticed that he wasn't alone. She could see an older woman beside him with long, shiny, grey hair, who helped him to prepare the lethal mixture that would change her forever. Anne Pauline did now know it, but this woman was a past incarnation of Patricia Murio, Belling's wife. This proved that Antha had been the spouse of the druid in different lives. The woman followed the hypnotic words spoken by Belling, and concentrated much more deeply. She saw Guinerve drinking the magic potion, after which the young Gaul fell on the ground and lost her senses.

After this vision, Anne Pauline remembered hearing Josef Salvaterra speak about his vocational theory. She now knew that she had to act in her past to change the personal consequences in her future, as what moved her now was her plan for revenge against Belling and all the evil he had done to her, namely that herbal potion. Anne knew that the druid possessed a vast knowledge of the main herbs that grew in his region. He had also demonstrated a basic knowledge of medicine that helped him to cure some illnesses, making Anne Pauline understand that Belling truly knew about the human body, as well as the soul. To change her past, Anne would need to find the texts that the druid kept and the location of his experiments. She ran for several miles across the plain to the small town where the druid could be found. Anne thought of the room where Guinerve, her own past incarnation, had been dancing. The young woman ran towards the town center, with its Roman temple of grand columns, and searched for a place where the druid might be working with Antha. Finally, on a narrow street behind the temple, Anne saw a small and sober building from where she saw the druid running with a pot under his arm. This was the same pot that the famed hypnotist would find, many centuries afterwards, inside a drawer of the Victorian desk in his consulting room on Sun Avenue. The priestly figure took an upper street, and as he disappeared, the green-eyed woman decided to sneak subtly through the door of his house.

As she entered, Anne Pauline took a deep breath. She was there on a mission and had to respect an alliance, and there was no time to lose. Anne saw a myriad of texts and drawings all over an old oak table, which was the formula for the magic potion that she had been obliged to drink. On another table, Anne found a recipe for the mixture of the local Marsiglia-grown herbs. The young woman read the name of a particular plant, *Nerium oleander L.,* on these pages, which Anne knew was used in the potion that confused her spirit during the course of her different lives. Throughout the house, she found texts and other coded scripts that confirmed his intense research into herbal alchemy. A thorough look confirmed he had recipes for herbal solutions, teas and combinations to promote health or cause death, as well as to induce people into a trance, using some method of ancient hypnosis. Another document was related to the sap of a tree that restored female fertility. The druid did have a vast knowledge of the power of herbs, which he had used to try and kill Anne Pauline, with a single goal in mind; to get his hands on the sacred feather from the Forgotten Island. Across another table, there were drawings of the moon in its various stages, symbolizing the continuation of life after death. Anne Pauline knew that she was in the right place to enact the alliance to Josef Salvaterra. Deep anger filled her mind when Anne realized that all the intention of gathering all this knowledge was to bring her back to the past with the magic feather.

The feather from the island was extremely sacred, and so much sought-after by so many. It should, however, be kept away from the Gaul priests. Anne Pauline saw candlelight flickering across the room. She grabbed it, knowing she and needed to act quickly. The druid could be back in no time at all and there would be nothing she could do then. Though she managed to control her trance, dominating her hypnotist was going to be a much more challenging task, as he was the future incarnation of her own druid. Anne turned to another table and organized all the scripts that contained different magic potions, herbal recipes, solutions, saps and herbal teas into little stacks. She let the candle fall on those manuscripts that contained enormous amounts of accumulated knowledge. Within a few minutes, the fire consumed them all, devouring each page and transforming the pieces of wisdom from several generations that had been transmitted over the centuries among the druids and druidesses, into an eternal void.

Anne Pauline knew it was time to leave that house. She left the candle where it first was, as the fire grew and rapidly turned the scripts into ashes. Anne left and ran up the street to the temple, which stood out from the surrounding buildings, left the city borders, and headed to the countryside. The golden plains stretched out to the horizon and the woman ran to the town of her birth, which she could see across the landscape, while waiting for Belling's voice to call her. Would Anne be able to return once again to her world? A column of smoke rose from the city she had come from and Anne knew exactly what was happening. Belling's voice now thundered across the golden fields of wheat and poppies, and Anne awoke from her trance, once more returning to the green couch in Belling's clinic. She had done the unthinkable. The past had, in fact, been changed, as she had promised to Josef Salvaterra.

Marcus Belling stood there, looking at Anne Pauline, and trying to understand if she was in catharsis after awaking from her trance, as was usually the case with this singular patient. However, this time, Anne didn't show any such signs. She looked tranquil and told the therapist of her return to her past life as Guinerve Dubra. Belling, however, didn't look convinced, mainly because his patient gave increasingly vague answers over the course of the sessions, which meant he could barely understand what had really happened while Anne fell into the deepest layers of her trance. The prominent hypnotist knew it was time to work on those memories from her past, even if he didn't know much of what happened to her during regression. He then told her, "I think it's time to understand how the memories from your past need to be released from your subconscious. I now ask you to take another deep breath… but slowly."

But rather than taking a deep breath to control her anxiety, Anne Pauline thought of how to hide her acts in their common past. As she looked her hypnotist in the eyes, Anne felt her body slowly falling asleep, as if he could hypnotize just by using his eyes. She couldn't remember anything afterwards. It was only after waking up to her normal state of consciousness, did Anne notice that Marcus looked more satisfied after having applied his relaxation technique to extract those extra-sensorial memories that were stuck in her past. Anne would never know what had happened but did not feel freer after this procedure. I hoped to feel freer, she thought to herself. Maybe Salvaterra is right; only this alliance will give me the freedom I desire.

Belling stretched his hand out to Anne and bid goodbye to her. Sofia threw her a suspicious look from across the room, not understanding why she kept coming there.

After this session, Anne Pauline went home, still not believing what she had just done. If the vocational and causal theories were right, something was about to change in her life as a consequence of her actions in the past, which frightened her. Anne would have to report those events to Salvaterra, but she still couldn't believe that she retained such power to change the past in her previous incarnations. She tried not to think of anything else, knowing she had an appointment with Salvaterra later that day.

After Anne left his clinic, Marcus remained on his couch and his eyes once more aimed the old Victorian desk. He stood up and walked to the desk, as Marcus usually needed to search that first drawer whenever a session with Anne ended. The hypnotist turned the key once more, opened the drawer, and saw the 1930 magazine and antique pot for religious use, and nothing else. There was nothing more hidden inside that part of the desk, but Belling didn't really believe it, and so used his hand to search all over the drawer for some other hidden object. This article could have appeared there after Anne returned to the present. Nothing more was there, however. Belling seemed disappointed, for he didn't understand how the magic worked inside his consulting room. Feeling upset, he immediately locked the drawer and left the clinic.

Marcus Belling arrived home later than usual on that day. Patricia Murio was getting ready for the concert that evening and her bump was getting more visible with the passing months. She had known about her pregnancy for quite some time. Belling took her hand and they left home together. As he closed the door, heavy rain and thunder started and the couple ran to their car. As their car drove out to the city center, neither of the two could imagine what was happening at his consulting clinic.

While the hypnotist was coming home, Rolland Ulm found himself in a secluded spot on Sun Avenue, where he took cover from the rain. He followed Josef Salvaterra's orders to stay near the office, but these orders were not clear. He was an obedient spy and so, as with any client, he didn't ask for explanations. He had clear instructions not to go near the woman he was in love with, but as he had told Sofia, his soul and his feelings didn't belong to the hypnotist and his wife. He was going through a rough patch in his life. He was forbidden to approach the people he was spying on. However, he wasn't able to keep his distance from her and intended to reveal details about himself to her.

After Anne Pauline left, she met Salvaterra and gave him a full report of that afternoon's session. The hypnotist now had information that she had just altered the past, and the consequences of this were very much beyond their expectations. Rolland Ulm was unaware of these backdoor deals. He was a medium-sized, middle-aged man with a curved moustache, which made him stand out from many other men of his age. He had been working as a spy and as a private detective for many years. He had been working for Belling for many years, ever since the hypnotist had established his clinic in the central avenue. His previous task consisted of spying on Belling's accountant, Vincent Torquay, who was the first to warn Belling that someone was spying on his every movement. Belling's staff had already reported this to the authorities. Salvaterra, however, denied the accusations of hiring an agent to spy on Belling. In the meantime, Rolland had the gift of passing by unnoticed, which made everyone get used to his subtle presence. In one form or another, Roland Ulm was more than a spy, he was now a private security guard.

Rolland stood under a roof, as the rain got harder. The thunder rolled and lightning flashes spread chaos over the city. An eerie silence had settled on the area. After some time, Rolland left his hiding place to have a better look at what had happened to Belling's clinic and noticed a small fire. After a neighbor's call, the firefighters arrived to see the fire had quickly spread over the entire floor. Rolland kept watching the events unfold from under a roof of Sun Avenue. The fire brigade forced the door into the consulting clinic to control the fire, which had now destroyed a small annex and another room. Salvaterra will surely want to know about this, he thought. The spy stood quietly as he watched the fire, delighted and amazed by an event that had never been seen before anywhere near the clinic. He waited until the firefighters had left, so that he could leave his spot to return home. A scared Marcus Belling ran towards the building with his wife by his side.

The next morning, Marcus did a careful examination of the destruction caused by the fire. Sofia Estelar and Patricia Murio, shocked by what had just happened, were with him. Thunderstorms charged with static electricity were common during summer nights, causing short circuits in some homes. But rather than the weather event, they were worried about the destruction caused by the fire in Belling's private library. No books were left intact, as they all had been reduced to ashes. It seemed very strange. The fire followed a specific direction to his library, turning the books to dust. The rest of the clinic seemed untouched by the fire, except for an annex.

"There may be some wiring inside this wall that leads directly to your library. Any electricity from the thunderstorm may have passed through those cables," one of the firefighters told him.

Marcus Belling wasn't convinced by this possibility, however. The strange fire had also taken the women by surprise, raising their suspicions about arson. But the clinic had adopted a tight security system and there was no evidence that the door had been forced. Belling looked once again at his library and noticed the loss of one of the major titles about hypnosis, the book by Thomas Hommas, entitled *Regression: A New Understanding*. It was the first book he had picked from his library after Anne Pauline came for her first hypnosis session. She had left him feeling uneasy from the beginning, which made him take the work by Hommas from the shelf. Belling felt the need to read it again, especially after that strange intuition he felt as Anne entered that door for the first time. The hypnotist guessed that he would need the knowledge contained in that book to deal with this young woman with the shiny and bright, green eyes. Without saying a word, Belling kept thinking there was a connection between this young woman and this disaster. There had been no object in that drawer after Anne's last session, which could only mean something that was beyond his comprehension.

In the meantime, Patricia and Sofia were still startled by the destruction of the library. All but two books had been reduced to ashes. One of them was *Brave New World and the other was Island* by Aldous Huxley. Belling didn't understand how this book could've remained intact, as it was placed in between other books that were consumed by the flames. Many questions went through his head, but the hypnotist couldn't imagine Anne Pauline destroying the druid's scrolls in one of his past lives, which led to the inevitable consequences. The books he kept in his private library were the key to his inner talent for hypnosis. Belling always kept reading, studying and researching to improve his techniques, making him a far more complete therapist than his colleagues. Marcus had always been an avid, innate and curious reader. But from the moment that Anne Pauline set fire to the druid's writings, blocking his access to the knowledge of herbs, potions and vegetal alchemy, this had inevitable repercussions in Belling's life. All the books that gave him access to the power of self-development and knowledge about humans and the world were now nothing but ashes.

Marcus Belling felt desolate and that all his knowledge was gone for good. Sofia and Patricia looked at each other as they tried to find possible explanations. They concluded that the clinic's security had been breached. It was time to talk to Maria de Burgos.

The night before, as the fire had struck Belling's consulting room, Rolland Ulm had tried to contact Josef Salvaterra to report the latest developments. Marbella was close by and she could see a smile growing on the face of her husband as Josef heard the last news from his spy on the phone. Marbella asked for the news he had just received from the spy and Salvaterra told her of the fire that had occurred at 27 Sun Avenue.

"Marbella, a fire has just consumed part of Belling's clinic," he said. "Rolland was there when it all happened."

"A fire?" the astonished woman asked. "Josef, this is the best news I have received from you all year!"

This was indeed the best news that Marbella could have received from her husband, but she wanted to know more details. Salvaterra told her everything that he knew, but kept quiet about his alliance with Anne Pauline, the woman who could change the past through hypnosis. At that moment, Josef Salvaterra was the only member of the National Council for Hypnosis who knew about people who could change any past events with future consequences while they were being hypnotized.

The following day, Anne Pauline and Salvaterra met again quickly. The two sat at a café close to where the young woman lived. Salvaterra told her that he knew everything that had occurred at Belling's consulting room on the central boulevard and was eager for more details of the girl's last hypnosis session. As he carefully listened to every detail given by Anne, Salvaterra became increasingly surprised with each revelation. He could barely keep his emotions to himself, as he felt that his career as a hypnotist was at a major turning point.

CHAPTER 6

THE ALCHEMICAL PERFUME

1

As soon as Rolland informed Josef Salvaterra about the fire that had broken out in Marcus Belling's clinic, the avenging hypnotist rapidly understood that his Theory of Change was much more real than he could have ever thought. It was highly probable that his other theories of vocations and bonds could be correct as well, which made it essential to keep his alliance with Anne Pauline, for she was the only person who could give him all the details of the appointments in the clinic at 27 Sun Avenue. Marbella also needed to be kept uninformed of any plans her husband might have, at least until he understood more about the power of Anne Pauline and what it could help her to accomplish on his behalf.

The fire in the consulting room of the famous Marcus Belling was widely commented on and reported by the media in the days after the incident. Maria de Burgos spent more time in the consulting clinic than in the headquarters of her consulting company, much to Argus Dubois's satisfaction, who kept watching her from his antique shop across the road. He couldn't really take his eyes off her. It had been years since he had developed a true passion for her and, therefore, Argus couldn't stop but thank this tragedy for Marcus Belling, as it gave him the opportunity to watch Maria for most of the week. But he hadn't corresponded with her… yet. Maria de Burgos noticed his presence, but the sheer scale of the events at the clinic made her forget anything related to love affairs. She had always been a busy woman and couldn't cope with the destruction of Belling's clinic. When Maria spoke to Sofia and Patricia, she rapidly realized that all three shared the same perspective about the event; it was a clear case of arson. This meant that someone had dared to enter the clinic and set fire to the library. It was hard to believe that a summer storm could've destroyed his shelves, mainly because the flames had followed a specific direction. The simple idea of an electric current flowing throughout the building until it reached the specific power cords right behind the books did not convince any of the three women. Such facts led them to meet and discuss the security and logistical system that was set up at Belling's consulting clinic. The hypnotist was absent from the discussion as he was worried about all the valuable knowledge that had been lost in the infamous fire.

"Sofia, something is going on and we don't know if it's once more related to h Salvaterra and that infamous spy who has watched our every movement for so many years," said Maria de Burgos.

"I know that you don't have an easy task in these moments," said Sofia.

"Imagine what the papers will say. Some say that the practice of hypnosis in the Sun Avenue is going to close... that's why it's so important that we find out the real cause of this fire," concluded Maria de Burgos.

At the same moment that the two women were arguing passionately, Patricia Murio arrived at number 27 Sun Avenue. It took all of the strength in her arms and hands, the ones that cured people every day in her work as a physiotherapist, to drag Maria de Burgos out to the waiting room, which still smelled of the smoke that had consumed most of her husband's library.

"We should take measures. Belling doesn't worry about them, as he thinks this is a one-off event with natural causes," Patricia said.

"I agree with you, everything just seems so strange," Maria de Burgos replied.

Patricia then appealed to her, saying, "You should be reminded of Rolland Ulm, the man hired by Josef Salvaterra to spy on my husband. That should be our starting point."

"Do you think that he might have something to do with the fire?" Maria asked, and was immediately answered by the confident Patricia.

"I guess that we let it get too far. We should know more about this man."

"What about Sofia?" Maria asked.

"She will also have to join the investigation; we'll speak to her immediately," Patricia answered.

In the past few years, they had tried every solution they could, even taking it to court to stop the constant vigilance, but with no success. The first time that Patricia Murio knew of the situation was through Vincent Torquay, her husband's now retired accountant. The bookkeeper was the first member of the Belling's entire workforce to notice the presence of a spy, and Patricia passed on every detail possible of this story to Maria de Burgos. One day, 15 years ago, Torquay had just arrived at his clinic, which was already in the building next to number 27. Heavy rain meant thick drips came down the clinic's window. Managing the revenues was far from easy, as there were not only sums large involved, but he also had to manage them within a transparent fiscal system. On that rainy day, Vincent Torquay adjusted his glasses and stood up to clean the windows with a cloth he had left by his desk from the day before. He could never work with his windows like that, so he carefully cleaned them in circles, which left him with a clear view of Sun Avenue below. Suddenly, the accountant saw a vulture watching his window and managed to see that he was a middle-aged man with a distinctive handlebar moustache. Torquay reported the situation to Patricia Murio, telling her that his gaze looked different, "His eyes were those of a falcon, almost as if he had been trained to look farther than any other person," he confessed to her.

Vincent was scared about what he had seen on that day. The spy seemed not to notice that he was being watched by Marcus Belling's accountant, who had hidden behind the dripping windows, trying to identify that strange man below who watched all his moves. This same man suddenly took a camera from underneath his trench coat to take a few photographs of number 27 before putting it back inside the coat when Belling suddenly left the building. All these gestures worried Vincent Torquay. The spy then sneaked along the walls so that he went unnoticed and disappeared without a trace behind another building.

Patricia Murio and Vincent Torquay discussed the day's events after research proved that Salvaterra and Marbella had hired Rolland to spy on Belling and his staff. They kept an attentive lookout, and some scandals later affected his career, which were related to this mysterious figure. Vincent then retired but the spy kept doing his work in the areas around Sun Avenue, although sporadically. Patricia spoke quickly, as if she felt the urge to report all this information to Maria de Burgos, who was both her friend and confidant. After describing the events in detail, it was now impossible not to believe in some sort of conspiracy that has been started by Salvaterra, his wife and their spy. Maria promised to Patricia and Sofia they would do deep research on that night's events in Belling's library.

In the meantime, the smell of burning had been sensed by Jasmine, a fortune-teller and visionary who was widely recognized in the entire city. She knew Marcus Belling's work well, for she was a close friend of Marbella Gorey, who consulted the oracle once every six months for a glimpse of her future. Each year, come early September, Jasmine returned to the city after several months of traveling. She lived in the outskirts, close to Anne Pauline. Jasmine was a short, black-haired woman in her fifties who loved anything that was related to the occult. She was dedicated to the tarot and was an oracle, visionary and fortune teller, whose knowledge wasn't known by most other people. She lived in her own world and only a few people were allowed in, Marbella being one of these rare exceptions, as she wasn't a believer in the occult.

Jasmine spent months traveling around the world accompanied by tarot readers and oracles who aimed to discover the meaning of life. So, for much of the year, she lived apart from society for she lived as a true nomad, with just her busts, medals and prayers that no one else could understand. Jasmine knew much of the world but always kept one place in her heart for a location – a small village which she traveled back to every year with her nomadic tribe. This location was Marva. Its light was unique and magical, attracting numerous people who longed to discover the occult meaning of the night in it. The small village was located at an altitude of over 800 meters on the near mountains of Sapoio, from where it was possible to contemplate the world. Many said that Marva was like a balcony to the universe. It was here that Jasmine called the spirits, anxious as she was to know the hidden meaning of life through them, while knowing that it was a very well-kept secret. Marva was also a one-off village where they could feel some special energy from the skies that scratched the tall peaks. One such magnetism came out of the ground and had the power to heal any disease, physical or of the soul. Jasmine had sensed this energy beforehand, using it for the remainder of the year. Such absorption of energies strengthened Jasmine's her ability as a visionary and her knowledge of the occult.

While in Marva, Jasmine felt she could retain the universe's energies, which was why she always returned to this special location, which was barely known even among those who claimed to know geography well.

Although she barely spoke of it, Jasmine considered herself a pagan. She believed in a multitude of deities and had, therefore, many different statuettes that traveled the world with her. These travels, which usually took several months, helped her to consolidate her beliefs, and after visiting Marva, Jasmine returned to the city in February and September. She then took off r walking and wandering in the mountains, plains and remote locations with her nomadic community. The occultist had just returned home when Marbella knocked on her door. She lived in a very narrow building, squeezed in between two other buildings. Salvaterra's wife knew perfectly well that September was the month when Jasmine returned to the cit. This made it her favorite month, as she would finally meet the only person who could really understand her.

Few people knew about the personal background of Jasmine, Marbella being an exception. She was introduced to tarot reading at the age of five by her mother. For many years, the family lived in the field next to the Castle of Marva, where her mother fought hard for their survival. Jasmine didn't meet her father but knew that he had been a farmer, and so perceived the power of nature more than ever. As she grew up, Jasmine started reading the cards at home, where many came for help, as it was considered that she had a talent for the occult. A few years later, she was able to improve her enormous potential in the field, thanks to her mother, who understood as Jasmine grew up, that her daughter was far more talented than she had ever been. Her mother encouraged her to develop her capacity to read the future and dreams, some of which disturbed her. Jasmine learned to control her anxiety to deal with the visions, which made her resist the inner turmoil that her skills could potentially bring about. Both mother and daughter started to do combined tarot reading sessions, which attracted more clients to them. Within a few years, Jasmine and her mother could finally leave Marva and seek sustenance in the city.

A few years after her mother passed away, Jasmine got to know Marbella and began to teach her about the occult. Salvaterra's wife had really been into this unknown world, which one could only disclose by means of a specific language. Marbella's new interest helped to change her husband's perspective on hypnosis, making him read more works about the connection between spirituality and hypnosis. This was the opposite to Marcus Belling, who maintained a more technical perspective of his work rather than a spiritual one. Using her practice, Jasmine came to know that Marbella, now a close friend and confidant, showed enormous power in this field. It was an obscure power, however, that was tainted by such dark colors that her friend would always use to achieve her most selfish goals. Her fear of having an enemy at the same level meant that Jasmine decided to hide any techniques from her that could develop own talent, a decision that would also protect Josef Salvaterra.

Marbella had always envied her husband, who was good in his field, and couldn't find any area that she thrived in. Years later though, his proximity to the occult allowed Salvaterra to perceive the inner gift that Anne Pauline possessed and the struggles that she fought. Marcus Belling didn't manage to see this so easily. Josef now had a competitive advantage, which helped him to understand such a unique power. It was undeniable that the close bond that existed between Marbella and Jasmine had deep consequences on the perspective that Josef Salvaterra adopted regarding hypnosis. Years after the start of this friendship, and thanks to the catalyst of meeting Anne Pauline, Salvaterra would be conscious of how this contact with the unknown world had such an influence on his work. What was beyond his understanding was that his wife had similar powers to Jasmine. The difference was, however, that she had never been given the opportunity to develop them, since most of her life had been dedicated to managing her husband's career. As Jasmine and Marbella were so similar, it isn't surprising that they shared common visionary abilities, especially through their dreams. Only they could understand these experiences, which was why Marbella so anxiously awaited Jasmine to return to tell her about the visions she had seen in recent dreams. These visions that had made her quite uncomfortable in the last few days.

It was three o'clock when Marbella Gorey rang the bell of the small, modest house where Jasmine lived. Her friend's black hair was tousled when she appeared behind her door, yet she showed an uneasy smile. Salvaterra's wife soon noticed how much Jasmine had aged since they last saw each other, and she knew that those travels around the world were taking a toll on the health of the occultist. Marbella concluded that her friend would soon need to stop going on such journeys, despite not knowing when she would return to the city for good.

When Jasmine opened the door and saw Marbella, she remembered how well they knew each other and why she hadn't taught the woman the arts of the occult. Salvaterra's wife possessed this dark and obscure force inside her, which should not be released on any occasion. A friend of the card reader had even let her know that Marbella envied her own husband for his talent in hypnosis, which could be seen in her gestures and words. As she opened her door to her friend, Jasmine found it odd to see the anxious smile on her face, which was quite rare. In a friendly fashion, Jasmine quickly took Marbella to the corner where she kept all the materials for her handcrafted perfumes. Her dedication to fragrances was known by any of the usual clients or people who visited the fortune teller, so it was an unknown fact that she preferred not to reveal. Only two or three other people in town sought her just for these handmade perfumes, and they paid a high price for these scents. One of these people was Georgine Gunderson, who sought a solution for her problem with different smells. She had also sought the perfume maker earlier in the day. Marbella was staring at the flasks that her friend used to stir her mixtures. This was a method that allowed her to create the unique fragrance that made her products so popular with those who used them.

"Hello Jasmine. It's so good to see you again. I always want September to come fast so that I can reach you. I see that you keep making your perfumes," Marbella said.

"Oh, my dear Marbella, you know well that this is an old passion I have," her friend answered, showing her unease as she spoke.

Jasmine had dedicated herself to making these self-made perfumes for many years. During her travels, she learned many different smells, how to gather nature-grown essences and test any possible combinations between them, while taking into account what nature had to offer. What Marbella didn't know, however, was that all the knowledge that her friend had accumulated for years was solely used to produce a unique scent, one that was different from all the others. This was a truly mesmerizing fragrance that could block every other smell around whoever used it.

This was why Georgine Gunderson had looked so avidly for it. The librarian's rare aversion to smells meant Jasmine's perfume was her last resort, as she struggled to work in a place where the aromas of ink, dust and pages resulted in a truly unbearable environment for her. Jasmine didn't need to provide such detail to Georgine, as she had told her friend of her passion. The history of her self-made perfume was a very well-kept secret.

However, Marbella hadn't come that day to talk about her handmade perfumes. The fortune-teller sensed her friend's inner anxiety and gave her meadowsweet tea for relaxation. The herbal infusion was one of the discoveries that Jasmine had made during her trips and she was now using it in her pagan rituals around the world, although not to the knowledge of her friend. Little by little, Marbella felt relaxed enough to speak openly about her frustrations regarding her own life.

"Jasmine, I'm here to ask if you envision anything about my future. I feel stagnant," she confessed.

"I'm listening. Drink your tea before it gets cold," Jasmine answered back.

Little had changed in the Salvaterra's lives since Marcus Belling had taken the spotlight from Marbella's husband, Josef. They had hired Rolland Ulm to watch the offices at 27 Sun Avenue and keeping them informed about everything that happened there. The precious information supplied by the spy had allowed the couple to infiltrate the life and work of Belling; after which they published the scandals and blatant lies they uncovered so the media would keep away from him. Maria de Burgos had, however, successfully solved some of these situations. Over the years, Marbella had developed a troubled relationship with Maria, much more than she had with Sofia, whom she kept a good distance from.

This didn't give Marbella much opportunity to move up the social ladder or get into the most exclusive clubs in town. Marcus Belling was not her only problem, though. In the last few years, many alternatives to hypnosis had appeared around the country, like experiential or existential-humanist therapies, which an increasing number of people were resorting to. Step by step, such alternatives were taking clients away from Salvaterra, as they needed new ways to heal their traumas and therapies that didn't require going into a trance, which scared the most skeptical patients. The situation for the couple was becoming, therefore, more complex and fragile. In addition, their financial background didn't make it easy for Salvaterra to progress in his career, since most of the other private consulting rooms had been closed due to the current situation in their field. Most hypnotists now gathered in clinics to share the costs and use a vast partnership network to lower their prices to clients. Many had preferred the latter system when they searched for a hypnotist. Marbella had fallen silent. While these circumstances had made her feel more anxious, they were not what had brought her to Jasmine. The fortune-teller was now both apprehensive and intrigued about Marbella's recent behavior. She knew that the wife of Salvaterra was hiding something from her.

"Dear Jasmine, I had a near-vision a few days ago," Marbella told after taking courage. This announcement left the oracle wide eyed. To make herself clear, she paused to explain that, "I don't really know if it was a vision, so that is why I called it a near-vision."

Her friend and oracle knew that there was no mention of this vocabulary in the encyclopedia of the occult, but she needed to listen to every word that her counterpart told. Salvaterra's wife said that, a couple of days before, she had dreamt that her husband had left their bed during the night, looking confused and anxious, and that he might really feel enormous joy inside. Afterwards, Josef opened the door and left their home. Marbella had followed him with her robe on and expected him to meet Marcus Belling. But at the end of their street stood a young woman with green eyes and black hair. Marbella couldn't recognize her face, as she looked unfamiliar. What disturbed Mrs. Grey, however, was the huge smile on her husband's face, as if he felt immense joy. It looked like he was deeply in love with someone he had known for a long time. Marbella didn't know how to describe the feelings shown by her husband in her dream towards this young woman, maybe because she hadn't known what real love was for a long time. The strangest thing in this dream, however, was a giant clock that had disproportional dimensions compared to any other existing clock. Its hands worked correctly so it showed the right time, nearly 11 o'clock at night. The young woman acted fast yet decisively and took Josef's hand, and he gave her an intense and disturbing stare. Then an invisible door opened in the wall of the clock and the two entered through it underneath the clock's giant hands. Suddenly, Marbella woke up. This had been her dream or, as she described, her near-vision, for it looked excessively real. This was the main reason she looked for Jasmine on that September day.

"What I would like to know is if it's only a dream or a true vision, or a near vision, as I prefer to call it. If it's a vision, I wish to know who this woman is and how she got to know my husband," Marbella said firmly.

"I now understand the anxiety that made you look for me. I could feel your spirit even before you climbed the stairs that led to my door," the oracle answered.

The conviction in Marbella's voice made Jasmine understand that her friend needed her services to unravel the secrets of that dream, which had intrigued the wife of Salvaterra.

"So, you need my help," the oracle whispered.

"What I would like to ask you, my dear friend, is that you try to use your visions to find out the name of this young woman who haunted my dream. Or my near vision," Marbella promptly answered. "I know that you've just arrived from your travels, but I urgently need your help."

The fortune teller had indeed just arrived from Marva, that special place where she refilled her energy sources. It had been a long journey with her nomadic group, and her age had started to take their toll on her body for the first time. These trips would not last for much longer and Jasmine knew that she would need to retire to her apartment in the city, where fortune-telling would then fill most of her time.

Jasmine suspected that her friend's cry for help was not for love but because there might be some secret pact that she wasn't aware of. It would not be fair to say that Marbella had never loved her husband, Josef, as this wasn't true. She had loved him, but over the years that feeling had totally vanished as egotism and greed had taken her over.

Jasmine asked Marbella to sit at the round table that stood in the middle of the room. Her most valuable medallions and statuettes from Marva and her travels around the world were on top of this table. Such symbols provided the power that she needed to have her visions. The statuettes usually answered her appeals but only when the cards were spread out on the other side of the table. Before sitting down with Marbella, Jasmine entered the annex, which she used to craft her perfume, or the Alchemic Perfume, as her customers called it.

Jasmine opened a drawer and took out a plant with large green leaves and a compressed stalk, from which drips of a yellow sap fell, spreading a unique fragrance. The fortune teller put it on the table for it activated her inner energies again. The truth was that Jasmine needed all her energies, and so placed all the available energy sources around her, to achieve the concentration needed for her visions, or at least those that carried some magnetic energy that could heal the soul. The plant had other near magical properties that allowed Jasmine to create a fragrance that could block all other surrounding smells. This was exactly what Georgine Gunderson has looked for and the reason the librarian became a regular and faithful client of the fortune teller.

Jasmine displayed the statuettes on her table once again. She then turned the stalk of the plant towards the cards, which was opposite to the direction of the images, which now gained life. The meadowsweet herb that Jasmine had used to make tea for Marbella was now helping to spread the oracle's visions in the empty space, thanks to its therapeutic function that no one could ignore. Salvaterra's wife observed this ritual with her full attention, for it would be the first time that Jasmine had revealed the meaning of her dreams. Before calling the visions, however, the oracle decided to be clear to her friend about her visions concerning Salvaterra and informed her about the content of his four theories of the past few years; namely, those of Vocations, Bonds, Casualties and Changes. Marbella was surprised, for she knew that her husband had only explained the results of his studies to her. The fear of the power of Jasmine haunted her but it also confirmed the full potential of her friend's powers, as she knew that these rituals were necessary to clear any ideas that would explain her dreams.

Silence fell between the two. Jasmine decided to tell Marbella about her own theory, one which could somehow complete those that had been elaborated by Salvaterra. At the base of this theory was the inner power of nature. The occultist revealed the knowledge she had gained from her many journeys around the world, the magnetic force of Earth she felt in Marva, and her attempt to understand the meaning of life, which led her to elaborate on her Olfactory Theory. This idea was connected to her Alchemic Perfume, and it explained why her fragrance, a by-product of the sap from the plant on the table, was so desired by her clients. Marbella was quite intrigued and listened carefully to every word her friend told her about this new theory. Marbella had never paid much attention to her husband's ideas. Their content would not only revolutionize any ideas from books or the National Council for Hypnosis, but they also seemed quite absurd. Her opinion was about to change, however, for Marbella saw Jasmine as an authority who should therefore be respected.

According to Jasmine, smells are tightly connected to remembrances, and this doesn't happen by accident. Each existing aroma is linked to deep-rooted memories that all people have. These memories transform into a unique scent that then transmutes into an element of nature, which is why alchemic perfumes are directly produced from the extracts of nature. It seemed that Marbella hadn't totally understood the so-called Theory of Smells, and Jasmine was prompted to clear her doubts.

"Dear Marbella, the strongest memories of your life will transform into a particular smell, or a unique scent from nature. This unique aroma can't be repeated, for the remembrance kept by one person is one of a kind. From the essence that forms, it should then be possible to elaborate a rare perfume. This perfume itself becomes an alchemic perfume, directly made from the elements of nature. This is the reason smells have always taken us back to various times of our lives."

"So, smells can take us on a journey back in time?" Marbella asked.

"Exactly," Jasmine confirmed, "This is why I consider it important to produce the alchemic perfume. I help my clients return to their past."

"So, can we say that you keep one's soul under your command?" Marbella asked, after a brief period of silence between the two.

"You might say that," Jasmine answered in a faint voice, astounded at the insight shown by her friend.

"I see it now," Marbella told her, now with a clear idea of her friend's true power.

Marbella Grey now understood the true sense of the Olfactory Theory, which could, at least in part, explain the power that her friend kept over the souls of other people. She couldn't imagine any mightier power above this one. She also came to finally understand why this green herb with a long stack and yellow sap was on the table. This sap was the ingredient of the alchemic perfume. The essence released by this fragrance transported Jasmine to some other moment, namely Marbella's near vision. This handcrafted perfume she found in the oracle's home was produced from unique elements of nature that she found on her journeys around the world, as well as in Marva, the place where Jasmine could sense the power of the universe. Upon arriving at this place, the fortune-teller had taken to other dimensions through a mysterious magnetic energy.

Just after revealing the contents of her own theory, Jasmine asked Marbella to close her eyes. With her arms in the air, the oracle held her breath and let herself be taken by the spirits that now transported her to another dimension. First came the mist and then, suddenly, the giant clock that had appeared in the Marbella's dream, with its giant hands showing the right time. The oracle concentrated even more and saw Josef Salvaterra and the green-eyed, young woman with the long, black hair, just as they were described by her friend. The eyes of Salvaterra showed true affection towards this woman, but Jasmine couldn't see if there were any signs of passion. There was, however, a close bond and complicity between the two, as if they shared a secret. At that moment, Jasmine knew that her friend hadn't seen a near-vision, but a full vision. There was a woman she didn't know who had become close to her husband. There seemed to be a secret pact among the two. The oracle raised her arms even more.

Surprisingly, the yellow sap used for the alchemic perfume started to drip all over the table, the statuettes seemed to have changed their position, and the sun shone brighter through Jasmine's window. Marbella was in awe of this ritual and, for a moment, wished she could take part in it. She remained silent, though. Jasmine directed her inner stare towards the tunnel of time that she was in and looked at the giant clock that stood behind Salvaterra and the young woman. She rapidly realized that the clock meant the past, but not only that, it was a door to both the present and future. What the image meant was that Salvaterra and the young woman were connected by time. This green-eyed woman could be one of his patients, someone who had done past life regression with him.

The truth was opening itself to Jasmine, but she still didn't know who this young woman was. The fortune teller focused even more, but it didn't require much effort to find out her name, as Salvaterra took her hand and said it aloud, "Anne Pauline."

At that moment, Josef and Anne were sat under the hands of the clock. Jasmine had a feeling, more of a premonition than a vision. Anne Pauline held this enormous power that was related to her past, enabling her to easily move between time periods. It was both a power and a gift, which when used simultaneously, could effectively change the future.

The sap kept dripping all over the table while the visions seen by the oracle became clear. Marbella's hands were now moving, as if she could now see the same visions and was being transported to a different dimension like her friend. An extraordinarily strong energy could be felt in the room. Jasmine doubled her efforts and again, saw Anne's alliance with Salvaterra. Her eyes opened, still in trance. This alliance focused on Marcus Belling. Once more, Jasmine was able to read all these hidden secrets. In the meantime, the clock kept showing the right time, as if the past and the future needed to be aligned for a single final destiny. Anne Pauline and Josef Salvaterra looked at each other and a seagull flew over the clock. The oracle felt an enormous power taking over her body. The visions and smells suddenly disappeared and her spirit was once more transported to her own living room, where the statuettes, silver medallions, and e thin-stacked plant awaited her. Jasmine opened her eyes and stared at Marbella, as if she was trying to understand how hard it would be to tell Marbella about her reading. Jasmine lowered her arms and put her hands on the shoulder of her friend.

"This issue needs to be addressed quickly," Jasmine told her.

Marbella held her breath before saying these words. This was a moment of *suspense,* and she didn't know what to think but this was most certainly a revelation. Jasmine sat at the table, put her medallions to one side, and took a deep breath. These moments were always intense, as she needed to trust her soul to the spirits. Returning from the trance and adapting to the reality always took her some time. A torrent of words now spewed out from Jasmine's mouth and the wife of Salvaterra understood that this mysterious woman seen in her near vision had signed a pact with her husband. It took some courage, but the oracle said, "This alliance is related to Marcus Belling."

"With Belling, really?" an astounded Marbella asked.

"And you need to act quickly," Jasmine warned once more. "This alliance depends on time and we don't have much of it left."

"Who is the woman who haunts my dreams?" Marbella asked, now becoming more intrigued by these revelations

"Her name is Anne Pauline," Jasmine answered seriously.

"Anne... Pauline..." Marbella whispered, as if she was already designing a plan against this menace.

The oracle told her friend about her vision but decided to hide two facts from her. One was the affection there was between her husband and this young woman, and the other was that the destinies of Marbella and Anne would meet someday. Jasmine didn't really know what Salvaterra felt for the green-eyed, young woman, deciding to keep her premonition to herself. Marbella listened to every word that the most famous visionary in town had to tell her, and it just confirmed that her near-vision was, in fact, a full vision. I feel that my power is growing, she thought to herself. As the oracle finished detailing her visions and rose to another dimension, she knew this revelation would mean that serious issues would arise between the Salvaterras. Such confrontation had never existed before and she could not know if their marriage would survive such information. Marbella stood up from her chair, but her eyes were much heavier than before the session, kissed her friend (or the globetrotter, as she always called Jasmine) goodbye. As she walked out of the door, the doorbell suddenly rang. Jasmine waited for another person.

This sound bothered Marbella, who could not imagine how she could use her occultist friend's help to find out more about this pact. What else could she discover by using such information? Mrs. Grey looked into the eyes of Jasmine on her way out and asked, "How can this alliance be related to me? What can we do?"

"It could mean positive things to you if we learn how to control the power held by Anne Pauline. It was this power that brought your husband to her. You'll finally have access to the most secluded clubs in town and bring new influences into the city and the National Council for Hypnosis, as you've always wished," Jasmine answered. "My visions can help us to achieve other dimensions. I can meddle with time and get to this young woman."

"Will we speak anytime soon?" Marbella asked

"Of course, we will. As I said before, we need to act quickly. It's all a matter of time," the oracle answered.

Marbella smiled. The two shared an immense complicity that was hard to explain. As she came down the stairs of the narrow building, Salvaterra's wife ran into Georgine Gunderson. It was the first time that they met and, as clients of the local legend Jasmine, they couldn't stop but look at each other in the eyes, as if they were studying one another. While Marbella was a short woman with black hair and dark eyes – that were almost black – which showing her clenched face, Georgine had the beauty of an angel and was much taller, with white and grey hair, and her eyes were velvety and large. The depth of her stare left Salvaterra's wife shivering inside, as her eyes had once more reminded her of Anne Pauline's, just like she had seen in her dreams. The intensity was similar, albeit a different color. At that moment, Marbella couldn't imagine how the destinies of all these women were inevitably and unpredictably connected with each other.

Marbella finally closed the entrance door to the building and left the dark veil behind that followed her everywhere. Georgine, the librarian, felt a very strange premonition. The dark eyes of Marbella showed nothing but resentment and hatred. Nothing good came from the presence of that woman. However, Georgine rapidly forgot the unpleasant feeling that haunted her as Jasmine met her with that open smile of hers and gently asked her to come into her humble home.

Georgine Gunderson was one of the very few in the whole city who came to Jasmine that didn't look for her skills as a visionary and fortune teller, but to acquire her perfume, which essence remained secret. Only a small number of people knew about her unique and rare perfume that could block out any other surrounding aromas, making it what she called a supreme scent. Whenever Georgine applied it in her daily routine, she knew that her problem with the library's smells, namely those of book ink, dust, and pages, would disappear. She felt ashamed and so had never seen a doctor to solve her problem, mostly because she was afraid of not being taken seriously. She had never met someone else with this disease, which had only started a few years ago after she began working as a librarian. Eventually there was no other smell that bothered her as much as the smell of libraries. The librarian then studied all the products that might help her to overcome her handicap, when she came across Jasmine's perfume. Georgine was sure that she could keep her work as a librarian from the moment that she first applied the "Alchemic Perfume". Thaddeus Borba, the shoemaker at Sun Avenue, had informed her there was a perfume made from such a rare essence that perfectly surpassed any other existing smells. Georgine believed the words of Thaddeus, who was also a visionary, like Jasmine, but far more famous for his Spells of Truth, which every client of his appreciated.

Jasmine asked Georgine to come into the little annex in her home. It wasn't her first time there, though. All the materials that were needed to create the perfume were on top of the table; test tubes, glass rods, flasks of different sizes to combine all the ingredients, glass funnels, filter paper, and an amber-made container with a lid for the maceration of all the components. For five years now, Jasmine had sold her own product to her most loyal clients. No one knew what the essence of this perfume was, but most of them recognized its efficiency. Jasmine gave Georgine a 90-ml flask of the precious mixture and immediately paid for it. The librarian had never paid that much for a perfume. She gave the money and held the bottle carefully for fear of breaking it or dropping it.

This was a precious delivery as Georgine Gunderson knew that Jasmine would be out of town by late September to go on her journeys, from which she would only return next year. She needed much more of this perfume than before as she worked at the old library. The old building where she now worked was full of dust, and the smell of those books was much more intense than at the new library. Each book had a unique smell or scent, and so did each corner of that old building, as if they could all tell tales of a distant past.

Not all librarians had really realized this, but each book had a unique scent that Georgine knew well. These aromas were intense or subtle or very particular, and only someone with an acute sense of smell could smell it. She had an aversion to so many fragrances and aromas, it seemed contrary to her profession. Georgine had tried to recreate the alchemic perfume at home but needed to know what essence Jasmine used, but the occultist kept that secret. Georgine had expected Thaddeus Borba to know of it, although she never asked him. She held the 90-ml jar of the perfume even closer to her, to be sure to bring it home safely. Gunderson kissed her goodbye and left her home. This freshening aroma would now help her to return to her work at the old council library.

2

In the meantime, while Jasmine was welcoming Marbella and Georgine to her home, Anne Pauline had once more returned to Sun Avenue. Before her return, though, Salvaterra had informed Anne of what had happened at the clinic. It took her a week to return to the clinic while the refurbishment took place to recover the elegance of the part of the consulting room consumed by fire. Anne Pauline's conscience bothered her, and she suddenly felt guilty. She had set fire to the scrolls of the druid in the past, and the fire in the hypnotist's library was clearly related to this. The Theory of Casualty had now been proven to be right. Whoever interacts with people from their past lives through hypnosis can change events in that dimension of time, resulting in future consequences. Anne Pauline couldn't have imagined having this power before she had started her sessions under the guidance of Marcus Belling and, truth be told, she didn't know how to control it. Anne didn't know of any similar case to hers. These events made her feel isolated. Anne Pauline was either alone in the world or the world was distant from her. The young woman didn't know which of the two applied to her.

A fresh breeze was now blowing through Sun Avenue. Anne Pauline was moved by the weight on her conscience and decided to see what had happened in Belling's consulting room with her own eyes. A loose, angled stone on the pavement caused her to trip and fall on the floor, which even her agile moves couldn't prevent. She was stunned at the unexpected way she fell, but wasn't hurt at all, and noticed that her celestial blue shoes were torn at the front. Unable to react to this situation, Anne saw a friendly old man close by who said, "I am a shoemaker. I can help you, come with me."

Anne just stared at this gentleman and kept silent. She got up and followed the man. The green-eyed, young girl didn't know it, but she had just met Thaddeus Borba, the most renowned shoemaker in town. Their brief dialogue was more than enough for Thaddeus to feel the occult power held by this woman, which didn't usually happen when someone came across Anne Pauline. Once again, he had a premonition. The shoemaker was reminded of the words he had told Marcus Belling not long ago, when he had explained that someone would arise and change his mind and convictions. He knew this green-eyed woman was the one that his spells had predicted. Once more, his words had only told the truth. Anne Pauline's gift, however, had a dark side. Only minds that were more open and freer from preconceived ideas could achieve the hidden power that she held. But they would hardly understand it, for it implied the acceptance of an eternal connection between the future and the past. Thaddeus Borba asked her name and from that moment on, the troubadour prophet would never forget the name of this young woman.

Anne Pauline followed Thaddeus to his small workshop that stood only a few feet from the spot where she had slipped. The workshop was discreet, had a wooden door, and a glass window, which allowed his clients and their shoes to come in as fast and efficiently as they could. Anne Pauline saw a small tile on his white wall that said; Knowledge isn't seen with one's eyes. Her thoughts were instantly connected to the Forgotten Island, or the Island of Wisdom, as it was also known, for the seagulls had flown around the world to spread knowledge to humans for many centuries, sometimes more successfully than at other times.

It wasn't just Anne who kept a secret. Thaddeus Borba had also been to the Forgotten Island, but he had never shared it with anyone else. He was unlike all those who had been taken to the Island of Wisdom and knew about it after their hypnotic trance, this process allowed him to equally know this island, so forgotten by man. The fact that Marcus Belling was a regular client of his allowed Borba to learn the basic notions and techniques necessary to induce someone into a hypnotic trance. The famous therapist helped him to understand the key to this method while his shoes were being repaired.

"Thaddeus, I'm going to teach you some methods of self-hypnosis. It's easier than it looks. One way or another, we have all been hypnotized," Belling once told him.

As he fell into his trance, the shoemaker came to meet the community of seagulls that inhabited this mysterious island and learned about their history. Contrary to Anne Pauline, he hadn't been given the sacred feather, nor did he know that she kept it in a pocket of her jacket. His visit to the Forgotten Island, however, turned out to be a very bitter experience, so he had forgotten that he had visited this location, which could only be found in another dimension of the world.

Anne Pauline carefully observed the room around her. There, she saw machines to repair shoes that the shoemaker used every day, but she totally ignored their exact function. Next to an annex, Anne noticed one more beautiful tile hanging on the wall. She carefully moved to see it better. Unlike the previous one, this was signed by Borba himself and showed an island covered in luxurious vegetation with three mountaintops, well detached from the landscape. A beautiful beach of golden sand stretched along the whole island, and the waves rolled smoothly on the sand, giving them an intense glow. Anne Pauline knew at that moment that the shoemaker had also made it to the Island of Wisdom and the first tile she had seen, depicting Wisdom, was related to his experience there. Anne was both surprised and moved, for it was the first time she had met someone who knew about such a place. The green-eyed girl felt no shame about simply facing the troubadour with the facts, "I see that you know the Forgotten Island."

To Anne's awe, Thaddeus Borba wasn't surprised by her discovery. From their first contact, he felt that she possessed this enormous power, something he had only achieved by the time he had traveled to the Forgotten Island through self-hypnosis. He couldn't hide this fact. However, Thaddeus ignored her question and asked her to take off her shoes.

"Please take a seat on this chair. It's quite old, but it's good enough for some rest," he said. "I will fix your shoes and you'll be able to use them again."

In any other situation, the shoemaker would have answered the question posed by the young woman by the means of a lay, but Anne Pauline was a unique person who knew the truth through her dreams. Contrary to any of his other clients, she *still* didn't need to listen to his lays of truth. As her power flowed through his workshop, Thaddeus Borba finally understood the content of the words he had dedicated to Marcus Belling just a few months ago, and reminded himself of the words once more:

> *It is better to know at times*
> *Than to just wait and see*
> *The one who will rise*
> *Will forever change your mind.*

Thaddeus, the troubadour, knew that Anne Pauline was the person who was meant to arise in the life of Marcus Belling, and made her a proposal, "Yes, I know the Forgotten Island. I went there many years ago. We are among the few who knew of its existence. As you can imagine, it should obviously remain a secret."

After this he took a deep breath and continued speaking. "I can also help you to control your power," he said, but now more firmly.

The voice of the shoemaker sounded hesitant and anguished as he waited for a positive reaction from her. Anne Pauline opened her eyes and looked astonished at his proposal. She now understood that both knew of secrets that, until now, had remained in the silence of time. It was also highly probable that Thaddeus Borba knew the power of the sacred feather and wrote of it. On the other hand, he had always envisioned the past and the future and, even more surprisingly, the shoemaker knew about her power.

These last few weeks had been very disturbing and intense for young Anne Pauline Roux. She had made a pact with Josef Salvaterra and changed events from the past in her life, as well as Belling's, so that she could test the truth behind the Theory of Vocations and the Theory of Casualty, which she now knew were both viable. Despite this alliance, Anne Pauline still felt isolated, as if she was still living her days on the Forgotten Island. Salvaterra knew her power and his goal was to use it to ruin Marcus Belling's career as a hypnotist. Only Borba knew who she was. He was an old man who repaired shoes with a passion and passionately told lays of truth. She now felt like she was on the high seas and didn't really know where she should navigate to. The green-eyed woman seriously considered the wise old man's proposal. He was someone she could trust, who shared similar mystical experiences. Therefore, Anne accepted the proposal as put forward by Thaddeus, the shoemaker.

The weeks went on and, during that time, the refurbishment of the clinic on number 27 Sun Avenue progressed quickly. The clients returned to their sessions with Marcus Belling and so did Anne Pauline. Her conscience weighed on her for she knew that the fire that had destroyed Belling's library had been caused by her actions in one of their past lives. Anne let herself be carried away by this strong feeling of power. As Josef Salvaterra had told her, it indeed was an immense power and no one she knew possessed such capacities or had gone through such an experience. Now she was no longer alone, as Thaddeus Borba had promised to help her to control this power.

While Belling's clinic returned to its old routine, Patricia Murio, Sofia Estelar and Maria de Burgos kept searching for explanations for the mysterious fire that had broken out in the library. The flames minded the books, which showed that someone had accessed the consulting room. No electrical storm could have caused such results. The three decided to take a trip to the home of Vincent Torquay, their retired accountant, who now lived in the countryside, away from the bustle of the city. One could say that the accountant knew Salvaterra well, for he had also done some work at the National Council for Hypnosis. After working in Sun Avenue for some years, Torquay had made a discovery that would forever change the rapport between the two hypnotists. He had found a spy whose name was Rolland Ulm, a middle-aged man with a handlebar moustache and a fit body, was monitoring each step taken by Belling and his working crew. From this moment on, there was no contact between Belling and Salvaterra anymore, though the spy kept subtly watching their windows on an occasional basis. The three women who protected Belling's work were inevitably worried about the presence of Rolland and linked him to the fire that had broken out in the library. Maria, Patricia and Sofia decided to visit Vincent Torquay to ask for any explanations for the events in the consulting room just a few weeks before.

Life in the clinic on Sun Avenue was slowly returning to normal. There was, however, something that could terribly change its day-to-day routine, as some strange phenomenon was now happening more frequently. After each consultation, the hypnotist experienced a strange regressive amnesia that made him forget what had happened in the previous session. He sporadically forgot even the most basic techniques of his practice, fundamental notions of hypnotic trance, as well as his practical knowledge of past life regression. He also kept losing his ability to use persuasive and hypnotic language, all of which made his attempts to induce patients into a trance take much longer. Such a thing had never happened to him before. He was a talented and famous hypnotist who could deal with any kind of personality, even those that were more resistant to hypnosis. The destruction of the books in his library seemed to have caused him to forget the knowledge he had built up.

His vast bibliographic catalogue had helped him to decipher the most complicated cases, the traumas and unconscious dramas that his patients had carried with them. Without any of his tools, Belling knew that his situation was fragile, and he feared he had lost his memory, as well as his books. Little by little, his patients gave their feedback, mainly to Sofia, who was now more of a complaints manager. It seemed her employer had somehow lost all his talent. He had the calling, but now found it hard to use it. Marcus" skills seemed to be locked between thick walls. Belling felt like he was trapped inside his mind, without understanding what was behind it, and so his frustration grew.

As time went on, Anne Pauline continued her sessions with Belling, who now felt increasingly discouraged. The fire in his consulting room seemed to have consumed a substantial portion of his knowledge in the field, or so he felt. His helplessness and incomprehension were rapidly sensed by Sofia, who tried to approach the issue with him, but was immediately rebuffed by a nervous Belling. He knew, after the fire in his library, that he had lost all the material he used to help him in the hardest situations. Anne Pauline was just one of many patients whose traumas meant he faced more complex dilemmas to unlock. It was not a mere material loss, however, but also a cognitive or knowledge loss that had come over him since the fire. However temporary it was, the truth was that, Marcus felt increasingly that he couldn't remember his techniques. He kept forgetting how to be a hypnotist and how to apply regression. Sofia received more complaints from many clients, some of whom showed their disappointment with the uncertainty and doubt showed by Belling. He stammered, contradicted himself and revealed a complete lack of command of the essential practices. He wasn't even able to get help from his books to solve the hardest cases and often ended his sessions in tears. He didn't understand what was happening and felt ashamed to approach the facts with the people around him, for his team depended on his talent and his knowledge to defend his name, which had been well known in his field for many years, and now being questioned.

The strange phenomenon that affected Belling caught the attention of Maria de Burgos. After consulting the information sent by Sofia, the Spaniard saw all the complaints that had been sent by patients who reported that their therapist showed uncertainty and doubt during their sessions.

"Patients have been reporting absurd happenings during the sessions. Some say that Belling has forgotten to wake them up from their trance, while others can't be hypnotized by him at all. We are talking about very faithful clients," Sofia said in a muffled voice to Maria. "Others have told how, for brief moments, he doesn't know what regression is used for. It looks like he's suffering from amnesia or blockade of information."

"Are you certain of what you're telling me?" Maria asked.

"Absolutely. I've never received so many complaints as in the past few days, it's nothing like in the old days anymore," the secretary said.

Maria de Burgos was advised by Sofia not to directly approach the issue with him at least for some time. It might only be a coincidental, temporary situation, maybe because he was still in shock about the latest events. The three colleagues promptly decided to visit Torquay as soon as possible so that they could discover more about this traumatizing incident that had shaken the lives of every member of staff that worked at 27 Sun Avenue.

Anne Pauline had noticed the strange environment in the clinic for some time. Since the day of the fire, her eyes were now minded each detail around her and knew, more than anyone else, what was happening to her therapist. Anne had been able to change the past and taken revenge for her death in her past life, the traumas and her uncertainty. She could not understand how intense her power was, which made the green-eyed woman think it could be even stronger than she thought and capable of changing the course of history or the state of the world. All this seemed too absurd, though. This power only showed when she was in a trance and it only allowed her to change events in her past lives, but this was something that not even Belling, a trained and experienced professional, could imagine to be real. One could say that Anne Pauline felt satisfied with what had happened at the consulting room and, reported to Salvaterra how Belling was feeling disturbed. Such news brought joy to Josef Salvaterra, which he hadn't felt for about two decades.

To Sofia's despair, the number of complaints filed by clients concerning Belling's behavior didn't stop growing. Such a system to sort out complaints had never existed before in their clinic on Sun Avenue, which made this an unheard of and unpredictable situation. No one could have anticipated these events. Sofia frequently reported the facts to Maria de Burgos, who considered this an appropriate time to see Vincent Torquay. But more unwelcome news arrived as they planned the trip to Torquay's home. This time it was from Ruben Mortsel, the new bookkeeper. He informed them of a drastic decline in the revenue of the clinic and of reimbursement requests from different patients who were not satisfied with their treatment. Sofia and Maria decided to postpone the discussion with Belling so as not to make it worse, but truth be told, their working system seemed to be crumbling.

After a session of past life regression with another client went terribly wrong, Belling decided to see a friend and neurologist. The explanation behind such a phenomenon might be related to some modification that had taken place in his cognitive and perceptive capabilities, and consulting a specialist was mandatory. The therapist became aware that his patients were dissatisfied with his sessions and started to doubt his own capabilities. No one invited him onto the usual television programs about past life regression anymore, in contrast to Josef Salvaterra, who was now under the media spotlight. Maria de Burgos avoided the publishing of news concerning her employer's situation, and only informed him that it was nothing more than a temporary situation and that further news would be given at the right time.

Just as the visit to Belling's former accountant was happening, Marbella decided to confront her husband about his alliance with Anne Pauline, which Jasmine had confirmed through her visions. Marbella confronted Salvaterra with the existence of this woman, who held such power over the hypnotic process, and was capable of influencing the spirit of Marcus Belling.

"I visited Jasmine who, as you may know, is the most talented visionary in town. From her visions, she told me that you know some woman called Anne Pauline, with whom you've forged some alliance or agreement. Moreover, that everything is related to Marcus Belling."

She felt more tranquil now. "How could you do this to me, especially without telling me anything?" Marbella asked, shocked by her husband's behavior.

Josef was astonished at his wife's courage. He knew that Jasmine and his wife were close to each other, but he had never guessed that such visions could allow someone to discover the truth about his pact. He had never liked Jasmine, for he thought she had excessive control over his wife. So, he told her, "I find it incredible that you consulted Jasmine with such intent."

The truth is that Salvaterra had decided not to hide more information from her. The reason was that, since the fire in Marcus Belling's clinic, Josef had felt that he had somehow lost control over the whole situation. Indeed, he did have a pact with Anne Pauline. For quite some time, the two had met regularly so that she could report on everything that had happened inside the clinic on Sun Avenue, as the agreement required. This system allowed him to access information that couldn't be obtained from any other source, not even Rolland Ulm. Marbella immediately understood that the power of Anne Pauline was rare and her husband's alliance with this woman could forever change the course of her life. There seemed to be a complex communication system between the past lives of Anne Pauline and Marcus Belling, which were linked by a circuit of time and space and gave them a secret passage between times. As Salvaterra had explained, the young lady's power only occurred while Belling kept her in a trance, which was why Josef never tried to hypnotize her. Josef suspected that the whole of Belling's working team could intervene in the past somehow. It was also probable that others who worked with him could interact with Anne's past. Josef had thoroughly thought over these ideas. The only certainty was that Anne Pauline could change her past through hypnosis.

Marbella listened to each of her husband's ideas. On the other hand, it took a rare moment of honesty to inform her husband that Jasmine knew the content of his four theories, and she took the chance to add one more, called Theory of Smells. Marbella explained its meaning to Josef, with the hope of understanding more about Anne Pauline's power. However, this theory on the effect that aromas had on people didn't seem to get his attention. There was, however, one matter of major importance that Marbella raised and she did so with her eyes shining out of sheer curiosity, "What I would like you to tell me, Josef, is how you'll ensure that Anne will follow her part of the plan?"

Marbella knew that her husband had already thought about this question, but he was still hesitant about revealing to her the destiny he had planned for the green-eyed woman. Such hesitation didn't please Marbella, who kept staring at him with her deep black eyes, as if she would not allow any more secrets in their marriage. Josef sighed deeply and decided, against his will, to tell her about his plan.

"Very well, listen carefully."

He was not pleased about having to tell her the truth, but it seemed impossible to hide this secret anymore. Josef ended up telling her that once he had all the essential information he required about the functioning of Belling's clinic, concerning the number of clients, monthly turnover, organization, and schedule, the plan was to convince Anne to let him hypnotize her. During her trance, Josef could then induce information into the mind of the young woman, which would become orders. Anne would, therefore, be obliged to keep the alliance secret and forget everything that she had communicated beforehand. Salvaterra aimed to use techniques that were regarded as less democratic than Belling's to induce amnesia. Less democratic, at least, from the perspective of many people, but Salvaterra didn't really take individual freedom into consideration, unlike his rival. Marbella was taken by surprise by the daring plans of her husband, as she finally understood why Josef wanted to control the mind of such a mysterious woman. Both were now clearly dependent Anne Pauline's gift to put those plans into action, which didn't really please Marbella, for she always wanted to control any situation around her.

Marbella hadn't understood during their conversation that her husband wanted to use these techniques to give Anne Pauline a positive destiny. He wanted the confidential information for his own benefit, but he had no intention to harm Anne Pauline at all. Whenever Josef thought of this young woman, he couldn't hide his feelings for her. Maybe this was because he had fallen in love with her, something he hadn't expected.

On the same day, Marcus left his clinic much later, watched by Rolland, the spy who now hid in a corner of Sun Avenue. The daily clinic's routine was now harder to follow, as Sofia received increased complaints about Belling or his apparent ignorance of the necessary techniques. The relationship between Belling and his secretary was now in a crisis, as the mystery surrounding Belling's so-called knowledge amnesia grew.

The hypnotist came down the building's three flights of stairs and closed the door behind him. Within a few meters, the hypnotist stopped by a café where he regularly went with Sofia when he was nationally recognized, thinking of how his special bond with his secretary now seemed like a distant memory. Belling asked for a coffee and looked around him.

People didn't approach him as much as they used to, and the women didn't ask for his autographs as they once did. This left Marcus Belling in a nostalgic mood and this was a rare opportunity for him to stop and think about his life. The truth was that he had not been able to enjoy the beautiful spots on Sun Avenue for quite a long time.

It was now October and the summer breeze had given way to a biting frigid wind. The days were much shorter now. At this time of the year, the many fountains along the avenue were no longer throwing up their sparkling water that had amused the passers-by and tourists in the previous months. After a last sip of his coffee, Belling watched a group of people flock towards the wall of another café next to him. Belling was curious about what drove all those people there and decided to take a closer look. As he pushed some people to the side, Belling saw an advertisement on the wall of the café where he read; Sessions of Hypnosis and Regression for very fair prices. I am a therapist by training and with years of experience. Please contact through 256 222 145. Bernard Deya.

A buzz could be heard among the crowd who read the advertisement. As they looked around, they immediately recognized Marcus Belling. His face was deathly pale, and his pupils dilated. He knew Bernard Deya had been an administrator in the National Council for Hypnosis clinic for many years. He was far from being a hypnotist, however, as he only worked in the setting up of events and conferences held by the Council. It was staggering how Deya could write such a paper offering his services as a hypnotist who, moreover, had skills in past life regression.

Marcus Belling realized how the rumors concerning his personal situation had spread through the whole of Sun Avenue and the city. His professional decline had given way to so-called hypnotists who had found an opening to achieve the fame that had been previously denied them.

CHAPTER 7

SCHOLA MEDICA SALERNITANA – MEDIEVAL ERA, ITALY

1

Marcus Belling felt desolate as he got home that day. Bernard Deya was a short, thin man who the hypnotist had barely met. He knew, though, that Deya organized events such as conferences, lectures, seminars and various other meetings at the National Council for Hypnosis, which discussed different issues, including new hypnosis therapeutics or the effects of regression therapy.

Despite all that, Deya dared to call himself a hypnotist, which showed how far the situation had deteriorated. Bernard Deya wasn't even a member of the General Assembly, which approved the action plan and annual budget. Though he wasn't an effective member of the working group, he surely had a deep need for personal affirmation. It was clear that the probable knowledge amnesia and the Councils already knew about the loss of technical skills that plagued Belling or, at least, to those who worked for the organization. This was an extremely dangerous situation. The people who had seen Deya's advertisement had no knowledge of the subject and were obviously being fooled by it, and Belling couldn't ignore the potential and impending danger that many faced if they decided to take such therapy sessions. Past life regression demanded the hypnotist to possess the knowledge and the techniques to do the job, which Deya didn't have.

Nevertheless, Bernard Deya was not Marcus Belling's only problem. After the fire in his private library, he closed his clinic for a few days. Upon reopening, Anne Pauline was one of the first patients to resume her sessions, as she was conscious that the actions in her past life had had consequences in the present. Josef Salvaterra, in turn, was perplexed with the young woman's power, but knew this was a unique chance to use his rare gift to change the position he had comparatively to Marcus Belling's.

When Anne Pauline returned to her sessions, she couldn't stop looking at the destruction that the fire had caused. Few books had escaped the flames. The remainder of the room seemed to have escaped the calamity, including the couch for the hypnotized. Its luxurious mahogany and green colors were fully intact, having escaped from the destruction at the other side of the room. From that moment forward, Anne Pauline knew that she couldn't be afraid. She had signed a deal with Salvaterra and promised to follow it. There was much more to be known about her past lives and her true identity. Once again, she lay down on the magic couch that had taken every person into a different reality before Marcus Belling's amnesia that had affected him since the tragic event. Anne Pauline let herself go and saw herself once again in the large tunnel. She walked a few meters, before finally opening a wooden door at the end. An intense ray of light flashed before her eyes and then immediately disappeared. Anne knew at that moment that she had come to another of her previous lives.

As the intense flash disappeared, Anne Pauline had returned to the 12th century and was in Salerno, a coastal town in southern Italy and the seat of the famous *Schola Medica Salernitana*. The academy operated in a former monastery and had adapted its facilities to receive students and patients from all over the world, who were searching for the wisdom to find a cure for diseases. For that reason, Anne Pauline felt unnoticed in Salerno. The town was busy, and she wasn't sure if people could see her... but they didn't, as no one stared at her. It looked like no one recognized her, in contrast to what had happened in the laboratory. Not even Anne knew how her power worked, and so hoped to learn some more from

Thaddeus Borba, the truth-telling shoemaker. Still, she did understand that, though she had this gift, not everyone in her past lives could interact with her; only those people she had some empathy with. It was, nevertheless, hard to define empathy and what it related to in human relationships. When she was feeling confident enough, Anne took the path to the monastery, where the medical school operated.

Anne Pauline was being guided by her instinct. She didn't know when this past life occurred, but she was aware of being in the Middle Ages. Upon arriving on the top of a hill, Anne could see the monastery. Here was the only medical school in Western Europe that included a treatment unit for healing illnesses of people who suffered years in agony. The monastery was right by the Etruscan Sea in the south of Italy. The school's lecturing body included doctors, professors, nuns and monks who wanted to create a medical school that would be seen as a reference in the West. Hippocrates and Galen had studied here, and the lectures and experiments on diseases and the functioning of the human body were conducted in other parts of the monastery. There were many people from different social classes and different parts of the world, both men and women, as well as ailing people who sought an answer to their long-suffered illnesses. Anne Pauline was aware of the cosmopolitan atmosphere and that the use of plants, animals and vegetables as potential cures for diseases was being studied. Experiments were done to develop the best medicine for each of the diseases for this reason. Anne Pauline walked through the corridors unrecognized, as if her power had temporarily become inactive. She was sure she had opened another door from the tunnel of time to another life that would drive Anne towards her identity. All this time, Marcus Belling's hypnotic voice could still be heard, and he asked her to walk through that monastery and to memorize every single detail, and so she did.

A door to the clinic of one of the lecturers of the *Schola Medica di Salerno* was open, so Anne Pauline decided to confirm that she had come to the most acclaimed medieval medical center in the West. On the top of a wooden table there, were books by Avicenna, Dioscorides, Aristotle, Galen, Serapio, and other authors, which showed that the teachings of diverse sources were regularly ministered there, including Byzantine, Greek, Arabic and Latin ones.

However, two fundamental manuscripts, whose pages seemed to have been turned over during someone's medical consultation or research, were peeking out from the pile of books. One of them, entitled *Antidotarium* by Nicolaus Salernitanus, lay open to a page where the pharmaceutical formulas in alphabetical order could be read. The other, called *Regimen Sanitatis Salernitanum*, was the most famous treaty produced by *Schola Medica Salernitana*, which consisted on a compendium of hygienic rules, nutrition and medicinal herbs, although Anne Pauline didn't know this. Both texts contained a large span of wisdom and were written in Latin. They collected the medical and pharmaceutical knowledge of the time, which indicated it was the property of doctor and professor, Thomas Godwynus, whose name was on a notebook kept on top of the lecturer's working table. Anne Pauline didn't know who he was, but the truth would be told to her when it was most suitable, as always happened during her hypnosis sessions. The number of ancient manuscripts lying on that table showed that she had come to the clinic of one of the most recognized experts out of *Schola Medica Salernitana*. All this kept Anne Pauline's attention.

She didn't have much time to observe the room, as the sudden sound of footsteps made her hide behind a nearby cabinet. The sound grew louder and soon Godwynus entered the room. He was a tall, middle-aged man with dark, even black, hair. He looked gaunt and depressed, but Anne could only see him in profile briefly. He laid some books on the table and then sat on the chair to thoroughly consult *Antidotarium*. He was looking for a specific page where there was a pharmaceutical formula of healing herbs for different symptoms was represented, especially the cure of anxiety. Psychological illnesses were usually thought of as being symptoms of the soul, which had brought the attention of a few doctors of the *university* to the works of Avicenna, especially the book entitled *Book of Healing*. They were working to bring together a full knowledge of the therapeutic effect of plants, yet it was a controversial issue.

Anne Pauline tried to stand still behind the cabinet, remaining silent, but couldn't help watching the master, who now stood up from his chair. She was surprised to find that Thomas Godwynus was Marcus Belling. He was a few years older, but his face was still easily recognizable. He was once more part of her past and both had shared a particular historical period. In this case, they were in Salerno, Italy, back in the 12th century. She didn't know it but Godwynus had been a doctor of *Schola Medica Salernitana* for some years, having studied there before, and was now following his career as a lecturer, teaching seminars on the healing power of plants. We're in 1160, Anne Pauline thought to herself. She looked back to Marcus Belling's aged face. He was a master, sage, and professor. She couldn't stop her thoughts from racing. Belling would somehow retain the typical posture as a professor many centuries later, when he would be a famous hypnotist whose goal was to demystify hypnosis for the public.

At that moment, it was clear to Anne Pauline that the Vocational Theory Josef Salvaterra had developed made sense. Belling's talent for hypnosis had been developed throughout his past lives and because of this experience, he was an expert in his field. The same had happened during the Middle Ages, where he was a doctor at the *Schola Medica Salernitana.*

Godwynus practiced healing and soul medicine for many years, having created this specialty to cure the most disoriented and grieving souls. He was even called the master of souls by some. Besides that, he was born close to England, with some records stating that he had family roots in Normandy. He traveled all the way to Salerno, settled there, and through his career, he served others there.

He enjoyed breathing in the fresh air from the sea because it took all his worries away. Thomas Godwynus knew he was privileged, as if he could foresee his future. The Middle Ages were harsh and unpredictable times. Not everyone was able to access the services of those who worked at the *University*, which welcomed both men and women, students, professors and doctors. For some, it represented the most open-minded place in Europe that hosted anyone who looked to cure their disease.

After consulting the healing formulas from some of his scripts, Thomas Godwynus sat back on his clinic chair and could only think of one person; an incredibly special patient who had undergone an unsuccessful treatment in the healing section of the monastery. That day, the professor had received a patient called Isabella who looked for help as she suffered serious anxiety, distress and apathy symptoms. These caused both general paralysis and deep wounds on her body. He knew immediately that this case was different because she had a spiritual disease that caused physical sickness. This was a result of the link between the psychological and physical parts of the human body, which works like a system that aims for a balance among all its elements. These were effects that not all the doctors were agreed upon, denying the merging of spiritual and physical energies. Despite that, Godwynus dared to develop different plant-based formulas to cure illnesses of the soul, making it difficult for his colleagues to fully understand him. In the meantime, to best develop a solution for the described disease, Thomas Godwynus asked his patients to study the books and pharmacology manuals at his on-campus clinic, specifically those of Nicolaus Salernitanus a reputed professor. Salernitanus taught healing medicine at *Schola Medica Salernitana* for decades before he passed away years before. It was the expert's book, *Antidotarium, where Godwynus searched for* a cure for Isabella.

As Anne thought about Isabella, the girl with deep green eyes came to the master's door and asked permission to enter. Anne Pauline peeked from behind the cabinet, curious to see the person Thomas Godwynus, who was also Marcus Belling, thought of so often. When the girl turned her face, it was easy to see that Isabella was Anne Pauline. It was as if Belling and his patient were together again, though the situations were slightly different and Isabella looked petrified, as if she wanted to run away.

As with Godwynus, little was known about this young, sick woman because many patients searching for a doctor in Salerno were too weak to tell their personal histories. In addition, most kept their identity completely secret so that they were anonymous. However, the first time Isabella had met Godwynus, she told him that she had traveled across Central Europe to meet him in Salerno. Thomas Godwynus immediately knew that his reputation had crossed borders. He was one of the few in his class who had developed cures for the so-called diseases of the soul. These were the most complicated of all illnesses to affect human beings, and Thomas explained to Isabella that this was why he was called the master of souls.

It was quite a scary moment for Anne Pauline to realize that she could understand Isabella's personal history just by focusing on Isabella's face, though it had never been told to verbally. Anne went through a parallel dimension, where she could hear the conversation between Isabella and Godwynus that had taken place the day before. Anne felt one hypnotic trance within a larger one. The next day, she wouldn't be able to define this feeling to anyone else, not even Josef Salvaterra. It looked like access to the past allowed the doors to other bygone periods to be opened, even if only briefly. As she closed her eyes, Anne Pauline immediately saw the druid who came to her in her other past life and understood that this past had also been part of Isabella's life. Anne felt a magnetic energy that came from the ground and gave her a huge sense of tranquility.

When Anne Pauline opened her eyes, Isabella had just come into the clinic and was politely greeted by Thomas Godwynus, who asked her to sit by the desk while facing him. He listened to her personal history. Isabella immediately felt comfortable enough to tell him that she had been plagued by incomprehensible dreams for many years, making her so anxious that all her muscles left her unable to move. The young woman then felt confident enough to say that she had once been paralyzed for two days and suffered excruciating pain all over her body. This had only been one of the extreme situations she had gone through. Another one had occurred when she was a little girl, as anxiety got so high, she had physical wounds that took months to heal. Doctors in her town couldn't find any physiological explanations for what was causing these strange reactions in the young girl's body.

For many years, it was difficult to give Isabella a diagnosis, especially as it was so hard to admit that her past lives could have an influence on her clinical condition. After hearing her description, Thomas Godwynus knew that he had a complicated case before him. It was the first time that a patient had told him they experienced total paralysis due to an altered state of consciousness and extreme anxiety, of which the reasons remained unknown. The expert was equally aware that patients in this situation would usually seek help from the occult, using recipes obtained from local wizards. Nonetheless, the he was unable to say that he knew the young lady's personal history, which wasn't the case of with Anne Pauline, who went through a trance during her hypnotic state. Images then came to her head. This was a double dimension, unknown to either Marcus Belling or Josef Salvaterra. As Isabella spoke again of her anxieties, Anne Pauline closed her eyes. She was now able to see the truth, which showed what a person never tells, and was important to understand her identity. The young girl was born with an innate talent much like Thaddeus Borba, who would later develop his Ballads of Truth, which his clients genuinely appreciated. As she noticed the truth, Anne Pauline realized that Marcus Belling's hypnosis sessions followed a chronological order as Isabella also had the Gaul's spirit.

Looking back at Isabella, Anne Pauline saw that she had a history that was similar to Salvaterra's, though she didn't fully know it. The girl had grown up an orphan. Her parents had been the subjects of a Lord, who welcomed Isabella into his own family when they died, leaving her obliged to pay him the dead hand tax. As she grew up, Isabella needed to work as a peasant in the Lord's lands, though she enjoyed some protection. However, she had become increasingly incapable of doing her job in the last few years in and out of the family that had hosted her after she was orphaned, especially because of the inexplicable anxiety peaks that had grown in intensity. Isabella had been given the opportunity to consult Thomas Godwynus at the *Schola Medica Salernitana but* was obliged to pay more taxes to cover her travel expenses there to look for an emotional cure. Despite the tough agreement, Isabella accepted its conditions. Anne Pauline immediately understood that her tragic childhood, existing economic dependence, heavy taxes, and lack of freedom had all contributed to Isabella's traumas.

While Anne Pauline discovered Isabella's personal history from her trance within a trance, Godwynus once again turned the pages of *Antidotarium*, prescribing his patient an herbal infusion to calm the nervous system. This was based on the theory of humors, which guided many of the teachings administered at the *school.* Isabella thanked him and then promised to come back the following day to tell him if the mixture cured her of her anxieties. As with all doctors who worked at *Schola Medica Salernitana,* Thomas Godwynus had studied the theory of humors, also known as the theory of the four humors. It had been used on many patients and became the main rational and medical explanation for health and disease since the fourth century B.C. It was based on the idea that corporal balance needed the following elements; blood, phlegm, yellow and black bile. These represented the heart, respiratory system, liver and spleen, respectively. Illnesses, either physical or of the soul, resulted from the instability of the humors produced by the distinct levels of each corporal element. In this way, the theory of humors tried to give a rational explanation for different human behaviors, which depended on the type of corporal fluids that existed. For that reason, Godwynus always kept a book by Hippocrates about this subject on his table, as it was especially useful for his daily work at the academy.

HYPNOSIS

After Isabella left the consulting room, the expert returned to his books, while considering whether the theory of the four humors could be affecting his patient. After thinking about the listed symptoms, Thomas immediately thought of bile-related problems, for which he had prescribed that infusion of healing herbs to her on that day. Then again, if Isabella suffered from bile, that could only mean her liver was functioning badly. This would show a controlled fury sparked by deep trauma, which might be causing her corporal bleeding of the soul. Nevertheless, the master of souls was far from knowing what spiritual dramas might be causing such a disease in Isabella's body, but he quickly understood that it might be related to experiences in her past. But Godwynus could not practice hypnosis as Marcus Belling did and in the Middle Ages, those who dared to perform such a practice were sentenced to death. Thomas surely knew nothing about the art he would develop some centuries ahead, so the only way to find out Isabella's personal history was by winning her confidence.

During this time, Anne Pauline remained hidden behind the cabinet, waiting for Thomas Godwynus to leave so that she could return to the center of Salerno, where she had arrived after being hypnotized by Marcus Belling. But the master kept nervously searching his texts and books, while still thinking of Isabella, or Anne Pauline. He could never imagine that his patient was behind his cabinet after returning to the past, thanks to an art of the occult, as hypnosis was seen back in that day. Neither could he imagine that one day he would become Marcus Belling, or that he had been a druid in a previous life. Anne Pauline understood that these life experiences could be behind Belling's interest in holistic medicine, the healing power of plants, alternative and holistic therapies, and consequently, hypnosis.

Hypnosis was a non-conventional therapy and so the teachings learned at the *Schola Medica Salernitana* had been essential in developing an understanding of the complex relationship between the body and soul. The knowledge transmitted by Avicenna, Galen and Hippocrates gave a broader vision of the human body, even though the Theory of Humors would be made obsolete in the 17th century. Pharmacology had always been a fundamental area of knowledge and wisdom in Marcus Belling's professional path, which pushed him towards pursuing a career in clinical hypnosis some centuries later. This did not seem to be a coincidence. Belling's past as a doctor at the *university* was of fundamental importance as it led to his future curiosity in hypnosis and its applied techniques. His previous life as a druid and his knowledge of healing herbs also seemed to have sparked his future interest in natural medicine and the world of therapeutic herbs. As she now looked at Marcus Belling in the 12th century, Anne Pauline had almost forgotten her plan for vengeance and the mission that she intended to execute with Salvaterra, through their alliance, to change the path of some events. Anne now looked at Thomas Godwynus as a good man who was willing to help her with his teachings and the resources he had, despite not knowing what she had been or done in her previous life.

One thing was certain, it was now clear that Marcus Belling and Anne Pauline had been in a hypnotist-patient relationship more than once over the course of their different lives, though not always in a formal setting. In fact, the two had met in an identical situation in the 12th century, at *Schola Medica Salernitana,* where Isabella had looked for the master of souls to seek comfort for her troubled spirit.

The following day, Anne Pauline would come back to Sun Avenue and planned to go back to Salerno again under hypnosis, and hear the conversation between Thomas and his patient, as she knew about the dramatic experiences that had led to this girl looking for help. So, she was just waiting for the right moment to leave Godwynus's office to return to the city center.

Thomas Godwynus stood up shortly afterwards, put some books under his arm, and left the room. Anne could finally move from behind the cabinet, where she had been hiding for about two hours. She opened the door and left unnoticed. Anne Pauline took a stone corridor until she left the monastery while a few medical students gathered on an inside patio to attend a class on healing herbs. Anne ran through the city as she heard Marcus Belling's voice, who was once more asking her to return from her deep, hypnotic trance. When she arrived in the center of Salerno, the sun struck her face. Anne then slowly closed her eyes and headed back through the tunnel of time before finally waking up on the couch in the office of the famed hypnotist.

2

After returning from her past life, she always did so with a surprised look on her face. After a few seconds, she noticed that Belling was staring at her with curiosity. He asked for some details of her regression, but her pact with Salvaterra once more prevented her from revealing that he had been a part of all her past lives. Anne, instead, described the events at the *Schola Medica Salernitana*, and the fact that she had been a patient who also sought answers to some of her anxieties, but without mentioning the existence of Thomas Godwynus. As always, Marcus Belling had no idea that he had shared his life with this young girl.

"Can you think of any more details? We have a good indication from these memories that this isn't the first time that you've looked for your identity and the reasons behind your concerns," said Belling.

Every time he ended an appointment with Anne Pauline, Marcus Belling had recently felt that she was hiding something from him. He didn't know, however, that Anne held a power that only occurred when she was under hypnosis. The only clues he had about her as a patient were the artefacts and other rarities he found after Anne Pauline went home. Belling decided to open the Victorian-style desk's drawer he kept locked, as if he could find out in there more about the past that the patient refused to tell him. That desk had survived the fire and he kept the objects he found there, deep in the drawer. Argus Dubois, the artwork antiquarian at Sun Avenue, considered both pieces to be of infinite value after examining them and he had clients who would be interested in buying them.

Once more, Anne Pauline hid most of her experiences under hypnosis from Marcus Belling. After Sofia had taken her to the door, the hypnotist stood up from his couch, turned the key of the desk's drawer and opened it very carefully. While thinking that this woman was a unique patient, Belling slowly studied the drawer with his hands, searching each square inch until he found a notebook with leather binding. When he took out the book, the hypnotist read its title, *Antidotarium* by Nicolaus Salernitanus. It was nothing more than an old book written on parchment, but it was extremely valuable. Belling knew he would meet Argus Dubois and Gembloux again after this new discovery.

Just after Marcus Belling discovered the old manuscript in his desk, Anne Pauline was meeting with Josef Salvaterra once more. When Anne started talking about her life in Italy during the 12th century, explaining how she had met Marcus Belling, Salvaterra could confirm his hypothesis that both shared a common past. The rival hypnotist understood that this past bonded them intensely, just as it had strengthened Anne Pauline's power, and this force only revealed itself when she was hypnotized by Belling.

Because of all this, Josef Salvaterra reminded Anne Pauline of their alliance and urged her to continue using her rare gift to keep Marcus Belling away from practicing hypnosis. Salvaterra took the chance to suggest how the past could be changed for their own benefit while also being enchanted by the young woman's green eyes. He once more recalled that, like Thomas Godwynus, Belling turned to his books many times, including his encyclopedias and the many compendiums that allowed him to understand more about the functioning of the human body and soul. In effect, these contained his knowledge about how the mind and body worked and gave him access to other information which, when put into practice, would give him enormous power. For this reason, Josef Salvaterra suggested that Anne Pauline destroy all of his texts, scrolls and annotations, just as she had done in her previous life.

"This master of souls, how dare he. He can't have access to books and knowledge that will make him one day Marcus Belling. You must destroy these documents!" Salvaterra said with conviction.

"He seems to be driven by good principles," said Anne Pauline.

"What are you saying? Get these ideas out of your head! Thomas Godwynus and Marcus Belling are the same person, and they can wisely handle the opinions of others. Can speakers convince people of the impossible? Don't forget our agreement," concluded Salvaterra.

Anne Pauline listened to every single word that Salvaterra said, but warned him how difficult it would be to put it into practice at this time because he was always surrounded by people at the *University*. On reconsideration, Belling's rival suggested that she intervene in the past by defaming him at the *Schola Medica Salernitana*, spreading rumors that he performed hypnosis to his patients, knowing that this practice was prohibited.

As Josef Salvaterra told Anne Pauline about his plans, she realized that after hiding behind the cabinet at Salerno for two hours, she had developed empathy towards the man who immediately offered to help Isabella, though he knew nothing of her past. Salvaterra was led astray. He noticed that his plans hadn't pleased Anne Pauline, so felt the need to remind her of their pact, which Anne should now follow until her last hypnosis appointment with Marcus Belling.

It was against his interests to see Thomas Godwynus die because of the rumors about his hypnosis practice, which was considered an occult practice back in the 12th century. Being a doctor and lecturer at *Schola Medica Salernitana*, Godwynus could always defend and save himself from those rumors and escape a tragic destiny. But it was essential to destroy all of the medical compendiums that prevented him from benefiting from the acquired knowledge of alternative therapeutic healing in the future. It was clear that, according to the Theory of Vocations, Marcus Belling would become a hypnotist by acquiring and accumulating knowledge from his past lives, either as a druid or as a doctor in the 12th century. In any case, there always seemed to be a relationship between Belling and the study of the human body, its functioning anatomy and the existing chemical processes of human physiology that lie behind different diseases, both physical and mental. The healing of those illnesses also implied a knowledge of the holistic dimension of the human body and the medication should always concern the natural properties of the existing plants in the world. The position of the master of souls showed that he didn't follow and apply conventional medicine, but he had full knowledge of the area. Anne Pauline carefully heard all that Josef Salvaterra had to tell her, as well as his interpretation of the revealed facts. She was stunned by the logical connection he built between the events, and understood that beyond a common past, Anne and Marcus Belling might share a common destiny. Based on these facts, Salvaterra revealed more, "From what you've told me, I can conclude that this isn't the first time you've been a patient of Marcus Belling, only now you're in a different period. To discover the effect of further events on your identity, you should go back to Salerno in Italy, because you've probably not seen it all."

It was, therefore, clear that the relationship between Anne Pauline and Marcus Belling dated back far enough that only hypnosis could reveal it all. Salvaterra kept reminding her of the need to continue her sessions because this alliance must continue until the end, even if Anne Pauline didn't want it to.

She returned next day with his words in her mind and eager to find out what had happened during her 12th century life. The reconstruction work was moving along quickly at number 27, so that the mythical place could return to its normal routine. In the meantime, Belling had welcomed some of his colleagues from the National Council of Hypnosis into his workroom. They then reported every detail to the

General Assembly and the Chairman. The fire had destroyed a well-respected clinic in the field of hypnosis, and made some followers come back to see what had happened after the tragic events.

While still worried about his knowledge amnesia, Marcus Belling couldn't imagine that there might be a pact between his patient and his rival colleague. Belling once more welcomed Anne Pauline and immediately asked her to take her place on the couch to be hypnotized. Once more, she fell into a full hypnotic trance at the sound of his words.

Anne Pauline could quickly return to her past lives when in a trance. When she took control of her consciousness under this state, and saw herself once more at *Schola Medica Salernitana*, where she had been in the last session. Anne quickly sensed a slight sea breeze. After returning to the past, she still didn't feel courageous enough to put Salvaterra's plans into practice, mainly because she had created a deep bond with the master of souls. Yet she wanted to discover more of her own history. The green-eyed girl walked around the *College*, attempting to find Thomas Godwynus, as she knew he had an appointment with Isabella to find out if the natural medication he had prescribed had worked something out in her soul. Once more, Anne Pauline's intuition guided her. The school had one single specialized room for the sale of pharmaceutical and natural products, where it was possible to acquire all the medications prescribed by the doctors. It was not hard for Anne Pauline to find this room, though it was tucked into a secluded wing of the monastery. It was a critical area for those who worked at the *School*, and especially for the patients who looked forward to curing their diseases there. There were few places in the West like this during the Middle Ages, and this is where the distinction between medicine and pharmacology as two complementary, yet distinctly different, sciences was being made. As Anne Pauline would soon learn, this room was known to all as the healing hall.

It was rare to find medication for the soul. All who suffered from spiritual diseases were obliged to live with their own anguish, so Isabella was conscious that she had been given a rare opportunity to try to cure whatever it was that she suffered from. There were few doctors who were able to diagnose the soul's wounds and to understand their influence in the human body. For that reason, there were scarcely any medicines for the soul. Godwynus had tried to develop an interesting combination of natural products, which he called dissolution mixture. This exact mixture was unique. He claimed when the herbs were dissolved in water, specifically, water from some streams in Salerno, and taken by the ailing patient, they could dissolve the anguish and transform negative feelings into positive ones. The master of souls had never been clear to his students about the notion of positive humor, but it was a phenomenon of spiritual regeneration brought about by the consumption of his magical natural combination. After he diagnosed Isabella's spirit, the doctor then decided to prescribe her something identical to promote the transmutation of her bitter emotions into pure felicity. He now waited for his patient to find out how she had reacted to the treatment.

After finding the pharmacology and apothecary room, Anne Pauline decided to go in and see what it was. The healing hall welcomed all patients who came to the school looking for treatment. It was one of the few places in Europe with such a range of healing products. The hall was extremely large, which was needed, badly illuminated, as there were only two small narrow windows that let some light into the room, and there were many shelves on the walls with jars on them. In the middle of the room was a small counter where patients waited to show their prescription from the *Scuola* after consulting a doctor for their disease. Behind the counter was a man of about 35 years of age, named Bruno Deluca, whose name was written on a small, wooden plate hanging on the room's entrance door. Anne Pauline understood that he worked as the pharmacist, helping to hand out prescribed medicines and removing the patients' doubts about their therapeutic effects.

Unknowingly, Anne Pauline had just met Vincent Torquay, the former accountant for Marcus Belling, who had also lived a past life in Italy during the 12th century. Torquay, who had never been hypnotized, had no knowledge that one of his past lives had been lived in Salerno, nor that he had met Isabella (who was actually Anne Pauline). Bruno Deluca, just like Thomas Godwynus, had studied medicine, but had decided to travel around Europe after graduating. He then established himself in Antwerp, where he dedicated his life to business. In the 12th century, a league in the Low Countries was being created that would be known as the Hanseatic League, which would later turn into an alliance of the mercantile cities that controlled the commercial monopoly in northern Europe and the Baltics. It was in Antwerp that Bruno developed more interest and experience in the management of expenses and profits, budgets, and economic predictions. All of this knowledge acquired in previous lives would be crucial for him to become a great bookkeeper. In this way, the vocational theory also applied to Marcus Belling's accountant, as his technical competence in management had developed during his different lives.

Anne Pauline had not yet interacted with someone from her past since her arrival in Salerno. Therefore, she couldn't tell if her inner power would appear in this past life. Thaddeus Borba was the only person who fully knew her power and only he could tell when and with whom it would become visible, which made Anne collaborate with him in secrecy. Salvaterra had on idea about this agreement and never would. While standing by the pharmacist, Anne Pauline saw the opportunity to go unnoticed among the crowd, who was focused on Bruno Deluca, as she didn't know who might recognize her. As Anne was drifting by in her thoughts, Isabella suddenly arrived and looked very frightened at the grandiosity of the hall. As the pharmacist came to the counter to deliver Thomas Godwynus's prescription, he looked at Anne Pauline twice before he gave her the jar of natural products.

Godwynus had given her a prescription of the dissolution mixture, which was hard to acquire outside the *Scuola Medica di Salerno*, even if it was distasteful for doctors to sell such a product at such a prestigious *school*. Isabella lowered her eyes and waited for the jar with the magical combination of herbs, while feeling ashamed for having a spiritual illness, which many times could only be healed by magic or witchcraft. To tell the truth, these spiritual illnesses were very badly considered at the time.

The relationship between Thomas Godwynus and Bruno Deluca had never been very sound, and it got even worse when Thomas started to be known at the academy as the master of souls. This was because, apart from the physical illnesses, he also treated quite a few patients with soul diseases. As a result, Bruno always thought that Thomas Godwynus practiced the occult outside his work schedule as a doctor at the *Schola Medica Salernitana but* could never gather enough evidence to prove it. On that day, the combination of therapeutic herbs that were written on the prescription presented to Isabella made him doubt if the doctor was dealing with the occult with that patient. Although the written combination of herbs was normally used for anxieties, Bruno Deluca had seen this same prescribed formula in an old alchemy textbook to treat spiritual problems, namely for those souls that travel between the past and the future. The dissolution mixture was composed of secret ingredients, but there were some theories by other doctors that revealed a formula for its production.

Anne Pauline noticed the pharmacist's restless posture when he saw the dissolution mixture, a kind of potion that transmutes the negative emotions into positive thoughts, on Isabella's prescription. As Godwynus said, this had all the essences and active ingredients to transform negativity into positive humor. It really looked like the expert talked in codes that took a lot to decipher. Despite her analysis of the situation, Anne Pauline thought that the Theory of Bonds, as designed by Josef Salvaterra, might not apply to this situation, as the empathy between Marcus Belling and Vincent Torquay hadn't existed for a long time. Thaddeus Borba had told her once of Torquay very briefly, so she knew which links existed between them. Maybe Salvaterra's theory was incorrect this time. Magnetic empathies between people might not exist along different lives and they might be capable of changing into something quite different. When Salvaterra presented his three theories, he hadn't mentioned exceptions to these theories, when they might not correspond to the possible hidden rules to what is visible in life. Each theory had an exception, but this didn't mean that the concept wasn't well formulated. The Theory of Bonds was well built, but one should take into account that, sometimes, a phenomenon called transmutation of sentiments might occur from one life to another; that is, the negative would turn into a positive and the positive would change to a negative. This exception had already been identified by Salvaterra, who named it the Theory of Opposites and it was meant to precisely explain the energy rebalance that exists between the different lives.

But Anne Pauline had to wake up quickly from her thoughts. She briefly had the feeling that Bruno Deluca could see her, even while she was under hypnosis. Once more, she understood that her power didn't work with every person in her past lives, but only a few. The pharmacist kept talking to Isabella, his eyes seemed to search for Anne incessantly, as if he were impressed with her strange presence. This proved that Deluca had recognized her, and so Anne Pauline ran away from the healing hall to the main cloister of the monastery. Isabella was being given small jars of different crushed herbs with distinct colors to take twice per day in lukewarm water, using the spring waters from Salerno, especially before she went to bed. Knowing that her presence had emotionally affected the pharmacist, Anne Pauline felt she should meet with Thomas Godwynus and rapidly ran from the room.

Anne Pauline saw Isabella coming out of the hall looking frightened. She already knew the Gaul but couldn't get used to the physical resemblance she shared with these women from her previous lives. All were Anne but it felt bizarre to see herself in other times, speaking and dressing so differently. Anne obviously needed to get used to this situation, as she was still required to continue her hypnosis appointments with Marcus Belling. But as she saw Isabella leave that room to meet Thomas Godwynus, Anne Pauline decided to go back and see the pharmacist Bruno Deluca. Anne Pauline was keen on knowing more about her power, and she could not waste the chance to communicate with a person from a past life who managed to see her while she was under hypnotic trance. So instead of following Isabella, Anne Pauline wanted to go back, as this might be an opportunity to form an alliance. At this time, the halls were empty, and silence filled every space in the monastery as night fell on the *Schola Medica Salernitana* and the whole town. After thinking for a few seconds, Anne Pauline took the risk and, without knowing what the result might be, she re-entered the room where the dissolution mixture could be bought.

Bruno Deluca had his back to the entrance, using the silence that had settled on the monastery to put the jars of plants and herbs back into place before he locked the room. His workday was over, but when the pharmacist turned his back, one of the jars he held fell to the ground and broke into pieces. Bruno was astonished by the presence of this young woman with large, green eyes and dark, shiny hair, dressed at odds with other women he knew. As he looked into her eyes, he realized it was the woman he had seen in the room, as he was talking to Isabella. Bruno Deluca couldn't know that both women were one. Surprisingly, Anne Pauline started speaking in Italian to the pharmacist, though she had no knowledge of the language, rapidly understanding that she needed this linguistic knowledge to tell him about her plans.

Bruno Deluca asked Anne about her origins, which she needed to give some thought to before answering. Anne wanted to be sincere without carefully thinking of the consequences of her decision, so she replied that she came from a distant future with one mission; to spread rumors at the *Schola Medica di Salerno* about Thomas Godwynus's witchcraft practices outside the Academy.

"I have always suspected that," said the Italian pharmacist.

"It may be hard to believe, but I come from the distant future and know enough about this famous teacher, named Godwynus," she said simply.

Anne Pauline carefully told the pharmacist that the rumor might not be true. She was just carrying out her alliance. The truth was that the master of souls had dedicated all his life to teaching medicine in the town and couldn't know that Isabella had arrived from a distant life with traumas that had caused extreme anxiety to her spirit. It was to solve those past life traumas that she needed to buy those jars with medicinal herbs for her soul. To Anne Pauline's surprise, Bruno Deluca wasn't dismayed about what he had heard, although he did doubt that this green-eyed woman had really arrived from the future. It was indisputable, though, that her looks and her way of speaking were strange and different, so he decided to keep an open mind.

Bruno Deluca kept looking at Anne Pauline with more than just an enormous empathy for her, as he suddenly felt an attraction towards her. After carefully listening to Anne Pauline, he remembered an old internal publication that had circulated around *Schola Medica Salernitana,* which could help to spread rumors of the master of souls' dedication to hypnosis when not practicing medicine at the *school.* Bruno, as he wanted to help Anne in this mission. The announcement could be done by means of parchment pamphlets, which could be strategically spread from strategic spots around the monastery, where most students and patients could take notice of such uncommon events. It would be possible to throw Godwynus out of *Schola Medica Salernitana* through this secret alliance. The pharmacist promised to help spread the news the next day, but asked Anne Pauline to keep passing by. He was in love with this woman who had appeared earlier that day in the healing hall. Anne Pauline had come from the future and Bruno didn't want her to leave him. He came closer to her, feeling no fear, took her in his arms and kissed her passionately. Though she was also Isabella, he had seen a different woman in her, who was much more attractive and interesting. Anne Pauline didn't want to reveal it, even to herself, but she had also fallen in love at first sight with the pharmacist.

I had to come to the past and while under hypnosis to fall in love, she thought quickly. It seemed so. Anne hadn't felt something so strong for anyone else during her 25 years of life and she even doubted if it was possible to love someone under hypnosis. It all seemed very real, though, and Anne really knew what she felt. Although she was in a trance, Anne Pauline knew that it was love. After that kiss, she and Bruno Deluca kept staring at each other with such an intensity. Though the Italian pharmacist didn't fully understand what was happening, they both felt that they had sealed an alliance with that kiss. Deluca needed to meet the green-eyed woman again, and so he gave her the key that he kept to open the door to the healing hall. That was the real name of this room where he worked daily, and all the jars of natural medicines were kept that were produced from combinations of curative plants. The key was made from a very ancient metal and had a hollow base. On this, the shape of what seemed like a small island with three tall peaks was drawn. Anne Pauline immediately understood that it was the Forgotten Island. The drawing deciphered something on the key, which showed it didn't only open the door to the healing hall. Bruno Deluca knew that he was giving her more than a simple old metal key, as it could reveal other mysteries to Anne Pauline's real identity. She kept it scrupulously in her pocket, together with the sacred feather that she had brought from the island a few months ago.

The key held a secret about Anne Pauline, but Bruno hoped that she would come to *Schola Medica Salernitana*. It was the pharmacist's way of telling her that he wanted to see her again. She didn't know if she would be back though, even after she ended her hypnosis sessions with Marcus Belling. Up to that moment, she had observed her previous lives in chronological order, which meant that she would travel to a subsequent period after she left Salerno. Bruno Deluca lowered his stare as he understood her doubts and decided to give her the key that would help her in the future. He felt a deep passion for her and didn't need to give many other reasons to explain his action.

Anne Pauline knew she couldn't tell Josef Salvaterra what had happened with the *University*'s pharmacist at the healing hall. She had broken the deal by becoming emotionally involved with a person from her past, while under the hypnotic effect. It seemed surreal, but it had just happened. On the other hand, she had sealed an agreement with the pharmacist, against Salvaterra's rules, as he had asked for her total fidelity to their alliance, which forbade any pacts with anyone else but him. Anne had gone against all parts of the agreement.

Anne was still in the healing hall when she heard Marcus Belling's voice. She knew the time had come to return to her present, namely Sun Avenue, and be brought back from the hypnotic trance. Anne said goodbye to Bruno with a loving kiss, ran to the monastery's central hall, closed her eyes, and was then driven by the hypnotist's gentle words, who asked Anne to come out of her altered state of consciousness. In the meantime, the pharmacist didn't understand what was happening to the woman he loved, who had quickly left him without any warning.

When she opened her eyes, Anne Pauline was again sitting on the green and mahogany couch. She subtly checked her jacket's pocket to see if the feather from the island was still there. Not only was the feather there, but also the key given to her by Bruno Deluca was carefully kept inside her pocket. What was beyond Anne Pauline's knowledge was how both these pieces of her past would be fundamental in finally unlocking her identity, especially after meeting Georgine Gunderson.

While Anne Pauline talked to Marcus Belling the events at the *Schola Medica Salernitana*, Bruno Deluca locked the cabinets in the healing hall, where some jars of Thomas Godwynus's dissolution combination were kept. He then remembered Anne Pauline, the green-eyed lady he had fallen in love with. He also thought of the alliance they had established, and for which he left work early to go to the town center. He thought of a professor he hoped to find there, someone who could help him spread the rumor about Thomas Godwynus's dedication to the occult outside of *Schola Medica Salernitana*. Bruno would not have any difficulty in finding doctors who were able to collaborate in his mission, as many disagreed with Godwynus's therapeutic methods and his theory that the diseases of the soul might cause physical illness.

In the meantime, as Bruno Deluca tried to put their alliance into practice, the remodeling of Belling's offices had finally finished. Routine returned to Sun Avenue step by step, and the library, which had been consumed by fire, was being put back into its place. This included the first books that he had bought to compensate for his dramatic loss. One day, Georgine Gunderson had come to deliver a box full of books, which she had brought from the former council library. This had been requested by the Mayor, who was aware of the events that had occurred at number 27 Sun Avenue. With the help of this gift from the city's authorities, Belling intended to recover his specialty books on hypnosis, regression and past life therapy to solve his knowledge amnesia, a designation he had found to describe his state of mind. Marcus Belling welcomed Georgine Gunderson as she entered his room, where Anne Pauline would later have her appointment, and left the books by the empty shelves. Georgine carefully laid the box and observed the green couch where Belling's patients were hypnotized. She briefly thought of how she also wanted to be hypnotized one day. Marcus noticed this with his astute mind, which was part of his practice as a hypnotist, and took the chance to tell the lady, "You can come whenever you feel ready. Sofia will know that you're to be first on my list," he said through a smile.

Georgine Gunderson blushed at Marcus Belling's words and quickly left the clinic, feeling embarrassed that her intentions had been so clearly noticed. She wasn't the only one to feel like this, however. He usually had this effect on people around him, who felt as if he could discover their most secret desires. But as she came down the stairs and closed the door to 27 Sun Avenue, something very strange was about to happen.

Marcus smiled at Sofia after Georgine left his therapy room; they worked well together. At that moment though, he wanted to be left alone, so he closed his door and turned to the books the librarian had brought over. He had waited anxiously for them, as all his books on hypnosis had been consumed by fire, as he wished to have them back in his personal library as quickly as possible. He really hoped that this book-filled box would finally solve his knowledge amnesia and he would soon be able to return to his work routine without any complaints from his patients about him not being the great hypnotist he once had been.

Belling even lost some of his patients to Salvaterra, who was now doing better than he had done for a long time. For many years, his rival hadn't made so much money from the hypnosis sessions, as he did now. Marbella Gorey would certainly be incredibly grateful for all those events. The news spread quickly around the city. We can now understand how important it was that Georgine Gunderson came to his office with all these books, as he hoped they would change his life for good. Even without knowing Thomas Godwynus, he could be experiencing what the master of souls called the positive humor. Belling knelt and opened the box, but what he saw left him both scared and in shock. The books were torn, some even cut in half, the pages randomly spread all over the box. He couldn't believe that the librarian would deliver the books if she had known they were in such a state. Once more, he didn't understand this inexplicable event and showed Sofia what he had just received. Upon his request, his secretary quickly came in and realized, just by looking at the box, that another mysterious event had taken place after Anne Pauline had been there.

"I can't believe what I see," said a surprised Sofia, who couldn't contain the sorrow that suddenly filled her again.

"Believe me, it's true. All of the books on hypnosis and natural medicine are destroyed!" exclaimed Marcus.

While Belling opened the box of books, tragic events had just occurred at *Schola Medica Salernitana* in the 12th century. Aided by a professor, Bruno Deluca had spread the rumor that Thomas Godwynus practiced the occult, specifically, hypnosis. As a result, more students and lecturers became aware and it reached the point where his offices were invaded; his classic works and other literature on his desk was destroyed. At that moment, the books inside the box brought by Georgine Gunderson were also destroyed, the pages torn and randomly spread inside the box. Sofia knew it was time to contact Patricia Murio and Maria de Burgos to unravel the mystery with Vincent Torquay. Only he could give them more clues about what was happening.

Anne Pauline had once more time intervened in the past, thanks to the Italian pharmacist, and used her ability to change future events. But Isabella, back in the 12th century, had been informed of the events in Godwynus's room, which only postponed her appointment with the famous doctor. She didn't return to Salerno, so she never got a chance to acquire more jars of the dissolution mixture, yet she already felt the quick feeling of lightness that seemed to tranquilize her anxieties and transform her state of mind into something like a calm sea. However, because of the events at *Schola Medica Salernitana*, Isabella wasn't able to receive a diagnosis for her wounded soul, which left her stuck with the same emotions she's had her entire life. Anne Pauline would remain unknowing of who she was.

As always, Marcus Belling couldn't know that this event was related to changes in Salerno during the 12th century. Once more, all of this had been planned during that last session, while Anne Pauline was under an altered state of consciousness, which left him with no chance to discover the power that his patient possessed. She had effectively been able to change the course of Belling's past life as a famed lecturer at the *Schola Medica Salernitana*, which enabled the knowledge amnesia to continue affecting his entire nervous system. Marcus Belling then understood that his normal work routine was totally lost and that the discontent of his patients would only grow. As he reflected on this, the hypnotist started hearing voices arguing outside, as Sofia did her best to shout above the clamor and keep the respectable authority she was known for. As Marcus opened his door, a group of people rapidly turned to Belling, while his personal secretary nearly passed out due to her effort. There were men and women of different ages, who had seen Deya's advertisement just days before, showing much lower prices than those charged by the other practitioners. They were angry, as they felt that they had been fooled, saying that it was Marcus Belling's fault.

The hypnotist well remembered the advertisement of Deya, who was a mere administrative staff member of the National Council for Hypnosis, but now deemed himself to be a hypnotist. Belling remembered how he had arrived home desolate, as the rumors made people everywhere believe in the infamous and unfair news about his inability to follow his life as a hypnotist. Consequently, other members of the National Council for Hypnosis had taken the opportunity to raise their prices, while other people like Deya, who were merely administrative workers, took advantage of the whole situation to fool the public. Chaos spread through the town, especially from the moment when it became impossible for Marcus Belling to recover from the amnesia that affected him. And now, with the destruction of the books inside the box, the last chance of regaining control over the situation that had spread across his daily practice of hypnosis was lost.

Some men and women were now closer to Belling, demanding an answer to the situation caused by Deya. Some people who were misled by the advertisement had been hypnotized by the fake hypnotist in an improvised room that didn't guarantee the minimum-security patterns required for such therapy. As they got into a trance, patients reported feelings of loss, pain and emotional drift related to a past that they couldn't understand. When faced with the uncertainty of those clients who couldn't deal with the experiences they were living during regression, Deya's vague words only caused them further hypnotic disorientation. Right at that moment, an older man came forward from the group and reported these stories to Belling, telling him that he had started crying convulsively at a certain point. Deya had just stood up from his chair, leaving his patient alone in a deep trance. Though he later safely woke up from that trance, the regression had dire consequences. Most of Deya's patients reported that they experienced emotional drift that had aggravated their anguish, as they lived out those dramatic moments of their past lives. Then each person said Deya had told them Marcus Belling was responsible if things had gone wrong during their hypnotic state, as he had been his mentor.

The furious group demanded Belling to repeat the therapeutic process they had begun with Deya. Sofia had tried to stop them but didn't know how to react, even though she had sworn to always protect him.

In the meantime, back in the 12th century, a group of doctors from the *medical school* had come to Thomas Godwynus to face him with the accusations made against him, namely his dealings with the occult and, especially hypnosis. One of his colleagues, whom he shared lecturing duties with regarding the subject of therapy through medicinal herbs, told him, "You should be aware that hypnosis is forbidden at the *school* as a therapy."

The famous Godwynus was astounded by these charges and asked to know about their source, but Bruno Deluca hid behind the crowds. He waited for the consequences of his action to have an impact on the future. The pharmacist hoped that Anne Pauline would quickly come back to his time and use the key to the healing hall to see him again. He would do anything to put his alliance into practice.

The crowd was pulling Marcus Belling outside his Sun Avenue building, as Sofia Estelar was desperately screaming and trying to protect him. It was beyond their imagination, but Thomas Godwynus was also being taken outside the *Schola Medica Salernitana* by some doctors and students, who demanded a quick explanation of his occult practices. The expert knew, though, that his reputation as a professor at the *Schola Medica Salernitana*, was destroyed, though he had never really practiced hypnosis.

The first snow was now falling in Salerno. The town was covered in a thick, white blanket, which gave the environment a silent tranquility that was so different to the hasty events occurring on that day. In one last attempt, Bruno Deluca looked up to the sky and tried to find out how the lady he loved, Anne Pauline, was doing. As they had plotted in the healing hall, their message plan was being put into practice. He somehow felt that both were still linked through time but couldn't know if his actions would have any effect on the future. Bruno set his eyes on the deep, dark blue sky and wondered where Anne Pauline might be at that time. Meanwhile, she was also looking up to the starry skies from her window, right at the top of her building, guessing that she could even touch the universe. Anne also thought of Bruno Deluca… but didn't know if she would ever find him again.

Chapter 8

ANTWERP IN 1520

1

The protest at the clinic had prompted Sofia to take action. She had no sympathy for Anne Pauline whatsoever. Since the woman had first arrived on that sweltering summer day, it seemed to Sofia that the entire network that had been set up to protect Marcus Belling for the past two decades had been put in danger. In addition to these suspicions, they were still trying to understand how Anne's presence had interfered with the hypnotist's emotional state.

It seemed like an unpredictable and unstoppable destiny had stirred up his life, but he could never have imagined that hypnosis was the mechanism of Anne Pauline's power. The past had become tangible but also dangerously mutable and volatile from the moment the mysterious young woman had shown her capacity to change events in her past lives.

The usual suspects who were normally involved in events that jeopardized Belling's career, namely Josef Salvaterra, Marbella and Rolland Ulm, didn't seem not to have any influence on these changes, so for the moment, they were off Sofia's guilty list. But that was only for now. In the meantime, Marbella had tried to convince her husband of the necessity to hypnotize Anne Pauline, a possibility that he had always rejected. She had considered using the alchemic perfume to release any memories she had of her past lives, which would push her to share all information about the development of Belling's calling. Secretly, Marbella had never believed her husband's vocational theory, though she had a passion for the occult that sparked her interest in the existence of different dynamics in other worlds. She could never imagine that this theory would grant her access to the mysteries of Belling's career. Marbella couldn't forget something that Jasmine had told her about the Theory of Scents, which sounded as if all the secrets of the universe were being revealed to her, as it allowed her to access the past of any other person.

Jasmine was right about her theory. The past and the memories of Anne Pauline had been transformed into a particular aroma that could only be found when she did past life regression. This one scent could only be smelled while under hypnosis, and the past could be deciphered through direct interaction with people from that same period. This obviously made it difficult for Marbella to find the scent because she could not be hypnotized. Josef had tried it on numerous occasions, but no one could take her into a hypnotic trance, because she felt the need to control all the circumstances that surrounded her. Marbella didn't intend to just sway around her subconscious, for that would be an unpredictable trip that she couldn't manipulate and dominate.

While all this was going on in the lives of the Salvaterras, Sofia carried a frightened look in her eyes, which showed that something wasn't going well in the consulting room. This was the first time that there had been a protest led by patients who were angry about the influence that Belling had on Deya's hypnosis sessions. He wasn't responsible whatsoever for the events, but Marcus Belling and Sofia Estelar were fully aware of the gravity of the situation. Belling's knowledge amnesia had haunted him for quite some time and had led to people doubting his hypnosis skills and the validity of his work in past life regression. This situation opened the door for true usurpers who were now taking on the role of hypnotist without the competence or the knowledge to do so. A real crisis had hit and no one on staff could link all these events to Anne Pauline.

Meetings of the National Council of Hypnosis to discuss the update to the code of ethics didn't consider the opinion of Marcus Belling. He, therefore, increasingly realized that his influence as a reputed hypnotist was no longer valued by his colleagues. Hypnosis seemed to have taken on a mercantilist spirit and the social mission that was inherent to these functions were increasingly devalued.

On the day after the insurgency, Marcus Belling needed the comfort of reading some old books on sale at the second-hand bookseller on Sun Avenue. This shop had existed for more than 15 years and was the property of a very friendly gentleman of 68 years of age named Maarten Gembloux. He was short but with a snub personality, but took pride in his business, and was famous for selling works of art that couldn't be seen anywhere else in town. He had a large smile on his face as he saw Marcus Belling enter his shop. Maarten looked for a book that would make the hypnotist forget the confusion in his consulting room. Belling felt the need for some emotional support from literature and shared his feeling with the bookseller, explaining his need to take away a book that could help him to disconnect from his everyday life.

"These last few weeks, especially yesterday, have been terrible to me. Do you have a book that would make me forget the outside world, if only briefly?"

Although it seemed strange at first thought, this was far from an unusual request. People bought books for many reasons. Many pretended to experience other lives through reading books and wanted to take their imagination to the limit. As he heard these words, Maarten Gembloux picked up an extremely old book from his work desk that had just arrived the day before, entitled *Antwerp in the 16th Century*. Gembloux pointed to the title with his index finger and gave a witty smile to the hypnotist, making sure that his suggestion fulfilled his client's request. It was a rare opportunity to have Belling in his shop and he told him, "I am sure that you'll find this book interesting. It's full of humor and irony, making the story very dynamic to the reader, for it tells the story of a famous doctor and alchemist from the 16th century called Paracelsus. It's set in Antwerp. No one knows who the author might be, maybe because it was banned in the Netherlands and all over Europe. It's now seen as a book for all those who enjoy reading it."

Marcus found Gembloux's description of the book compelling and flipped through its pages a few times. He ended up borrowing it, for it fascinated him. Maarten was very accessible and didn't mind letting some books be taken for free. As the hypnotist left the shop with the book under his arm, the book handler confirmed the recent rumors that circulated in the town that something was happening to this man, who was known for his television talks about past lives.

The confusion in Sun Avenue's consulting room caused some plans to be hurried. As soon as Sofia informed Patricia Murio that some people from the National Council for Hypnosis, such as Bernard Deya, had taken advantage of her husband's amnesia, Patricia knew that it was now time for Sofia, Maria and herself to take action. A plan was set to stop the progressive professional decline of Marcus Belling. Ruben Mortsen, the accountant, was being kept away from the ladies' message operation. His role was still fundamental, though, as he controlled the finances of the famous therapist and kept them inaccessible to Josef Salvaterra, Marbella Gorey and the spy. The latter kept wandering about Sun Avenue. Prudence was now the watchword. However, no one was yet connecting the arrival of Anne that summer to the change of routine of him and his staff. They suffered collectively from a group amnesia, which prevented them from understanding the events around them.

Sofia told Patricia knew every detail of the events in the consulting room during the massive protest, as they shared all their confidences. It was now clear that the knowledge amnesia that affected the hypnotist for about a month was causing devastating and unpredictable damage. This had led to disturbing situations after Deya had wrongly implemented hypnosis techniques on patients. The blame for such acts was being pinned on Marcus Belling. What Patricia Murio and the remainder of the staff didn't know was that Anne Pauline was changing the past during each of her sessions, rewriting her own personal history and that of Belling. Only

Josef Salvaterra and Thaddeus Borba knew of Anne Pauline's power, therefore, it remained a secret. The two women felt that something needed to be done, although they didn't really understand the force they were dealing with.

Day after day, Patricia became more worried about the situation and its consequences for the business if certain members of the National Council found out about the events at her husband's consulting room. Belling's wife decided they needed to contact the retired accountant. He was the only one who could help answer some of their questions. They had thought of contacting him for some time, but now it became necessary.

Vincent Torquay had known Belling for years and had taken on the role of professor and personal guide in the life of his friend. No one could question his influence in Belling's career, and no one knew the routines better than him. There was, therefore, an urgent need to visit Torquay. Patricia Murio had developed a hypothesis concerning the main suspects who could be responsible for bringing down the career of Belling. They were obviously Josef Salvaterra, Marbella Gorey and the spy. Together, they had tried to decipher the logistical strategy implemented in the Sun Avenue office for many years.

When Marcus Belling came home with *Antwerp in the 16th Century* under his arm, Patricia informed him of her intention of going on a business trip with Sofia and Maria de Burgos the following day. She didn't give him much information because his focus seemed to be on the book he had borrowed from Maarten Gembloux, the bookseller she didn't know very well. This message trip would be used to unlock the circumstances that might have caused the fire in the library, as well as the protest of the clients against Belling. The goal of Patricia was to heal the regressive amnesia that had hit her husband, before it was too late. On the other hand, though she didn't verbalize it; they wanted to understand the hidden forces that influenced the mind of Marcus Belling.

The following day, Sofia and Maria met out front to discuss the details of the day's journey. Vincent Torquay now lived in a small village just two hours away from the city, in an old palace, a recluse from the outside world by his own choice. The three women intended to find out how the fire in Belling's library could have affected his knowledge in his field, as it did not seem like an isolated incident. It was more like one of a line of events that they didn't understand yet. At first, they fell silent. None of them knew the possible outcome of their investigations, but their goal was to understand the logic behind the events that surrounded the hypnotist. Some strange force seemed to be at work, bringing him close to certain events, while the reality itself combined with the dynamics of other parallel worlds. As the time ticked by, their hope that Torquay's explanation would provide the answers was increasingly important. It was this hope that drove these three women into the unknown. Patricia, Sofia and Maria de Burgos were slowly awakening from these unique circumstances and gradually entering the spirit of their shared journey.

It had been a long time since the three women had been together, although they often saw each other in the office. While Sofia and Patricia shared all their confidences, Maria de Burgos liked to feel free from any dependency loop, whether that was professional or personal. It had been a long time since this woman of Spanish parents had decided to convey certain secrets only to certain people, and she intended to keep these out of her professional life. Though she had a great empathy with the two other women, she knew that it was the career of Marcus Belling that had joined them together. Maria de Burgos understood the natural proximity that had developed between Belling's secretary and his wife, who was a more controlling person, more than anyone she could imagine. Patricia Murio knew the work of her husband well, the revenues that were generated and the women who were interested in him. She was very discreet in helping to drive her husband's business, but he didn't see it as a business.

"You're both very quiet," said Patricia.

"We're thinking," replied Sofia and Maria simultaneously.

Gradually, the three women started a conversation about trivial matters to forget the anxiety they were feeling. The children, their loves and relationships were always the themes they spoke of together. Meanwhile, it didn't take long to arrive at the village where Torquay now lived. The car drove around the former town hall, an old building that was topped by two dome-like structures, which pointed out from the skyline of the village, followed by a small square. The women then went straight to the edge of the village. The former bookkeeper now lived in a refurbished villa, surrounded by leafy bushes and a vast garden, just a few miles from the village center. Before entering his palace, they still had to drive through the massive gate that separated the house from the main street. Maria de Burgos rang the bell and the gate opened, letting the car finally arrive at their destination.

Vincent Torquay was now 70 years old, but he was both proud and fit, and didn't look it. His relaxed attitude and discretion would make someone who was unguarded question his relationship with Marcus Belling, or at least those who thought that he still did the books for the business. He knew about their journey through Patricia Murio, to whom he was closer, and so asked his guests to take a seat in his elegant living room. It was a large room with geometric figures printed on the wallpaper, as well as animals and flowers. A massive chandelier hung from the ceiling, which was the key element in his décor. There wasn't much time for fine words, so Maria de Burgos started their conversation straight away.

"You must have been informed by now of the sad events in Belling's consulting room. We need you to help us understand the most recent events. We share many questions, which lead us to think that none of this was accidental. We don't know if you're aware of it, but Marcus's private library was destroyed. We find it strange that the fire started in an annex, and only then moved in the direction of the books. The worst part, however, was what came next. The texts were turned into ashes and, in the following days, Belling started to suffer from a kind of knowledge amnesia. We suspect the usual people but can't understand how Salvaterra and Marbella could have caused such damage."

"What do you mean by knowledge amnesia?" Torquay asked, looking intrigued.

"I'll explain in detail. It might seem strange, but the fire seemed to have made Belling forget his skills as a hypnotist. We know it's hard to believe, but it's true. Sofia started receiving complaints from patients who reported that Marcus no longer had a grasp on the techniques for each case. There was recently a massive protest by people who were not satisfied with his work. I'll give you an example. He slowly found it difficult to answer questions from patients on past life regression and even contradicted himself by using information that is part of the induction into the hypnotic trance. It's as if the fire has deleted his knowledge, making us consider this to be some type of knowledge amnesia. A strange phenomenon," Maria de Burgos sighed, without adding anything further about the situation.

"I didn't know that it had got to such a level," he replied. "From what you just told me; this seems strange. I believe there's no reason to suspect Salvaterra, Rolland and Marbella, even though they are the most likely suspects. That is what drove you to meet with me, so that I could share my opinion on this situation, given that I worked with Belling for 20 years."

Suddenly, an intense feeling of nostalgia filled Torquay, after which he returned to the place where he had stopped. "Whatever words I have to tell you about that spy won't help your investigation. However, there may be something more relevant to be told, which I had never told anyone previously. But before that, let me tell you something more about the first time that I saw that spy," Torquay said.

Vincent Torquay had now caught the attention of his three guests, who were anxious to hear the latest information that could help them to discover the reasons behind Belling's knowledge amnesia. Patricia Murio knew, more than anyone else, that the retired accountant was a man of unbreakable honesty and loyalty. She still clearly remembered the morning the accountant arrived after greeting Marcus Belling. The accountancy department was already separate from the remainder of the consulting clinic. They had rented an apartment next door to function more safely. It needed to work this way, because of the large income. Those sessions had always been very profitable, but Belling refused to call his public mission a business. Any resulting profit he made was only known to the hypnotist and to Torquay, which contributed to the strong trust and loyalty that existed between the two during all those years.

When Vincent retired from his work, Ruben Mortsel took his place, albeit with a lack of experience that meant Patricia Murio assumed more control over the turnover of her husband's sessions. From that moment on, she spent more time on Sun Avenue, controlling anything that happened through the information given by Belling's personal secretary. Some might say that such circumstances could've slightly changed her soul, although such issues were never discussed. The truth was that Belling's wife only understood how profitable the practice was after the former accountant left. Both Sofia Estelar and Vincent Torquay knew that one day, Patricia would control the profits made in this consulting room, the way it happened between Marbella and Josef Salvaterra. Little by little, Mrs. Murio started to take a fundamental role in the career of her husband. As Torquay often said, "Belling needs Patricia to see the world that he doesn't want to see and, most of all, accept it."

This was the precise enigmatic sentence that he would frequently use to end his conversations with Sofia and Maria, as he closed the door.

The encirclement set up by Salvaterra and Marbella had become more intense since he left the clinic and the team bid farewell to one of the Belling's most loyal companions.

Torquay put down his glass of wine on an antique *gueridon* that stood next to the leather sofa he sat on. The retired accountant was about to speak of one day in particular. This story was gossiped about by his guests, but now they had the chance to hear it first-hand. The day before, Vincent had seen Rolland Ulm wandering around the building, taking photographs of and peeking through Belling's window. An accountant who worked on the other side of the street also saw this mysterious figure with a handlebar moustache and a camera in his hands looking through the. This colleague had seen this man talking to Josef Salvaterra, and accidentally uncovered their espionage scheme. Marcus Belling had been warned about this man.

A few days later, Vincent Torquay was told the name of this spy. Rolland Ulm was a former agent of the national secret agency, but now worked for specific clients, selling espionage and competition control services to them. The latter had become his true specialty in his field. The spy tried to act secretly to interfere in the market's regulation, through partnerships that favored his clients. This was the reason behind his collaboration with Josef Salvaterra and his wife, from whom he earned considerable commissions for giving them information on Marcus Belling's work or the business he performed in his consulting room on Sun Avenue.

One could really say that, over the years, Rolland Ulm had become a constant presence in Marcus Belling's life. Although this situation was uncomfortable for his whole working team, it dragged on for over 15 years. One day, Vincent bumped into the spy and was so embarrassed, he immediately ran into his accounting firm. They exchanged looks but the spy never suspected that Torquay knew about him, as he wandered around without being noticed most of the time.

Vincent Torquay then told his three guests of how he was approached by the shoemaker, Thaddeus Borba, the day after this incident. Thaddeus's routine was fixing the shoes that his clients delivered to him, while singing lays to them. The shoemaker was known all over the city as the Troubadour of Truth, or as The Bard. The accountant had always tried to keep a distance from him because they believed in his capacity as an oracle. At this moment, Patricia, Sofia and Maria knew they were about to listen to the revelation that had prompted them to drive down to his villa. They were shocked that the explanation for the events that affected the hypnotist was also known to the shoemaker.

Vincent and Thaddeus had kept a cold distance from each other, which was about to be breached. The shoemaker invited the bookkeeper into his workshop, supposedly to polish his shoes, but he really had a much different proposal in mind. The bard had clearly seen destiny coming after Torquay as he walked down Sun Avenue and found it impossible not to speak about it. Destiny always assumed different shapes, be it an animal or a plant related to the person, or it could come in the form of a scent that was so notable and intense that it allowed Thaddeus to connect it to the past of the man or woman. The shoemaker could see destiny coming after Torquay in the form of the 12th-century herbalist, Bruno Deluca, who still carried a key and a glass bottle with a mixture of herbs that smelled of cinnamon, apple and cloves. The shoemaker had known Deluca for some time, especially as he had appeared in many of his dreams. But until that day, he didn't know who he really was.

Contrary to Anne Pauline, Thaddeus couldn't travel in time through hypnosis, although his journey to the Forgotten Island had been done by the process of self-induced hypnosis, which didn't always work out. It was for this reason that the shoemaker could not confirm the identity of Deluca, who reincarnated the destiny of Belling's former accountant. As he worked as an herbalist, Thaddeus felt his role was to give out this key to someone who could change the past and, in consequence, the future. Thaddeus also knew that this person could only be Anne Pauline. These visions confirmed his thesis of a past common between her and Vincent Torquay.

The shoemaker had seen both the past and the future of this aide of Belling and felt the need to tell him the truth. Vincent's stare became deeper and more intense while he revealed these stories to Patricia, Sofia and Maria, as he was reminded of his good times at the clinic with the hypnotist. Meanwhile, his three guests kept listening to every word he had to say, waiting for the revelation that confirmed that someone had caused Belling's knowledge amnesia. But the accountant was so thrilled by having an audience that would listen so intently to his life stories, he started telling of how Thaddeus Borba invited him to his workshop for the first time.

The accountant went quiet and a sudden silence fell on the four people. It was now time to tell Patricia, Sofia and Maria about the event that would help them to solve the case of the fire in the hypnotist's library. Torquay took a deep sigh before speaking of the facts that he still couldn't understand. The first image on his mind was of the precise area of the shoemaker's workshop on Sun Avenue. It was wide but narrow, with a wooden door that separated two different areas. On display along the corridor were shoe trees of all sizes, as well as nails, leather polish and ink, layers for leather or wooden soles, wood shavings, awls and a hammer. The accountant marveled at all that he saw, for he didn't know that shoemakers worked with such a wide array of materials, which reminded him of a painter or sculptor that uses different tools to recreate a new reality. It was then that Vincent knew that shoemaking was a true art.

He had never seen the inside of the troubadour's workshop before and marveled at all that he saw, and so had kept this wonderful discovery in his memory. Finally, after so many years, Torquay was willing to finally meet the shoe repairman, who he had seen working every day in Sun Avenue and gave him a different and intense look. Thaddeus Borba understood the meaning of the stare that he received from the accountant; his guest was ready to listen to the truth. Vincent's eyes opened wide with curiosity, as he knew that he had been called inside for a purpose, and then remembered what had people said when Thaddeus was about to recite a lay, which meant that a major revelation about one's life was about to happen. Belling's accountant was now much more curious and listened to every word the repairman said:

> *A dream is yet to be confirmed*
> *That travels at par with wisdom*
> *Through fire alliances shall be forged*

Not all in flames is a vague hope
Knowledge is lost in this secret
Through a woman who handles the plot
This name I shall not tell you
Though engraved shall it be
Changing the past is indeed rough
But harder shall it be to decide in truthfulness
Past and future are connected
We shall be valiant; unexpected adversity
shall arise ahead!

Vincent Torquay was surprised that he still knew the lay, just as Borba recited it to him many years ago after he had been invited into his workshop. The bookkeeper couldn't believe that he could still sing it just the way it had come out of the shoemaker's mouth. Sofia, Maria and Patricia were surprised by what they had just heard, though none of them knew Thaddeus, the Troubadour of Truth, in person. The retired accountant then gave his own personal input about the verses he had just spoken of. This was to his own surprise, given the fact that he knew it full detail, "In my opinion, the fire referred to in these verses means the flames that would soon destroy Belling's library, which means that the shoemaker predicted one event that would happen years later. I can't comprehend how it works, for as I just told you, this meeting took place several years ago. There is also reference to some woman who holds the truth but whose name should remain unknown. It's my opinion that this woman alone can explain what happened in the consulting room," he finally concluded.

"Are you telling me that there's a woman behind this sudden amnesia that affects my husband?" asked a furious Patricia Murio.

"Yes, there is, although the relationship between the two may seem distant. There's something connecting them, but I don't know what it is. I just remembered these verses after the events at the library," said Torquay.

"As the verses say, past and future are interconnected. Can this be what brought them together?" Sofia asked, to which Torquay simply responded, "I don't have a clue. It's a long time since I recalled such verses."

"The only thing I can safely say is the past and the future are very intense in the Sun Avenue office. I can't believe..." Sofia said deeply. She continued, "I do a rigorous screening of all the people who pass through. I can't believe there's someone who was missed when I made my choice of patients."

"We don't know who this woman might be. All we know is that she holds the truth and that her identity should be kept secret. Unless, as the verses say, we can see her name in written form," said the former accountant.

"What is that supposed to mean?" Maria de Burgos asked.

"I don't really know," Torquay answered.

"This must be the woman we should look for," Patricia murmured.

Nothing more was to be added after these words. It was now clear that a woman was involved in whatever issues that were troubling the mind of Marcus Belling, which made Patricia Murio alert. She recalled the patient that her husband had taken into his care called Anne Pauline a few months ago for past life regression. Her case had really started to take over her husband's emotional state, but with time, this issue was discussed less, which made Patricia think that it was nothing more than a false perception. But such circumstances couldn't be ignored by Sofia, who looked at Patricia closely. It was clear that both shared the same perspective on the meaning of the poem. It was very plausible that Thaddeus Borba had seen Anne Pauline in his visions. That same destiny which took the shape of a person and followed behind the former accountant as he walked along Sun Avenue could not just be Bruno Deluca holding a bottle of wine and a key, but also his loved one, who felt lost in time. Such circumstances of the past had always been a heavy burden on Torquay, who never got married. As he used to say, he had never found the love of his life. This woman in the lay that had been recited by Thaddeus was the one behind the regressive amnesia that hit Marcus Belling.

As they all tried to make out the meaning of the verses, they also clearly saw that Salvaterra, Marbella and Rolland had not interfered in the dramatic events that hit Belling's library, which left Maria and Sofia disappointed. They had always nurtured the worst opinion of the said people. The three women knew that they now fought a new and unknown kind of battle, as the agent behind all this was unknown. They strongly suspected that Anne Pauline could be behind it, however. The protective network built around Belling seemed to crumble because of several circumstances that seemed to be only connected to the occult. Maria de Burgos then remembered to ask Vincent one important question, "At the end of it all, you were worried about repeating Borba's verses when he first told them to you. The question is why?"

"I can't tell you. The truth is that I just memorized them," the accountant said.

To be fair, Vincent Torquay felt that he would need the verses sometime in the future, although it was nothing more than a mere premonition at the time. He now saw that his intuition was right. Belling's former accountant understood that this meeting with the three women who were part of the hypnotist's life, would certainly happen, although he didn't know if they had the same impression. The last verse in the lay kept repeating in his brain and, every time it happened, Vincent could feel danger, "Unexpected adversity shall arise ahead," Borba had said. But what did the shoemaker mean by these words? What adversity was he referring to? The former accountant decided not to warn the three women before him with such a question. Patricia Murio felt uneasy and decided to put an end to this meeting.

Vincent Torquay drank his last sip of wine and put down his glass on his oval table, which he had bought from the antique trader, Argus Dubois. He felt sad that his guests were leaving his palace, leaving him once more to his solitude. He hadn't contacted anyone for years and missed those years when he did accounting for Belling. He occasionally felt that there was some strong connection of love that had been lost in his chain of time, and he needed this love to leave his own seclusion. Where was it, though?

As the four left, and the old accountant and Sofia spoke to each other, Patricia Murio took the time to whisper in the ear of Maria de Burgos the existence of Anne Pauline. Apart from Sofia, none among the ladies had never ever interacted with the mysterious patient. This young, green-eyed woman seemed to be behind all the recent events. With the secret now unveiled, the three women drove past the imposing gates that separated Torquay's palace from the outside and made their way back to the city. Deep in her heart, Patricia Murio knew that Vincent Torquay had predicted that this meeting would occur, but this was based on his relationship with Thaddeus Borba, the antiquary. In the meantime, the retired accountant went back to his routine in his *villa*, always waiting for this woman from the past that he knew existed. He just didn't know where she could be found.

As Patricia, Sofia and Maria drove back home after such a clear and revealing conversation, Marcus Belling kept reading *Antwerp in the 16th Century*. It all seemed vaguely familiar to him, although he didn't know why. Maarten Gembloux had been extremely generous in offering this book to him, or was he predicting the future, just as Thaddeus Borba had done before? This question wasn't what Belling thought of, though, as he kept reading.

The book accompanied Marcus Belling to his office the day after Patricia Murio returned from her so-called business trip with Maria de Burgos and Sofia Estelar. Despite the protest by some of his patients, Belling kept working as a hypnotist and tried to keep his appointments as normal as possible. He saw Sofia just as he arrived at the entrance door. She had decided to keep the trip to Torquay's *villa* secret, and, after their conversation, something told her that Anne Pauline might be responsible for all that was now occurring, though she didn't know why. There seemed to be no way of stopping her, at least while Belling accepted any patient that reached him. Nothing that she could do or say could help him to change his mind, however.

Sofia looked at Belling from another perspective that day and, for the first time, questioned her relationship with this man she had worked for more than two decades.

After a brief silence, he asked her, "Do you know Antwerp, Sofia?"

"No, why do you ask?"

"Oh, nothing really. It's because of this book that Maarten Gembloux lent me. All seems so familiar to me. I would like to go there one day," he said, with a strange feeling of nostalgia.

"You've been asking rather some strange questions," Sofia said, feeling suspicious about his strange behavior.

Marcus Belling remained silent, as he thought of everything that he had read since entering the shop of Gembloux, the well-renowned second-hand book trader. His personal secretary interrupted the silence to open the door and let the hypnotist enter first for one more day of work. Sofia began by organizing the papers on top of her desk, displaying the files by date and the alphabetical order of the names. Moments later, she knitted her brows at Anne Pauline, who had just come in and immediately stepped into the consulting room where Belling was expecting his patient. Anne entered the room and Sofia smiled restlessly as another session started. This young woman could never imagine that years ago, she had been mentioned in the verses of the shoemaking troubadour. What kind of secrets did this woman hide?

Belling put down his book about old Antwerp on top of his Victorian-style desk and asked Anne Pauline to sit back on the couch once again. At this same moment, Maarten Gembloux was about to witness one of the most enigmatic hypnosis sessions ever to be performed there. As Anne heard the calm, persuasive voice of her hypnotist, she started to close her eyes until she fell into a deep trance. This process took only a few minutes. The patient could already see the tunnel of time as usual but this time she found three golden doors, which was surprising. Each of the doors had a different destination. One said Gaul, the other said Salerno and the third said Unknown Destination, which surprised her. She didn't know how to react. She hadn't experienced anything like this since the first session with Marcus Belling. She needed to choose one door and quickly, so she reluctantly decided to open the Unknown Destination. It made no sense to open the remaining doors to the destinations that she had already been to. Anne wanted to be brave and face the uncertainty of her journey through the world of hypnosis.

2

As Anne Pauline opened the door, she tried to concentrate all her strength, both spiritual and of the soul, on visualizing the plate that shone under the brilliant light. She read it clearly; *Anvers*. Anne knew her European history well enough to know that she had arrived in Antwerp at a time after the Middle Ages. This could be confirmed by the date under the plate, which could be read for a moment before disappearing; 1520. Anne Pauline had made it into the 16th century and listened once again to the hoarse voice of Marcus Belling resonating in her mind, asking her to follow her path under his hypnotic trance. The young patient stood outside the door. This wasn't an unknown destination anymore.

With this simple gesture, Anne Pauline started wandering through the streets of Antwerp, looking for any corners and places that might have been part of her past life. These streets were indeed related to her. Within a few minutes on foot, the young woman finally reached the maritime harbor, which was a European and international reference of the time from a mercantile point of view. Anne wished to stop the hands of time to observe the harbor that bustled with life. She could rapidly understand from the view before her that the city was on the path to economic and commercial success and was enjoying enormous prosperity. Poverty existed, but there was also much wealth. Anne had still to discover how her past was related to this province of Flanders that she had only discovered during her studies at university. What was her real world, after all? Was it this one in her trance or her real life? Both worlds seemed real to her, mainly because her power meant she could interact with people and be something more than a mere shadow. Anne kept listening to the voice of her hypnotist asking her to keep exploring the terrain. She stopped and asked herself how she could discover her past in this city.

This question was important. At that moment, Anne felt that she was lost in her hypnotic trance. It seemed that her thoughts had been somehow heard, as a boy no older than 10 came over and gave her a short pocket-sized book, called *Religion in Antwerp: The Role of the Church*. She wanted to reject the offer at first, but the worried look on the young boy's face convinced her to take and read it. When the shape of a female figure stood out over the lower right-hand corner, Anne Pauline focused all her attention on the image. She was astonished to find it was her own shape represented on this print mark. The name of the typographer was also written on there. The author was Gotthelf Tory. As Anne knew, such print marks that distinguished the work from that of the author was usual at the time. Many of these markers were highly enigmatic, so some of their meanings are still unknown. The boy stood by her side until she unveiled his truth and then immediately disappeared into the city.

Anne Pauline had no time to ask him any questions. There was an answer to her question, however, from her intuition that said she needed to meet Gotthelf Tory, a typographer in Antwerp. Although she was under a hypnotic trance, the young woman could still talk to a few people and it took her no time at all to find the address of his workshop. This was her only known destination until now. Anne walked some time until she noted that she wasn't that far from the sea harbor.

The door of her Unknown Destination had now become that of a known destination, as she was in Antwerp in 1520. Anne Pauline walked to the west side of the city, where she easily found the address of Tory's typography. This small, discreet workshop was located on a street populated by many weavers, potters and goldsmiths, which was why the locals called it the street of artists. Such names were for typography was a kind of art, although the printing of books wasn't often seen by the people. The truth was that many typographers compared their importance to that of painters or sculptors.

The aesthetic influence of books with large circulations was wider than any other artistic movement at that time and, therefore, any person who practiced this craft was conscious of the power that was in their hands. Anne Pauline kept listening to Marcus Belling's voice, which asked his young patient to describe everything that surrounded her, which Anne did. Every typographical detail of the print workshop was told to him. The young patient had decided, however, not to report the printing marker that she had found inside the book the young boy had given her earlier in the day. She would not report her connection to the typographer Gotthelf Tory, for this was a personal discovery that not even her hypnotist could know about.

Anne Pauline's power had started to show again, allowing her to interact with anyone in the city. At first, not all people could see and recognize her as she walked around Antwerp while under her trance, except for the young boy who gave her the book printed at the workshop of Gotthelf Tory, which couldn't be possible for anyone who had returnéd to the past under regression. Anne had greeted him very naturally and he had returned the greeting, which meant that the power was working, as predicted by Josef Salvaterra. She could engage people in conversation, as if she, too, lived in 1520.

Some people recognized her and even answered her question, "Where is the typography of Tory?" However, others don't even notice her presence. For them, Anne Pauline Roux was another shadow they saw on the ground.

Anne Pauline finally found the typography workshop owned by Tory within a few minutes of walking around the western area of the city. It was on a hidden street and had a narrow window. Anne peeked through it to see a man and a woman behind him who seemed to argue with each other.

This man, who was resting on his printing machine, could only be Gotthelf Tory, but his face was covered by a shadow, which prevented her from seeing clearly who the people inside were. Suddenly, Anne felt someone pulling her back and she turned her head to see who it was. This time, there was an even younger boy, much thinner this time, who gave her another book, this time about astrology and alchemy. It was now clear that she had a special gift that was only revealed when in a hypnotic state. Anne accepted this book from the boy, who disappeared after running up the street.

Meanwhile, two potters who worked close to Tory's typography looked at each other and turned their attention to Anne Pauline, who immediately knew that they had seen her. Once more, the green-eyed woman couldn't believe how she could be seen by others in her past lives, those same people who had also been part of her numerous pasts. They all interacted with each other at the same time.

Anne held the small book as firmly as she could. Anne now had two books that seemed to be related to her past life in Antwerp and the printing workshop. Anne went through its pages, as she had done with the first book, and looked for a print mark at the end, which could identify its printer. To her surprise, Anne was able to find it in the lower left corner of one of the last pages. Such a fact could only mean that there was another printer in this town that could somehow be connected to her life in the year 1520. She was surprised to see that the marker this time was in the shape of an island with seagulls flying around it. Anne Pauline knew this was the Forgotten Island. Belling's patient decided that she needed to know the person behind this marker. Her time, therefore, should be used to discover all the circumstances of this past life before she was awoken from her trance. She looked at the image of the Island of Wisdom and noticed that shade was blocking her view. Anne turned back to see the stern face of one of the potters that she had seen moments before in the street of artists. He then told her, "Some people say that these books this young man distributes should not be read. Take care before accepting any of these forbidden texts. The

Church disapproves of them and it's why Christopher Beck is disapproved of by some locals and religious figures. I could even tell you that this was the reason the little boy ran away in such a hurry. These are forbidden books," the man said for a second time.

As he finished his warning, the potter retreated into his workshop, which was located only a few feet away from the typography workshop owned by Gotthelf Tory, and he quickly disappeared through its door, filled with an inexplicable fear. Once more, without any warning, the power of Anne Pauline had become evident and, during this time, she discovered more about herself. People from her past communicated with her by written and spoken word, as well as subliminal messages. Despite the dramatic warning that she had just received, the young woman was satisfied with this interaction, as it gave her some more relevant information. In 1520-era Antwerp, there were two notorious names related to her past in this city; Gotthelf Tory and Christopher Beck. Both men were typographers who printed books, although in vastly different fields. Tory printed works on Catholicism, Orthodoxy and Medicine, while the books produced by Beck defied established dogma. Anne Pauline knew immediately that she should get acquainted with both men if she ever wanted to discover her real identity.

This was an unknown world. The young woman decided to take another look through the narrow window into the interior of Tory's workshop. Anne wanted to know more about this man, who could unlock the mysteries of her past. The man himself had finally turned around another way and she could clearly see his face. Anne was amazed to see that Gotthelf Tory was Josef Salvaterra, and the woman beside him, assumed to be his wife, was her. To her shock and surprise, Anne Pauline quickly turned her gaze away from the window to reflect on what she had just witnessed. With this simple gesture, Anne had discovered how she had lived her life in Antwerp during the 16th century, and that she had married one of the most renowned typographers in town. Anne didn't know yet, but her name was Simone Estienne, a woman known for how she influenced the work done by her husband.

It was then that Anne Pauline understood that the rivalry between Salvaterra and Belling had persisted throughout the centuries. Christopher Beck (the printer the potter had spoken of) could be a past life of none other than Marcus Belling. Everything made sense. Just as Belling always intended to challenge his community by questioning some of the dogmatic knowledge about hypnosis, Beck also acted unconventionally in his field. The two famous hypnotists had taken part in the life of Anne Pauline.

The two printers worked in opposite areas of the city and, just as any typographer of their time, had developed print markers to identify the workshop of origin in their books. It was this symbol that enabled Anne Pauline to identify both in Antwerp, or else it would have been impossible to find either of them and to understand that the relationship between Salvaterra and Belling had a common past.

It was with this information in mind that Anne decided to find the workshop of Christopher Beck as well. This was a grueling task for she only possessed the little book with its print marker. Anne had instantly recognized the unique geography of the Forgotten Island with its two tall, green peaks, the golden beaches, as well as the flying seagulls. What Anne couldn't decipher was the set of letters and symbols next to the island.

The young woman tried to focus on her faint memories of the island to try and remember anything that could help her take on this personal mission. As she already knew, both Josef Salvaterra and Marcus Belling were typographers in Antwerp in this past life of hers, each one was publishing books that differed in the kind of knowledge and teachings they provided, leading to very different perspectives of the art of printing, as well as the goals their work achieved. This made it highly probable that Beck and Tory would know each other, and their families would frequent the same public areas in town, and even share each other's secrets.

This simple argument made Anne Pauline remember to close her eyes. Although she was hypnotized, it might be possible to remember moments from the past simply by focusing on these memories.

It was not the first time that Anne Pauline had fallen into an even deeper hypnotic trance during her therapy, for it was the only conceivable way to access memories from the deepest pockets of her subconscious. Closing her eyes during hypnosis was all she needed to achieve such a state, and so Anne did. The young patient let herself be rocked by the hypnotic voice of Belling, who kept hypnotizing her in his consulting room of Sun Avenue. Anne didn't fully understand the process. As soon as she closed her eyes during her trance, Anne could access her memories from the past, as if she was in another dimension. Each dimension was a different, yet parallel world that intertwined with one another. While still listening to the voice of Belling, Anne Pauline started to be reminded of her life as it happened in Antwerp, back in 1520.

Anne let her mind be conducted by the hypnotic words of her therapist, and as she focused on her past, the patient was reminded of her own name; Simone Estienne. The first image that came to mind was that of a few people who she spoke with in a small room. Their faces were not familiar to her, however. Anne tried to focus on the issue being discussed, as it seemed to be of immense importance. She noted that the discussion was about a print marker used by the famous typographer, Christopher Beck, a past incarnation of Marcus Belling, the meaning of which no one could seem to decode. Suddenly, an older man who also sat in the room said to all those who were present, "The information that was given to me says that Christopher Beck got inspired by a marker drawn up by William Caxton. Caxton is known as the introducer of typography in England. This could help us to clear the mysteries behind this marker."

The man, about 60 years old, seemed to be well informed about the personal path of the typographer, and told his audience about Beck's past as a commercial agent in the Netherlands, which left everyone in awe. He conducted business in the city and often traveled to Antwerp, where he later got closer to typography. William Caxton would pass away in 1491, but Beck had developed an interest in the enigma surrounding his print marker, and then started making an elaborate marker of his own, one that was rather mysterious. There seemed to be similarities between the signature markers of both typographers. At this moment, the man whose name was unknown to Anne Pauline, but who seemed to be of major importance within this group, informed all the others in the room that Christopher Beck had once chosen Zakstraat to conduct his business in typography, as Caxton used to frequent this area during his business trips. Beck seemed to search for inspiration from the latter, as well as a sign that would recognize the influence of Caxton's ideas on his printing work. Everyone in the room, including Simone Estienne, looked at each other in awe at the words that they had just heard, which meant that this should stay inside the walls of this room. Why should such information be this important, Anne thought to herself. The more she knew about each typographer, the more she would understand about her own identity.

Anne opened her eyes at this moment. She had once more experienced a state of trance within a trance. She could barely explain such a strange phenomenon to Josef Salvaterra. Anne Pauline knew that closing her eyes during her therapy with Belling was enough. The vast sea harbor of Antwerp stood before her eyes. She now knew which way she should take. Her destination was Zakstraat, the street where Christopher Beck had his printing workshop. Knowing the truth about her history had only become possible after Anne was reminded of a conversation she had been involved in during the 16th century while she was Simone Estienne, while the voice of her hypnotist had helped her to find a way to her past. Belling was sitting next to his patient in his consulting room, while he drove her into the hypnotic trance, but totally ignored the events that happened during that process of hers.

Anne Pauline caught her breath once again. The image of this man who had shared a secret about the marker used by Christopher Beck was still fresh in her mind, and she would not easily forget the strange feeling that was caused by her memories of her life in the 16th century. Everything was completely different. Despite understanding what people said back then, their language was archaic, and their behavior seemed bizarre to her. Once more, Anne took a deep breath, as she needed to find Zakstraat, where she would still need to find the printing workshop owned by Beck, as well as some more of her own past.

It didn't take long for the green-eyed woman to find the street in Antwerp where William Caxton, the master of Christopher Beck (the past life of Belling), had wandered up and down just 30 years ago. It seemed incredible how everything seemed to match in her life, and, for a moment, Anne thought that it hadn't been by chance that she looked for this hypnotist in Sun Avenue. Anne rapidly understood that the information that she received in her second hypnotic trance now seemed much more important for an understanding of her destiny in this city and in her life. It had become one of the most precious pieces of information that she would later transmit to Salvaterra as soon as this session ended, as it allowed him to understand how the vocational theory (which was now apparently becoming more exact) seemed to explain the success of Belling.

Zakstraat was a short walk away from the sea harbor of Antwerp and the workshop owned by Christopher Beck (albeit closed) was rightly signaled as a typography. Anne Pauline stood there a few minutes, still feeling anxiety about meeting this previous incarnation of Marcus Belling in this other time. It took 30 minutes for Anne to see a tired man, yet with vibrant and lively eyes, that looked similar to those of her hypnotist, walking quickly towards the workshop. Anne Pauline immediately knew that this was Christopher Beck himself. Next to him stood his wife, who Anne recognized as Sofia Estelar in a past life. The suspicious look in her eyes as well as her thin body didn't leave much room for doubt; the personal assistant to the hypnotist had been his wife in a previous life. This could explain their complicity when they showed their work at the consulting clinic. Anne had never fully understood their proximity, which resembled that of two lovers. What the young patient didn't know was that Sofia had sometimes felt attracted to his charisma, as many other women had before. She had pledged an oath to protect him, however, that left her no room to develop their proximity. They had developed a unique relationship; which Anne could see had crossed time and distance.

In 16th century Antwerp, Sofia was Marie Veldener, the wife of Christopher Beck. No matter what time she lived in, her wide, vibrant and smart, yet suspicious, eyes would always be noted. This woman showed inborn personality traits, despite the 500-year gap, which was a considerable time difference. The difference in the physical features between this woman and the version Anne knew from the consulting room were impressive, and no one could question that the two had been married during this time. In 1520, Marie Veldener was a major rival to Simone Estienne, both being the wives of celebrated typographers in town. Both helped their husbands in their respective print shops and defended their ideals as well, searching for authors whose texts would reach the largest readership. This could explain the permanent suspicion between Anne Pauline and Sofia, and match Josef Salvaterra's theory on the development of empathies through time. Such past connections explained the close bond between Sofia and Belling, as well as the secretary's troubled relationship with his patient. This mystery now seemed to have been solved; it was as though the criminal had been caught in the act. Everyone, including Anne herself, Sofia Estelar, Marcus Belling and Josef Salvaterra, seemed to share a common past. The mysterious young woman understood that nothing in life happened by chance.

Back from the lethargy of her thoughts, Anne Pauline gathered herself to drive her mission ahead. Before she could get closer to the workshop owned by Christopher Beck, the young woman felt someone pushing her hard, only to find that this time, it wasn't some random young boy distributing books. As she looked back, Anne saw a much shorter woman with dark hair smiling at her, as if the two had known each other for a long time.

"Please do excuse me for bothering you, but I must ask you a question. Do you know Josef Salvaterra?"

Anne Pauline had to ask the woman if she could repeat her question. She was in utter shock. How was it possible that someone from the 16th century would know Josef Salvaterra? Josef would only become a hypnotist some centuries later. This simple question left Anne Pauline quite startled regarding the identity of this woman in front of her, who kept staring at her with large, curious eyes. Her face was thin but seemed to possess an immense inner strength, as if she could read the past and the future, as Thaddeus Borba could.

All that was happening to Anne Pauline had once been predicted by Jasmine in one of her journeys to the subconscious, driven by her alchemic perfume. The young patient of Belling might not know this yet, but she had just met Beatrix van Edegern, the single daughter of one of the most famous jewelers in Antwerp, whose name was Jacob van Edegern. The rich trader had also been a close friend of Gotthelf Tory for many years, mainly because the latter had specialized in publishing texts on minerals and jewelry, a subject that caught the attention of Mr. van Edegern. The jeweler had always tried to keep up to date with the latest trends on jewel and diamond production, and so was keen to know all the information regarding discoveries and new extraction methods for minerals that would be then be used in the production of jewelry. Jacob van Edegern had always developed his partnership with Gotthelf Tory, who printed new texts with the aim of reporting on the development of jewel production in Antwerp.

The small books on jewelry that were printed by Tory's typography for Mr. Van Edegern but didn't have much public demand, however. These prints were merely sought by a small yet influential group of traders who used them to develop techniques for the improvement of their techniques and the development of their trade. The work of Gotthelf Tory as a printer would, however, help to increase the circulation of jewelry and the sale of diamonds in the Low Countries consequences for the regional economy. Such development would help Tory to become a much more influent typographer than his colleague, Christopher Beck, who was an opponent of the mercantile environment in Antwerp, despite also benefiting from it. The goal of the latter was to keep using his craft to oppose the deep-rooted dogma that swept his society, he published new books from unknown authors, who kept using his services in every conceivable way, sometimes even secretly. Beck and Tory were both typographers with a public mission. Christopher would always back the idea of accepting every manuscript from any author on any subject, independently of any monopolies in his trade.

Each typographer in Antwerp had become specialized in certain fields, which generated partnerships with other professionals who focused on those same subjects, as was the case with Gotthelf Tory. Such a development led typography to have a tremendous impact on the regional treasury. Printing was used to develop each branch of the economic activity that flourished in Antwerp, which was the mercantile and economic center of Europe. Christopher Beck aimed to keep up to his neutrality, which Tory would never fully understand.

Beatrix Van Edegern, the petite young lady who gave Anne Pauline a curious smile, would use the long-established partnership between her father and Gotthelf Tory to take over the local jewelry and diamond business. She too held a unique power but, unlike Anne Pauline, didn't require hypnosis to perform it; in the meantime, it was almost inevitable that she and Marcus Belling would cross paths.

When Anne came across Beatrix in Antwerp under the influence of hypnosis, she started to logically work out the family tree of the different families. This same genealogy would confirm a few theories proposed by Salvaterra. Beatrix was the only daughter of Jacob Van Edegern, a rich jewel trader who married Rebecca Clifford many years ago. She was an English woman, who had moved to the Low Countries at the age of two and gone on to established herself and her family there. This woman was dedicated to the trade of spices, namely cloves and cinnamon, having established economic connections in the region that allowed the distribution of her goods all over Europe, therefore granting her family considerable influence in Antwerp. Both the van Edegerns and the Cliffords would benefit from the services of Gotthelf Tory. One could then say that they both had permanent contact with the art of typography, whose social mission was so often poorly understood.

Every person from Anne Pauline's present life had a role in her past. This, she would learn while consulting the registry at the council library after ending her therapy with Belling. Beatrix Van Edegern had been Marbella, Rebecca Clifford had been Maria de Burgos, Jacob van Edegern was a past life of Ruben Mortsel and, as she knew it already, Gotthelf Tory had been Josef Salvaterra, Marie Veldener was a past life of Sofia Estelar, Christopher Beck corresponded to Marcus Belling, and Simone Estienne was her own past incarnation. Each member of Marcus Belling's staff played a part in this past of hers, as Vincent Torquay had been Bruno DeLuca, a character from another dimension of time and space of her life. Anne Pauline would soon consult a forbidden and mysterious book with two centuries of history, which would give her the truth.

Beatrix recorded her past lives but had also developed a unique capacity to anticipate her future lives. Something bizarre happened to her while she was asleep; she inadvertently fell into a hypnotic trance, as if someone was guiding her, as Anne had been. Beatrix could then see both past and future and, on one night, she was able to see that Anne Pauline would soon arrive in Antwerp through hypnotic sleep. Beatrix van Edegern could read the disorientation that was felt by Anne in the tunnel of time, as she got to the Unknown Destination. This green-eyed, young woman was Simone Estienne, the wife of Gotthelf Tory, the printer with whom her father kept a long-aged partnership. Both helped to increase the economic power of jewelry and diamonds in Antwerp.

Beatrix quickly perceived a strategic interest in Anne's arrival. She would have to meet this mysterious green-eyed, young woman while she was under hypnosis, and couldn't pass the chance to make a deal with the wife of Tory, which could make her the leader of the jewelry business in the city during this period. Beatrix van Edegern would have an advantage over every other jewel maker in town and later take over her father's market. Beatrix was tremendously greedy and hadn't much of a moral compass, which only worried her father, who kept telling her, "Your greed is so great that it scares me. I don't even know how to describe the feeling I have or how to explain it to your mother, Beatrix."

His daughter kept ignoring him, though. The trance state that Beatrix reached during her dreams allowed her to develop such foresight that she r understood she could reach her goals in life by using her power of accessing different dimensions simultaneously. Most important still was the fact that this power helped her to make firm pacts with important people from both her past and future, to assume control over the trade and business of jewelry in Antwerp. This power was as strong as the one held by Anne Pauline.

Anne herself was still shocked by the question posed by Beatrix van Edegern. The mind of the green-eyed, young woman was still bewildered by this woman, who she had never seen before, asking if she knew Josef Salvaterra. Yes, Anne Pauline obviously knew him, as he was the hypnotist with whom she had entered into an alliance with the goal of discovering the different past lives of Marcus Belling. Beatrix stared deeply at Anne, as if she knew what her mission in the 16th-century Antwerp was. The daughter of Jacob van Edegern did know of the pact between Anne and Salvaterra, or Gotthelf Tory. Given the Anne Pauline's silence, and despite her shock, Beatrix took the chance to introduce herself. Young van Edegern had a proposal for Anne and so came forward to present it to her in her hissy, grating voice, which irritated anyone who heard it.

"You don't have to give an immediate answer. I see that you're in shock, but I don't want you to feel upset about it.

Anyone with such a mighty power as you should be used to such situations. I have a proposal for you. I would appreciate it if you joined me in this pact, which should remain secret. I know that you would like to interfere in Marcus Belling's career by using past life regression and hypnosis."

"How do you know all of this, of both Salvaterra and Belling?" Anne asked, furious with that high-pitched voice of the other woman.

"The parallel world in our subconscious and its mechanisms through the different time periods is nothing new to me, dear Anne Pauline," Beatrix answered.

The shock felt by Anne Pauline then transformed into an immense fascination about this woman, who was aware of both her alliance with Salvaterra and the mission that had brought Anne to Antwerp during her trance. Beatrix took Anne Pauline's sudden interest in this conversation as an opportunity to present her proposal, "I know that you can use your power to change major events in the past. I ask you to consider my proposal very carefully. Insert these metal medallions inside the typographic machines that are inside the workshop of Christopher Beck on Zakstraat. They will make the machines stall. I will also give you this flask containing hydrochloric acid, which you should place on top of the type plaques that are used in such movable presses. The acid will end up destroying the metal and no more new books will ever be printed. You'll then see whatever happens in the future. You can be sure that such actions will reinforce the alliance that you've entered into with Josef Salvaterra and bring you much success. It will also allow you to finally achieve the revenge that you've always wished for. Don't worry much about what happens in the consulting room. You might not believe it, but the destiny of Marcus Belling has been set for a long time."

"What do you mean?" Anne Pauline asked.

"What I mean is that his destiny had already been set, even before you rang the bell that summer day."

"How can you know all this?" Anne asked once more, now frightened of the presence of Beatrix van Edegern.

"I don't know it, Anne. I see the truth that is hidden through time," Beatrix finally answered.

Anne Pauline knew that she should not insist anymore. Beatrix spoke through intrinsically coded messages, which were often difficult to read. Having already made a decision previously, and taking all this into consideration, Anne accepted the proposal from Jacob's daughter. She knew, however, that the demands of this woman had not been revealed. Anne and Beatrix made a pact, which made Anne uncomfortable about moving between such different worlds. The woman then grabbed the metal medallions and agreed to complete the plan to destroy Beck's mobile print machines as soon as she entered his workshop.

"Use your power," Beatrix finally said, before disappearing along Zakstraat, leaving an impression of being someone with uncontrolled ambition.

As soon as she left, Beatrix had taken more than Anne had realized. Ms. van Edegern had taken a second flask that was empty, but which she captured some air into. Not the common air that we breathe, but a specific one. This scent would one day become a memory. Since Beatrix was Marabella in a past life, one night, during a hypnotic trance, she became aware of the Theory of Scents by Jasmine. Beatrix knew just how efficient this alchemic perfume was. It consisted of a secret combination of essences that could release all memories of the past. Such a capability would give anyone who possessed it an enormous power to dominate other humans.

Anne Pauline had kept hearing the voice of Marcus Belling all this time, and she knew she would have to speed up. Hearing Belling as he fidgeted during the patient's trance meant that he was impatient and hoped to finish the session quickly. Belling was looking through the pages of the book that he had left on top of his table, the title of which Anne had read just before she fell into a deep trance. Surprisingly, the title of the book was *Antwerp in the 16th Century*.

CHAPTER 9

THE TYPOGRAPHY AND PARACELSUS – 1520

1

Anne Pauline didn't know if the fiction had taken account of reality, or if reality had transformed into fiction. When she returned to the session of hypnosis with Marcus Belling, after her experience in Antwerp, she contemplated the book that he was reading. This had been her last remembrance, before entering the deep hypnotic trance.

The book that had been delivered to Belling by Maarten Gembloux, the well-known bookseller of Sun Avenue, felt like a scary omen about what would happen after the sessions of hypnosis. Before being induced into hypnosis, Anne Pauline had a clear image of that book, without realizing why it had become so important to her to recall the title of that work. Now everything made sense.

Although she didn't want to wake from her trance-like state, she had maintained control of her consciousness as always. As he had told her in the first session, she would not lose her freedom, even if she were in a deep state of hypnosis. However, she no longer knew what freedom was. Yet, she didn't want to leave the streets in Antwerp, in the middle of the 16th century, partly because this was a way to keep hidden away in her past. She awoke to the persuasive words of Marcus Belling and knew he would help her recovery. He would have to know everything that had happened during the period she had been hypnotized. The truth is that she couldn't hide everything, but also couldn't say anything. In the face of this dilemma, she decided that the most notable events could only be disclosed to Josef Salvaterra, as was determined by the pact that they both had established. Anne Pauline knew that Belling would try to access the memories of her subconscious, and her attempts to conceal the most relevant information, meant he would be even more likely to question her. How could she escape this? It was exactly what had happened the last time she had sat on the couch in the Sun Avenue office. Upon exiting the hypnotic trance, Belling questioned her in depth about her journey through the past and received the same vague answers that stopped him from making an accurate and detailed diagnosis of his patient. It was the first time that he succeeded.

"Tell me, Anne Pauline, did you find someone in your past?"

"Not that I've noticed, no."

"Maybe if you really concentrate, you'll be able to observe someone who is also part of your life today. You're my first patient to whom this happened," Belling said, not fully convinced by the answer from the young woman.

"Sometimes, I can only see blurry images," Anne Pauline quickly responded, afraid that the hypnotist had unveiled the hidden truth.

"I see. Let's move on to other memories," replied Belling, realizing that he would not be able to extract more information in that session. And then, officially, told her, "As I said in the first session, trust is essential between patient and hypnotist."

Marcus Belling didn't know how to manage that situation. On the one hand, he had to respect the freedom of his patient, since she wasn't obliged to talk about everything that she had seen and felt. However, he also knew that those sessions couldn't wander into the unknown, without knowing exactly what the deal was. Everyone should ask questions about their own ethics. Even the Code of Ethics that the National Council of Hypnosis followed referenced a situation like this. Anne Pauline knew that trust was particularly important for those traveling between the past and the present by hypnosis. It was precisely this trust that was at the base of her agreement with Josef Salvaterra. On the other hand, session after session, Marcus Belling distrusted the events that were reported by his patient more each time. He knew from experience when a patient didn't feel comfortable enough to convey all of the events from their memories. For a moment, he thought about confronting her with everything he thought of her, from her attitude to her lack of confidence. However, as ironic as this might seem, he didn't have the confidence himself to express his distrust, maybe because he had never encountered a similar case to this in his entire professional life. Marcus Belling had never felt as incapable of treating a patient as he now felt. These circumstances contributed to a new experience with Anne Pauline.

Marcus Belling was gradually changing his point of view about the potential of hypnosis as a therapeutic method without realizing it. For the first time, he had a strange feeling about the relationship between the mind and the hypnotic state, especially after his amnesia of knowledge. He seemed unaware of anything in this process, and Anne Pauline surpassed all the knowledge he had acquired during his life. The sessions of hypnosis with his patient were different from any session before. These uncertainties had already led him to question his profession, especially in this case, but unlike with other situations, he still had no reason to think otherwise. For the first time, hypnosis had become an unknown world for him.

This last session of hypnosis had revealed much more about Anne Pauline's past than she could ever have imagined. This began a thread between all the people who were part of his team and his past. It could not be a coincidence! During her stay in Antwerp in the 16th century, she had discovered that Marcus Belling was the well-known typographer called Christopher Beck, that Sofia was his wife named Marie Veldener, that Josef Salvaterra had been Gotthelf Tory, and that he was married to Simone Estienne. And she was Mrs. Estienne. To complete this network of links, Marbella had been Beatrix van Edegern, daughter Jacob van Edegern, who had married Rebecca Clifford, who was Maria de Burgos. In her mind, she had already outlined all the existing connections between their identity, and the people who worked with the highly respected Marcus Belling.

Once again, Marcus Belling had shared a past in common with her, being a typographer in this life who was opposed to the dogmas of the society of the time, which seems to have surprised her. However, this time, the ride to Antwerp was in many ways more complex than all the other previous lives. More people were connected to the life of Belling who appeared to also have been part of his past. Therefore, in this sense, the theory developed by Josef Salvaterra about regression and past lives had now proved to be correct.

Since she had touched the bell of number 27 Sun Avenue, so much had changed in the life of Anne Pauline. She now knew more about herself than some months ago. This whole trip was to become both mysterious and exciting.

Even before leaving the hypnotic state through the persuasive words of Marcus Belling, she still had time to realize something. She no longer remembered her last action, when she returned to focus all his attention on the book, *Antwerp in the 16th Century*. The torpor of her return to reality had accompanied her for a few minutes, while she realized that she was no longer mesmerized in her past. She still had time to put into practice the plan that had been established with Beatrix Van Edegern and put the medallions of metal into the mobile presses of Christopher Beck. Anne Pauline was amazed by her own power.

In Antwerp, she hid behind big baskets that were scattered throughout the street of Zakstraat and waited a few minutes for movement in the workshop proofs of Beck. A few minutes later, Marie Veldener appeared at the bottom of the street and entered the workshop, whose doors were semi-open. At that moment, Anne Pauline left the baskets and, in quick movements, slid to the foot of the door. She listened and quite clearly heard the name Paracelsus. The well-known physician and alchemist was passing through the city and wanted to meet up with his typographer friend of several years. Christopher Beck was to align types on his machines for the next prints when the woman came into the workshop and said, "Paracelsus is in Antwerp. Now is the time to find the two."

"Good news, Marie," smiled her husband.

Anne Pauline knew the work of Paracelsus well. He had for some time had contact with some of their studies in alchemy but was unaware of the relevance of the information transmitted that morning by Marie.

The visit of Paracelsus to Antwerp would not take long, because he would have to go, within two days, to Switzerland to deepen his knowledge about the healing power of various medicinal plants in a meeting with botanists and other interested parties on these issues. Paracelsus was a physician, astrologer and alchemist, who had known Christopher Beck a few years ago, after he had assumed the task of publishing some of his texts on natural medicine, alchemy, astrology and botany hides. This was a thankless job for other printers as they were afraid of publishing the texts. Not all printers in the Netherlands wanted to print texts of the theories of Paracelsus on a parallel world, which produced a language of its own. For this reason, Christopher Beck had become a close friend of the reputed physician and alchemist, who spent his time traveling through Europe. Inevitably, the printer's contact with the themes investigated by Paracelsus made him interested in and curious about the same subjects. The two friends decided to meet once a year in Antwerp, when a rare opportunity existed.

Anne Pauline cringed at that moment on the street corner. Sofia Estelar and Marcus Belling, i.e. Marie Veldener and Christopher Beck, closed the door of the workshop and walked down the street, excited about the news they had received that day. Although it was still possible to recognize the typical features of their faces, the tough times had matured them. Their movements were also different and cruder, as they dragged themselves. Christopher Beck limped slightly from the right leg and Marie Veldener helped him to walk, putting an arm on his shoulder as they turned into a street that ran parallel to them. What would think Belling if he were here, the young woman with green eyes thought to herself.

Anne Pauline realized that this was her opportunity to introduce the characters in the workshop and realize the plan that she had established with Beatrix van Edegern, before Marcus Belling asked her to leave the hypnotic trance. So, she sharpened her gaze and noticed that the potters and craftsmen were working hard in their workshops, and it wasn't possible now to see anyone on the street. She slid slowly up to the door of the workshop and with a slight tug, was able to open the door. With discretion, she entered a large space where it was possible to find eight typographic machines, specifically mobile presses. By observing all of the space, Anne Pauline realized that the workshop was divided into four specific areas, which were all duly organized and mechanized to each phase of the printing process; casting, printing, binding and engraving. One corner was more discreet. Here, Christopher Beck practiced his woodcutting and used wood as the matrix that allowed the reproduction of the image recorded on the paper. Anne Pauline realized immediately that it was so that the printer could manufacture your bookmark printing, which was so enigmatic that it became almost impossible to decode.

The time had come to finish the plan. Anne Pauline poured the contents of the vial that had been delivered by Beatrix van Edegern into two of the presses. Gradually, the acid began to eat away the metal. She then held in the medallions of metal and placed them strategically in locations within the machine that could only be triggered by the manual force of Christopher Beck's employees, to stick the system pressure. It took only 10 minutes to complete her mission. By evicting the last vial with the acid, Anne knew that she was breaking the alliance that she had signed with Josef Salvaterra, who had asked her not to establish agreements with people from her past lives.

"I advise you not to encourage partnerships between people with whom you communicate through hypnosis or during the manifestation of your power," he told her once. "You don't know the full potential of your power to keep agreements with the people of your past lives, nor do you know what this could mean for them in the future," he concluded.

Despite not knowing well the power of the young woman with mysterious green eyes, Salvaterra seemed to know how this worked. The long years he had spent studying his four theories had enabled him to provide for some actions of human nature. He also hoped this warning would stop Anne Pauline from violating the pact that had been signed between them; if this were to happen, he would follow Marbella's suggestion and mesmerize Anne, without her knowing it. Then, he would have to extract the relevant information and give misleading suggestions, to stop her from being hypnotized by someone else. However, despite his words, Anne Pauline had achieved her mission and knew that this had breached the agreement with Josef Salvaterra. This wasn't the moment to question the actions that would certainly bring about consequences for the future.

After leaving the workshop of Christopher Beck, Anne Pauline clearly heard Marcus Belling ask her to exit the state of hypnotic trance and finish a further session of hypnosis. As a result, she ran down the street Zakstraat, which gradually started to disappear from her mind, and she looked once more at the door where the words 'unknown destination' were written on a tablet. She closed the door behind her with bang and knew at that moment that she had already left Antwerp. When she opened her eyes, her hypnotist looked at her as if several centuries had passed. On his table was the book, *Antwerp in the 16th Century*.

Sitting on the sofa, Anne Pauline briefly reported to Belling what had happened during the hypnotic trance, choosing frivolous details that never revealed her real actions. For this reason, Marcus Belling remained in total ignorance about the memories released by the subconscious of her patient and the events during her sessions of hypnosis and regression. Despite not being able to confront Anne

Pauline with his suspicions (as he didn't seem to have the confidence to do so), he felt certain that when he finished a session of hypnosis with Anne, an ancient relic would appear in the drawer of his Victorian-style desk.

Over the past few months, this strange phenomenon had become an indisputable truth. Something that belonged to the past of that patient was returned during hypnosis. So, when Anne Pauline left the clinic, Belling resumed his routine of opening the closed drawer, putting his hand inside, and checking the interior. This time, he found a medallion of metal, which had the appearance of being as old as the others. This was a puzzle.

The next day, as always, Marcus Belling would eventually see Argus Dubois, and requesting an explanation and market assessment for the object that had appeared in his desk after finishing a further session of hypnosis with Anne Pauline. After this last session, his patient had also taken the opportunity to reflect a lot on the importance of their past life in Antwerp during the 16th century. According to Josef Salvaterra's Theory of Vocations, Belling's talents had developed along different in the past and therefore his work as a typographer seemed to have been fundamental to building his Vocation, in some way.

There were skills in the art of typography that would one day later lead to Belling becoming a famous hypnotist, including the need to spread the knowledge to a wider audience, the willingness to contribute to expand horizons, and permanent contact during his different lives with therapeutic methods that were alternative to conventional medicine. His close friendship with Paracelsus also seems to have been crucial for Belling, as he was interested in themes, such as hypnosis, that hadn't generated a consensus of popular esteem. Anne Pauline related all these ideas and it seemed increasingly that the theories of Salvaterra were correct. For this reason, she continued to trust him and informed him about everything she saw and heard within the medical clinic of the Sun Avenue.

Anne Paulin's past was linked to Marcus Belling's, but also to that Sofia Estelar's. This proved again Josef Salvaterra's theory that Belling and his team were somehow connected to the woman with the power to change the events of the past. In turn, Anne Pauline understood now that her empathy with Salvaterra and his apparent attraction to her was because both had been married in the 16th century. For a moment, she thought about omitting this information to him when they met up the next time, especially since Marbella now had knowledge of the agreement established between them both. She had still had not given much thought to the matter; what would the Salvaterra's wife think of the pact that she had kept with her husband? At this point, Belling's patient had realized who had established an agreement in the past; the only person who could know Josef Salvaterra during the 16th century was Marbella. She hadn't yet had the opportunity to meet her in the real world. After all, she was the only person who could know about the agreement with Belling's rival. Then, she suddenly realized that she two agreements; one with Salvaterra and another with Marbella in another dimension of the mind. All of this was extremely confusing for her. For a moment, she decided to forget about it.

Anne Pauline had decided to forget Marbella Gorey, but Marbella wanted to meet the woman who had established an agreement with her husband. For the first time in decades, she had not been consulted by Salvaterra and felt that she didn't have any influence on what was going to happen to Marcus Belling. If things were up to me, Belling would have ceased to exist a long time ago, she thought to herself several times, wishing that Anne Pauline could be hypnotized by her husband, as this would allow her to control the mind of this woman who she had seen in her near-vision.

Anne Pauline's power had been described and seen by Jasmine. It allowed her to intervene in the past and understand the development of Belling's career. Despite the agreement that had been reached, there were no guarantees that Anne Pauline would not be convinced by Belling's generous side and decide not to complete her mission. Neither Marbella nor Salvaterra knew her real movements when she went into a hypnotic trance. That was why it was so important to control her mind.

After Jasmine had taken advantage of traveling the world, Marbella was once more left to herself. She tried to convince her husband several times that it was important that Anne Pauline be mesmerized by him. However, Josef Salvaterra didn't agree, especially as he had to prove the correctness of his four theories, which was the work of a lifetime. To do this, he needed this woman with free thought to embark on that journey to the past.

Marbella knew it was important to control Anne Pauline's mind. One night, she returned to have a quasi-vision and appeared in her dreams. Beatrix Van Edegern knew, in some way, that she was already inside Anne Pauline's dream. Everything seemed far fairer, as she became aware that she could unexpectedly control the movements of the young woman.

When she got home, Anne Pauline sat in her room at the foot of the library. After her experience in Antwerp, it became clear that Marcus Belling had benefitted from the knowledge and teachings transmitted by various masters of various eras that had passed. Lessons learned during the different centuries were fundamental to the creation of a so-called Vocation, which would transform a carrier of success in the distant future. Apart from Paracelsus, William Caxton was the first typographer in the United Kingdom, and he had a vital influence on the work of Christopher Beck. For this reason, Anne Pauline withdrew a book from the library on cryptography, which mentioned the enigmatic marker of the Typesetters of Caxton. This was compared to Beck's marker, where the contours of the Forgotten Island were drawn. On this printing device, Anne Pauline managed to read for the first time a series of numbers and letters that seemed indecipherable; **W80V**. She then removed a piece of paper from her coat and wrote down the code in the following order; **CNPP.14.1** and **W80V**. However, it lacked another code, which Georgine Gunderson found when she opened one of the first boxes of books to get to the defunct municipal library a few months ago, but Anne Pauline was unaware of its existence. The other part was **BO18**. Now, all the circumstances of Anne Pauline's life came together so that she could find out the truth about herself, something that she had wished for throughout her whole life. The first code in their possession had been found in one of the books of J. Johnson, which she kept in her library without ever having noticed the set of letters and numbers that were contained in those pages. This discovery had happened many months ago, since she had started the sessions of hypnosis with Marcus Belling. She knew deep down that all these sequences of symbols, numbers and letters were related to each other and that one day, they would lead to a destination that still wasn't known. So, she followed her intuition and wrote down the codes that she knew on the sheet of paper, without realizing what the purpose of all these discoveries would be.

Sitting on the sofa of her private library, Anne Pauline continued her research into the significance and development of the enigmatic called vocation. She discovered that not only had William Caxton and Paracelsus had a crucial influence on the work of Christopher Beck, and therefore later Belling, but also Thierry Maertens de Alost, who considered to be the man who introduced printing to the Netherlands. In 1473 came the first establishment in this typographical area of Europe, which disseminated the art of bookmaking by other typesetters, as was the case with Christopher Beck in 1520, some decades later. Anne Pauline made a brief study of typography in the college, which allowed her to immediately relate to this set of ideas. Everything now made more sense. It became evident that Paracelsus, William Caxton and Thierry Maertens all had a decisive influence on the construction of the professional career of Marcus Belling centuries later. However, the presence of these experts in this life was still not enough to explain the common lifework present in all of his different lives. Just as the teachings conveyed by the different experts in the Renaissance were central to Belling's success as a hypnotist, it was now visible that the historical conditions of this time were decisive in this outcome.

The historical context in which Belling lived in Antwerp in the 16th century helped him to have contact with different arts, such as prose, theatre, sculpture and painting. So, sitting at the foot of her small library, Anne Pauline concluded that it was very likely that Christopher Beck would have been influenced and inspired by the figures and movements that were characteristic of his time; perhaps, the paintings of Albrecht Dürer, the sculpture of Claus Sluter, the theatre comedian of Cornelis Everaert, the Praise of Folly of Erasmus, the poetry sung in the Rhetoric Chamber, the classic paganism that was introduced into culture and inevitably, the international capitalistic spirit in Antwerp in the 16th century. In 1520, the city was at its peak before the decay of Bruges, and it transformed into an economic capital, with the social development of the Netherlands representing a real turning point in the economic history of this area of Europe. Anne Pauline had some books in her private library that explained this transformation and the birth of new ideas of Reform that appear to have influenced the spirit of the famous typographer, Christopher Beck. This spirit was already back to dogma. With these new elements, Anne Pauline was able to better understand the course of the development of Marcus Belling's Vocation and put her mission in the past into practice.

It wasn't only the historical context of the season that could explain the development of Belling's Vocation. As she went through the sessions of hypnosis, Anne Pauline realized that life is an intricate web of relationships, which may have been born in the distant past. The young woman with green eyes understood in this way that the emotional links which exist between people are repeated several times, life after life.

Since Anne Pauline had gone back to the times of the Roman Empire, she had developed a theory that came to supplement the teachings of Josef Salvaterra. This new theory was given the name of the Relational Theory, and it was more complex than the ideas developed by Salvaterra because it took into account a variable he hadn't taken into consideration; that of love. She was inclined to change the name of his theory to the Theory of Love, but for some reason, this term seemed to be a little too scientific for her. She never talked about love with Marcus Belling, not even when it was presented to her in the first sessions. He didn't have a great love in his life, and he deduced that she was a woman who lived alone. This issue was not mentioned in her conversations with Salvaterra in a cafe near their home, although she sensed his attraction to her. The turning point in her life was the moment when she met Bruno Deluca at *Schola Medica di Salerno*. At that moment, her perspective on her power and ability to change past events had changed significantly. The only knowledge that she had was through hypnosis, nothing would be able to change the love that existed between two people. In this way, her power wasn't as great as she thought, because she now knew that there would be situations that resisted the pursuit of great powers, even those under a cosmic force. She knew she had fallen in love and was equally aware that even if she used her gift to change this reality, it would not work. Anne Pauline didn't know that Bruno Deluca was Vincent Torquay, the former chief accountant of Marcus Belling, now retired. She had a love who was lost in time, and so did he. It was difficult for her to speak with Belling on the love she felt for the one-time herbalist and botanist, who she had met at *Schola Medica di Salerno* during the 12th century. Her constantly fleeing could have been in response to this. When Bruno Deluca sought in the vastness of the universe, the woman he loved and who came from the future, he was no longer able to find the direction in this aspect of his life. The two were looking now for one another, without knowing if the longed-for reunion would ever succeed.

However, Relational Theory was a closely guarded secret of Anne Pauline, who didn't intend to share it with Josef Salvaterra. Instead, she would exclusively share it with Thaddeus Borba. The well-known shoemaker of Sun Avenue was the only person capable of guiding the path of her gift's domain and who suggested a way of using the experiences during hypnosis, to find her identity, and the truth about herself. Despite not knowing what love was, Anne Pauline thought that Josef Salvaterra would not understand, because he could consider it dangerous to love someone from her past life with such intensity, as if everything was real at a given moment of time. However, in this respect, Anne Pauline was wrong. Josef Salvaterra loved Marbella, more than any other woman in the world, regardless of her character and multiple defects, and in spite of the inexplicable empathy and attraction that he felt for Anne, without ever knowing that he had already been married to her when she was a well-known typographer in Antwerp during the 16th century. The rival of Marcus Belling knew what it meant to be in love, and everything that it entailed, but Anne Pauline decided to only share her new discoveries regarding the Relational Theory with Thaddeus Borba. She sometimes took the opportunity to talk about the power of love with him.

"Tell me a little more about this Relational Theory," said the shoemaker.

"It has everything to do with the love," replied Anne Pauline. "This is the only thing that resists this power. It isn't slaughtered by the intensity of distance, or time, but remains intact, even if it can't change past events when I am mesmerized."

"Does Salvaterra know about these ideas?" the shoemaker asked curiously.

"No," the young woman replied simply.

"Don't tell him, then. Gradually, you'll discover the limits of your power, and at the bottom, your own limits. The aim is to discover your identity," said the shoemaker quite wisely.

During her visits, Anne Pauline had the opportunity a few times to find Thaddeus Borba, who remained, as was his habit, reciting his troubadours of truth. The shoemaker waited for her every day in expectation so that he could teach her a more important lesson of how to control this great and rare gift, but the truth was that the past was to precipitate them uncontrollably. In each new session of hypnosis, Anne

Pauline made new discoveries that led her to realize that all of Marcus Belling's team, and him as well, had been part of their past lives. So, her trips to number 27 could not be a coincidence. One day, the shoemaker gave her this advice, "To continue to control your power, be careful not to be hypnotized by Josef Salvaterra. His wife, Marbella, will use this occasion to block your path to discovering your own identity. You, Anne Pauline, are a precious resource for her, more so than you ever could imagine," he concluded in a warning tone.

Anne Pauline didn't have much time to chat with the shoemaker but took into consideration the warning that he had made the day before she had discovered that one of her past lives had lived in Antwerp. Thaddeus Borba sometimes conveyed useful lessons that gave her a better understanding of her travels to the past and interaction with distant people.

One day, he said, almost in a whisper, as if he was about to reveal a secret, "When you get to *Schola Medica di Salerno* and someone delivers a key, accept it without asking any questions. And wait for the most opportune moment to use it, because you'll need it later for your freedom."

The notice contained an omen. When the time came to meet Bruno Deluca in one of the past life therapy sessions with Marcus Belling, he gave her the key to his workroom so that the woman he loved could find him in the future. The key was kept at home at the foot of her private library, but on days when she had a session of hypnosis with Marcus Belling, the young woman brought the two *items* with her inside her jacket pocket. She never knew when they might be needed. In this way, the relationship of Anne Pauline and Thaddeus Borba was developed through the use of a subtle language and imbued with codes and signs, because a power like that could not be revealed through a system of common communication, even vernacular. The shoemaker's warnings were an omen of the future and an alert that made her aware of what was happening around her.

HYPNOSIS

Thaddeus Borba was a true philosopher, who had a very modest profession. Inside him, he kept the secret of the Forgotten Island and other mysteries about human nature.

For some time now, he knew that Marbella Gorey sought to take control of Anne Pauline's mind, although that didn't give her the right to intervene in the power that belonged to this woman. For the first time in a long time, the young woman with green eyes could release her thoughts freely while being hypnotized, although many people sought her with the objective of seeking her gift, but the goal in these cases was only to serve their own interests. They were not interested in the welfare of Anne Pauline Roux, since she wasn't anybody in the world, and soon, she was at the mercy of the personal ambitions of others.

Anne Pauline's power was unquestionable, no matter how displeasing this was to Marbella Gorey. That being so, Thaddeus Borba decided that he would guide the young woman regarding the past, giving her recommendations about the operation mechanism of her gift that should only serve to discover her identity. Deep down, he knew that she was a good person, but the circumstances of her life were made it difficult to find her identity. For lack of courage at times, she had let others say who she was. So, for the first time in a long time, someone who didn't want her to be evil would show her the right way. The Troubadour of Truth had decided to take on this role, without wishing to obtain any benefit for himself.

Anne Pauline was undoubtedly curious about her past life in Antwerp during the 16th century and wanted to know more. However, before she could answer the various questions that floated in her mind, something profoundly serious occurred at that moment in the accounting firm of Ruben Mortsen, the bookkeeper of Marcus Belling. A few hours after destroying the jam with the medallions of metal of Beatrix Van Edegern in some of the presses at the workshop of Christopher Beck, a set of consequences had been felt at that moment. A few hours after these actions in the past, 10 years of invoicing was destroyed. What had caused this situation was unheard of. This time, one of the windows of the accounting department opened with a gust of wind, and a flock of birds entered, destroying all the meticulously organized files. This was a strange phenomenon. A curious and unique combination of constellations that night had cast in darkness what some who are interested in esoteric themes have called the recipe for the fury of animals. The stars, the moon and all the heavenly bodies aligned in a certain way that made the animals unstable, causing a change in their behavior. This modified their animal instincts and thereby create a widespread fury that led to the manifestation of bizarre events. The birds streamed into the office of Mortsel, pecking the papers to pieces. The destruction of documentation erased a decade of revenue records, much like the fire in Belling's library.

In the face of this destruction, Mortsel immediately turned to Vincent Torquay. In that tragic moment, the young accountant needed the support of his mentor, the one who had taught him everything before he had taken on those crucial functions in Sun Avenue. In light of the information that had been transmitted, and the tone of the hissing voice with which he heard every report, Torquay quickly realized that he was watching the implementation of the Troubadour of Truth, mentioned by Thaddeus the shoemaker a few years ago. Although he was surprised, Belling's former chief accountant took this opportunity to turn to Patricia Murio, informing her it had become increasingly important to find the woman who was referred to in the verses of the shoemaker. Now, yes, her identity would be revealed. With this, Patricia Murio, Sofia and Maria de Burgos all realized that it would be necessary to find and confront Anne Pauline with all of these events and, even, if necessary, prevent her from continuing to attend the hypnosis sessions with Marcus Belling. However, the damage had been done. Belling's practice again suffered the setbacks of actions committed in the past, and although the patients didn't have a full awareness of what was going on at that moment, Ruben Mortsel was in a panic.

2

A few days later, Anne Pauline returned to Sun Avenue. This time, the face of Marcus Belling looked absorbed, gazing into the void. He felt that he was fighting against invisible forces that would gradually destroy his career. For some time, Salvaterra had taken note of what had happened at the accounting office and he warned Anne Pauline that she would have to be discreet the next time she sat on the couch to be hypnotized. There was no doubt that his power continued to manifest itself with intensity, fulfilling the objective of destabilizing Belling by using the principles that had been studied in the Theory of Vocations and all the other theories elaborated by Salvaterra and Jasmine. Even Anne Pauline, after traveling to the past by hypnosis, had developed her own theory.

On the day that Anne Pauline underwent a further session of hypnosis, Belling was gradually able to convince himself that he had lost all the techniques and knowledge he required to practice his profession. Inevitably, he began to have doubts about himself. Even so, in an attempt to overcome the latest from his accountant, he simply continued his work. A long time ago, Sofia had felt it was time for him to refuse treating the patient anymore, but nothing was able to change his mind. The hypnotist again induced Anne Pauline into a deep, hypnotic trance and, through his melodious voice, she returned once more to the past.

When she closed her eyes, she was immediately taken back to the street Zakstraat, where the workshop Christopher Beck was located. As with her visit, the street maintained the impressive medieval features and the intensity of the smells that filled it. When she sat on the couch, she never knew what the fate of this journey would be, but during her consultations with Marcus Belling, she would eventually follow a timeline that was quite fixed and consistent. The trip to their past, was like being told a story or watching a movie.

On returning to Antwerp, it was inevitable that Anne Pauline would remember Simone Estienne and Gotthelf Tory. In many of the dreams she had had throughout her life (which she was now able to remember more clearly), she had seen Tory as a typographer, who published manuscripts on religious orthodoxy, and she knew that he was very close to Anna Bijns; a strong opponent of the ideas of the Reform advocated by Luther that began to spread through the city at this time. This relationship was important for them both. The truth is that Bijns had a crucial influence on the work of Josef Salvaterra in his past life as a well-known typographer in Antwerp in the 16th century. Paracelsus and William Caxton inspired Christopher Beck to bring new books printed for the Netherlands and Europe, which questioned forms of being in society, and the dogmas that had been installed during the Middle Ages.

Anne Pauline was aware that the two typographers were leading contenders in the art of typography in Antwerp during the 16th century. When she returned during the hypnotic trance to the street Zakstraat, she knew also that her past was connected to the street, because that place somehow held hidden secrets about her identity. She admired every nook of it. While several artisans and potters worked beside her, a few yards further on, the art of basket-making was practiced by women who were hardened by the misery and poverty of the times; and without exception, they were all true artists. Then, an older man with blue eyes lifted the face of the vessel, which was still damp from the mud that was used to manufacture the parts, and beheld Anne Pauline with particular interest. He was the only person on the street who had noticed her presence, while all the others continued to work. This man was called Jacob. Like no other, he knew about the heart of every person he spoke to, or of those he observed from afar. With the ability to see the soul of each person, he had been able to see Anne Pauline, a slender woman with green eyes that held secrets. There she was, at the bottom of the street, with black hair and bright green eyes that shone in the night; all this combined to create a sense of mystery about her. Jacob knew that the woman wanted to find out about her own truth. This was hidden by symbols, coded messages or in dreams that became reality. Above all, he saw that Anne Pauline had no fear of the truth. Precisely for this reason, she had managed to develop a unique power through hypnosis.

Anne Pauline tried not to be bothered by the intense look from Jacob. She continued to have a mission to complete. She was directed to the typographic workshop of Christopher Beck and noticed that the door was closed. Wasn't there anyone there? There had been no movements for two days. A strange calamity had destroyed five presses, and this has hampered the progress of the well-known typographer. In the background, Anne Pauline knew she was solely responsible for that situation due to her alliance with Beatrix Van Edegern.

For a moment, she felt very guilty for that. As she watched Marcus Belling over the course of their various lives, she realized there was something in him that Salvaterra and Marbella couldn't understand, perhaps generosity or compassion. Regarding her hypnotist, she had conflicting emotions. She didn't enjoy the fact that she has been part of his past. On the other hand, his life was linked to hers so intensely that she could not avoid returning to the clinic. Is this freedom? It seemed to her that it wasn't, when it wasn't possible to refuse her destination. To forget about this, she tried to concentrate on her mission. The last time she was there, she remembered clearly that Marie Veldener had informed Christopher Beck about the visit of Paracelsus in the city. Several meeting places would be possible, such as the Stock Market Trading, the Vleeshuis, or the fortification known as Het Steen. These were emblematic sites of a city that was said at the time to be the principal focus for the commercial, economic and cultural development of Europe. Anne Pauline knew she had to find Beck and Paracelsus and followed the path to the port of Antwerp, in the direction of the Scheldt. This was a special place. When she was here last time, Anne closed her eyes in search of her way, and went back into trance, inside her own hypnotic trance. This time, the image that appeared to her was of Josef Salvaterra meeting a woman, who she wasn't able to identify, next to the Town of Rhetoric in the city, where they both exchanged views on a recent manuscript that had been published in the workshop of Christopher Beck. The woman that Anne Pauline had noted in her short trance was called Anna Bijns, whose face she began to gradually remember as Simone Estienne's, Anne she knew she was married to Gotthelf Tory. Indeed, she had become accustomed to Tory's frequent presence in her house. The couple had known the successful writer from the Netherlands several years ago. Currently, in 1520 to be precise, she was 55 years old, and only a few years older than the typographer. Bijns was also the owner of a reputable school in Antwerp, so she was just as familiar with the art of books and typography. Anne Pauline remembered that the relationship between the writer and Gotthelf Tory had already lasted several years, and she had benefitted from typographic art to disseminate her texts, poems and prose. In order to appeal to the workshop of the typographer, Bijns was also able to disseminate and share the ideals of the Counter-Reformation with a speed that would not be possible without the precious help of typography. As Tory quickly realized his publication needs, there was a tacit agreement between them that lasted for several years. On the day when Anne Pauline watched Anna and Gotthelf, with her eyes still closed in a double trance, she realized that they both seemed uncomfortable with the content of the text published recently by the typography of Christopher Beck. Something in this situation was no longer curious and she thought that it would be related to her past. She needed to find Tory and Anna Bijns and so she opened her eyes and tried to find her own way.

Before Anne Pauline came to Antwerp for two weeks, Christopher Beck had completed a draft of typographic projects. During his time in contact with Paracelsus, he began to take an interest in subjects, such as the causes of occult disease, the influence of imagination in diseases, and the connection between the pain of the spirit and physical pain. The well-known typographer had decided to use his profession to widen existing knowledge of these subjects by using the writings of Antiquity and the Middle Ages. Many years ago, while interested in the manuscripts of Avicenna and his ideas, he had thought for a long time about using the knowledge of the art of the characters to make them more accessible. In this follow-up, Christopher Beck decided to publish *Book of Healing* in Latin, a kind of encyclopedia of science and philosophy that was written in the 11th century. In this book, Avicenna had intended to compile all philosophy, dividing the text into distinct parts; logic, natural science, psychology, geometry, astronomy, arithmetic, and music. It was a basic treaty written during the Middle Ages that he had always found interesting and which he hoped to print so that he could share the unique knowledge of the author. For some time now, Tory Gotthelf had known about the secret project of his rival printer. In this respect, Antwerp revealed itself to be the ideal city to achieve all these plans, because 1200 works were printed here, in contrast to the 200 books in the rest of the country. Because it wasn't possible to halt the publication of several volumes of *Book of Healing*, Tory had decided to meet with Anna Bijns at the foot of the Rhetoric Chamber. Once gathered here, the two wanted to discuss the rapid and urgent printing of new texts on the church and religion to muffle a successful piece of work developed by Beck.

"These are dangerous ideas," Gotthelf Tory said several times to Simone Estienne when dealing with the subject of his rival's publications, and a day later, he would make references of the Belling's working methods to Marbella. So, when Anne Pauline arrived at Antwerp under hypnosis, an important meeting was already underway between Gotthelf Tory and Anna Bijns. Both were displeased with the publication of works by Beck, who defied the natural order of things. These plans revealed what Anne Pauline had already noticed for the first time since she came to Antwerp, that the relationship between the two known typographers was quite troubled. On the other hand, this relationship was already being influenced by the first internal upheavals that had been experienced in the city during the 16th century between those who advocated Protestantism and those who preached the Catholic religion. In this sense, Christopher Beck had clear empathy with Lutheranism and Calvinism, which was struggling against the dogmas of Roman Catholicism, and he wore typographic art in an attempt to liberate the spirit of the dogmas that were installed in a society that had not long progressed from the Middle Ages, while Tory turned to the print shop to disseminate religious texts with the help of Anne Bijns. This meant that when Anne Pauline came to town by way of hypnosis, there was already discord between the two printers.

Somehow, Anne Pauline realized that her past was undoubtedly related to the historical context that was alive in Antwerp in the 16th century. But her state of mind also helped the troubled relationship between Tory and Beck, as well as the life and work of Paracelsus and Anna Bijns. The different experts and the new religious movements, such as Lutheranism and Calvinism, had a strong influence on this past life of Anne Pauline, who was known at that time as Simone Estienne. Early on, Simone had known the functioning of typography well, as she belonged to the family of Henri and Robert Estienne, the well-known French typographers, which meant she was in early contact with the new versions of the Bible that had been published in Latin. For this reason, she knew the background of the work done by her husband, whose interests gravitated around religious themes and the Church. Simone Estienne was deeply Catholic, due to the mystery that had always surrounded her dreams, which were encrypted, using symbols and strange codes that she never had the chance to unravel. As Anne Pauline would be advised centuries later, through her dreams, she would have to seek her identity in a hidden past. Many nights, the names Aurélie, Guinerve and Isabella constantly ran through her mind, without her ever knowing the source of them. So, she went on to attend the Church more assiduously, fulfilling all the cults and reading regularly one of the Bibles that had been printed by the cousin, Robert Estienne, who had kept her informed of corresponding new versions or typographical improvements. During the 25 years that Simone had been married to Tory Gotthelf, she preferred to just keep up with the intensified developments in the field of typography, and helping her husband in whatever way she could, even in his workshop sticks. The story would be printed and translated into several books that, in future, would be published by Tory. One day, Anne Pauline would discover her life story in a file that she couldn't access at the city's municipal library. A day later, the Marcus Belling's patient would have the help of Georgine Gunderson who would help her to continue to unravel all these links from the past.

As Simone Estienne was Anne Pauline, she had been married in a previous life to Josef Salvaterra, which explained the unexpected empathy that was generated between the two on the first day they met. Anne Pauline decided not to disclose this secret to Salvaterra. There were secrets that she thought should remain hidden. She had promised an alliance and this action seemed to defy it. That is why she began to think about all the different contexts and historical figures of the time that had shaped her life in the past. She quickly realized that the close friendship between Paracelsus and Christopher Beck had been crucial in the development of the Vocation of Belling. The incursion of Paracelsus into the occult and alchemy had effectively made him a pioneer in these different areas of knowledge, and his influence was felt in fields as diverse as medicine, chemistry, homoeopathy, botany, and surgery. Thinking more deeply on these influences, Anne Pauline was particularly intrigued by the connection between Paracelsus and alchemy, especially as it was highly likely that Marcus Belling (or Christopher Beck) would keep precious teachings in this field to himself. Knowledge that might have contributed to the belief that hypnosis could serve as an alternative therapy that is complementary to conventional medicine. Alchemy, the precursor of chemistry, often awakened the ambitions of unreasonable kings and attracting other vested interests of artists and secret societies. The close relationship between Paracelsus and the famous typographer must have been marked by intense discussions about these topics, which explained, in turn, the interest of Beck in investigations that were carried out by his doctor friend and alchemist. Consequently, he made the workshop sticks available to facilitate the dissemination of the writings of Paracelsus and other authors of antiquity who had, somehow, contributed to a new outlook on men, their infirmities, and possible cures.

Anne Pauline confirmed through her reflections that Christopher Beck was oblivious to all dogma in general. For this reason, the well-known printer developed a language through his bookmark printing that was so enigmatic nobody was able to unravel it. Everyone, except Anne Pauline, because she knew about the Forgotten Island and had already been there. She realized that he used a language made of symbols and mysteries. So, Anne Pauline made the decision that she would have to go back to reading some books from her library, or others in the new municipal library (where Georgine Gunderson had used to work, but had now been moved to the now-defunct city library) to unravel this encrypted communication. Although this was not yet fully revealed, it became clear that Paracelsus and Christopher Beck shared deep affinities and interests through the experience of having lived different lives, Marcus Belling would eventually become the receiver of a hidden knowledge centuries later.

Anne Pauline was lost in her thoughts at this time, but her eyes were already open. This wasn't the first time that this had happened when she was hypnotized. It sometimes seemed to her that she lived a trance in a trance. However, she decided to react to the stimuli around her and began to walk around the city, being quite attentive and watching the cosmopolitan movement that existed in Antwerp during the 16th century. The street Zakstraat was too far away and the seaport had already fallen behind her. Antwerp was not a strange city. During trips to Europe, this was one of the cities that she had become more familiar with, and that's why she had purchased a sofa that would later be placed in her private library. She would sit when she wished to consult a book on hypnosis, regression and past lives, constantly searching for her identity. While walking through the streets of the 16th century, Anne Pauline became aware of the wealth that existed in Antwerp and its cosmopolitan movement. This was spurred on by numerous theatres, concert venues and trades that gravitated around various products, such as cinnamon, ginger, chili pepper, sugar, pepper, copper and silver. Charles V was the sovereign who ruled the Netherlands at this time, and she often heard his name mentioned at numerous festivals that excited and stimulated the city. From anywhere in the city, it was possible to observe foreigners, especially the Portuguese, Spanish, Germans and Italians. At one point, Anne Pauline passed by the Portuguese settlement. Registered in the house in Kipdorp, it had been given by the Portuguese in 1511 to board trade and products that came to Europe from the East. The house in Kipdorp played a fundamental role in the city by helping to make Antwerp the economic center of Europe. In a few minutes, Anne Pauline left the factory behind and continued to walk through the city expecting to find Gotthelf Tory and Anna Bijns somewhere.

At this moment, a strange smell began to emerge throughout the city. The scent that hung in the air was probably a result of the many products traded in Antwerp. It was a mixture of cinnamon, apples and cloves; products which could be found scattered throughout the city. Anne Pauline stopped in the middle of a busy street and to think about the enigmatic smell that was increasingly becoming ingrained into her clothes and skin. Then gradually, without realizing it, she lifted her nose as if she had sensed a familiar scent. It was fantastic and intense, which strangely made her think back to her life before starting the sessions of hypnosis with Marcus Belling. She realized then that her life had changed very much since she had rung the bell of Belling's office. She tried to concentrate a little more to see if she could identify the source of her memories, which were vague and recessed in time. She had no doubt that this was the smell that woke her up in the middle of the night. It tormented her because she didn't know its origin, yet she was able to sense it, night after night. These sensations were more distressing than any others she had ever had and were why she sat for hours in her private library, looking for answers to her inner truth in the books there.

Anne Pauline opened her eyes. It had happened once again, same as before; the trance within a trance. It was strange how she had found that smell in Antwerp during the 16th century, which only confirmed that her past and her identity were linked to this city. The mystery seemed to have been finally resolved. The smell that seemed so familiar was composed by a mixture of various scents, such as cinnamon, apple and the harpsichord, and she didn't remember ever having used a scent of this composition before. For this reason, she had never encountered it, despite making many searches to different perfumeries in the city. Therefore, she could only have smelt it while she was Simone Estienne. If smells are connected to memories, then this smell was undoubtedly related to her past in the 16th century. It seemed that the truth had been revealed while she was in a hypnotic trance. Anne Pauline decided once more that she would keep this secret for herself and would not inform Marcus Belling, whose voice still guided her (although it now sounded increasingly distant). Jasmine had known long ago this truth about Anne Pauline, i.e. that her identity was hidden in the lives of the past, which could only be accessed by hypnosis. Through her Theory of Smells, she realized that this enigmatic smell that had accompanied the young woman with green eyes every night since childhood was the result of the transformation of her memories. The memories of this forgotten past had remained hovering over the years. In the 16th century, Anne Pauline used to attend the large markets of Antwerp. This was especially because they were places of passage where people could reach her typographic husband. As the years passed, the mind had absorbed the smells around her and created these memories of the aroma that had chased Anne Pauline in another time, as she was growing up. This was the truth that Jasmine had discovered after using the scent's alchemy.

The mysterious smell came then to a past life of the young woman who lived in Antwerp, during the 16th century. The same smell now flowed around Anne Pauline and she decided to follow its course until its last trace had disappeared. She walked this way for several minutes, and when the smell finally and completely abandoned her, she found herself unexpectedly in front of a small and discreet house on a little street in the bustling city center. Her goal was to find Gotthelf Tory and Anne Bijns, she was instead in front of a small house, with no printing workshop. Contrary to what she thought, there was inside a makeshift laboratory, as Anne Pauline would find out a few minutes later. This had been the venue for Christopher Beck's meeting with Paracelsus.

At the exact moment that Anne Pauline arrived at this small house, Beatrix van Edegern appeared at the bottom of the street. It was time to find out her true intentions, as these had been unclear since she had seen Anne Pauline for the first time and asked her if she knew Josef Salvaterra.

"Hello Anne Pauline, I think that we should talk about our pact," said Beatrix.

Anne Pauline confirmed to her that the acid and the metal medallions Beatrix had given her last time had indeed had consequences in the future, by causing destruction in the accounting office of Ruben Mortsel, who worked with Marcus Belling. She told her how all the invoicing of the last 10 years had been destroyed by a flock of birds. The information wasn't surprising to Beatrix and she finally revealed her true intentions.

"As you can see, I kept my part of the deal. Now I need to hear what you can do for me," Beatrix said.

Finally, the thoughts of this woman who knew the secret of Marcus Belling's patient would be revealed. Many centuries ago, she had hoped for this moment. Many years ago, she knew that Paracelsus was studying the theory and method of transmutation of metals, like lead, into gold, among other discoveries, such as the production of the spagyrical elixir.

Access to all this power would enable her to monopolize the trade of gold in Antwerp, which she had always desired. For this reason, she believed that the famous alchemist, born in Switzerland, had decided to meet with Christopher Beck in the improvised lab to show him his latest innovations and discoveries in this field. This was, therefore, an important day.

The purpose of Beatrix van Edegern was immediately clear; that Anne Pauline would be an intermediary between her and Paracelsus. The objective of this alliance was to get the doctor and Swiss alchemist to explain to Beatrix how the process of transmutation of the lower metals into gold worked. In exchange, she would give them several pounds of precious jewels to invest in the most diverse studies and investigations. The plan seemed both bold and intelligent. However, to achieve this, Anne Pauline would first have to go inside the house, where the meeting between Paracelsus and the well-known typographer was taking place, and then force them to leave the vicinity to continue with their negotiations. Anne Pauline could confirm that the two were actually

compounds used for the manufacture of the spagyrical elixir, and they were guarding the method of transmutation. After what had happened with Marcus Belling, who had once again been affected by changes in the past, the young woman with green eyes knew that she couldn't refuse this alliance.

Beatrix van Edegern was confined to a small corner of the street, as she watched Anne Pauline enter stealthily inside that house, which held men with experience of alchemy, whose goal it was to produce gold through the fusion of different other metals. The door was open, so the young woman with green eyes decided to take the risk and enter; with a few rare exceptions, nobody recognized her. The house was cramped inside, quite dark, with two floors. On the second floor was clearly heard the voice of Christopher Beck and another man, Paracelsus. Pauline had to concentrate to decipher which one was speaking at that moment. With care, she ascended the narrow stairs up to the second floor and hid behind a cupboard, while she could clearly see the two figures who spoke among themselves. She soon realized that these two figures were Christopher Beck and Paracelsus, who at that moment seemed to be conducting an experiment in a laboratory. This lab was different from the university at the time when he had been Aurélie Caen. However, the two men were performing experiments seen with Caen and Rosalie, so Anne Pauline concluded that there should be a link between all of these of different lives from the past. They were all looking for the same thing. In the past, people looked at the method of Paracelsus in the hope that it would transform lower metals, such as lead, into gold. As Georgine Gunderson would find out for herself, the very history of Sun Avenue was intricately linked with the past of both Anne Pauline, Marcus Belling and those who had worked with him.

The second floor of the house was transformed, not into a workshop, but a true laboratory, where Paracelsus wanted to show the results of his covert investigations. This explained his trip to Antwerp. Anne Pauline decided to remain hidden behind the cupboard, because she never knew who would be able to see and interact with her when she was hypnotized. After what had occurred at *Schola Medica di Salerno*, it was clear that only a few people who were linked more directly to her heart seemed to be able to recognize her. This was exactly what had happened with Bruno Deluca, the man who was in love with her.

On that day, Christopher Beck had met with Paracelsus and enjoyed the opportunity to speak about his work in the workshop of the characters, including the texts of different authors that had been published. At one time, the typographer confessed to him that he intended one day to print a text in which the law of cause and effect and the Law of Rebirth was discussed. The laws state that human beings evolve as they experience new lives and we reap always what we sow. Anne Pauline, who was still hidden behind the cupboard, was surprised by this revelation because it showed that Beck was already interested in past life regression and logistic regression, though he was living in the 16th century.

Paracelsus was interested in the ideas of Beck, but there were other reasons why he had sought out his typographer friend. The well-known physician and alchemist had worked for many years with an unknown formula that gathered together salt, sulfur, mercury, earth, human bile, water, gold, silver and other ingredients. This allowed him to create what he called the spagyrical elixir, which could enable him to remove quintessence; this is the fifth element that is composed of the world, beyond earth, fire, water and air. Quintessence would be the ether that simultaneously represents a kind of energy, which explains the expansion of the universe. Through this brief explanation, Christopher Beck quickly understood the importance of what he had heard. Anne Pauline realized, at that moment, that Paracelsus had traveled to Antwerp to explain to the well-known typographer how to extract quintessence from the spagyrical elixir by using an improvised laboratory that was in a busy, small town. However, all was not yet revealed. After resting a hand on the shoulder of Beck, Paracelsus said, "I would like to publish the results of this experiment, using your typography."

The printer couldn't deny this request, although he knew the risks.

The conversation between Christopher Beck and Paracelsus ended abruptly when they saw a liquid seep into a small, glass jar that had been placed underneath a volumetric flask, which served to collect the liquids that were generated through experimentation. In contact with air, the collected liquid quickly evaporated completely before the incredulous eyes of the printer and famous alchemist, who couldn't contain their happiness that the experiment had worked. Or at least, so it seemed. The result would have to be kept secret, at least until it was published and had reached those people who could understand the importance of this discovery. However, Anne Pauline remained hidden behind the cabinet, and although she had never practiced alchemy, she could perceive the relevance of what was being spoken about and tested in the laboratory. In this way, she had demonstrated the need for there to be an intermediary in the situation, as she had asked Beatrix. Paracelsus asked Christopher Beck to publish the results of their research, so that they could share the knowledge of how quintessence could be removed from the spagyrical elixir. The printing machines that were installed in the workshop of Beck on the street Zakstraat would play a fundamental role in realizing this project, as they would help them to disseminate their knowledge, which in the words of Paracelsus, he "intended to be universal". With a nod, Beck agreed to cooperate with Paracelsus and help him to publish the results of their research. From that day on, everyone would know how to produce gold through the transmutation of lower metals.

It was important to know this method of the transmutation of base metals into gold, and the trials that had been conducted to extract the quintessence were a significant help. However, Paracelsus didn't have enough time to show Beck how he carried out this entire process, but instead explained all the phases of transmutation, showing him a map that he himself had designed. The well-known alchemist now wanted Christopher Beck to publish the results of his investigations very discreetly, in such a way that it would not be possible to identify the source of these discoveries. The transmutation would have to continue to be a closely guarded secret. Thanks to the words of Paracelsus, Anne Pauline understood the importance of typography throughout the process. The time had now come to realize the plan she had outlined with Beatrix van Edegern.

The smells of the different elements and minerals that had been mixed in the laboratory through a complex system of distillation and evaporation were now agony for Anne Pauline. She wanted, at that moment, to leave her hiding place and go down the stairs to the first floor of the house and tell the daughter of the well-known jeweler of Antwerp everything that she had heard. She slowly started to stir all the muscles of her body, preparing to descend the stairs, but in stretching one of her legs, she knocked over a decorative glass bottle beside her, and the sound of the glass smashing echoed around the building. Immediately, Christopher Beck and Paracelsus fell silent and realized that there was someone else in the house. The power of Anne Pauline had once again manifested itself. Contrary to what she had thought, her power was becoming increasingly strong because there were now more people aware of her existence. They were able to recognize all her movements while she was subject to the hypnotic words of Marcus Belling. She could never have assumed that the well-known printer and the alchemist would be able to hear her movements and discover her. With agility, she succeeded in getting down to the second floor without being noticed, but Beck and Paracelsus were already on her trail, looking for the person who seemed to be hiding in the house, which had now been converted into a makeshift laboratory that could produce gold through the spagyrical elixir. When Anne Pauline opened the door of the house, her face was quickly seen by the printer and the physician. She had to run into the street to escape the two men. The two stared at each other, not knowing who the woman was and what she had been doing hidden in the house. In view of this, Beatrix van Edegern decided to follow her, but then realized that the woman under = hypnosis had been discovered.

Running through the streets of Antwerp, Anne Pauline knew the two men were carrying the secret about the production of the spagyrical elixir and drinking gold, something that she had already experienced when she had observed the couple, Caen and Rosalie, at the laboratory of the university in another time. This was, therefore, a great secret, which was also linked to both their identity and their inner truth, though Anne Pauline still couldn't understand how yet. For a moment, she thought about not sharing this information with Beatrix, but quickly realized that this would not be possible because she could see Beatrix running behind her, as well as Christopher Beck and Paracelsus.

All that time, Anne Pauline was continuing to listen to the voice of Marcus Belling and, in an impulse, turned back and watched the eyes of the typographer, which were overpowering, almost hypnotic, like those of Belling, who was sitting in his medical clinic in Sun Avenue. At that moment, he had created a tunnel of time, which linked the past and the future.

Christopher Beck surrendered to the green eyes of Anne Pauline. Something about her seemed to be eerily familiar, as if he had seen her before. Annoyed by that look, Anne Pauline decided to follow the trail of the familiar smell of cinnamon, apple and cloves while passing through one of the markets of Antwerp and knew that this had somehow always been present in her life. She was aware that these memories would lead to Gotthelf Tory, her husband in this life, and Anna Bijns. They would be next to the School of Rhetoric, which was preparing for a new spectacle the following day. Beck, Paracelsus and Beatrix realized that they were heading toward a common destiny. This would be a specific location where, to their surprise, they would discover the true potential of the power of Anne Pauline.

Anne Pauline had achieved the unlikely power through hypnosis. In the middle of the 16th-century, in Antwerp, she'd just been where a group of people whose pasts were linked had been, though their ideas, ideologies and personal stories varied greatly. This was an incredibly special meeting.

When Anne Pauline stopped running and started to walk toward the house of rhetoric, she could clearly see the shadows of Gotthelf Tory and Anna Bijns, who were discussing the printing of new religious texts and theology and their subsequent dissemination at a school that Bijns owned and operated in the city. When the young woman with green eyes arrived next to Tory, her face showed absolute amazement. This face was remarkably similar to Simone Estienne, his wife. It was difficult to define the feeling that he felt. Christopher Beck, Paracelsus and Beatrix van Edegern all now gathered in that space, and looked at each other with a mixture of surprise and disbelief, as they were all, without exception, able to see and recognize the young woman with green eyes; the woman who had traveled to the past by hypnosis.

something strange was happening in the hypnosis practice on Sun Avenue. At that moment, Marcus Belling had closed his eyes, and inexplicably, went into a hypnotic trance. He had been induced into the hypnotic state by his own voice. This rarely happened to hypnotists, but sometimes, it could. A brief time later, he traveled through the same tunnel as his patient and came to three wooden doors, one of which had the lock made in gold that gave access to an Unknown Destination. He felt, deep inside, that this was the right door to open. For the first time, Belling would have the opportunity to finally find out what was happening to Anne Pauline during those sessions of hypnosis. With curiosity, he tried to open the door of the Unknown Destination but failed to realize that the resistance was greater than he thought. So, he decided to wait for some time for a person on the other side to open it. However, on the other side of the trapdoor that Marcus Belling was to climb through was Anne Bijns's foot. Due to the uneasiness of the moment, Gotthelf Tory and Christopher Beck, the well-known writer of the Netherlands, had realized that someone was trying to exit through the rocks in the street rather than a door. This wasn't even a street. It simply gave access to other dimensions that had yet to be discovered.

While Marcus Belling expected to be able to open the door of the unknown destination, the group of people that was next to the School of Rhetoric began to show signs that they needed a quick explanation of what was happening. First, Gotthelf Tory was angry to find Beck, who had assumed that his meeting with Anna Bijns had been unveiled. Meanwhile, Beatrix van Edegern hadn't stopped to look for Paracelsus, who wanted to remove all the information that he had on quintessence and the secret of the transmutation of metals into gold. He knew the knowledge about the functioning of this process could guarantee him the monopoly on the route of jewelry and diamonds throughout Europe. In the middle of the group, Christopher Beck couldn't take his eyes off Anne Pauline, and nor could Tory, as she bore a strong resemblance to his wife, Simone Estienne. Everyone knew of Anne Pauline, but in reality, no one really knew her. Then Marcus Belling finally managed to open the door of the Unknown Destination. At that moment, Anna Bijns was startled to see that someone was trying to climb through the rocks of the street. The arms of a man caught hold of the ground, looking for something to hold onto. Anne Pauline wasn't able to contain her astonishment when she saw Marcus Belling arrive in Antwerp, in the middle of the 16th century. With his whole body already off the ground, he asked the inevitable question, "Where am I?"

CHAPTER 10

MAGNETISM THERAPY – ANTWERP, 1520

1

The inert bodies of Marcus Belling and Anne Pauline could be found in 27 on Sun Avenue after both had finished traveling to the past by hypnosis. Effectively, a phenomenon similar to self-hypnosis had made Belling enter a deep hypnotic trance soon after the mesmerized Anne Pauline did so. However, he didn't self-hypnotize, although he could and knew how to do it. The hypnotist knew all the techniques inherent to his profession, having taught some of them to Thaddeus Borba, but this was a quite different situation.

Sofia never suspected what was really going on in the office, otherwise, she would have opened the door immediately. The hypnotist and patient had passed to a parallel world that few people besides Jasmine and Thaddeus Borba knew of and wasn't described in any compendium prepared by the National Council of Hypnosis. On the other hand, as this was a lost dimension of hypnosis, it meant that both could interact with people from their past lives without being stopped, at least for some time. Already in this other reality, Marcus Belling had discovered a brave new world that he had ignored throughout his career. When he opened the door of the Unknown Destination, the hypnotist remembered Aldous Huxley's, *Brave New World* again. At that moment, he realized that this was part of the life that Anne Pauline had inhabited since she started the sessions of hypnosis with him nine months ago, ignoring even her pact with Josef Salvaterra. When he opened the door into the tunnel of time, Belling was first confronted with a parallel world that was only accessible by hypnosis, and he couldn't contain the questions that flowed through his mind.

"Where am I?" asked Belling.

"You're in Antwerp," replied Christopher Beck.

"But what time am I in?" asked Belling, wondering about the smells, the people and the place that now surrounded him.

"At what period?" asked Beck. "1520," he said finally.

"I never thought that this could happen," replied Marcus Belling, in a tone of amazement. He continued, "I don't believe what I see..."

He realized immediately that he had returned to the faraway past. Everything was so real; it was impossible to doubt what now surrounded him or the people he spoke with. At that moment, he quickly realized what had happened at the session of hypnosis with Anne Pauline; finally, he now had access to a world that had been previously hidden by his patient. Never in the books and teachings given by the National Council of Hypnosis could he imagine that hypnosis allowed such effective access to the past of one of his patients. He doubted for a moment that he was in Antwerp during the year 1520. However, after looking at the face of a surprised Anne Pauline, he had the final confirmation that the young woman with green eyes had known about long ago this other dimension of his profession. How was it possible that he had never been aware of what was happening in those sessions of hypnosis? Maybe he didn't want to see what had always been in front of him. For a moment, he felt cheated.

Although Marcus Belling had never returned to his past lives through hypnosis, he quickly realized, what had happened with Anne Pauline when he mesmerized her. She could return and communicate with people from her past and it was all real. Then, he remembered the first time that he saw her and the intuitive feeling of surprise she had caused. Suddenly, an image appeared to him of Patricia, nine months pregnant. She was about to give birth, and they conceived their son on the day that he met that patient. A feeling within him told him that he had just encountered a dimension of hypnosis that he hadn't experienced yet in his career. However, if it was true that access to other worlds through hypnosis was a reality before he Anne Pauline, why had it occurred only now? He felt confident that this wasn't possible with all his patients, otherwise he would have seen it before.

However, the typographer, Christopher Beck, was absolutely amazed by how much he looked like the man who seemed to have returned from another dimension. He didn't know what he should think of everything. He and Paracelsus had pursued Anne Pauline through the city in an attempt to understand why she was hidden in the house with a makeshift laboratory. separate to these events, Beatrix van Edegern was more interested in the successful formula to produce gold, which had been developed by the alchemist through the extraction of the so-called fifth essence. On the other hand, the typographer, Tory, was totally confused with this situation, and couldn't understand how it was that the meeting between him and Anna Bijns had been discovered. He was also surprised by the similarities between Christopher Beck and Marcus Belling. During all this time, Anne Pauline remained silent and looked askance and ashamed at Belling.

After a few minutes, Belling gathered the courage to ask Anne Pauline, "Can you explain what is going on here?"

"I don't know to explain this, but the truth is you just go back to one of your past lives," she said.

"I don't understand any of this. This is a past life of mine? This gentleman is much like me," said Belling, pointing to Christopher Beck. He continued, "Are you telling me that it's possible, through hypnosis, that I can communicate with and be recognized by people from my past?" asked Belling, increasingly surprised with the unknown world before him.

"Yes, but I didn't know you were also able to return to these other worlds by hypnosis. I thought that this only happened to me," said Anne Pauline, realizing that it would be impossible to hide her secret any longer.

"So, this is what has happened during our sessions of hypnosis?" an intrigued Belling asked.

This question of Marcus Belling was the most relevant of all questions he had just asked. There was no doubt about it, and Anne Pauline couldn't give him an answer that would satisfy all the questions that now rose up in his mind. Through the uncomfortable silence, Marcus Belling knew he had asked a prohibited question and he would never hear the answer, or at least the truth. However, deep down, he felt he already knew what it was, but he was still too incredulous and skeptical to relate all the events of the past nine months during his hypnosis sessions with Anne Pauline. Briefly, but now with clarity, everything made more sense in the mind of Belling about the strange events that had taken place; from the fire in the library to his knowledge amnesia. This confirmed that everything that had happened in the last nine months and almost ended his career is related to his ability to intervene in the past.

Once more, Anne Pauline was motionless, and a long silence settled between her and her hypnotist. As always, the truth wasn't verbalized. Even so, Marcus Belling's brown eyes intensified, as if he desperately needed to hear confirmation from his patient that everything that had happened was her responsibility, because she had a power that he hadn't yet the ability to understand or even accept. Anne Pauline's special gift defied everything that Belling knew about the effects and the potential of hypnosis, and he had never known a similar case through the National Council of Hypnosis. He felt cheated and betrayed.

"As I said to you in the first session, trust is the basis of all sessions of hypnosis with my patients. Even if this world were unknown to me, you should have said something. Who knows about this?" asked Belling.

"Josef Salvaterra and Marbella," Anne Pauline replied simply.

When he heard that answer, Marcus Belling wished he hadn't learned the truth. At that moment, he felt trapped in that city, aware that there was an alliance with the objective of destroying his career. Many years ago, he had known Salvaterra, but he could never have guessed that he would put a plan into action against him that was so cruel. Using the power of Anne Pauline to intervene in the past and cause unpredictable consequences in the future was diabolical. Belling was thirsty for answers to his many questions. He didn't need much time to understand that most people he had known and worked with at Sun Avenue had been part of his past lives. Despite everything though, he would never know of the existence of the Theory of Vocation, which had served as the basis for outlining Salvaterra's plan to intervene in his career as a hypnotist. He also would never know he had been a prominent physician and professor in *Schola Medica di Salerno*, or that his former accountant had been Bruno Deluca, who had fallen in love with Anne Pauline. To some extent, he preferred not to know the whole truth, because he didn't know if he would be able to deal with the revelation of all this information. At that moment, he was incredulous about the pact that his patient had established with Josef Salvaterra and understood that his rival was intending to use the changes made in the past to his advantage. There was, therefore, a question he had to ask Anne Pauline, as he still hadn't realized the reason she allied herself with someone who had always placed obstacles in his career, "Why did you agree to cooperate with Josef Salvaterra?" he asked.

Once again, she gave no answer. Anne Pauline had the opportunity to tell the hypnotist everything but had no intention to. Instead, she would keep the past nine months to herself and she wasn't prepared trust her hypnotist as she promised to in the first session of hypnosis. Contrary to what Marcus Belling thought, she didn't want to be cured. At least that was what she thought, taking into consideration her own behavior. The hypnotist realized that his patient had agreed to ally herself with Salvaterra and Marbella because she had discovered that he had been responsible in part for her past insecurities, tragedies and uncertainties. Anne Pauline didn't like the idea that he had been part of so many past lives of hers; it seemed that one way or another, she always ended up meeting Marcus Belling. Because of this, she felt enclosed, a true prisoner of her destination. She didn't want a cure, which meant she didn't believe in hypnosis as a therapeutic alternative method to conventional medicine, or as a method of therapy at all. She had discovered this long ago. Even so, Belling was willing to show her otherwise.

This desire inside him surprised Belling. Despite everything that had happened in the last few months, he continued to believe that he would be able to bring more fulfilment to the life of his patient. Despite the discord with Sofia, he felt that he had to finish what he had started. Follow-through was a philosophy he lived and worked by and he would not abandon it over Anne Pauline's power. On the other hand, after this experience in his life, nothing seemed improbable to him, not even the possibility of a cure in another dimension, or in another world during the state of hypnosis. Clearly, this was a unique case. His patient had demonstrated her unique power to interact with people from past lives, including the ability to change the course of events that had taken place in the past. Since he had started the sessions of hypnosis with Anne Pauline, she had moved into a dimension completely different that was known to most people, and other hypnotists. For that reason, Marcus Belling was still in shock about all these revelations.

Belling wasn't the only one surprised by everything that was happening. Christopher Beck and Gotthelf Tory looked at each other, seeking answers as to what was happening and, briefly seemed to forget the rivalry that existed between them in the field of typography. That morning, Tory and Bijns combined to have a meeting at the foot of the Rhetoric Chamber, which was located in an area in an airier part of town, at the foot of small streams that were brought together in the maritime port of the city. In the distance, they could see some small bridges that crisscrossed Antwerp and stood in the stunning city, giving the city its existing medieval appearance. Behind one of these bridges there began to emerge the figure of a woman who appeared to be looking desperately for someone; in this case, Gotthelf

Tory. Effectively, this woman, still in the shadows, had seen that Christopher Beck move quickly to the place where Tory was going to meet with Anna Bijns and soon realized that the plans that existed between the two could be quickly discovered. With agility, Simone Estienne arrived with her elegant step next to the Rhetoric Chamber and Marcus Belling stared at her; the physical likeness of this woman to Anne Pauline was awesome.

No one in the group was able to hide their amazement about this unprecedented encounter in Antwerp. Christopher Beck, Gotthelf Tory, Anna Bijns and Simone Estienne didn't know who Marcus Belling and Anne Pauline were, as the two continued to discuss the events of the last nine months. On the other hand, they didn't suspect everything was linked to a common past. One person in that group had been impressed with the event. Beatrix van Edegern had already seen that moment through her visions of the future, although Jasmine's powerful alchemical scent had intensified these visions. Beatrix had already been at the door of number 27 Sun Avenue, but unlike Anne Pauline, still could not interact with people from the past. Christopher Beck then took courage and asked, "I don't understand what we are all doing here. Why is this gentleman so familiar to me? He pointed to Belling.

"We're the same person. I am you," replied the famous hypnotist.

"I don't understand," said the typographer incredulously.

"You don't need to understand, because I don't understand. Anne Pauline is my patient. I am a hypnotist. She searched for me so that she could undergo hypnosis to discover the truth about her past. This is her past, and my past. It could be just a mirage, but I feel this is all very real. Now I find out that my patient, who has attended sessions of hypnosis with me for nine months, has the ability to interact and communicate with people from the past."

"I don't know if I can understand what you tell me," said Beck, still stunned by these revelations.

"Try to realize that we came from the future and we don't belong to this era," said Marcus Belling categorically.

"So, in this case, what are you here to do?" asked Christopher Beck.

"Today, Anne Pauline sought me for a further session of hypnosis and I somehow entered a deep state of hypnosis. This is what I am trying to find out. I don't know what I am doing here. I never imagined there was another world through hypnosis," said Belling.

"I think this is the question that you must seek answers to," challenged Beck.

"I turn to hypnosis to heal my patients when conventional medicine can no longer provide more solutions. In this case, Anne Pauline sought me to go in search of her past. Her identity was lost. However, what happened was different. She used a unique power to harm me. Now I can see it," said Marcus Belling.

"Why does she need a hypnotist to be healed?" asked the printer, increasingly interested in the conversation.

"The experiences of past lives are sometimes stored in the subconscious. What I try to do through past life regression is to look to the past through another dimension, then understand it, and give it a new perspective. Hypnosis helps to give a greater clarity to us about the person we are, and who we want to be."

"I think we'll also need your help, one day," murmured Christopher Beck.

"Perhaps at another time. In this case, I have a mission to fulfil," said Belling.

It's true that Marcus Belling had a mission to accomplish, like Anne Pauline. At that moment, everyone was staring at Christopher Beck and Marcus Belling, not understanding how the immediate empathy between them had arisen. However, Anne Pauline tried to pay attention to everything that was being said about herself and his life. She had become aware that the alliance she had signed with Josef Salvaterra was a huge mistake on her part, and that this experience in the past had shown that there was something more important that had to be understood. This was the message that the seagulls of the Island of Wisdom had tried to convey to Anne Pauline when she visited there in a state of hypnosis. It isn't always advisable to seek out responsibility for the past, whether it is possible to change the present and the future or not. On the other hand, the seagulls know that man's power lies in his very nature and in spirit, if it's his priority to find out his identity. In addition, the definition of what he is depends only on him.

At that moment, the present and the future were related to each other. In another time, the statue of the phoenix in Sun Avenue began to acquire a different coloring, before the astonished eyes of the people of the city that were passing by. As Christopher Beck and Marcus Belling continued their conversation in the middle of 16th -century Antwerp, the statue was turning into something quite different. It seemed full of life, while the bird's eyes glowed in a way that almost made it take flight. The phoenix was ready to fly away from Sun Avenue. In Antwerp, Anne Pauline remembered then that she had received the feather of a phoenix when she was on the Forgotten Island. This lost island inhabited the only phoenix known to the modern world.

"I think that you have to ask yourself why you also came to the past," said Christopher Beck.

"I feel that I still have this mission to fulfil. Anne Pauline is the most striking case of my career and defies everything that I thought I knew about the potential of hypnosis," clarified Marcus Belling, expecting to be understood.

"Perhaps you've come here to complete your work. Not with your patients, but through your own past," said the printer.

"What do you mean by that?" asked Belling.

"This case requires a new method of treatment that is different to the one that has been practiced up until this moment. At least, this is what I see. To heal Anne Pauline, you also must be mesmerized," replied Beck.

"I think that all of us have realized the purpose of this conversation," Beatrix then said, interrupting the conversation between Beck and Belling, already annoyed with the empathy there now existed between the two. "I have a proposal to make to Paracelsus, which is more important. Is that not true?" she asked Paracelsus.

"What are you talking about?" asked the doctor, surprised.

"Well, we both know that you save the formula of transmutation of base metals into gold. That was the reason for meeting Christopher Beck at the lab today," said Beatrix confrontationally.

"I don't have any formula. If I did some experimentation, it was only to understand the human soul. The idea IS that at certain times of life there is an inner transformation OF spirituality within us," said the reputed alchemist.

"What do you mean by this?" Beatrix asked, surprised with that response.

"I want to say that everything in the world boils down to a transformation, from inside to outside, in nature and in man. The same is true in chemistry, medicine and alchemy," he replied.

"You're telling me that everything that relates to you, from the discovery of gold water to the spagyrical elixir, boils down to a metaphor for life? There isn't any chemical formula?" asked Beatrix, increasingly indignant.

"Precisely. The formula that I discovered was a treatment for the soul, not to increase the greed of men. Each one of us must find this formula to achieve our own inner transformation. In the laboratory, I just tried to remove the pure elements through the impure ones. Nothing more. Many have thought that I have found the life elixir or the philosopher's stone, or discovered the formula of transmutation, but this isn't true. The transmutation of metals merely rehearses the spiritual transformation, it's in the background," explained the alchemist.

Paracelsus was increasingly upset with the questions of Beatrix van Edegern, mainly due to the fact that she had exposed to the group his meeting with Christopher Beck, which had taken two years in preparation, and it had been revealed to everyone who was by the Rhetoric Chamber at that time. To complete his ideas, Paracelsus had also decided to add something, thinking that the conversation with the daughter of the jeweler was over.

"In reality, there is no phenomenon of transmutation of base metals into gold, because the transformation is always within us. It is, as I said before, the formula that I have found to treat the soul only."

"I don't believe in anything that you say. Tell me then what hides there? I understand you were preparing the formula of the spagyrical elixir, which can transmute lead into gold," said Beatrix van Edegern.

"You're going too far in your statements," Paracelsus shot back.

At that moment, Gotthelf Tory and Anna Bijns began to look desperately to one another, perplexed by those revelations, unable to understand how typography could serve the purpose of transmutation. Actually, there were only a few texts on alchemy and transmutation of metals that circulated through Antwerp, since these were themes were still viewed as obscure and forbidden arts of the occult. Paracelsus intended to use the workshop proofs of Beck to spread his knowledge and his more recent discoveries in this field. However, this fatal encounter at the foot of the Rhetoric Chamber had exposed their plans. Beatrix van Edegern then took advantage of the confusion of all those minds to submit a proposal that surprised the whole group, including Marcus Belling, who contemplated the faces of all those who had been part of his past life.

"I have a proposal for you," Beatrix said to Paracelsus.

"I am not willing to accept a proposal on your part," he said.

"I think that you'll think differently. What I must give you in exchange will allow you to finance your studies and investigations in various areas of knowledge for the rest of your life," concluded Beatrix.

"Paracelsus won't accept your offer, but say what you have in mind," challenged Christopher Beck, interrupting the conversation.

"In exchange for the formula of transmutation and the spagyrical elixir, I will give you 20 pounds in jewelry at this first stage, and I promise you much more if you immediately deliver to me the result of these searches. I don't accept that these experiments in this area are just a metaphor for life," said Beatrix van Edegern.

"As I have said, they're a metaphor for life. My experiences in the laboratory aim at removing the material of pure minerals and nothing more, and then watching what is happening with the men. I then apply forms of extraction, like those that exist in our world. For all this, my years of study in this field serve me by providing new means of healing my patients, after analyzing first the functioning of nature. It's possible to achieve this state of inner transformation by removing the impurity of men. This is how I learn more about medicine," said Paracelsus.

"I understand that perfectly well," said Marcus Belling, who interpreted the words of the recognized physician, as he applied those guidelines to his profession. He used his technique and his art to help all those who seek him for whatever reason. For him, it was more important to treat the illnesses of the soul than to find the right formula to mesmerize someone. However, he didn't know whether Paracelsus would have even discovered the process of transmutation of metals into gold, but if this had happened, he would never reveal this to the daughter of the city's best-known jeweler. He didn't doubt that the reputed physician and alchemist had discovered something about human nature, and that their experiences in the laboratory helped to unravel the mystery of man. Belling also quickly realized that Marbella was Beatrix van Edegern, not only by their physical similarities, but also because her nickname in this life, chameleon, suited her perfectly. Her greed, which was known to all, was also present. Marcus Belling had witnessed many situations where Marbella insisted on getting involved in the life of Josef Salvaterra, particularly by wishing to intervene in the decisions taken by the National Council of Hypnosis and the revenue generated by their sessions of hypnosis. He knew well the risk to everyone if Paracelsus gave away the secret formula of gold production, because it would be put in danger in the future. In view of all this, the doctor maintained the authority in his voice and his decision not to accept any proposal from the daughter of the goldsmith. Without this alliance, he would have more difficulty sustaining both his travels in Europe and his multiple investigations. There were other ways of funding his research.

However, Anne Pauline understood immediately why, in her past life as Aurélie Caen during the 18th century, she easily discovered the correct mixture for the production of potable gold. It was no coincidence. It was clear that there was a relationship between her life as Simone Estienne and Aurélie Caen, and that they somehow shared knowledge about the transmutation of metals through the course of time. That being so, it might be sensible to consider what Paracelsus had to say about the transmutation, that the true transmutation of metals to gold didn't exist as a chemical process, but only concerned the change that occurred in the spirit of man when he drew the unclean from the clean. After traveling to different places and periods through hypnosis, Anne Pauline realized that in everything the past had served to better understand the soul of men, such as the well-known physician who used, instead of the hypnotic trance, the products that nature offered him in its most natural state to reach the deepest human spirit. To understand all of this, it was necessary to resort to wisdom, as Thaddeus Borba had already realized many years ago. The shoemaker of Sun Avenue could see the truth behind human existence and, perhaps because of this reason, he was the only person who could teach her to control her unique power. Anne Pauline then immediately remembered the Forgotten Island, also known as the Island of Wisdom. This was an important event, and not just a coincidence. The gulls were several centuries old and spread the wisdom of men, so that men could see further beyond the state of living, beyond their routines and their habits. Was it possible that Paracelsus had also discovered this truth, hence his desire to remove the pure from the unclean during the various experiences that he had had during his life? Anne Pauline had doubts, as did Marcus Belling, if that formula would be the same.

Anne Pauline wasn't sure if Paracelsus had also had the opportunity, one day, to know the Forgotten Island. It was only possible to her through hypnosis, and not from alchemy, but even so, that process might apply to the human nature in the laboratory. Nevertheless, that seemed more difficult to make real. How could it be possible to extract the pureness of man through his impunities? In some form, it seemed that the known alchemist could extract, through a chemical process, everything that was polluting the human soul; excessive greed and uncontrolled ambition. He had shared this formula with Christopher Beck. Such knowledge would be a mystery to maintain, such as the existence of the Island of Wisdom.

2

The thoughts of Anne Pauline were abruptly stopped. All of a sudden, Beatrix van Edegern came over to Christopher Beck, who at that time was lost in his thoughts, and, with a frightening agility, stripped him of the sheets of paper that he held a long time ago in his hand, which she assumed to contain the formula of transmutation. In a few seconds, she was already in the possession of the hidden secret of gold production, drinking water, and raced toward the seaport. Paracelsus and Beck ran after her in a desperate attempt to recover the sheets that had served as the basis for the experiments in the laboratory that morning. Not only was it a secret formula about quintessence that Beatrix had stolen that day. She now carried with her the secret of human existence; that wisdom is the human virtue that enables us to reach fullness, to discover the pure through the unclean, and to find the path to happiness. Indeed, the formula contained the secret of how the phoenix was reborn from the ashes, and at that moment, the statue located on Sun Avenue became a true incandescent bird. However, the daughter of Jacob van Edegern was aware of the seriousness and gravity of her acts; she had just committed a crime by taking ownership of something that wasn't hers and served only her highest purpose and profit. In possession of those sheets, which contained phrases and number mazes, she could figure out how to transform base metals into gold, and thereby, control the market for gold and jewelry in Europe, taking over the monopoly that her father had built up over the last 20 years. She had seen it all through the dreams she had when she saw Anne Pauline arrive at Antwerp. The desire to get hold of that enormous secret was stronger than her.

Without regretting her actions, Beatrix van Edegern wished to escape from the city with the formula of Paracelsus and, therefore, began to run to the bridge that was closest to the one that gave access to the seaport. The goal was to hide in one of the boats moored in the harbor, and then head toward an unknown destination. Behind her now were Paracelsus and Christopher Beck, who had joined the group behind of Tory Gotthelf, Anna Bijns, Simone Estienne and Anne Pauline, while Marcus Belling decided to stay back to observe everything that was happening. He felt that, somehow, he should not intervene in the past. More than anyone, he knew that he could get damaged. Over the past few months, Marcus Belling could never have imagined the different, dynamic worlds with which his patient had come into contact, without ever suspecting he had been a part of it.

From afar, Belling realized that Christopher Beck had already grabbed Beatrix van Edegern from a bridge in the city and struggled with her to retrieve what she had stolen from him. When Paracelsus arrived, the daughter of the jeweler withdrew a pair of scissors with encrusted diamonds from her jacket pocket; a gift from her father a few years ago. At that moment, Gotthelf Tory also approached the confusion that had been generated by the threatening words of Beatrix, especially because he had known her father for many years and was, therefore, trying to avoid the family's misfortune. However, the words of Tory had no effect. The printer felt that Beatrix would use all the resources at her disposal to stay in possession of the formula of Paracelsus in order to know about the mysteries inherent in the transmutation of base metals into gold and to ensure the monopoly of trade of jewelry in Antwerp (and in Europe). Beatrix van Edegern then showed the scissors to Christopher Beck and threatened to kill him if he continued to try to grab it. After looking deeply into his eyes, and without waiting for his reply, she touched the scissors against his belly, before the eyes of a scared Marcus Belling. If something were to happen to Beck, Belling would die too! He didn't know what to do. He was several meters away from the group and if something dramatic happened with the well-known typographer, he would die during the hypnotic state. With nothing to hand, Gotthelf Tory then grabbed Beatrix by the waist, while she kept the tips of scissors pressed with more force against the belly of Beck, the two fought against the bridge. Losing her balance for a few seconds, Beatrix van Edegern dropped the scissors and fell from the bridge, her screams wrenching their ears as she was carried away by the strong flow of water. Within just a few minutes, she disappeared forever. Before the event, Christopher Beck, Anne Pauline, Simone Estienne and Anna Bijns addressed disbelieving bystanders along the bridge, knowing there was nothing they could do to prevent the dramatic outcome. In the distance, Marcus Belling couldn't believe that he had survived the attack, as if he could still feel the scissors ready to take his life.

When Beatrix fell into the water, after losing her balance on the bridge, Belling noticed small sparks of electricity that seemed to disappear quickly into the air, as if the body of the daughter of Jacob van Edegern was surrounded by a cloud of electricity. The phenomenon, however, wasn't strange to Belling, who quickly returned to thinking about Anne

Pauline. She and the two typographers were returning to him now, absolutely horrified by what had happened.

I never thought that she could've considered the possibility of killing me, Christopher Beck thought to himself. Without the intervention of Gotthelf Tory, he would have died, meaning Belling would have died as well because the two were one person. The group was now in silence. All around them echoed the screams of an anguished Beatrix, who had disappeared into the water completely, as if the world had taken her away. She had taken with her the papers that had been in the possession of Christopher Beck; the formula of transmutation was lost forever.

The truth, which was hard to accept, was this; Beatrix van Edegern was willing to do anything to be in possession of one of the most coveted formula ever. Her death had immediate consequences in the distant future, which were still unknown to the group that now turned to gather next to the Rhetoric Chamber. At the precise moment that the daughter of the goldsmith fell to the water, Marbella fell lifeless to the ground at the entrance of the Free Center on Sun Avenue, after protesting the payment of their quotas. That morning, she had decided to become a member of the city's most democratic club, against her own expectations. Over the years, she had given up trying to integrate herself into the most elitist and reserved groups in her society, as to admit that she would have to accept her economic possibilities and modest status. However, this behavior didn't reveal that something had been transformed in her, but instead she would use her influence as the woman of Salvaterra to control the Sun Avenue's "Free Club". After the club's demand for the payment of jewelry and an annual quota, Marbella protested in an effusively. A few minutes later, she lay lifeless on the ground. She would not rise again. The events of the past had dealt her the ultimate blow.

However, Marcus Belling tried to overcome his shock at the death of Beatrix, thinking about the strange phenomenon that had occurred when she fell into the water, as this gave him the idea for a cure for Anne Pauline.

Some years ago, at the beginning of his career as a hypnotist, Belling had developed some studies and conducted some sessions of treatment. It was a therapeutic method, which had also complemented alternative medicine, based on the idea that there's a magnetic fluid in the human body, which is able to regenerate not only physical pain, but also psychological pain. This became known as the Theory of Healing Magnetism. There were very few times that he could apply these techniques. These reflections were important, since neither Belling nor Anne Pauline could awaken from their hypnotic trance alone, without first achieving the goal that he had proposed in the first session of hypnosis nine months ago, to free the patient from her past. However, Marcus Belling didn't know yet how he could realize his plan because he was in a latent state of self-hypnosis. Still, he knew he had to take that opportunity to heal Anne Pauline.

In recent months, Anne Pauline had become part of an underworld that Belling that Belling didn't know existed by hypnosis, though he had practiced the therapy of past lives for many years. He wasn't able to forget one of the first questions that Christopher Beck had asked him; *why was he there*? The only possible answer was that he was on a mission to liberate Anne Pauline from her past. To release his patient, it was necessary to protect his career and his entire team. It was worth a try, but he would need help to do it. So, while his patient remained on the bridge, reflecting about the covenant she had established with Beatrix van Edegern and her tragic death, Belling took the opportunity to speak with Christopher Beck, Gotthelf Tory and Anna Bijns about his plans. In a general way, he reinforced the need to heal Anne Pauline. While explaining this, Simone Estienne approached Anne Pauline.

Everyone was shocked by the death of Beatrix, but it was necessary to act quickly and prevent the power of Anne Pauline continuing to produce effects over the course of time. The two typographers and the writer listened carefully to what Marcus Belling had to say but were not yet fully prepared to accept the idea that these two people had traveled by hypnosis to Antwerp; the commercial, economic and cultural center development of the European Renaissance. Belling took the opportunity to present himself to the people from his past, as well as to reveal everything that had happened in the last nine months of his sessions of hypnosis and regression with Anne Pauline. During this time, his patient and Simone Estienne had continued to talk to each other at the bridge, accepting more readily that they were a single person, separated by eras of time. Paracelsus now understood that his formula for quintessence and the spagyrical elixir was somehow related to the past of Anne Pauline, as she also needed to transform her past into gold. However, it was gold water that was the substance in question. The doctor and alchemist realized that the young woman with mysterious green eyes needed to, but this time to be cured of her past. Christopher Beck, Paracelsus, Gotthelf Tory and Anna Bijns listened to Anne Pauline's story, as told by Marcus Belling, and agreed that it was necessary to find a cure. Then the hypnotist drew their attention to the strange phenomenon that had occurred when Beatrix van Edegern fell into the water.

"I can assure you that there is here, in Antwerp, a magnetic fluid that is transported by water and is present in men and in nature," said Belling.

"And what magnetic fluid is this?" asked Gotthelf Tory.

"It is the fluid of life. It is an energy that we find in all living beings, which regulates our mood, our temperaments and our diseases," said the hypnotist.

"I don't see how it's able to heal Anne Pauline," said Anna Bijns.

"If this energy is in Antwerp, I could apply it more easily and efficiently. It's magnetism therapy; healing using the energy flowing through our bodies," replied Marcus Belling.

"And this energy is able to heal spirits and souls disturbed by the past? asked a skeptical Beck.

"Yes, if this energy has sufficient intensity, it can regulate and treat her," replied Belling.

"I think we should try this track. From what you've just said, the two must return to Sun Avenue briefly, but the power of Anne Pauline must be stopped," Paracelsus concluded.

"To stop this power, I have to heal Anne Pauline. Otherwise, this power may manifest itself in a disastrous way if she is hypnotized by another hypnotist," said Marcus Belling.

After some initial effort, these people from the past had finally realized Marcus Belling's mission and the need to halt the power of Anne Pauline. Luckily, there was a different energy in the city that could heal the young woman with green eyes.

Belling had experienced sporadic contact with the Theory of Healing Magnetism, also called biomagnetism, after it was formed in clinical hypnosis. He had learned these ideas from reading, especially the studies of Franz Anton Mesmer, who advocated it as a way of imaging or as a magnetic fluid, which influenced the health of the human body. The mesmeric gestures could transform the universal fluid in magnetic fluid and this, in turn, could produce vital fluid; or as Belling would say, vital energy. He knew that this was the treatment indicated for Anne Pauline. it became necessary to halt her enormous power so that she couldn't continue to change the events of the past. In turn, this was a power that only condensed her questions about her identity, which would help her to find her way. The magnetic fluid that Anne Pauline had would be transformed into vital energy. The work of Marcus Belling as a hypnotist wasn't finished. This was his only certainty. He knew the sessions of hypnosis could not finish without him treating Anne Pauline, and for that, he would need to use a technique that had never used on a patient, since at least the time he had devoted himself to hypnosis exclusively.

Paracelsus suggested that Belling use a magnet to balance the magnetic fluid in the body of his patient. He had also already been studying something like a fluid that flowed through the veins and seemed to influence the state of mind of man, although a few centuries later, all these theories were compiled into the well-known magnetism therapy. However, he intended to use the mesmeric gestures to find the vital energy in Anne Pauline as the first phase. Magnetic therapy was used to restore both good physical and mental health and, as learners of this therapeutic method knew, Aristotle approached this in his work, Treatise on the Soul. Here, it was stated that the action of magnetic forces on the human body also had an influence in the case of the soul, which reacts equally to the action of a magnet. Both Paracelsus as Marcus Belling knew quite well the theories of Aristotle on the performance of the technique of magnetism in the soul. The two realized that it was through the past that he should find the solution to the case of Anne Pauline.

To successfully apply the technique of magnetism therapy, Marcus Belling would induce Anne Pauline into a magnetic sleep, but he wasn't sure if it was possible to perform this, since she was already in a hypnotic trance.

Back at the Sun Avenue office, Sofia wondered about the long silence from Belling's office. However, given that the session of hypnosis hadn't yet been completed, she didn't intend to interfere with it. Inside, the bodies of Anne Pauline and Marcus Belling were motionless, while something disturbing was happening in the past. When Beatrix had fallen from the bridge, both Anne Pauline and Belling had been alarmed at the tragic event and were almost awakened from their trance. Even so, they remained mesmerized. Marcus Belling tried to think quickly of a way to induce Anne Pauline into a magnetic sleep and considered mesmeric gestures; another form of hypnosis. In addition to being a good hypnotist, he was also a good magnetizer. It was time to test his ideas and, therefore, it was necessary to check the movement of the energetic, young woman with green eyes and then reverse it in a positive direction.

Suddenly, Paracelsus made a gesture to Gotthelf Tory. The well-known typographer dragged Anne Pauline to Marcus Belling and he quickly put his hands on her shoulders. Suddenly, a different energy and intensity began to circulate through the body of the young woman, who gradually started to feel increasingly quiet and relaxed. Soon, she closed her eyes. He had done it; he had induced a patient into magnetic sleep while she was in a hypnotic trance, confirming the past opinion of some that he possessed a great power. Marcus Belling was now a hypnotist and a magnetizer.

Gotthelf Tory and Paracelsus then helped Belling to throw Anne Pauline over a small pile of straw that had been lying on the street. Her eyes were now closed, and she breathed calmly. Suddenly, a strong smell of cinnamon, apples and cloves invaded the whole city area where the group were, while several Dutch and Portuguese merchants crossed the street without even noticing the presence of Marcus Belling and Anne Pauline. This surprised Tory and Anna Bijns. Although they already knew that those people (from the future) had arrived in the city through hypnosis, they hadn't realized that not everyone could recognize them. However, Marcus Belling continued with his hands over the shoulders of Anne Pauline, kneeling next to her, without the inhabitants of the city realizing what was happening at that location. He would now use magnetic therapy to reverse the power of the young woman for a load that was vital and positive, with the objective of gradually stopping her power. Then she would not be able to change the past, even if she was hypnotized.

The hypnotist, now also a magnetizer, gently moved his hands a few centimeters from the body, following the determined routes for some time. He then returned to put his hands on top of Anne Pauline's belly and turned them clockwise in order to strengthen his vital energy, to intensify the movement of the magnetic fluid. Gradually, Belling noticed that his hands and the body of the young woman were becoming increasingly hot. An unknown chemical process was now affecting both, but the therapy was not yet complete. The magnetizer now turned his hands in the opposite direction, anticlockwise, under the penalty of reinforcing the negative magnetic, that action already existing in his patient. After waiting a few minutes, Belling returned to move his hands a few centimeters from the body of Anne

Pauline and, to her surprise, she began to squirm slightly, as if her body was reacting to the treatment. Paracelsus and Gotthelf Tory focused and paid close attention to everything that was happening, realizing that Belling had identified the major nerve center of Anne Pauline. There was a lot of time before the curative magnetism began to produce its effects. The patient began to move restlessly, as if she were having a seizure. The magnetic fluid had actuated her cells, transforming her power to change the past by hypnosis into vital energy. With this new energy, it would be possible to heal the trauma of her past lives and she would not be vulnerable to these memories anymore. Through the use of magnetism therapy, Marcus Belling could proceed to cellular repolarization, which would also contribute to the polarization of the soul. The electricity that exited from the water when Beatrix Van Edegern fell from the bridge showed that Antwerp had the right charge of positive energy to treat the pain of the soul of Anne Pauline.

The healing process was now almost finished, but the magnetizer let his hands float a few inches above the belly of his patient. Anne Pauline tried to adjust the imbalances that were not only occurring at the cellular level, but also at the level of her mind. To this day, it can be said that there was a system of depolarization that functioned in the body of the girl, which had contributed to accentuating her anxieties and her sorrows. However, with Belling's technique, it was possible to make both the polarization and the balance magnetic. Slowly, the magnetizer slid his hands out from the body of Anne Pauline and knelt at her side, waiting for her to wake up from her sleep, which happened a few minutes later. The young woman gradually stood up and contemplated Belling with a questioning air, without being able to understand what had just happened to her. With her were Paracelsus, Christopher Beck, Gotthelf Tory, Anna Bijns and the Simone Estienne, with whom she shared a lot of physical similarities, who couldn't look away.

Marcus Belling explained to Anne Pauline what had happened during those 20 minutes. He had used the technique of curative magnetism to induce sleep and restore the vital fluid that flowed throughout her body. In this way, he had started the polarization of her cells and her soul, which was only possible because Belling was a good magnetizer, as well as a good hypnotist. At that moment, Belling was reminded once more of the work he had read of Aristotle in the Treatise on the Soul and hoped that he had achieved, with his technique and knowledge, his objective and finally cured Anne Pauline. However, she was still stunned by what had happened, because the vital energy was running through her body for the first time and she could clearly feel that liquid flowing throughout. It was a sensation that was difficult to explain, but she felt both light and happy at the same time, as she had never felt before. She sat on the floor smiling. Marcus Belling had never seen Anne Pauline's smile before and could feel that she was now a new person. A vital energy and positivity began to take care of her soul.

Paracelsus was surprised and thrilled with the technique that Marcus Belling had used to heal the pains of the spirit and this discovery was more important than his formula for the production of potable gold. It seemed that the hypnotist had extracted the pure through the unclean, which he himself had done various times in laboratory experiments. With these thoughts, Paracelsus turned to Christopher Beck and told him, "I would like to publish something about what happened here in Antwerp. I thought that magnetism would only work using a magnet directly to the patient," said Paracelsus.

"In this case, the energy moves around here in this area with great fluidity. This is what I saw when Beatrix fell from the bridge. It might not have worked, but I had to try," said Belling.

It would have been much easier for Marcus Belling to heal all his patients in recent years by using only magnetism therapy. However, the profession would not have been so committed and interesting if he had succeeded; on the other hand, the case of Anne Pauline was different from all the others, and therefore required a therapeutic approach that he had never been attempted before. What he could now understand was that the spirit is connected to energies, so that the treatment of the soul passes by redirecting the heart in the right direction. Now, and in the way that best suited her, Anne Pauline would find the way to discover her identity. Knowing who she was, she would have a chance of achieving happiness.

The technique of mesmeric gestures had surprised Paracelsus, who now showed interest in using the workshop sticks of Beck to publish his studies on this therapy. Gotthelf Tory looked askance at this, as if he appreciated the famous doctor and alchemist's idea, but as always, he couldn't prohibit the texts that were printed in the workshop of his rival. Simone Estienne gave no reaction. Anne Pauline hadn't understood what had happened after Belling had resorted to therapeutic magnetism for the cure. She approached her husband, as if she feared that she too was subject to some sort of trance and hypnosis or magnetism. What she had seen that day went beyond her imagination. Gotthelf Tory's wife showed him, with a quick gesture, that she no longer wanted to be around these people, for she didn't know what strange powers she had witnessed.

It was this subtle movement of farewell to Simone Estienne that put an end to the journey of Anne Pauline and Marcus Belling to Antwerp. The young patient was standing only with help from her hypnotist, the session having zapped her strength. The weakness gave her a new appreciation for how important positive energy was to the well-being of the soul. The only assurance that she had was that she had never felt so light in her life. Her wide smile continued to fill her with happiness, and she felt no fears or anxieties, although she knew there were past lives that had been responsible for the events of her past. However, at that moment, Anne Pauline felt full and in tune with the world and all other sub-worlds.

In another time and another space, Sofia had decided that it was time to enter the room and alert Marcus that the session with Anne Pauline had ended a long time ago. Upon entering, she was incredulous. Anne Pauline and Marcus Belling were in a deep state of sleep hypnosis (and magnetic), while a strange light of electricity surrounded them. They had been clearly mesmerized, although she didn't understand how he could've stayed in that state. Her intuition told her to get up them immediately from that state, but she didn't know if this simple act would interfere with something that could be happening in another dimension that she hadn't known about. Still, something would have to be done and she remembered about Patricia Murio and Maria de Burgos, who were near Sun Avenue that day. It was certainly important they should be informed of what was happening, especially after the Ruben Mortsel's conversation with Vincent Torquay about recent events in the accounting office, located right beside number 27.

In a few minutes, Patricia Murio replaced Sofia Estelar on Sun Avenue. After some time, she opened the door and saw what Sofia had seen; he and Anne Pauline had been hypnotized and there was a strange energy flowing around them. Due to the knowledge amnesia that affected Marcus Belling several months ago, they decided not to intervene. They waited a little longer for Maria de Burgos, who arrived shortly afterwards, accompanied by Argus Dubois. In recent times, the two of them had developed a closer relationship since she had been going to Sun Avenue with increased frequency, hoping to find a solution to Belling's faltering career. The antiquarian couldn't help but stare at her whenever she appeared at number 27, and one day, had gained courage and invited her to meet him. When she went into his shop, they fell immediately into each other's arms, as if they had been waiting for that moment for a long time. They had been waiting for the right opportunity to speak to one another. They had fallen in love. In time, Maria de Burgos told him everything about the investigations she had made along with Patricia and Sofia with Vincent Torquay. Argus Dubois understood well his state of unrest when he came to visit him in recent times, as it would expose the truth about the controversial news that Belling was no longer the hypnotist he used to be. Dubois then told Maria de Burgos the history of the rare and valuable pieces that Belling always had, and which were, in some way, related to Anne Pauline. All the objects were stored in one of the drawers of the Victorian-style desk in the hypnotist's office.

Now that they were together, Patricia Murio, Sofia Estelar, Maria de Burgos and Argus Dubois had the opportunity to open the door of Marcus Belling's office. Sofia wanted to see what they thought of the whole situation. Everyone looked at each other and quickly realized there was only one person who could help in this situation; Jasmine.

Jasmine was very well known in the city. People said that she was capable of intervening in the past. So, the group decided that she was the right person to consult in that situation.

Patricia Murio found the house of Jasmine with both agility and speed. She had returned a little while ago from Marva, where she had remained for some time with her nomadic and shifting groups of people. The fortune teller opened the door and received the four people into her house, who explained they wanted her to intervene quickly in the hypnotic state that Anne Pauline and Marcus Belling were immersed in. Argus Dubois took advantage of the opportunity, as he always did when he went into the house of someone, to evaluate the furniture and the more valuable objects that Jasmine had there. He never knew when there might be an opportunity for a good deal. However, the oracle only had flea market items in her home, since, like Josef Salvaterra, she had little interest in antiquities, preferring instead to collect objects that had already belonged to others. This practice meant she could feel the energy that was associated with each of these parts, so only chose those ones that had a positive effect. Jasmine quickly realized that Argus Dubois was looking for something in particular and asked him about this.

"Nothing, nothing," replied the antiquarian, ashamed at being discovered, while Maria de Burgos looked at him with a questioning face.

"Come, sit down," said Jasmine to her four guests.

"We need your help urgently. Marcus Belling is lost in the past. We think he's been mesmerized, and his body is currently in a hypnotic trance at the clinic. We need to intervene immediately and get him back to the present securely. At this time, we don't know what kind of dimension he's in, and it could be dangerous to wake him up without us first being aware of what is happening," said Maria de Burgos.

"Is he accompanied by someone else?" asked Jasmine.

"Yes, with a patient, Anne Pauline. We believe that she's responsible for certain events that have happened to my husband over the past nine months," replied Patricia Murio.

"We undoubtedly need your help," Sofia added, reinforcing their request once more. She already had tears in her eyes, as she remembered seeing Belling in the office.

"Well, I say that Marcus Belling and Anne Pauline are both in Antwerp. The two have returned to the 16th century," said Jasmine.

"In Antwerp?!" they all said in unison.

It was a shocking surprise that Jasmine already knew where Marcus Belling was. She also knew through her visions that he had used therapeutic magnetism to heal Anne Pauline and that she was now free of the events of her past. She saw all this when by wearing the alchemical perfume, which enabled her to watch everything with an enormous foresight around her. In this way she could see Marcus Belling, who was indeed the best hypnotist in the country. He had used his knowledge and therapies to cure a patient during the hypnotic trance, after finding himself mesmerized. In addition, magnetism therapy had never been practiced at the Sun Avenue location before, which is what made this event even more unusual. She knew that Josef Salvaterra couldn't have achieved this result, although she would never have said that to Marbella. Marbella... Jasmine knew her friend died with the fall of Beatrix van Edegern from the bridge in Antwerp, but she kept this secret to herself. As for the tragic death of her friend, nothing could be done. The only thing that remained to be done was to bring Marcus Belling and Anne Pauline safely back to the present.

Jasmine was prepared to bring them back, but nobody knew of her true motives. Why was she so keen to help them? At that moment, the important thing was to bring Belling and his patient to the city, more specifically to the hypnosis office, but behind this act of salvation was a dark secret. Jasmine wanted to steal the sacred feather that Anne Pauline had always with her, the one from the seagull and the one from the phoenix, which she had been entrusted with on the Forgotten Island. It had been a planned to put this idea into practice a long time ago and quickly realized, when her guests entered her house and asked for her help, that this was her opportunity. The feathers contained an enormous power, even though the Anne Pauline was weak from therapeutic magnetism. If she gained possession of either of the feathers, Jasmine could become an even more powerful oracle.

The visionary spread the alchemical perfume around the house in front of Maria, Sofia, Patricia and Argus Dubois, who gave her curious looks. The five closed their eyes in hope that this simple gesture could bring Belling back to his world and his team. Jasmine then whispered unclear words, while murmuring speech that was difficult to understand; she engaged all her guests in a hypnotic trance. Now she could see Anne Pauline perfectly, accompanied by Marcus Belling, Gotthelf Tory and Paracelsus, whose existence she had learned of since returning to the past in Antwerp. To wake Anne Pauline and Marcus Belling, she spread more quantities of alchemical scent around her. This time, the scent evaporated in a strange way and formed a heavy grey cloud that culminated in a slight precipitation. A ray of light full of electricity then illuminated every corner of the house. Suddenly, the room cooled down and a smell of cinnamon, apple and cloves spread around the five, which came directly from the market of Antwerp. At that moment, Jasmine knew with certainty that Marcus Belling and Anne Pauline had awakened from their hypnotic trance. They looked at each other in surprise, knowing what had happened before during their visit to the 16ᵗʰ century. It was clear that the young woman with green eyes was cured because she beamed with an open and spontaneous smile. The sun shone now as intensely as it had shone on that summer day when she touched the door of 27 Sun Avenue for the first time. However, it mattered little to Jasmine that the magnetism therapy had worked. She would be thinking of a way to obtain for herself the powerful feathers of the Forgotten Island that would finally be hers.

CHAPTER 11

THE FINAL OUTCOME

1

After nine months, the sessions of hypnosis with Anne Pauline had ended. As soon as Jasmine managed to bring Marcus Belling and his patient back to the present time, the two never met again and the mission had been fulfilled. After what had happened in Antwerp and the strange phenomenon of self-hypnosis, the famed hypnotist had finally realized that he knew little about the real potential of hypnosis and began to doubt his career. Josef Salvaterra had increasingly integrated himself into the activities of the National Council of Hypnosis, especially after Marbella had died from cardiac syncope, which took her life in mere seconds. Life had changed quickly because the convictions of the hypnotists had also changed radically, especially since Anne Pauline had entered their lives. Belling had never met anyone in throughout his career that could change the past by using hypnosis and past life regression. All of this was unheard of for him, and it was a frightening situation.

Two weeks after he had returned from Antwerp, Marcus Belling took a crucial decision in his life. He didn't need any period of reflection before deciding to end his career as a hypnotist and sell his practice at number 27 Sun Avenue to Argus Dubois, who was now married to Maria de Burgos. The antiquarian would use that space as an administrative basis for his antique business, which continued to attract the wealthiest customers in the country. This also allowed him to finally put forward a proposal to acquire the rare and valuable parts than Marcus Belling had kept locked away in the drawer of his Victorian desk, namely the vase that had belonged to a druid, a magazine of rare skill, and some unique metal medallion, that dated from the 16th century. Marcus Belling's hypnosis office had become a place of pilgrimage for people who sought hypnosis and regression as an alternative to conventional medicine. There was, therefore, both a prestigious and historical aspect that was inherent to number 27 Sun Avenue, which made the sale price of that space more expensive for Argus Dubois, who acquired it without even trying to renegotiate the price. He knew well the market value of that space, but this would always be the place where Marcus Belling had dedicated his life to hypnosis. After his marriage with Maria de Burgos, the two began to form a partnership for life, with the aim of rewriting the history of the most famous doctor of hypnosis in the country. The sale of the clinic took place shortly after Anne Pauline had ended her sessions there. Marcus Belling was relieved about the speed of the process and quickly received the last books in his library stacked inside one of the remaining boxes.

The same could not be said of Sofia, who nurtured a strong antipathy about all the events that had led to the closure of the famous medical clinic. However, she now had other functions. After her marriage to Argus Dubois, Maria de Burgos had also become a member of the empire of antiques and decided to invite the former secretary of Belling to work with her. Sofia accepted, but with deep sorrow in her heart. She upheld the oath of loyalty that she had made to Belling for decades but she knew the fate of both had already been mapped out.

This was not the only major change in the life of Marcus Belling. A few weeks after selling his hypnosis clinic at number 28, something special happened. During a spring night when there was a smell of flowers hovering around the city, his daughter, Isabella Murio Belling, a pink and cheerful baby, came to fill the family home with new animation. After this birth, both Belling and Patricia Murio knew that Anne Pauline had been involved with some intervention, although they didn't know how. Perhaps it was no coincidence that his sessions of hypnosis with her had lasted nine months.

However, the mysteries that surrounded Anne Pauline had still not all been unraveled. Although she had been healed through magnetism and vital energy, Anne Pauline continued to save the strange codes that she had found throughout her period of regression with the famous Marcus Belling.

One day, she walked down the street, not far from her home, when Georgine Gunderson inhaled a familiar smell; it was the smell of cloves, cinnamon and apples that Anne Pauline had known in 16th century Antwerp while she was under the influence of the hypnotic trance. When the librarian passed by her, she knew exactly who she was, so she followed her for several meters until she realized that she worked in the now-defunct municipal library that, today, looked more like an abandoned building. She wondered how anyone could work there. The building had been closed to the readers of the city for many years and so it was rare that anyone had gone there. Georgine Gunderson, however, had been studying the hidden history of Sun Avenue for several years, and for that reason, used to visit many libraries in search of answers. One of her more pertinent queries was why the place was called Sun Avenue. In an ancient book discovered in the now-defunct municipal library, she discovered that an event of the utmost importance had taken place there many centuries ago. In some papers of the period, it was recorded that, in the middle of the 16th century, Paracelsus had left a bottle with gold water spilling in the street after developing the formula of quintessence and the spagyrical elixir. She came to discover that in the coded language of alchemy, the sun means gold. The librarian discovered that Sun Avenue signified that this was *the place of gold*, i.e. the area where the formula for the transmutation of metals had been spilt. After many readings, Georgine knew the truth without ever suspecting that the person who had followed her in the street that day was the same person who had observed this rare moment in the past; Anne Pauline was a witness of what had occurred in the 16th century.

Georgine Gunderson continued to walk down the street, always inhaling that smell. This smell contained a mixture of an alchemical scent that had been developed by Jasmine over the years. A few minutes later, she ended up climbing the stairs that gave access to the port of entry to the defunct library; this was a door that stood at the bottom of the sumptuous staircase. The librarian entered the building. Her contract for the provision of temporary services that had been signed some time ago was now almost finished, but she still received the latest uploads of books that would be stored for several years in the library. While there was a reshuffle in the new library, they would have to be stored in this building, as this was the decision of the director. Anne Pauline followed her with curiosity. That smell reminded her of the experiences and revelations that had taken place in Antwerp and her thoughts turned to Marcus Belling, who she hadn't seen since her sessions had ended. Thaddeus Borba had told her that the hypnotist had sold his hypnosis clinic to Argus Dubois, who had been married to Maria de Burgos for a short time. The Troubadour of Truth was almost abandoning his noble profession of shoemaking but promised to continue singing the ballad of truth through the city.

After entering the now defunct municipal library, Anne Pauline lost Georgine Gunderson, who had disappeared completely down the dark corridors of the building. At that moment, she was lost and didn't know how to find her way in a library in which there worked only a single employee, and the smell of mold and abandonment was everywhere. Suddenly, Anne Pauline remembered to check her coat pockets. She found an old sketch on which she had written a few months ago the strange codes that appeared under hypnosis. She was in possession of a real map, armed now with the latitudes and longitudes to find Georgine Gunderson in that library, and therefore, a piece of herself.

Anne Pauline looked at the paper she held in front of her, and with her attention fully focused on the codes that she had written, tried to uncover the path to Georgine Gunderson. The set of codes appeared before her eyes; **CNPP.14.1, W80V, Room Aldous Huxley**, but now, she didn't know how she could find any coherence between all these symbols. Then she raised her face, wondering if what she was doing was right. At that moment, in front of her, she saw two distinct corridors, both poorly illuminated, and she didn't know which one would be the room where the librarian was working. On the left-hand side, she saw some names that were illegible because of the dim light that stopped her from viewing in detail what was written; however, with enough effort, Anne Pauline managed to read; W99A, W78A, W80V. There it was! The last code was written on her paper. She now understood that the code was an indication of the corridor she should follow. She then walked down the W80V corridor. The hallway had several rooms, all of them closed, but each could be identified by the name. That being so, she would have to find the Aldous Huxley Room because that was what made the most sense out of all of the symbols she had found during the nine months of hypnosis. To her right, there was a wooden board that indicated the orientation of the different rooms in the library. So, she tried to be led by these guidelines. The long hallway was dark and empty, but as she went forward, she began to see some light without knowing where it originated from. The smell of Antwerp was no longer able to guide her now. Certain places in the hallway were pitch black and the old red carpet that lined the ground of that majestic building had been scoured for quite some time, letting her see the gradual destruction of its interior.

Finally, after walking for 10 minutes, Anne Pauline stopped in front of the Aldous Huxley Room and looked back at the paper in front of her; now she would have to find something with the reference CNPP.14.1. The young woman opened the door of that mysterious room and saw a small focus of light at the bottom. Despite it being daytime, the windows were all closed. The room was magnificent. It was enormous, while at the same time majestic, and lined with wooden shelves along most of its wall. The room seemed to collapse within itself in the center and a spiral staircase gave access to a lower floor, where there was a chair and an old table, and on this chair, Georgine Gunderson was sitting.

The librarian walked at a rapid pace down the corridor W80V every day and went into the Aldous Huxley Room, borrowing the name of the place of the defunct municipal library. When Anne Pauline entered, Georgine was packing many boxes of books that were handed over by the mayor each day. The librarian was a fine employee, which was why she had been assigned to carry out those functions while working alone in a closed library for nine months. However, these were now her last days in that place as her contract would not be renewed. It was with some nostalgia that she looked around the Aldous Huxley Room, the most beautiful room in that building.

When Anne Pauline came downstairs, Georgine Gunderson noticed immediately that the girl with green eyes was just behind her. When Georgine had been with Jasmine the last time to collect more quantities of alchemical scent, the fortune teller and visionary had warned her that Anne Pauline would appear briefly in the former city's library. The librarian had been waiting for Anne Pauline for several days, although she didn't know when and how this sighting would happen. For that reason, she had worn the scent of jasmine in recent days to attract the presence of the woman who had come looking for a book at the library nine months ago. Georgine Gunderson turned back and saw the face of Anne Pauline for the first time, her long, black hair and her green, magnetic eyes. This was the person who had caused Marcus Belling to end his career as a hypnotist. She was surprised by her presence and appearance. Anne Pauline was younger than she expected, making it difficult to associate her with a power so great. Still, she tried not to look scared, but the truth was that she was shaking on the inside.

Anne Pauline came to Georgine Gunderson and could smell and feel that scent that she knew so well from both her past and her dreams. Throughout her life, it had accompanied her during endless nights, without her knowing where it came from. She extended her hand in greeting, but the librarian was in a state of shock that Jasmine's forecast was so accurate and real; Anne Pauline was there in front of her, holding a piece of paper that contained a set of symbols and codes. The young woman with green eyes noticed the scared look on Georgine's face, presented herself quickly and explained that she was looking for something, but that she didn't know exactly what it was. A book, because she was in a library.

"If you're looking for a book, do you have some reference with you?" asked Georgine.

"Yes. I have the code, CNPP.14.1, but I don't know whether it's sufficient," replied Anne Pauline.

"Don't be discouraged. This is the numbering system for the books. With this identification, we'll quickly find what you're looking for," responded the librarian.

"I am happy to know that," replied the lively Anne Pauline.

"Moreover, this book is inside this box here, BO18. This was the first box that got to the library when I started working here nine months ago," replied Georgine.

On the table was a box labelled with the code BO18, and the librarian, given her experience of several decades in that field, knew that this was the box that contained the book with CNPP.14.1. She opened it quietly before the watchful eye of Anne Pauline and began searching for the book. Without knowing it, this was a piece of her own personal history. It was quite an old book, written more than two hundred years ago, and on the cover could be read; *Liber Transcriptus*. However, this couldn't be easily opened because it was closed with an old lock that seemed just as old. Anne Pauline tried to understand the next steps that should be taken to access the contents of the book. In a few seconds, she remembered the key that had been delivered by Bruno Deluca in Salerno and opened one of the doors of *Scuola Medica di Salerno*, where he worked at the apothecary. she recalled the wise and true counsel of the shoemaker, Thaddeus Borba, who told her to use the key when necessary.

After considering all these experiences, her intuition told her what she should do, and she immediately withdrew the key from her pocket, and inserted it into the lock of the book, which was hiding a secret that was about to be revealed.

Anne Pauline opened first the lock and then the book with curiosity. Despite being written 200 years ago, it was in an excellent condition and the text was accompanied by images of the functioning of the human body. The book described in depth all of the nerve centers of the human body, the formulas and the investigations of Paracelsus, the history of *Scuola Medica di Salerno,* and the technique of magnetism therapy that was used by druids and later developed by Franz Anton Mesmer. The book even contained vast notions and knowledge about natural medicine, astronomy, alchemy, the power of the imams, the influence of imagination in human diseases. It even approached subjects like hypnosis, psychology, geometry and mathematics. This was, therefore, a genuine treaty of natural sciences and humanities that was of incalculable value to society and contained references to sporadic concepts that were difficult to define, such as positive touch and magnetic sympathy. Everything seemed strangely familiar to Anne Pauline, as if it summarized all the experiences of her past lives and of her present life. Feeling increasingly curious, Anne Pauline flipped through the book until she reached its last pages. Here, she found a disturbing passage that said:

Here we list the names of those who have proved in the past 200 years to have special powers of intervention in the past when hypnotized. These experiences challenge and put into question the whole knowledge that exists about the world and of man. Therefore, in this book, you can find some names these are the people who surprised doctors and healers over time with this extraordinary gift. For this reason, this work was considered a secret that should continue to be kept only by those who understand the value of knowledge found in this book.

1. Jacques Piquet
2. Clara Moussa
3. Eveline Gilles
4. Samira Zarco
5. Georg Buchert
6. Matthias Bass
7. Ludwig Barbro
8. Annelise Champs
9. Florian Hans
10. Mary Rose
11. Carlos Murio
12. Josefine Belem
13. Alexandra Blau
14. Gustav Salvatore
15. Marcelline Mull
16. Joan Albrett
17. Andre Robert
18. Peter Adam
19. Charles Platin
20. Richard Blum
21. Ricarda Valle
22. Laurent-Xavier Theodor
23. Teresa Silber
24. Diana Dionisio
25. Oscar Salerno
26. Francisca Rodriguez
27.

Anne Pauline realized that number 27 contained no name but seemed to be waiting for someone to add one. She understood dramatically that she was number 27 and remembered then that this was also the port number of Marcus Belling's office on Sun Avenue. Finally, she remembered the familiar feeling the number had always given her.

All of a sudden, Georgine Gunderson pointed the finger to Anne Pauline's jacket pocket, where paint was dripping, already leaving a spot. Anne Pauline placed her hand inside her pocket and withdrew from there the feather of the seagull, whose harsh tip was filled with ink. There was a reason she had received the sacred feather of the Forgotten Island. The secret had been revealed in the presence of the librarian. Quietly, but with concentration and emotion, she printed her full name; *Anne Pauline Roux*. With this simple act, she became the 27th person to appear in *Liber Transcriptus*.

The discovery was much more important than it seemed because the manuscript proved for the first time that Anne Pauline wasn't the first person capable of changing events of the past by hypnosis. After all, she wasn't alone. Perhaps this was the message that the gulls wanted her to know when she came to the Forgotten Island; that nobody gets overlooked in the world, even if at times, the seagulls are the only ones who know this great truth.

The Forgotten Island. This mysterious island was now completely out of the reach of Anne Pauline, especially after Marcus Belling had resorted to magnetism therapy to stop the development of her power. She no longer knew if she would have a new opportunity to go back. This was a place where only people could travel through hypnosis. The truth was that never she had ever felt so at peace as when she was on that wonderful island.

After trying to contain the emotion inside of her, Anne Pauline turned to look for the *Liber Transcriptus*, where her name was now written delicately. Anne Pauline witnessed that she was one of the people who could change the events of the past through the state of hypnotic trance. Now nothing was a surprise, but she had been amazed when she realized that the seagull's feather in the pocket of her coat was filled with ink for her to complete her name in that mysterious book. What Anne Pauline didn't know was that this feather was sacred for that very reason; the goal was to write and rewrite her story. The feather of the Forgotten Island wanted to mark her life and leave no blank sheet. The story was written with truth, firm and hard. As she was.

At that moment, Georgine Gunderson closed the book, picked up the key that had been delivered to this woman by Bruno Deluca in Salerno and decided to put it back inside box BO18. This box would forever remain closed in the defunct municipal library. Anne Pauline looked now to the librarian in a dramatic way, as if she had taken away a part of herself, her identity, when she removed that book from her hands. However, there was a specific reason that Georgine Gunderson had decided that the time of Anne Pauline of that sacred book was complete. Behind them was Jasmine, who had waited for this moment for a long time.

2

Jasmine asked Georgine Gunderson to withdraw from the Aldous Huxley Room. Since Marbella had visited her regarding the alliance of Salvaterra with Anne Pauline, Jasmine had followed the path made by that young woman with mysterious green eyes, even when she was in a state of hypnotic trance. The visionary had seen her signing her name to *Liber Transcriptus* and witnessed the strange phenomenon in which the feather of the seagull of the Forgotten Island was filled with paint so that she could sign her name. In this way, Anne Pauline had become number 27 on that list. The power of the feathers was enormous, which was why she longed to take control of them, even if she had to travel between different times. So slowly, she began to descend the stairs to the lower floor and Anne Pauline. She noted a chair and an old table; on top of this was box BO18, which contained the key to the secret, prohibited book that revealed the existence of a unique gift. To know Anne Pauline, it was necessary to accept that there's a spiritual dimension and holistic human existence that is sometimes difficult to understand. Although Anne Pauline knew exactly who Jasmine was, the powerful visionary decided to take advantage of the opportunity to talk a little bit about her personal history.

"It's good that we are here. I'll introduce myself. I've been searching for you for a long time," she said.

So, Jasmine began to inform her listener that she had known Marbella, Josef Salvaterra's wife, for many years and consulted her some time ago about certain behaviors of her husband, who in some way, seemed to be hiding something. She was able to sense this through her near vision. Through her dreams, she could feel that Salvaterra had an agreement with someone, but she couldn't figure out who that person was, so Marbella had searched for her. However, none of this now made sense. After Belling sold his hypnosis clinic to Argus Dubois, his rival had also decided to make a temporarily departure from hypnosis, especially as he had been traumatized by the unexpected death of his wife. However, life had a different destination for him now.

Jasmine decided to be honest with Anne, who was listening to her attentively in the former municipal library. The truth was that Jasmine always knew about the alliance that Anne Pauline had kept with Josef Salvaterra during her nine months of sessions of hypnosis. The visionary then asked Anne Pauline to sit in the chair, before continuing, and said to her, "I need you to sit down and listen to something, and to understand why you're here."

Anne Pauline was about to hear a story that would surprise her, despite believing nothing special could happen to her after she had finished the sessions with Belling. Apart from being a visionary, Jasmine was also a producer of perfumes, especially one in particular, which was known by the name of alchemical perfume by her more loyal customers. The perfume was rare, because its essence was rare. Having realized this, Jasmine began to produce it by hand and had a few good customers who were willing to pay her a fortune for that fragrant elixir, which was a dominant scent. This was the case with Georgine Gunderson, who had suffered from intolerance to the smells of libraries, even though she had always worked in one. There were several types of intolerance, but Georgine's one was extremely rare, and she was only able to overcome the difficulty of working in a place full of books with the alchemical perfume. It seemed ironic, but it was true. However, she took pleasure in her work, but as nobody would understand her problems with the smells and didn't want to be dismissed, Georgine decided to look for Jasmine after hearing about this scent that worked miracles. It was so.

The very alchemical scent had a story behind it and that was related to the rarity of the essence that was used in its preparation. Jasmine confessed to Anne Pauline that she had stolen the essence from Thaddeus Borba, the shoemaker of Sun Avenue. The young woman with green eyes couldn't believe what she was hearing. When the shoemaker traveled to the Forgotten Island, he discovered by accident a rare plant with a green stalk long, dark and slender, which exuded a smell that was different and a little aphrodisiac; it was a mixture of cinnamon, apples and cloves. With the authorization of the gulls of Forgotten Island, the shoemaker brought back various plants, but a few days later they were stolen from his workshop by Jasmine, who knew of its potentialities. From that moment on, Thaddeus Borba decided never to speak with Jasmine again, despite their close relationship before this episode. They were two oracles who often shared knowledge that each one had about the world. The theft would dictate the distance there was between both. Shortly afterwards, Jasmine began to produce the alchemical perfume and dominated the industry of scents in the city in the process.

However, this wasn't the only revelation that Jasmine had to make to Anne Pauline. Through this perfume, the visionary had noticed that her extrasensory powers now grew so rampant, she could now travel between the past and the present, as Anne Pauline was already doing through hypnosis. So, when Patricia Murio, Sofia Estelar, Maria de Burgos and Argus Dubois sought to save Marcus Belling, she decided to use the perfume to return to Antwerp and release the hypnotist and the patient from their trance. Anne Pauline was surprised by this revelation.

At this time, Anne Pauline shifted in the chair where she was sitting, feeling fairly restless and uncomfortable with everything that she was hearing. The face of Jasmine was familiar, perhaps because she didn't live far from her home, although Anne Pauline had never seen her with Marbella, nor with Josef Salvaterra.

"Speaking of Marbella," the fortune teller began, as if she had read Anne Pauline's thoughts. The mole had died in the Free Center as a consequence of Beatrix van Edegern falling from the bridge. In this respect, Anne Pauline wasn't surprised. Everything that she had modified in her past and of the past of Marcus Belling had resulted in a catastrophic event in the life of the hypnotist, who had now decided to abandon his career. Suddenly, she remembered Belling and felt nostalgic about the times when she had attended his famous sessions of hypnosis.

The time had come for Jasmine to reveal to Anne Pauline her real wishes and to ask the Georgine Gunderson to lead the young woman to the defunct city's library, which was in a near state of abandonment. So, she pointed the finger to the pocket of her coat and told her, "Give me the sacred feather and you can leave here with *Liber Transcriptus* and the truth about yourself. You may well prove to Marcus Belling that there are more people like Anne Pauline, which may be a huge relief to you. In addition, through my visions, I can help you whenever you want. You just have to give me those feathers," said Jasmine.

Anne Pauline would not deliver the feathers to Jasmine and, therefore, pressed on the pocket of her coat with more force, which made the fortune teller move closer to her, dangerously. At that moment, Anne Pauline no longer knew what she could do. She had been taken to the municipal library, which was closed, so that no one could come to her rescue, even if she screamed. Anne Pauline lowered her gaze. She felt lost. She didn't know what to do at that moment, but only that she couldn't deliver the feathers to Jasmine. Once the fortune teller was in possession of them, her power would increase more than she could ever imagine. Anne Pauline began to cry.

When she lowered her head, the young woman with green eyes saw a small trap door beneath her feet. She could clearly see this because the edge stood out among the carpet that covered that area. At that moment, without knowing how, she remembered Thaddeus Borba telling her to use the key. He had said this to her several times during the nine months of hypnosis she had with Belling. Anne Pauline never noticed how insistent the shoemaker with these words, but she now understood them perfectly. The key that Bruno Deluca had given to her in Salerno served not only to open *Liber Transcriptus*, but also the trap door that was under her feet, and that would allow her to escape from Jasmine. But how? How could she get away from Jasmine when she had her eyes focused on her? At that moment, Georgine Gunderson appeared again in the Aldous Huxley Room and sprayed huge portions of the alchemical scent in the air which made the fortune teller feel baffled; actually, the smell was so strong that it mixed up all her extrasensory capacities.

Jasmine screamed in pain, not physical but of the soul, when she saw that much alchemical perfume was being sprayed in that dark room, and her visions mingled with the past of Marcus Belling. At that moment, through the power of the scent, she suffered all the pain of the souls who had traveled into the past. She felt herself fall on the Forgotten Island, as if she couldn't prevent this sudden drop. Anne Pauline realized this and so looked to Georgine Gunderson and knew that this was her chance to use the key of Bruno Deluca, the only man who had truly loved her. It was he who was going to help. She quickly withdrew the floor carpet, uncovering the trap door that she had seen while Jasmine had been talked to her. Anne Pauline knelt down, grabbed the key, entered it into the slot and opened the trap door, letting herself fall through it. Without knowing what the destination would be, Anne Pauline ran through the narrow, hidden corridors, which existed under the Aldous Huxley Room.

HYPNOSIS

Anne Pauline found a door at the end and realized this led outside to the former city library. Jasmine remained closed in the library, having been nearly blinded by the quantities of alchemical scent that Georgine Gunderson had sprayed in the room. It was even possible to hear her agonizing cries of pain from the corridors.

Anne Pauline ran. She ran like she had never run in her life, past the library, down Sun Avenue and past the hypnosis clinic until she left the city limits. Already exhausted, she picked up a ride with a group of itinerant people who were traveling together and asked them to take her to the village where she lived with her parents. The sea had been waiting for her for a long time.

It had been a few years since she has come to town, she and she had never seen the sea again since then. Now, as she approached the village where she had grown up, her thoughts focused solely on the horizon. The sessions of hypnosis with Marcus Belling had finished a few weeks ago and she was now finally a healed and full woman, ready to enjoy a whole brave, new world that was waiting for her. The wind whipped against her face, wiping away her anxieties. The fear of returning to find Jasmine seemed to fade with time. Now she could feel the taste of the sea clinging to her thoughts and memories of childhood. Anne Pauline just wanted to go back to the place where she had always belonged.

Upon reaching the village where she had grown up, Anne Pauline quickly moved to the beach where the boat, both colorful and dazzling, was still anchored. The *Argo* could be found on that deserted stretch of sand, as if it had been waiting to take her far from her torments, towards the fullness of her soul. At that moment, without her realizing it, Vincent Torquay had reached the village, after having better understood the verses that Thaddeus Borba had recited many years ago. After decoding the words, which were, in reality, a love letter, he finally found the woman of his past after an intense discussion about the recent events on Sun Avenue. Anne Pauline was more beautiful than one might think, and on that lonely beach, his eyes filled immediately with emotion. He had decided that he would not bother her when he saw her walk along the path to her happiness. Anne Pauline pushed the boat out to sea and then jumped inside it, rowing faster and with more agility, observing now how far it was to the village where she had been born and spent her childhood. Sailing onward, the young woman stopped only when she felt she should, and her strength began to fade. Vincent Torquay stayed on the beach to see her swim to the far horizon, feeling that love, instead of departing, was coasting along exactly in his direction. When the woman understood who she really was, she would be available for love, no matter what time it was. On the other hand, Jasmine was far away, in the city, now blind with her alchemical perfume.

When she finally stopped running, Anne Pauline sat down, exhausted, on the *Argo*. She contemplated the beautiful end of the day and saw how the line of the horizon had become a mixture of colors, dark yellow and orange. Carefully, she removed the sacred feather of the seagull from her jacket pocket; the one that, with courage, she had always been able to save from various people who belonged to her past but were also part of her present. Somehow, she felt that she had now returned to the sacred place where she really belonged. Therefore, she lifted the feather in the air, waiting for the wind to take it. However, it wasn't the wind that took it, nor the sea. At the bottom of the line of the horizon appeared a lone seagull that flew in her direction, focusing only on its purpose to come and get the closely guarded secret of the Island of Wisdom. The seagull went to her and swiftly grabbed the feather.

In this way, Anne Pauline knew that a thousand years could pass, and the Forgotten Island would continue to exist, even if man had forgotten it. She had observed and learned, in recent months, how persistent the seagulls were in order to spread their wisdom around the world. On that day, the young, curious, green-eyed woman had realized that the holy things are not to be forgotten and that, in this way, there's always a chance to be happy.

HYPNOSIS

Dear Reader,

You can now open your eyes slowly. By opening your eyes, this means that you can wake up to the world that surrounds you, with a new understanding of who you are.

Relax deeply while being aware of this session. Store away the paper, pen and pencil because you will not need them anymore. The session of hypnosis with Anne Pauline has ended, as has yours and, although this isn't Marcus Belling, consider that you might have been mesmerized by these words. The words, these will continue to be written for as long as there are truths to be told, even under the effect of hypnosis.

LETTER TO THE NATIONAL COUNCIL FOR HYPNOSIS

1st December 1998
From Marcus Belling
Subject: *Liber Transcriptus*

Dear Sirs or Madams,

You must have by now received the information from Argus Dubois that *Liber Transcriptus* will be deposited in the library of the National Council for Hypnosis. Georgine Gunderson has received orders to deliver the book to a member of the General Assembly.

Liber Transcriptus is 200 years old and was submitted to a thorough evaluation of its condition by some of the most qualified second-hand booksellers and the antiquarians of Sun Avenue, who have considered it to be in an exceptional state of preservation. This is something unseen for such a rare book that dates back to 1798. This isn't its only exceptional characteristic, though. It's covered in old leather and is singled out by a print marker that is similar to those of the typographers Christopher Beck and William Caxton (at that time, such a marker wasn't so regularly used by typographers), and the cover shows an indented symbol of what seems to be an island. For us, the meaning of this island continues to be an enigma that, we judge, this book isn't going to reveal that easily.

After all the steps have been taken, I shall guarantee to the Council that Argus Dubois is now doing intense work with reputed specialists 18th and 19th-century books to try and decipher the encrypted messages that seem locked in *Liber Transcriptus*. My participation in the first phases of the inspection of the book has allowed me to observe the resemblance between this rare manuscript and some other pieces of work, such as *Corpus Hermeticum* and *Hermetica*.

Both texts do seem to gather diverse yet complementary knowledge of medicine, botany, occultism, magic, theology and philosophy. *Liber Transcriptus* still shows us one more upsetting fact, however; an exhaustive list of names.

We don't always know which men and women they refer to in this list, although the short description that precedes them makes it obvious that the case of Anne Pauline isn't unique. This is disturbing for me.

This being the case, and despite its exceptional workmanship and unquestionable market value, you shall know that, due to the content in this book, I hereby present you with this letter, which I hope will be rapidly delivered. It's the first time that I have seen such an exhaustive list of names in a book from such a period and which is also a real encyclopedia of knowledge. As you may guess, it's a very disturbing sensation for me and Argus Dubois, this being the first time that we've ever seen this. It's something that defies everything that we think that we already know.

I already have it settled in my mind, but I can't deny that this event helped me realize intention; I have decided to retire from my career as a hypnotist. It is the most appropriate way to formally express my distance from some of the measures that were taken by the National Council for Hypnosis relative to the practices of hypnotizing. I have repeatedly tried to show my disapproval to the President and the members of the entire assembly for the last 10 years.

It is equally necessary to warn you that the Anne Pauline case may not be the only one to occur in the years to come. I can shamelessly declare that I was naive in the handling of this case. without ever considering the consequences of the techniques that were directly used with one person who showed a special power under hypnosis. In this sense, I did not recognize the limitations of my knowledge. While recognizing my own responsibilities in this process, I shall also take the opportunity to suggest the adoption of other orientations to the Council in such situations; I think that hypnotists should have the right to know that some people can control the hypnotic trance in a different way. What I mean by different is the capacity to intervene in the past and, at least for those who practice Therapy of Past Lives, to change those events. In this sense, perhaps the Code of Ethics of the National Council of Hypnosis may take this point into account. In this case, I refer to the ability of the patient to intervene in the past, which should be an alert for those who practice past life therapy.

Despite what happened in this case, I shall also warn you that Anne Pauline acted under covenant with another hypnotist from this Council to harm me. I would like to warn you of the dangers of such a situation in case the organization doesn't possess all of the facts.

I shall also declare that Anne Pauline is now living with a fuller feeling (though we could not affirm if she is totally cured), which I confirm from the experience of my 20-year career in hypnosis. It is likely that her power might show again for brief moments, but the extreme anxiety that led her to look for my help will hopefully not haunt her again. If so, I shall ask you to not subject her to any sort of experimentation to confirm what is written in *Liber Transcriptus* and to let her, as a patient, live her current life in plenitude. In this way, I hereby request that you carefully evaluate the information contained in *Liber Transcriptus*; this seems to have been hidden for more than 200 years and as such, should be carefully preserved. This doesn't necessarily mean that it should be kept in total ignorance. It is for the National Council of Hypnosis to decide, in accordance with the Code of Ethics, the natural development to be made in this case.

I can't end this letter, however, without showing my sadness at retiring from my career as a hypnotist, which, despite all obstacles, always fulfilled me professionally. It is only with a clear mind and reflection that we can follow our own paths; mine and the Council's, this time, without any magical potions or hypnotic trances.

I would also like to inform you that I have chosen to become a writer.

Yours faithfully,
Marcus Belling

www.ingramcontent.com/pod-product-compliance
Lightning Source LLC
Chambersburg PA
CBHW051635180726
48284CB00006B/1731